THE
PROTOCOL
LAST

MANE
FICTION

THE LAST PROTOCOL

ANDRE SEGURA

MANE Publishing
2248 Broadway #1868
New York, New York 10024

This book is the sole creation of human artists.

No part of its text or artwork was A.I. generated or manipulated.

MANE Publishing believes that art in all forms is a uniquely human endeavor. It is created by the artist's perception and communicated through a choice of words, purposefully placed brushstroke, or interestingly angled perspective. This is how art connects us on a deeper, more emotional level, which cannot be replicated through LLMs or A.I. image generation.

A.I. cannot create. It can only regurgitate what has already been created by human artists, while lacking the capability to discern artistic purpose. Thus, it steals and devalues the countless hours of work an artist puts into creating their art and learning their craft. More worryingly, the use of A.I. to generate art not only threatens artists' livelihoods but also denigrates artistic expression in favor of homogeny and easy profit.

By purchasing this book you are supporting actual artists.

MANE Publishing asks that when considering the art you consume, to please be mindful of its source. Only through our collective rejection of A.I. generated "art" can we hope to protect true artistic creativity and expression.

Thank you.

For Jessica.

You are as much the author of this book as I am. Thank you for a lifetime of constant love and support. You have been, and will always be, my best friend, my compass, and my every desire. I miss you every day.

Goodnight, my Love Eternal.

Acknowledgments

This book wouldn't be half as good if not for the input and assistance of several friends and family who took the time to read this novel in its infancy and help me craft it into something to be proud of.

First and foremost, thank you to Ann Segura. Without her input and editing expertise this book would not be half as legible or thoughtful. She read and reread this manuscript more times than anyone should rightly be expected to do.

Additionally, my thanks to Aron (Sherbert) Miller for sitting down with me multiple times over beers and offering his sage advice on several chapters in this novel. It was with his suggestions that I was able to craft some of its most important and climatic scenes.

Also, to Mark Segura, who read more than one iteration of this novel and offered his heartfelt guidance as it slowly took form.

And finally, a big thank you to Ivan Molton for taking the time out of his busy schedule to read my manuscript and offer his considerate suggestions.

CHAPTER 1

Keeping low to the ground, Morrigan crept forward in a crouch, slinking through the tall ferns that covered the jungle floor. Sweat dripped down her body, the air oppressively humid despite the scant leathers she wore. She tried to hear past the cacophony of buzzing insects, bird calls, and the howling of monkeys, listening intently for something more specific. Carefully pushing aside a palmetto frond, she focused on the shadows just beyond the dense undergrowth and gripped her spear tightly, muscles taut and ready for action as she spied her prey.

Giving short snuffles as it hunted along the ground with its snout, the tapir rutted about, oblivious to her presence. Carefully adjusting her stance, she lifted the spear and gauged the distance between them. If she timed it right, she could take the animal before it realized she was there. Holding her breath, she leveled the spear over her shoulder and made ready her throw.

A sound to her left was the only warning. From the underbrush, a giant shape leapt at her. She had just enough time to see the shadow of an enormous ape—twice her height and many times her weight—looming above her, backlit by the sun. Morrigan whirled to face it but knew she was already too late as she tried desperately to set the spear between them.

Suddenly, the ape froze, hovering in mid-leap only a couple of feet away. Morrigan blinked in surprise, still fueled with adrenaline, her mind trying to register what had just happened. Seeing the beast frozen in place, its lips curled back and arms raised above its head, the fantasy of the moment was stripped away. With it the persona of Morrigan the Barbarian faded, returning Samantha to reality.

"Why'd you do that?" she demanded, turning to face Marcus as he walked towards her out of the undergrowth.

Like her, he was dressed in leathers and furs, his bare chest more muscled than in reality. His hair was long too, hanging to his shoulders, unlike his actual shorter cut. However, behind the fantasy trappings, he still looked like the man she loved.

"Because it was definitely going to kill you," he said with his familiar smirk, eyebrows lifting in a way that always reminded her of a puppy.

"Maybe," she said dismissively, standing up and letting out a hard breath. "Or maybe I would have done something awesome and killed it. But now we'll never know."

"Are you angry?" Marcus asked, surprise in his voice.

Sam gave out another sigh. "A little. It kind of ruins the fantasy, you know. And isn't that the point of all this? I was really getting into it."

Marcus gave her a sympathetic look. "I know, baby. I'm sorry. It's just… we were only testing out the newest patch today, and I'm still not sure about the death protocol. This might be a bit much."

Sam walked over to inspect the detail of the ape, marveling at its realism. Diego had done an amazing job. "But that's what I wanted to try out the most! No more just lying limp and paralyzed for an agonizing five minutes instead of dying. I'm excited to see what happens when I die."

Marcus gave a grunt at her words, his smile replaced with a look of pain.

"I'm sorry. I didn't… you know what I mean," she said softly, immediately regretting her choice of words.

"I know. It's fine," he replied. "But I am still a little apprehensive about all this. First, it was adding the pain sensation. Then you wanted that increased. And now, the death feature. I don't know."

"But that's the point! You can't lose yourself in the fantasy if you feel invincible. There need to be consequences."

"I'd have thought you'd had your fill of consequences," he said bitterly, glancing down at his feet.

"That's not fair, Marcus," she replied, feeling frustrated tears well in her eyes.

"I know… I'm sorry," he said, walking over to her and reaching out to gently take her by the arms. "It just creeps up on me at times. But you know I do all of this for you."

Sam nodded, trying to will her tears to stop. He smiled at her affectionately and she couldn't help but smile back.

"So? What do you think of the upgrades?" he asked.

She looked at the world around them, her eyes widening as her excitement came flooding back. "It's amazing: the sounds, the heat, the smells! It's so much more real than the previous versions! Tell Diego he implemented everything perfectly."

"Well, he was building off your input too. But yeah. His team is pretty good."

"Are you sure they have time to do all this?" she asked, a little knot of worry tightening in her stomach.

"You know Diego. I've made Sam's World the current priority and he agrees. He just treats it as a training opportunity for creating assets that we might experiment with in Elysium. Which isn't technically incorrect, and we have Evan's blessing," he said with a pleased grin. "So you like it?"

"Very much. Though…" she looked down at her clothes. "This outfit is a little ridiculous, don't you think? This was *your* input, wasn't it?"

Marcus stepped back giving her a long considering look from head to toe, taking in the leather loincloth and skimpy top. "I don't know. It is the jungle after all. You can't be burdened with too many clothes. Just needs to cover your important bits." He shrugged feigning innocence. "Looks good to me."

"Oh, I bet it does," she laughed.

"I can fix it if you like," he offered.

"No. It's fine. I actually kind of like it. Sexiest I've felt in a long time. But I think I'll design some other options to choose from too."

"No problem. This is your world, after all."

Sam gave him an amused smirk. "Now, you gonna let this big boy go so we can test out the death feature?" she asked, lifting her spear to ready herself against the giant gorilla.

"If you…" Marcus stopped and cocked his head, and she knew he must be getting a call or notification. After a moment he smiled and looked back at her. "Sorry. Just a message from Evan. He's got something he needs to talk to me about, apparently."

"Everything okay?"

"Yeah, no. I'm sure it's fine."

"He didn't say what he needed to talk to you about?"

"No. He just wants me to stop by and see him soon," he said with a shrug.

"Maybe you should go then. It might be important."

"Maybe," he replied, letting out a short sigh. "I guess we've been in here a while, haven't we? I suppose I should get back to work."

"We'd have gotten started sooner if you didn't delay us when we first got in," she said arching an eyebrow with a quirk of her lip, trying to hide her disappointment.

"Hey, you seemed as eager as me."

"Touché," she replied. "Well, fine. Go do what you have to do and leave me here. I'll be fine."

"You know that's not how it works. Not yet," Marcus said with a twist of his lips. "Plus, you need to eat and take your pills."

Sam gave a snort, lowering her spear. "Fine. But we're coming back and getting right into it. No getting side-tracked with sexy time until after I've fought this bad boy. And you're *not* stopping the gorilla next time."

"As you wish," he replied with a playful bow.

Stepping closer, she reached up to wrap her arms around his neck, pulling him into a long kiss. The sensation was arousing and familiar, just like the countless other kisses they'd shared over the last twenty years, and she couldn't help but marvel at the accuracy of the simulation. Not unlike their lovemaking earlier. That too had felt just as real as in life, with all the messy details. Though she supposed such things, so ingrained and familiar to her brain, should be the easiest sensations to reproduce.

Pressing herself into the kiss for a second longer, she disengaged as she felt Marcus' hands begin to wander.

"If we don't have time for the fight, we don't have time for that," she said giving him another arch of her eyebrow.

He let out a small sigh and grinned guiltily. "Fine. See you on the other side, little one."

In an instant, the world blurred and then darkened. Slowly opening her eyes, as if waking from a dream, she waited as the room around her came into focus. Sitting up in the bed, she flexed her hands and wiggled her toes to ease the numbness in her limbs. It was always jarring when he pulled her out of the simulation. It was an unpleasant side effect of using the SynAPP, but paled in comparison to the rest of the sensations that came flooding back. Taking in a deep breath, she tried to suppress the involuntary gasp that accompanied the returning pain stabbing at her ribs and spine but instead began coughing uncontrollably, only amplifying her torment.

Marcus sat up suddenly from the chair beside her bedside, his eyes wide and bleary as he quickly turned toward the sound of her distress. Forcing himself to stand unsteadily, he rushed to the table next to the bed and poured her some water from the pitcher.

Holding her side to try and lessen the pain, Sam sat forward and took the glass from him with a weak smile. With a pitying look, he waited until she was finished drinking to take the glass back. She hated that look. It wasn't his fault. She knew how much he loved her, but it was always a reminder of how their relationship had been changed by the cancer.

"I'm going to order us some lunch. You feel like anything in particular?" he asked from the doorway.

"No. Whatever you choose will be fine," she replied. "But don't you need to get back to Evan?"

"It's okay. I'm sure whatever it is can wait until I've got you fed. Be right back."

She watched as his shadow moved down the hallway, then leaned back on her pillows. Her thoughts returned to the jungle and the gorilla, and how alive and capable she'd felt there. There had been no pain. No weakness. She'd felt like her old self: strong, agile and confident. Now she was weak and basically bedridden again. Returned to the new normal. Her heart sank at the realization, and she tried to force back the tears that welled in her eyes.

The sound of Marcus' voice drifting in from the other room caught her attention. It wasn't how he sounded when talking to a restaurant or delivery person. It was more controlled and deliberate. His conversation was brief, and after it ended, he remained silent in the other room. It was probably Evan. She wondered what their friend might be calling about, a little knot of worry tightening again in her stomach. It had to be something with the simulation. She hoped it was something regarding Elysium, but whenever anything unexpected came up, she always worried that it might have to do with Sam's World. Impatiently, she waited for Marcus to return, desperate to know what was going on.

As if on cue, Marcus stepped through the doorway. "I got us Greek. I hope that's okay."

"Two orders of spanakopita, right?" she asked, mocking a serious expression.

"Two spanakopitas, two pitas, and lots of tzatziki," he confirmed with a smile.

Smiling back, she studied his face for any signs of distress.

"I heard you talking to someone. Was it Evan?"

His smile remained, but she could see his brow tighten a little. "Yeah. Well, Janice technically. Apparently, he wants me in the office ASAP. I told them I'd need an hour. So I'm afraid I'll have to eat and run."

"Do you know what it's about?"

"Nope. Classic Evan. Probably some new idea that he's really pumped about and wants to reveal face-to-face. You know how he is."

"You should tell him to wait. You can't just drop everything whenever he calls."

"Well, he *is* the CEO."

"So? He wouldn't have this company without us. He knows that. You need to push your weight around more."

Marcus shrugged. "It doesn't hurt to indulge him. The happier he is, the less involved he feels he has to be."

"I suppose that's true," she said, trying to hide a wince at the sudden jolt of pain that stabbed along her spine.

It didn't elude Marcus' attention, though, and he rushed to the side of the bed.

"You need more pillows?" he asked helplessly.

Sam shook her head and gritted her teeth, pushing herself up. "No. It's fine. I just need to reposition."

Tentatively, Marcus reached over to help guide her as she moved, though in truth it was more a show of support and didn't do anything to lessen the pain. He so desperately wanted to help, she knew that, but sometimes she wished he'd just let her deal with it on her own.

With another wince, she settled back on her pillows. The pain wasn't entirely gone, but it was a little less sharp than before. Looking into his worried eyes, she was reminded of the first time they met. He hadn't even been her "type", but there had just been something in his eyes. Something that had told her he was the one she needed in her life. A bond they'd both felt instantly and couldn't explain. They had never looked back.

She smiled and took his hand, lacing her fingers with his. Grinning warmly, he lifted her hand to his lips and kissed it.

Pointing at her head, she said, "Kiss it."

Marcus' smile widened, and he leaned over her to kiss the bald skin on the top of her head.

"How's the implant feel?" he asked, running his fingers down the back of her head to the base of her skull.

"Just fine. No change. Like every other time you've asked," she said, reaching behind her head to take his hand.

He nodded and squeezed her fingers.

A blip sounded from his phone and he looked down to where he'd laid it on her bed.

"Food's on its way," he announced, before leaning over to kiss the top of her head again. "You want water or soda with it?"

Sam's mouth twisted. "I should have water…"

"But?" He drew the word out teasingly.

"Soda."

"You got it, beautiful. I'll be right back."

"I'll be right here," she said quietly to herself as he disappeared through the doorway.

She listened to him futz around in the kitchen for several minutes before there was a knock at the door, followed by the sound of Marcus' voice drifting down the hall as he paid the delivery driver. After another minute he returned with a tray, the smell of the food wafting in before him. The familiar aroma of fresh pita and spinach would normally have drawn her interest, but instead she found her stomach growing queasy at the thought. He placed the tray in front of her, stopping to kiss her once more on the top of the head before leaving to grab his own plate.

Sam stared at the food, prodding it with her fork. It all looked as she expected, but as she breathed in the spice, her stomach became even more unsettled. At Marcus' approaching footsteps, she forced herself to pick up a piece of the pita and dip it into the tzatziki, shoving it into her mouth just as he entered the room. Her mouth full, she gave him a smile, forcing the churning of her stomach to the back of her mind. He smiled back and settled into the chair beside her, placing his own tray before him and lifting the remote to turn on the TV. She forced herself to swallow the mouthful and started cutting the spanakopita with her fork. No need to make him worry.

After they were done eating, Marcus moved to gather her tray and stopped, looking down at the half-eaten portions remaining on her plate.

"Was it not good?" he asked.

"No. It was fine. I'm just not as hungry as I thought," she said, smiling softly.

He stared at the food again for a moment, then looked at her.

"Are you feeling okay?"

She could see the worry in his eyes but twisted her lips and gave a shrug.

"As okay as I can be, I guess."

The worry in his eyes changed to sadness and he gave a nod, lifting the tray off her lap.

"Okay, little one. You let me know if you start feeling worse, or if I can get you anything else."

She nodded, trying to settle the churning in her stomach. He stood there for a moment and smiled down at her before turning to take the dishes to the kitchen. Sam watched him go and focused her attention on keeping her food down as she listened to him washing up. She wished she could go back to Sam's World. When she was there she didn't feel any sickness or weakness. She felt like herself again. Better than herself, actually.

She wished Marcus would give her the ability to go there whenever she wanted. He was so worried something would happen to her there if she was unsupervised. He wanted to control every variable and didn't realize how patronizing it was for him to basically require her to have a chaperone. He meant well, she knew that, and wouldn't see it that way. But if he could go in any time he wanted, why was it any different for her?

Not for the first time, she wondered what he would do once she was gone. He was so afraid of losing her, but she'd learned from this experience that sometimes you have no control over what will happen and just have to let things run their course. She wasn't sure he was capable of accepting that realization and worried that, when forced to face it, it might destroy him.

A sharp pain stabbed at her stomach, causing her to involuntarily wrap her arms around herself. She could hear Marcus finishing in the kitchen, and as he approached her room, she forced herself to let go of her ribs and leaned back into her pillows. His smiling face appeared in the doorway.

"Alright, boo. I should probably get over to the office and see what Evan wants. You got everything you need? You have enough water?" he asked, glancing at the pitcher by her bedside.

She nodded with a tight smile, swallowing down the bile rising in her throat.

"Do you wanna go spend time in Elysium while I'm gone?"

Sam shook her head. "No," she said, trying to keep the discomfort from her voice. "Compared to Sam's World, there's nothing to do there. Besides, most everyone is so much older than me."

"Well, maybe technically, but they don't look it."

"Trust me. It doesn't matter what they look like. We have nothing to talk about outside of pleasantries. Don't get me wrong. They're all nice enough, but there is nothing to do there. Can't I go back to Sam's World? I promise I won't do anything reckless."

Marcus gave her that pitying look again. "Sorry, baby. There are just too many variables and unknowns right now. But when I get back, we'll jump in again. Okay?"

Sam let out a sigh but nodded as her stomach tightened again. "Okay. I think I'll just try and get some sleep then."

"Alright, little one. I'll try not to be too long." Stepping over to the bedside, he kissed the top of her head before turning to walk out the door.

Sam watched him disappear from sight, then listened for his footsteps and the sound of the front door closing. Jumping out of bed, she rushed to the bathroom, barely even registering the lancing pain in her back, and made it to the toilet just in time to vomit up the contents of her dinner.

CHAPTER 2

Marcus stood at the window, waiting for Janice to finish her phone conversation, and looked down at the throng of people moving along the street below. How many were just going through the motions of the day? They were all probably dealing with their own problems. Problems considered big to some and small to others. It was a matter of perspective, he supposed. People were inherently self-absorbed. Any problem that affected them would always seem more important, despite how trivial it might be, compared to people with real problems. Did anyone ever think about the problems of the people they were passing on the street? Or would it even matter?

"Sorry that took so long," Janice called from behind, jarring him from his thoughts.

Pulling his attention away from the window, he turned to face the older woman and gave her a sympathetic grin.

"Don't worry about it. Can I go in?"

"Looks like he's still on his call," she said, looking down at the red light on her phone and shaking her head. "I've messaged him that you're here though. Hopefully it won't be too much longer." She offered an apologetic look and an awkward silence fell between them.

Janice's gaze drifted back to her desk and Marcus could hear her fingers tapping on the wooden surface.

"How's Sam?" she asked, her voice lowering unconsciously the way it did for everyone when they brought up uncomfortable topics. Marcus supposed he had been guilty of the same behavior before Sam's illness.

"You know, it's hard," he said. "She's got good days and bad. She's a fighter though," he said, forcing a small smile on his face in response to the pained look on hers. "She's still a troublemaker."

"If anyone can beat this, she can," the older woman said, her face brightening.

"Absolutely. How's John doing?"

"Oh, bored out of his mind. He doesn't know what to do with himself most days. I told him retirement was finally his chance to relax and do the things he always wanted to do. But after thirty years of doing the same thing every day, I think he's just used to having a set schedule. I warned him he'd better figure out how to spend his time before I retire, or else I'll decide what he can do every day," she said with mock seriousness before barking out a hoarse laugh.

"And how much longer is that for you?" Marcus asked, trying not to think about the very real possibility that he and Sam would never have the luxury of retiring together.

"Oh. I've got another ten years. John's a bit older than me. So he's got some time to figure things out. It's kind of an empty threat," she said with another laugh.

A sudden buzz from her desk interrupted the moment, followed by Evan's echoing voice. "Call's done, Janice. Is Marcus still there?"

"Yes. We were just chatting. I'll send him in."

"Thank you."

Janice motioned with her head to the door. As Marcus stepped past her desk, she reached out and grabbed his wrist, looking up at him with a sympathetic smile. "Let Sam know we're all thinking about her."

"I'll do that. Thank you. And say 'hi' to John from me."

Janice nodded, letting him go, her eyes reddening. Opening the door to Evan's office, he walked in, trying to ignore the sound of tissues being pulled from a box.

"Marcus!" Evan said with a broad smile, standing up from behind his desk to walk over and slap a hand on his shoulder. "Thanks for coming. Sorry to call you in with so little warning. You want a drink?"

Evan didn't wait for his answer and walked over to the mini bar tucked into the wall of his corner office. He'd had it installed after watching a TV show about advertisers in the 1960s. Every time Marcus saw it, it just reminded him of how Evan had missed the point of the show entirely. Not that it was any surprise. Evan was a great guy but had always been full of ambition at the expense of just about everything else, namely introspection. However, all that ambition had gotten his friend pretty far in life, and he supposed himself too, by proxy.

"Are we celebrating something?"

"Indeed we are, buddy," Evan replied, pulling out some bourbon and pouring a generous portion for each of them. Walking over to Marcus, he handed him a glass, clinking his own against it.

"I'm almost afraid to ask," Marcus said, looking down at the brown liquid.

"Oh drink up, sourpuss."

Marcus let out a long breath, then followed Evan's lead as his friend downed the whiskey in one swallow. It had been a while since he'd drunk anything heavier than beer, and Marcus winced a little at the stinging in the back of his throat, but he was proud of himself for not coughing. Taking his glass, Evan poured two more and motioned for him to sit.

"Mr. Nguyen, if I didn't know any better, I'd think you were trying to get me drunk," Marcus said, taking the refilled glass from him.

"Just trying to take the edge off. I know how hard things have been lately," Evan said with a sympathetic sigh, moving to sit behind his desk. "Figured you haven't had a proper drink in a while."

Marcus forced a smile on his face and took a sip from his glass. He knew Evan was just trying to be understanding, but he had no concept of how hard things had been. That was just something people said in the hopes that they'd come across as supportive. He didn't resent him for it, or anyone, but the words always rang hollow in his ears.

"How's Sam? She's really been missed," Evan said, leaning forward.

"She's doing her best. Not much more she can do, really. We're hopeful that her new treatment will start to have some effect."

Evan nodded. "God willing."

Marcus felt his teeth clench. "God has nothing to do with it," he said bitterly, taking another drink.

Evan's brow twisted sympathetically. "I just mean. I hope the new treatment works."

"I know," Marcus said, taking another sip. "Sorry. Things just haven't been very encouraging lately."

"Hey, man. You've got nothing to apologize for. I get it. How bad is it?"

"It's not good. I don't think you'd recognize her if you saw her. She's still Sam, but it's taken its toll on her. On both of us. I see her every day, so I don't notice it as much, but there are times when I walk into the room and it hits me."

"I'm sorry, man," Evan said, staring into his own glass somberly.

"Don't be sorry for me. Sam's the one who's dealing with it every second of the day."

"I know. And I'm sorry for her, too. I'm sorry for you both. I've always considered you guys as a unit. That's how everybody sees you. It's always been obvious how important you are to one another."

Marcus nodded, feeling guilty about putting his friend on the spot, and took another sip from his glass.

A smile grew on Evan's face. "I was just remembering our trip to Vancouver the other day. What was that? Fifteen years ago? We went to that club. Sam kept trying to convince women to dance with us," he said with a laugh. "It was great for me, but she really got a kick out of how uncomfortable it made you. You kept telling the women that you were with Sam, and she just kept smiling and saying 'It's just a dance. What's the big deal?'"

"She's definitely got a mean streak," Marcus said with a chuckle.

"Then she got drunk and tried to start that fight with those two guys."

"To be fair, they were looking for the fight. She just interjected herself."

Evan laughed. "Totally! And they were so thrown off when this girl got up in their faces and started talking shit to them. The stuff she said! What was that one thing she called them? Oh yeah, 'limped-dicked sister-fuckers'. It didn't even make sense."

Marcus smiled, remembering the moment. "Yeah, and I remember having to keep an eye out for those guys for the next three blocks while we tried to find a taxi."

"Sam was always fun, if maybe a little psychotic."

"She definitely has her moments," Marcus said, remembering the vibrant young woman he'd fallen in love with so many years ago, a stark contrast to how fragile she'd become. She was still the same woman, but the cancer had stripped away her physicality and, with it, some of her vibrancy. In the simulation, however, the old Sam came out again.

"So? Why'd you want to talk to me?" Marcus asked, pushing his other thoughts away.

Evan took another drink and put down his glass.

"What do you know about Clive Ellison?"

Marcus shrugged.

"What everyone does, I suppose. Made his money in tech, starting back with the internet boom of the late nineties. Created Dux Machina, and sold it for billions."

"Well, he learned about the research we're doing with the SynAPP and expressed his interest in its potential. He is very interested in Elysium and wants to get on board."

"How does even know about Elysium or the SynAPP?"

"Well, I kind of told him about them."

"You what?" Marcus exclaimed, sitting up in his chair.

"Calm down and just listen. Okay?" Evan said, holding up a hand to stop any further protests.

Marcus pursed his lips but stayed silent, arching a dubious eyebrow.

"Listen, he already knew about us. Not everything, but more than you'd expect. I guess he's been sort of following our progress," Evan said, putting down his drink. "He and I met a couple of months ago at a fundraiser in Austin. When I realized he was there, I introduced myself and we got to talking. He told me he was looking to invest in the next big thing. Turns out he's big into AI next-gen development. Believes it's the next step in human evolution. So, I insinuated that we might have something in the works that was in line with his interests. That's when he told me that Synerdyne was already on his radar. He was excited by what he had heard about us."

"And what had he heard?" Marcus prompted.

"Nothing solid, it seemed. But he knew we were working on an AI that dealt with human consciousness and synaptic transference. And he was interested in learning more about us."

"So, you told him?"

"No. I didn't tell him," Evan said in a mocking tone. "Well, not right away."

"We already have a contract with Medirnus, and as I was led to believe—by *you*—a pretty tight NDA. So why is he even involved? And what did you tell him?"

"That's the thing, Marcus. Medirnus is pulling out."

"They're what?! What are you talking about? They can't do that. Can they?"

"Not cheaply, no. But I have it on good authority that they're going to remove us from their portfolio at their next quarterly meeting. Apparently, they don't see a dependable profit return from experimental therapeutic care or our research - not in the near future anyway - and want to focus on more 'traditional' therapies."

"But they're the ones that wanted us to focus on the medical side of things."

"Well, not anymore."

"When did this happen?"

"I'd heard rumblings for the last few months. Well, the last year, really."

"Why didn't you tell me?"

"You've kind of had a lot on your plate, and none of it was certain. I didn't want to add to your worries. Besides, even if I had told you, what could you have done?"

"I don't know. Prepared myself? Considered other avenues of development with the team? I have a right to know what's happening with the company. You might have bankrolled it, but we are all invested in Synerdyne."

"Call it an executive decision. But you're right. I might have started this company, but it was you, Sam, and the others' ideas that were the catalyst. You're as much a part of these decisions as I am. I just didn't want to worry you prematurely. But that is where Clive Ellison comes in. With his support we don't need Medirnus. And he is *very* interested."

"I don't know, Evan. It's one thing to work with a company that has a long history and an executive board. It's another to rely on a single investor. What do we even know about him? Can we expect him to be reliable? Guys like him tend to be cowboys about this stuff and want to be the ones in control. What if he decides to throw his weight around? If he's a major investor, he could potentially have a lot more influence over our research."

"Nothing's been decided yet. And as far as I'm concerned, nothing will be without your consent. I'm not talking as CEO to R&D Director, just Evan to Marcus. I understand your hesitancy. Just remember, Ellison has spent millions on innovative technology companies and made a fortune doing it. Some are now household names. Why should we be any different? What we're doing is revolutionary. It only makes sense he'd be interested. That's why I want your take on him. Just feel him out and let me know what you think. All I ask is that you keep an open mind about this."

Marcus let out a long breath and stared into his glass.

"If you're willing, he'd like to take a tour and get a real sense of our research."

"A tour?"

"Elysium. He wants to see it for himself."

"He knows about Elysium?" Marcus balked.

"Not exactly. But he wants to see our research in practice. He knows we have a testing environment and wants to see it for himself. It's not like we haven't given tours before."

"Sure, but those were for a very select group of people."

"I would argue he fits that description. Plus, he'll sign an NDA."

"Yeah, I don't know, it just feels different with someone of his notoriety. I'm worried it'll just be like an amusement park ride for him."

"If so, then no harm no foul, and I'll keep looking for investors."

"Is there anything else he knows about us?"

"I couldn't tell you exactly. The guy has ways of finding out things. But I guess what I can confidently say is that he knows we have an experimental therapy involving patient brain stimulus using the Waxman-Li mapping."

Marcus let out a long breath. "You want us to take a walkabout in Elysium? Fine. But Sam's World is off the table."

"Of course. I have no reason to believe he's even aware of it, and I haven't said anything about it. We shifted away from the entertainment aspect of the SynAPP pretty early on, and it hasn't been our focus for a long time. There's no reason to think he knows anything about it. So, you'll do it?"

"Yeah. Okay. If we're losing Medirnus, I suppose I can't be picky about these things."

"Thank you, Marcus," Evan said with a relieved smile, his glass forgotten. "How is everything functioning, by the way? Anything I should know about?"

"No reports of any issues. The parameters haven't changed, and the patients have been active users. One hundred percent participation. Currently we are in development to add more activities to Elysium. We're worried that once the novelty of the simulation wears off, it may impact the patients' experience."

"What sort of activities?"

"Diego's team is working on a hiking trail and some rock climbing. We have plans to integrate a beach and ocean as well. There's even been discussion of skydiving."

"Skydiving? Most of these patients are elderly, right? Are you sure they won't have some sort of adverse reaction to that kind of stimulation? I'm thinking heart attacks specifically."

"Claire doesn't think so, as long as we screen them ahead of time. She says psychologically it could be therapeutic. Anyone with a heart condition will be denied access, of course. At least until we know more. But as for the physical exertion, there is no reason to worry. It's no different than running or being active in a dream. The simulation doesn't tax their actual physical body, at least not the musculature. Though respiration and heart rate can be affected. That's why we'll screen first."

"What does Sam think of it?"

"She doesn't really spend much time there anymore. She tends to spend most of her time in Sam's World. And when not there, she's resting outside the simulation. She says she finds it boring in Elysium. It was her suggestion that we add the activities. She said there was only so much gardening and walking around she could do."

Evan barked a laugh. "I suppose that makes sense. Sam's World was her baby, after all. And she's probably right about Elysium. Glad she still feels like part of the team, despite everything. Well, I'll be interested in seeing what Diego comes up with," he said, lifting his glass and downing the rest of its contents. "Okay. I should let you get back to it. Sorry again about calling you in on such short notice. I'll keep you in the loop about Ellison and send you any new details I get. Just promise me you'll give him a fair shake before making any judgments."

"All right," Marcus said, standing up and giving a nod. Placing his glass at the edge of Evan's desk, he turned to leave. "I think I'll look in on the team while I'm here."

"Good idea. I'm sure it'll be a morale boost to see you in the flesh."

"More like a cautionary tale," Marcus said with a grin.

"Hey," Evan called as Marcus stepped through the doorway. "Tell Sam we're all rooting for her."

Developers looked up as Marcus walked through the warren of cubicles that made up the entirety of Synerdyne's third floor, some of them greeting him while others just watched in curiosity. There were a lot of faces he didn't recognize, and he was sure they didn't know who he was either. His attendance at the office had dropped off significantly over the last year and a half, now that most of his work was done from home. When he did pop in, it was usually late at night, after everyone had gone home for the day.

From the glass walls of their offices, his team leads spotted him as well. Oswald was the first, and he hurriedly got up from his desk to come out onto the floor.

"Marcus, I didn't expect to see you today," he said with a broad smile, his interest in why Marcus was there more apparent than any happiness to see him.

"Yeah, neither did I. Just popped in to discuss some things with Evan."

"All good, I hope?"

"Yeah. Nothing to worry about," he said, giving him a lop-sided grin. "Thought while I was here, I'd check in."

"Happy to have you back. It's certainly been a while. How's Sam?"

"As well as she can be, under the circumstances."

"Yeah," Oswald said, letting the silence grow.

"Everything running smoothly?" Marcus asked, looking around in an attempt to break the awkward silence.

"Yeah. We're ahead of schedule in fact," he replied with a slight lift of his chin.

"Great. Good job. I figured you had everything under control."

"Are you lost?" A familiar voice called from behind, and Marcus turned to see Claire approaching.

"Yeah, I was looking for the bathrooms," he replied with a smirk, pretending to look down at the key card around his neck in confusion.

"Oh no. You're in the right place. You can shit in there," she said, pointing to his office door. "That's where everybody goes."

"I should have suspected as much," he said with a laugh as she stepped in for a hug.

"What are you doing here?" she asked.

"I had a meeting with Evan…"

"Marcus!" called another familiar voice from across the floor, as Diego emerged from his office.

Hustling between the cubicles, his friend threw his arms around him, squeezing him tightly. "It's so good to see you, man," Diego said excitedly. "I mean, you know, in the flesh."

"It's good to see you, too. All of you," he said, gesturing to his friends and the rest of the floor.

"How's Sam today? Man, we really miss having her here in the office," Diego said, putting a sympathetic hand on his shoulder.

"Not much different than when we last spoke. But it's been hard on her. I can tell," Marcus said.

"I'm sorry, man."

"Yeah. I know," Marcus said, patting Diego on the shoulder and giving him a somber grin.

"You said you had a meeting with Evan?" Claire interjected, cocking her head to the side, and making Diego raise his own head in curiosity.

"Yeah. We should probably have a talk. We just need to grab Amir."

"He's been in his office all day," Claire said. "He was already here when I got in this morning and hasn't left once."

"Yeah, he's focused on something," Diego added.

Marcus looked across the floor to Amir's office and noticed the curtains were drawn. Instinctively, he looked down at his phone and realized he had six notifications that Amir had called.

"Shit," he said under his breath. "Okay. Let me pop in on him and see. I need to have a chat with the Senior team. You guys wait for me in the conference room."

Claire and Diego nodded, while Oswald's expression flattened in disappointment. All three watched as he walked over to Amir's office.

Giving the door a couple of knocks, he waited. He thought he could hear some movement inside, but Amir gave no answer. He knocked again, this time saying "Amir. It's Marcus."

Inside the movement grew louder, and within seconds the door opened to reveal Amir's face, his eyes anxious and bloodshot.

"Hey, man. Sorry I didn't get back to you sooner. I…"

"It's about time," Amir said, opening the door and grabbing him by the shirt to pull him into the office. "Get in here. I have something you have to see."

CHAPTER 3

With the curtains drawn, Amir's office was dark, illuminated only by the light from his three monitors. Nothing else seemed abnormal about the office, but Marcus immediately picked up on Amir's agitation as his friend moved to sit down at his desk.

"Is everything alright?" Marcus asked cautiously.

"I suppose that depends on your definition of 'alright'," Amir said, scooting his chair under his desk and immediately beginning to type.

"Is it something to do with Elysium? Or the SynAPP?"

Amir turned to look at him, his eyes serious.

"It has to do with everything. Here. It's easier if I just show you," he replied, waving him over to his monitors.

Marcus moved to the desk, standing behind Amir's chair, and looked at the images on his screens. He recognized the familiar patterned lines and nodes that spider-webbed and connected on one monitor. On the other he saw the image in another view, creating the outline of a brain as though drawn by connecting the dots. "Okay. I see the SynAPP mapping protocol."

"No. You are looking at an artificial mapping created by the SynAPP protocol."

Marcus looked at the images. "I'm not sure I understand. What's the difference? The function of the SynAPP is to create artificial stimulus through cognitive mapping to guide function in the hippocampus, right?"

"Right. But this is not an image of stimulus on a patient's cognitive map. This is a completely artificial, self-functioning, replication of a patient's cognitive map."

Marcus stared at the screen, his eyes searching the image as he took in Amir's words.

"Wait. You're saying that this is a *copy* of someone's brain patterns? Not just a recording?"

"What I am saying is that not only is it a copy; I believe it is a functional copy. As in, using the SynAPP, the AAIP has replicated user mapping on a level we never imagined. With such detail that it, in essence, has the ability to potentially create another functioning brain."

Marcus' eyes widened as the implications started to sink in, and for a moment he had to clutch the back of Amir's chair in order to steady himself.

"So are you saying that this facsimile can *think*?"

"Maybe. I surmise that it has the potential to function in an environment that does not require a biological vessel."

"I don't understand how this can happen," Marcus said in wonder, leaning forward to look more closely at the data.

"I suppose we should have considered the possibility, despite how unlikely it seemed. After all, in order to function the SynAPP has to have a pattern map of the brain, not just the stimuli from the hippocampus. That information is then sent across every neuron to stimulate physical sensation and reaction. The AAIP then records those reactions in the neurons so that it can then interpret the signals into a specific, consistent reality experienced by participants in the simulation. To do this regularly, it must keep that mapping in a permanent file."

"Right. That's why mapping takes so long. But it is only a map used to guide the AAIP."

"But that's just it. Every time a user enters the simulation, the AAIP continues to map their neural patterns in greater detail. Those are just electrical signals. At a certain point it seems that the mapping might become as functional as the real thing."

"Have you tested this?"

"Fuck no! Are you crazy? Not only do we not know what would happen, but there are ethical concerns to consider."

"So are these facsimiles functioning on their own?"

"No. There is no stimuli to which they can react. And when used in conjunction with a participant, the mapping acts as it should, as a bridge between the AAIP and the brain, only increasing the efficacy of the SynAPP through continued use."

"So there is no danger to the participant?"

"None that I can determine, nor any seemingly from patient feedback."

Marcus took a deep breath. "But what you are saying is that the AAIP is creating an identical copy of each participant's brain pattern and neuron engagement. One that may be able to function on its own within the simulation?"

"Exactly."

"So we are preserving consciousness?"

"I don't know. Maybe."

Marcus moved from behind Amir's chair to drop onto the couch across from his desk. The implications were astounding, and his mind immediately turned to Sam.

"Is Sam recorded in the same way?"

Amir stared at him from behind the monitor with a knowing look. "I don't know. So far, I've only looked at the data from Elysium. Since Sam's World is on its own server, I only have a partial of her time spent in Elysium. But I don't see why it wouldn't be the same. I'd need to check the data from Sam's server first."

"So you're saying that the AAIP might be able to preserve her consciousness even if she were to die?"

"I'm saying that scenario might be a possibility, but I can't say for certain. Nor do I fully understand all the implications."

"But it might be possible."

"Perhaps. All I can say is we *may* have created a way to preserve memory and cognitive function when biological function ends. There is still too much we don't know, and we have no idea how this may manifest. I see two possibilities: one, we are creating the most precise and detailed map of the brain's function that has no ability to manifest as a self-aware consciousness; or two, we have developed…"

"A way to cheat death," Marcus finished.

"Don't get ahead of yourself. It is not the same thing. Death will still occur."

"To the body, sure. But in the simulation, you don't need a body. That's kind of the whole point. In a dream you can be anything and do anything. The rules are not the same."

"There are still rules. And the AAIP is only a simulation of the dream state."

"A simulation we control."

"Look. We need to figure this out. There are so many questions we still have to answer. And on top of that, there are innumerable ethical concerns here. We have to proceed slowly and carefully."

The image of Sam, smiling at him as she ran through the jungle—strong and vibrant again—filled his mind, before shifting to thoughts of her gaunt and frail body lying in bed. Though he never let his imagination linger there for long, he couldn't help thinking about the possibility of her death, causing a sharp pain in his chest. He immediately sought happier memories. Recollections of their youth, the two of them laughing together on car rides and long walks. Reminiscing about the vibrant woman she became in her late teens and early twenties. He could save all that from being lost. He could give her the second chance she deserved.

"Let's keep this between the two of us for now," Marcus said, pushing himself up from the couch.

Amir nodded, glancing at the door. "I'm not the only one with access to this data, Marcus. I'm just the one who noticed it first."

"Good point. But there isn't much we can do about that without drawing the very attention we don't want. So for now, let's hope you're the only one intelligent enough to deduce the possibility. We'll handle it as it comes." Marcus gave him a tight smile he hoped seemed reassuring. "As for the mapping. I want you to make it your sole focus from here on out. And keep me informed."

"Of course. Not like I'd be able to focus on anything else."

"I also want you to start devising a way for us to test your hypothesis."

Amir swallowed but nodded. "Alright."

"Okay. Good." Marcus said, taking a deep breath. "Now, I need you to join us in the conference room. I have to talk to you guys about something."

"Can't you just fill me in? I want to keep at this."

"For this news, it's better that you're there. Otherwise, it will seem suspicious that I didn't include you."

"Is it bad?" Amir asked, his brow raising in concern.

Marcus leaned forward on Amir's desk, his face lit by the glow of the monitor.

"Actually, I think it might be exactly what we need."

Claire and Diego were waiting in the conference room when Marcus and Amir entered, and both of their gazes shifted to Amir, their curiosity apparent. For his part, Amir gave them a wave. Marcus' eyes swept over them, but in his head his thoughts were reeling with the possibilities of what Amir had told him. Could they really be preserving consciousness with the AAIP? Different explanations and their possible outcomes also swirled in his head, some troubling, others exhilarating. He ignored his friends' expectant stares and gave them a bland smile as he walked over to the coffee maker. As expected, Diego had made a fresh pot. Good ol' dependable Diego.

Marcus grabbed a mug and poured a cup, giving himself time to gather his thoughts. For a moment, he forced his mind back to his meeting with Evan. There were so many variables to consider, and this thing with Clive Ellison made it even more delicate. Could he really save Sam? He tried to keep his mind on the facts as he had them, hesitant to open himself up to the possibility, well aware of the pain that would come with it if it didn't pan out.

"Everything alright, Marcus?" Claire asked behind him.

He could hear Diego whispering to Amir, but he didn't hear the other engineer respond. Turning around, he forced a broad grin on his face. His two friends were looking up at him expectantly, but Amir was staring off.

"I guess that depends. That's what I wanted to talk to you guys about," he said, taking a sip of his coffee. "So, as you already know, I had a meeting with Evan this afternoon."

Amir looked up, his curiosity suddenly piqued.

"Apparently Synerdyne has been approached by Clive Ellison. He is interested in investing."

"Fuck no," Claire said immediately, her jaw set.

"The tech guy?" Diego asked.

Amir just looked at Marcus. Though he didn't say anything, Marcus could see his friend slowly piecing together the potential implications.

"Now, don't jump to any conclusions," Marcus went on. "I'm hesitant, I'll admit. But Evan has given me his word that we will have input in this decision."

"It's Clive Ellison, Marcus. Everything he does is for headlines. He'd just make our research into another supposed 'innovation' on his part," Claire said sharply. "What is there to consider? Besides, Medirnus would never go for it."

"Medirnus is out."

"What?!" Claire exclaimed, followed quickly by Diego.

"Apparently, they don't see Synerdyne as a viable profit stream and want to cut ties. So much so that they're willing to take a hit to do it."

"Jesus," Claire whispered, folding her arms and slumping back in her chair.

"Well," Diego said softly. "That certainly changes things."

Marcus nodded. "That was Evan's argument as well."

"Evan just wants to guarantee funding and Synerdyne's bottom line," Claire said dismissively. "And he'll work with anyone he thinks can do that."

"Well, that is his job, Claire," Marcus countered. "But also, there wouldn't be a Synerdyne without him. The SynAPP might have been our idea, but it would still just be a patent without his funding and belief in the program. So maybe give him a little more consideration than just branding him the money-hungry CEO."

Claire let out a hard breath. "Look. I know you guys go back further than the rest of us, but that doesn't mean I'm wrong about his motivations."

"Maybe. But he won't make any move without my approval. He can't, really. That's the benefit of being as small as we are."

"Yeah, well, we still have shareholders," Amir interjected. "That capital didn't just come from Evan. He's just the one who knew how to acquire it. We've got people to answer to, and that means we are at their mercy."

"Sure. You're right," Marcus conceded. "But Evan believes in the project, and I trust his word when he tells me that we have input in the decision."

"This can only turn out badly," Claire muttered. "Ellison buys companies and takes all the credit for their research."

"Does he know anything about the program? The SynAPP or AAIP?" Diego asked, glancing at Claire.

"We're not sure how much he knows. He wants a tour of Elysium, and we're giving him one. Evan thinks this could be a game changer. He just asks that we look at it with open minds before we make any determinations." Marcus took another sip and looked around the table. "So for right now, it's just business as usual, yeah? I literally just left his office and came straight here. I wanted you guys to be in the loop."

Claire's glare eased a bit and her posture relaxed, while Diego and Amir both nodded.

"Did you tell Sam?" Diego asked.

"Not yet. I'm not sure if it'll do her any good to know, honestly."

"You have to tell her. She's still part of this, even if she's not here," Claire said, sitting up. "She's a founding member too."

"I know. But things haven't been good lately," Marcus said. "She's not eating as much and getting thinner. Like scary thin. She tries to hide it from me, but I notice. Looking at photos from just a few months ago, the difference is striking."

Claire's face softened, and after a moment she looked away.

Diego's eyes reddened, but he put on a sad smile. "We've got to jump into Sam's World with her again soon."

"She'd love that," Marcus said, a familiar tightening growing in his chest. "When she's there, she's the same old Sam. She doesn't even think about being sick. It doesn't change reality, but inside the simulation she really does get relief from her pain and worry." He glanced at Amir, and couldn't help but think that maybe it *could* change reality.

"How does she like the upgrades?" Diego asked, his smile broadening.

"She loves them. She specifically wanted me to tell you that she thought the latest patch was amazing. We hopped in this morning and played around a bit in the new environment. She's eager to kill the ape," he said chuckling.

Diego's smile grew even wider. "Well, you let her know I'm working on something even bigger and more special."

"Do you ever sleep?"

"Nope. Sleeping is for the weak. Sam taught me that," his friend said chuckling. "Plus, it's not only me. I've got a whole team of minions to do my bidding now."

"What do they think about the project? Do they have any idea about Sam's World?"

"No. They think it's for a new environment in Elysium, which isn't a lie. Though I have to be careful with some of the assets we are creating. They don't seem like the sort of thing you'd find in just a jungle biome."

"Like what?"

Diego held up a finger to waggle at Marcus. "Now, now. I don't want to ruin the surprise, do I?"

"You can't not tell *me*," Marcus insisted. "I have to know what she's going to encounter and make sure it's not too much."

"Give over, you control freak, and let yourself be surprised. That's the point of the simulation, after all," Diego chided him.

"Not with pain reception, it isn't," Marcus pointed out.

"How is that working out?" Claire interjected.

"Sam says she likes it. Says it's better than before when it was just invincibility. But I worry about it. I'm afraid it might create a cascade effect on her nervous system that, in her weakened state, might have some unforeseen circumstances."

"Well, we ran the simulations, and you and I both tried it. It's unpleasant, for sure, but the tests showed it doesn't create any sort of physical impact beyond some neurological stimulation. No different from pleasure stimulation, really. Just the opposite side of the coin. And I know you aren't interested in removing the pleasure stimulation," she said teasingly.

"I don't know what you mean," Marcus said, burying his face in his cup.

"I know Sam. There's no way you two aren't using the simulation to get your freak on. No judgments. I'd do the same in your situation.

I'm only glad you have the option," she said reaching over the table to pat his hand.

Marcus lowered his cup, giving her a lop-sided grin.

"Yeah, boy! Smash!" Diego added with a laugh.

"Well. I, for one, find your sexual deviance disgusting," Amir said, crossing his arms in mock disapproval.

"Alright. Alright. Enough talking about my intimate relations. But yes, Claire, I take your point. That's basically what Sam said. She says it felt weird without the pain before, and now things seem more natural. Though we still haven't tried the death feature."

"It should function just as in the tests. When the pain threshold reaches maximum tolerance, the SynAPP triggers unconsciousness. The subject is then ejected from the simulation as if they had ended it by choice."

"I know. Still, I can't help but worry that something will go wrong with Sam. You and I are both relatively healthy, but Sam's got so many other variables to contend with. I worry one of them will throw something off."

"I get it, and I can't tell you that you're one hundred percent wrong," Claire said. "But we made Sam's World under her direction, as a testing ground. One she willingly wants to participate in. And the data we get from her can help us with other patients down the line, many of whom will have similar physical impairments. I know it isn't clinically sound, and to truly get good data we have to run trials like in Elysium, but it at least points us in the right direction. Just keep an eye on Sam in the simulation and we'll keep recording the data. If you think she's going too far, or believes she's expected to push herself, then we'll pull back. But these were her requests," Claire swallowed and took a breath. When she continued her voice was tight and pained. "And I can't bring myself to deprive her of any request. Nor can I see the outcome as being worse than what she's dealing with."

Marcus held his cup in both hands before him and let her words sink in. What she meant was: 'She is dying. If she dies in-game enjoying herself, is that any worse than the alternative?' He didn't resent her for the statement. Part of him knew it was a possibility, but he couldn't entertain the idea that it was inevitable. He still clung to the hope of turning things around and ignored the ever-present darkness that told him otherwise.

"We'll give it a go soon. Probably tonight or tomorrow. Sam's not going to be put off from it much longer," he said with a sad smile. "But I don't think that's why I'm hesitant. I… the thought…," he swallowed as his throat tightened. "I don't know if I can handle seeing her die. Even just in-game."

Claire nodded and patted his hand again, while Diego stood up and walked around the table to pull him into a tight hug.

"That makes perfect sense, Marcus," Claire said softly. "But psychologically, experiencing that outcome in-game, where she is returned afterward, might actually help you process all of this a little bit. I'm not saying it won't be painful, or that it means you'll be more ready to accept such an outcome in real life. But it may help you face what I imagine has been your greatest fear for the last two years."

Marcus let out a long breath as Diego released him, blinking back the tears from his burning eyes. "Maybe. Yeah. I don't know."

"Remember, I'll monitor her physical response when she is ejected, and let you know if I find anything concerning. Ask yourself: is denying Sam what she wants fair to her? Sometimes you have to give up your control and just let things happen. I hope for the best, but in truth, Sam's fate is beyond our control."

Marcus stared down into the dark pool at the bottom of his cup and thought about what Claire had said. As if summoned by her words, a darkness seemed to grow in his thoughts. *Sam's fate is beyond our control.* However, with Amir's discovery, maybe it didn't have to be.

CHAPTER 4

Sam perked up at the sound of the front door opening and the jingle of Marcus' keys. She'd tried sleeping on and off since he left, but the pain in her spine made it so she could never get comfortable. She wished she could use the simulation to sleep, but it didn't work that way. However much sleep she got in Sam's World or Elysium, she still came out of the simulation as tired as if she had been awake the whole time. It had something to do with the SynAPP's stimulation of the hippocampus. Sort of like expecting to double your sleep by dreaming while in a dream.

Gritting her teeth, she pushed herself up into a sitting position on the bed, pain lancing up her back. Just as she settled back on her pillows, Marcus peered in from the doorway.

"Hey there, little one. How are you doing? Did you get any sleep?" he asked, his soft eyes meeting hers.

"Not really," she said, still trying to make minute adjustments to find the most comfortable position. "A little maybe. Mainly, I just watched some shows and browsed the internet."

His mouth twisted in sympathy. He walked over to the bed and gently reached out to grab her toes over the covers to give them a squeeze. It was one of the few things he could do to show his affection that wouldn't potentially cause her pain. The tumors that littered her chest were not only slowly draining her life away; they were simultaneously keeping her from finding comfort from the touch of those she loved. Any pressure that moved her unexpectedly would send sharp stabbing pain through her body. So hugs became squeezes to feet and hands, and kisses moved from her lips to the top of her head. It wasn't the same, but it still meant everything.

Smiling at him, she tried to keep the pain from her face. She knew it would only make him feel helpless. A reminder that there was nothing he could do to stop it. He smiled back, but she could see she wasn't fooling him.

"Did everything go okay with Evan?" she asked, trying to change the subject.

"Yeah, actually. Nothing bad. In fact, it might prove to be something really good for the project."

"Really?" she pressed, her interest piqued. "What was it?"

Marcus' mouth twisted into a grin. "Well, it's all still being figured out, and we may not go through with it." He pulled the chair over to her bedside, careful not to snag it on any of the wires that littered the floor.

"Are you going to tell me?" she prodded, frustrated at his evasion. She scrunched her face up in mock annoyance and twisted her lips, knowing he would find it cute and that it would weaken his resolve.

On cue, he smiled and twisted his own lips in response.

"I'm afraid it's top secret."

Narrowing her eyes, she glared at him and pursed her lips.

"Are you serious? Spit it out. You can't *not* tell me. Did you tell the team?"

"Yes," he admitted.

"Well, I'm part of the team too. You can't tell them and not me." Balling her hand up in a fist she shook it at him cartoonishly, playing to his affections while hiding the stabbing shocks that needled along her spine.

His smile grew and he took her fist in his hand, leaning forward to kiss it.

"Okay. Okay. But there's not that much to tell right now. I don't have any details. And bear in mind that not everybody is on board with the idea." His face grew more serious, his eyes searching hers. "It's kinda controversial. You might not like it either."

Sam's own expression sobered, worry replacing curiosity.

"What is it?"

"Evan was contacted by Clive Ellison. He's interested in the SynAPP and our simulation work."

Sam let out a breath, her mind immediately seeing the pitfalls of having the billionaire get involved in their research.

"Now we don't yet know his exact interest. But apparently Ellison is already aware of our research, and Evan wants me to give him a tour of Elysium."

Forcing her concerns to the back of her mind, Sam tried to see the opportunities Clive Ellison might bring to the program and Synerdyne. However, her thoughts kept returning to the idea that it all might threaten Sam's World and her access to it.

"This is a really big deal," she said.

"Yeah, but it also means potential funding on a scale we couldn't hope to achieve anytime soon."

"But what about Medirnus?" she asked.

"They're out?"

"What?! Can they do that?"

"Apparently."

"Shit," Sam said in surprise, letting the word linger. "How do you think it will affect our autonomy? Medirnus was pretty hands-off, all things considered. But you know what they say about this guy."

Marcus sat back in the chair and ran a hand through his hair as he let out a long breath. "Yeah, I know. Maybe I'll have a better idea after I meet him."

"If Evan gets any more details, you let me look at them. Okay?"

Marcus' eyes drifted over her, and she could tell he was worried about involving her in her present condition.

"Marcus," she prodded, giving him a serious look. "Promise me."

"Sam…"

She sat up, the pain in her back an afterthought.

"Promise me. This concerns me just as much as everyone else. More so."

Marcus let out another long breath, his eyes softening with a sad grin.

"Alright, baby. I promise."

Sam felt the tension ease at his words and let herself settle back on her pillows. She glanced over to Marcus and found him staring at her. It made her wonder what he was thinking, but as she opened her mouth to ask, he sat up in his own chair and smiled broadly.

"Want some dinner, little one?"

Sam felt her queasiness grow at his question. Food was the last thing she wanted. The thought alone made her stomach twist.

"I'm not hungry. Can we go back into Sam's World?"

Marcus' smile fell for a moment, replaced with familiar worry, before he forced it back onto his face.

"Come on, baby. You have to eat something."

"I did earlier," she said, omitting the fact that she had thrown it all up.

"Maybe just a little something?" he prodded. "I'll make you a shake. A little one."

Sam stared into his eyes, seeing the concern in them.

"Okay. A little one."

"A little one for my little one. You got it," he said. He stood up and his face brightened.

Sam couldn't help but smile back.

"But when I'm done we're going to Sam's World."

"As you wish," he said, stopping in the doorway to give her a wink before heading to the kitchen.

Morrigan looked down at the pool of water at the base of the waterfall. Beside her on the bluff, Aer moved into position. Bare-chested and clad in a simple leather tasset, he stared down at the scene. Below them, the giant ape made his way to the edge of the pool, cupping his hand into the crystalline water before bringing it to his mouth to drink. The beast seemed peaceful enough at the moment, but she could tell it was capable of great violence. They needed to be careful in their approach.

"Alright, boyo," she whispered. "I'll flank it on the left from those rocks, while ye go over there to the right." She pointed to a steep cliff that sat almost directly above the pool. "Ye get its attention, and I'll take it from behind."

Aer shook his head. "If something goes wrong, I won't be able to back you up from there."

Morrigan arched an eyebrow, the left side of her mouth curling upward. "Don't worry yer pretty face about that, boyo. Ye do yer part and I'll do mine. Just get its attention."

For a moment, Sam shifted out of character and looked him in the eye. "Remember, no stopping the simulation. If I die, I die. Let me see what the death protocol is like."

She didn't wait for his reply and started climbing along the ridge, keeping her body low to the ground to avoid being spotted. Luckily, the roaring sound of the waterfall was loud enough to hide the scrapping of her sandals on the flaking stone as she moved into position. Giving a glance over her shoulder, she saw Aer watching her, his mouth tight. Giving him a wink, she gestured to the right cliff with her chin.

Below her, the ape seemed oblivious to their presence. It was at least twice as tall as she, with massive arms and a barrel chest. If she was careless or moved too slowly, that thing would tear her apart. She felt a shiver run up her spine at the thrill of the thought, adrenaline coursing through her veins. Looking across the gap, she caught sight of Aer getting into position. Meeting her gaze, he gave her a nod to tell her he was ready.

She offered her own in return and began to slowly climb down the rocky slope toward the pool. Aer's gaze moved from her to the ape and back, watching as she drew closer to the beast. Once she was halfway to the pool, he suddenly shouted and threw a rock down at the monster.

At his provocation, the creature stopped its drinking and spun to look up at the cliff face, letting out a mighty roar that echoed over the sound of the waterfall. Morrigan took advantage of the distraction to scramble quickly down the rest of the slope. As she reached the pool's edge, she moved to close the distance.

Continuing to keep its attention, Aer flung more stones at the monster and shouted loudly. As she had suspected, the sheer cliff on which Aer perched did not offer any direct path for the beast to reach him. The ape let out another bellow, lifting itself to stand on two legs as it pounded its fists against its chest in frustration.

With a roar of her own, Morrigan ran at the creature, leveling her spear to strike. The beast only had time to turn its head in her direction before her spear sunk deeply into its muscled back. The ape whirled around, roaring in pain and yanking the spear away with its movement.

Morrigan was nearly pulled off her feet as the spear was torn from her hands. Above her, Aer yelled for her to run, throwing his own spear down at the monster and catching it in the shoulder. If the wounds it received did anything more than anger the ape, it didn't show, and its gaze turned to Morrigan. Wide-eyed, she scrambled away from the creature, fumbling to pull her knife from her belt. At that moment she felt fear, but it was dwarfed by a greater sense of exhilaration. This was it.

Dropping back on all fours, the ape let out another bone-rattling roar and charged, pulling itself forward with its massive arms. Morrigan was only dimly aware of Aer's distant shouts. She pushed them from her mind, tightening the grip on her knife and turning all her attention to the fast-approaching beast.

It all happened in a blur. She attempted to leap away, but the ape was faster, swinging a massive arm that sent her reeling onto the stony ground. She only had time to register the ape's shadow looming over her and roll away enough to take its second fist in the shoulder instead of the chest. Pain washed over her. Strangely, a small part of her analyzed it in the back of her head as the rest of her body instinctually took over. Was the pain as severe as she anticipated? Or was it dampened? Could the human body really take such punishment?

She moved with the blow, found her footing and rolled into a crouch. Knife still tightly held in her grip, she launched herself at the ape instead of trying to flee. The beast's massive body slammed into her vastly smaller frame, nearly knocking the wind from her as it wrapped its trunk-like arms around her torso. The sound of Aer's shouting and the roar of the waterfall faded into the background. All she knew was the crushing weight of the monster's arms around her and the feel of its leathery skin and coarse fur. Its breath was hot against her skin as it roared in her face, spraying her with spittle.

Morrigan screamed right back, driving her knife into the monster's neck. The attack did not stop the ape, and she felt her ribs cracking under the pressure of its arms. Pulling the knife out of its flesh, she stabbed again, yanking the blade out to drive it in again in quick succession. The pain only existed in the back of her mind as she continued her attack, the animal's neck becoming a grotesque mass of blood and fur. The beast, however, did not let go. Darkness began to press in at the edge of her vision, threatening to overwhelm her.

As her knife strikes slowed, she couldn't help but smile with the realization that the ape's breath didn't smell like anything. Just air. As the last moments of consciousness fled, she made a point to remember that she'd need to mention that to Diego.

Sam woke with a start, the sound of the ape's roar still ringing in her ears. With bleary eyes she searched for the creature, slowly coming to recognize the familiar shapes of her room and furniture. Letting out a long breath, she relaxed back into her pillows and winced at the sudden jolt that ran up her spine. Despite the pain, she smiled. It had worked!

In the chair beside her, Marcus let out a groan, his slouched body beginning to stir. Slowly his eyes opened and his body rose into a more seated position. His gaze moved about the room groggily, and after a few blinks, settled on her. Eyes wide, he sat forward, reaching out to take her hand.

"Are you okay?" he asked, concern in his voice.

"Don't worry. I'm fine," she said with a smile, taking his hand in hers. "It worked, Marcus! It worked!" she exclaimed, squeezing his hand, barely able to contain her excitement.

His eyes searched hers before sliding down to inspect the rest of her body. The action was irrational. The simulation wouldn't have caused any actual wounds, but she knew he was just acting on instinct. Something embedded deep in the lizard brain. She reached out a hand to pet his cheek.

"I'm okay," she reaffirmed with a laugh.

Looking back at her face, he seemed to relax. He took her hand and kissed her fingers. Then he sighed and gave her a relieved grin.

"That was brutal," he said. "I'll need to tell Diego to tone it down."

"No," she said quickly. "Don't you dare! It was perfect."

"There's no way you can take that thing on. Even with the two of us, it killed you."

"So? That's the whole point. I'm tired of hunting animals that don't fight back. There are only so many tapirs and stags I can hunt. It's the challenge of the thing that's important. I'll kill it. You'll see," she said, feeling her face split into a smile.

Marcus' brow twisted and he pursed his lips.

"How are you feeling?" he asked, changing the subject. "Anything weird or residual?"

"I feel the same as ever," she replied. "No better, no worse."

"What was the experience like for you? How was the pain?"

"It was sort of like falling asleep. Or maybe how it feels to have narcolepsy? You know, when you're so tired you can't keep your eyes open. No matter how hard you try," she said, trying to remember the last sensations she'd felt. But just like in a dream, some of the details were already beginning to get a little hazy. "The pain was… not what I expected. It didn't hurt as much as I thought it would. Are you sure you increased the threshold?"

"We did. But we put it on a tiered scale."

"You were supposed…" she began to protest but Marcus held up a hand.

"It was something the rest of the team agreed upon. There was some real concern that if some level of control wasn't kept on pain reception it could have some unforeseen consequences. There's a very real possibility that, without some set parameters, the AAIP could actually interpret pain reception in a way that could increase it beyond even normal thresholds and have a lasting effect on your neurological pathways."

"Think of it this way. In the simulation you're a hero, right? Well, heroes fight well beyond the pain that normal people can withstand. Doesn't mean you don't feel pain, it just means you feel it in a way that doesn't debilitate you. But only to a point. The pain is tiered so that as it amplifies, it begins to dampen. Allowing you to continue to act. In real life, one hit from that ape would have crippled you. So which would you rather? Be the badass? Or be like everyone else?"

"Part of being a badass is pushing yourself onward when other people would stop," she said glumly.

"Believe me, Sam. You're as badass as it comes. You handle pain every day that would debilitate other people. And you're no different in the game. I know how it was designed and have control of the simulation. But even I was scared to deal with that ape. You jumped at that beast without a second thought. And it's not like it didn't cause you pain, right?"

"Yeah," she agreed, unable to keep her mouth from twisting into a smile as her disappointment began to fade. "It was pretty intense, I guess."

Marcus' eyes widened. "Intense? I didn't even try to fight that thing after it killed you. I looked at it and just 'noped' out."

Sam laughed, but it was cut short as a sharp twinge stabbed at her side. She tried to hide it but saw the worry it caused on Marcus' face. Holding up at hand to let him know she was okay, she took a second to let it subside then smiled at him again.

"Can we go back and try again?" she asked hopefully but immediately felt disappointment looking at the expression on his face.

"Let's give it a little rest. We should probably analyze your neuropathic response before trying again. Just to make sure there isn't anything problematic." Seeing her disappointment, he leaned forward to rest his chin on her lap and looked up at her. "It won't be long, I promise. I'll have Claire and Amir analyze the data first thing. But we have to be careful whenever we test a new feature. You know that."

"Yeah," she said with a sigh.

"We'll go back and do it real soon. Claire can probably give us the green light tomorrow."

She let out another long breath, dreading the hours between now and whenever Marcus was comfortable enough to try again. Her chest tightened at the thought of just sitting there, bored and in pain. Her eyes began to sting, and she turned her head away so that he wouldn't see her tears.

"Hey, baby," he said, picking up on her distress. "Don't cry."

At his words, the dam broke. Her frustration and sadness washed over her. Letting out a choked breath, she turned back to him, her tears flowing.

"I just sit here, day after day, trying to manage the pain and waiting for our chance to play again. In the simulation, I get to forget all that. I can forget the pain and fear. When I'm there, I feel like myself again. Better than myself." She sobbed, trying to explain it in a way he might understand, but knowing he couldn't fully understand it. No one could, really. At least not anyone healthy who wasn't going through something similar. It wasn't his fault; he tried. But try as they might, 'cancer muggles' would never fully understand.

Tears slipped down Marcus' cheeks, his own eyes growing red. With a pained expression, he reached out to squeeze her hand.

"I know, baby. I hate that you are going through this. My only wish is to make it better for you. Listen, just because we can't fight the ape again doesn't mean we can't go back into Sam's World. If you're okay with just exploring and hanging out there, we can go back."

Sam felt her disappointment starting to fade at his words, and slowly her tears began to subside. He really was trying; she knew that. And deep down she also knew he was right about studying the data. She just wished he'd stop worrying and insisting on being in Sam's World with her and let her go there on her own.

"You just want to fuck," she laughed weakly, reaching up to wipe the tears from her cheeks.

"Well, I'll never say no to that. If you're offering," he replied with a smile, reaching up to gently turn her face to his.

Looking into his eyes, she wanted to cry again. Not out of sadness, but for the love and pain she saw there. He loved her so much. She only hoped he knew how much she loved him back. She felt her tears begin to flow again.

"God damn it," she said, choking out a laugh as she reached up to wipe her face again. "I get so damn emotional all the time now."

"It's okay, sweetness," Marcus said, getting up from the chair and leaning forward to gently kiss her lips, careful not to bump her.

She returned the kiss, reaching up to keep him from pulling away, ignoring the twinges of pain that lanced down her back. They lingered in the kiss for a long moment before Marcus reluctantly disengaged.

"You wanna go back?" he asked, his face inches from hers.

"Yeah," Sam said with a nod.

"You got it, little one," he said, returning to his chair and picking up his tablet.

"Oh, before I forget," she added, holding up a hand to stop him. "Tell Diego the ape needs to have bad breath. Right now it just breathes hot air."

Marcus smiled at her broadly.

"I'll do that," he replied, lifting the tablet and engaging the SynAPP.

CHAPTER 5

"As you can see, in Elysium our participants can experience a simulation of reality devoid of whatever pain they might currently suffer in their daily lives. Using the SynAPP we can control their experience in a tailored way," Marcus said, gesturing to the neighborhood of perfectly manicured lawns and white homes around them.

In those yards and houses, people moved about, tending to gardens and mowing lawns. Above them the sky was blue with only the thinnest wisps of clouds. There were no roads or sidewalks, just one wide silvery avenue that cut between a row of homes on either side. Tall trees lined the path, their green leaves fluttering as if in a gentle breeze. Several of the people stopped to watch curiously as Marcus and his guest strolled past, a few waving, and Marcus returned their greetings with a smile.

"For those who suffer from physical disabilities or unmanageable pain, the SynAPP allows us to block those impairments or sensations within the simulation. Our research is not meant to be used for standard impairments, but for those that affect the quality of life. So primarily people who are bedridden or impaired physically. Some of our participants are in palliative care: whether due to organ failure, cancer, or some other cellular degeneration. Likewise, we have participants who have suffered traumatic injuries. A few of whom are veterans who received their injuries in combat."

He looked over at the man beside him, but Clive Ellison didn't seem to notice him, and Marcus wondered if the man had heard what he'd said.

"And this is all generated in their hippocampus?" Ellison asked, gazing at the scene around him.

"In essence, yes. However, your experience is different from theirs. Were you using the SynAPP, the experience would be more akin to a living moment."

Mr. Ellison stopped walking and looked over at Marcus. "How is it different?"

"Well right now you are in a simulation pod. So in some ways you are experiencing the simulation as a virtual reality construct. Think of it as one, or more accurately, several hundred steps removed. You're experiencing this more like a video game. They're experiencing this more like a dream. If that helps."

"But you said the pod would let me experience the simulation to the fullest extent. It's why I agreed to put on that ridiculous helmet and suit and sat in that egg filled with water."

Marcus' lips curled into a smile. "Well, you're still in that 'egg', sir. And using the pod is the closest way for someone without the SynAPP to experience this environment. With it you can experience auditory, visual, and physical sensations in the simulation. But in truth, yours is an altogether different experience. You are experiencing a static simulation, crafted to represent what is being experienced by the participants."

"I think I understand," Mr. Ellison said. "Correct me if I'm wrong. With the SynAPP implant, the participant experiences sensations as if they existed in this environment. However, they aren't placed into this environment. Instead, the simulation is created in their mind, like a dream. You set the parameters for the basics of

Elysium to help guide the brain's creation of the environment, but the participant's mind is generating all sensations and experiences. In the pod, the suit and helmet are generating what I see and feel. Thus, the depth of my experience is external and limited to the pod and hardware's design capabilities. Whereas the SynAPP stimulates the hippocampus to generate an experience within the participant's mind crafted to your specifications."

"Uh, yes. Exactly," Marcus said, stunned at the accuracy of the man's description. "With the SynAPP, all their senses are engaged with no limits, save the ones we have designed. In this way, we can turn off the pain receptors in the brain so that people are no longer hindered by their nervous system. People who can no longer walk can do so with ease. People who can no longer see or hear can use those senses again. The helmet and pod can't do that."

"I think I understand," Clive said, beginning to walk forward again. "What about people born blind or deaf? How do they react to the SynAPP?"

"Well, that's not the purpose of the device, so we haven't tried it in that capacity. This device is to help people adjust to loss, whether it be motor or sensory function or cognitive loss. People born without certain senses are not considered to have lost anything. I can't say for certain, but the most probable outcome would not be what you might think. The SynAPP can only stimulate activity using the participant's already existing brain patterns. So if we were to generate the simulation for a patient who had never experienced light-based sight, their hippocampus would not process things the same way. Nor would they see or hear things as we might expect, as their brains have learned to perceive the world a little differently than someone who was born with functional eyesight or hearing. I can't say categorically they wouldn't experience the same thing, but there is no telling without further research. But that does lead to my other point."

"And that is?"

"That when using the SynAPP, each person's experience is unique to them. The fundamentals remain primarily the same, based upon the parameters we provide, but what each participant experiences is ultimately formed by their brain's interpretation of the information. Again, this is not the same with the helmet and pod, where you are provided with a fully constructed environment that is exactly as we designed it."

"So the people using the device see different things?"

"Essentially, yes. We can't see through their eyes, so there is no way to say for certain what they experience, but a bit of variation is bound to happen based on their own brain's interpretation. However, we do extensive and routine evaluations with the participants where they describe their experiences to us in detail. Additionally, each patient is expected to record a video journal after each visit to Elysium," Marcus explained, as their path brought them to a pond filled with clear blue water.

"The same thing happens in the real world. What you see is based upon your brain's interpretation of the signals picked up by your retina and sent through your optic nerve. An innumerable number of variables: light, genetics, macular degeneration, cataracts, glaucoma, astigmatism, all of these can alter what you perceive compared to another person. The details might be so small that two people can identically describe the same image, but it isn't their eye alone that determines what they see, it's the signal sent to their brain and how it interprets that signal. With the SynAPP it is similar. The entirety of the experience is just a construct of signals, uniquely interpreted by each individual participant's brain."

Clive Ellison stopped and turned to face the pool. "So, when looking at this pond, one may see blue water and another green?"

"Well, perhaps. In the real world that would depend more on the cones in a person's eye. However, here it is more likely they may see it as varying shades of blue, maybe one greener than another.

The variations aren't so great that someone would perceive the environment entirely differently."

"So, in all functional respects, what you see is what you get," Clive said, turning to face him.

"Essentially, yes."

"Good. No need to muddy the waters with insignificant details."

"Sir?"

"Despite popular opinion, I'm no scientist, Mr. Avery. Though I am sure it is fascinating, I'm not sure I could keep up with all the intricacies of the science. What I am here to see is how the SynAPP is used and what it is capable of. After that, I'll have a better understanding of its possibilities."

"Alright," Marcus said with a shrug. "Then let me tell you about how the whole process functions."

"Didn't you already do that?" Clive asked, his brow furrowing.

"No. That's only one half of how all this works. I only told you about the SynAPP's functionality, not how we create the experience. The implant is how we get the signals to the brain, but it doesn't create the signals. For that, we have the AAIP."

"AAIP?"

"The Autonomous Artificial Intelligence Program. It's the core of the simulation, and the SynAPP is its delivery system. The AAIP uses assets designed with multi-dimensional properties to not only simulate the assets in our participants' perception but also replicate them. Once given the parameters for a specific asset, it can extrapolate those parameters to other things, using the SynAPP to send those signals to the brain. It is the heart of the simulation, and without the AI, the SynAPP would be useless. On top of that, the 'autonomous' part of AAIP denotes that the AI learns on its own, based upon the information it receives, not only from our team but also the participants. For instance, if we tell it that a wall is made out of stone, and we give it parameters for the weight, density, smell, taste, color, and texture of that stone, it can replicate other things using the same stone that will contain those details. Thus, we never have to make an asset twice."

"Taste?"

Marcus smirked.

"We try to consider all aspects of an asset's composition. You never know how one thing might affect another. Or if anyone's going to try licking it," he said, grinning at the man.

Mr. Ellison looked back at the pond, apparently unamused. Marcus' grin faded and he cleared his throat.

"So basically, the AAIP is the true architect of this reality," Marcus continued. It has nothing to do with the SynAPP. The SynAPP only allows for a more authentic and visceral experience. Right now, you are only experiencing the AAIP construct."

"What is involved with the SynAPP implementation? Is it a dangerous procedure?"

"No, not really," Marcus replied. "The implant itself is a small rod, not much larger than a needle. Forty-five millimeters in length and two millimeters wide. It is inserted into the limbic lobe, more specifically the hippocampus, from the base of the skull. The outpatient procedure takes about an hour, without any invasive surgery, and only leaves a small scar. After that, in the following days and weeks, we perform a series of tests, slowly training the patient's brain to recognize the signals from the implant and monitoring for any adverse effects."

"And have there been any adverse effects or problems?"

"Early on, when in development, we had a number of failures but none that were a threat to patients' lives or function. The primary side effects that have been reported are disruptions in dream function, which makes sense. And headaches."

"And is there any long-term damage to the hippocampus?"

Again, Marcus was surprised by Mr. Ellison's specificity.

"None that we've observed."

"And extraction of the implant?"

"That is more difficult than the insertion," Marcus admitted. "It requires more invasive surgery to remove the SynAPP. Imagine the difference between pushing a needle into something and pulling it out. However, it can be deactivated remotely, and the user always has active control of the device."

"Active control?"

"A user has the ability to disengage from the simulation at will, preventing them from being trapped against their will."

"How does that work?"

"Through a conscious trigger. Part of the initial orientation process for patients with the implant teaches them how to do this. Each pattern is unique to the participant, and it takes some time to get the implant to recognize this command. But it requires no words or action from the user, just conscious thought. So, when a participant is ready to leave the simulation, they may do so at any time."

"And engagement with the simulation? Can they do that as well?"

"Yes and no. Engagement is reserved for certain hours of the day. However, within that time, participants may enter and leave as they like."

"And have you had this surgery? Or are you also in a pod?"

"I have had the surgery, and I am currently using the SynAPP," Marcus said with a nod, reaching up to pat the nape of his neck.

"Is that the same for your team?"

"Yes. My senior team all have the implant. They are also the ones who helped develop the prototype for this technology."

"That is a strong endorsement. What about others on staff? Mr. Nyugen, for instance."

"No, Evan doesn't have the implant. He's always been a little hesitant about it, to tell you the truth. Though he'll be the first to tell you how much he believes in our technology and our mission. He just participates using the pod."

"You mentioned earlier about inhibiting pain reception. Does that mean you can't feel pain here?"

"That's right. In Elysium, we prevent and control all pain reception. This way our participants don't have to fear hurting themselves in the simulation and can take all the risks they like. We haven't added them yet, but we are currently working on several activities such as: hang-gliding, rock climbing, and skydiving. All of which will be safe for the participants."

"Hmmm," Ellison said, looking back to the neighborhood. "Is that only for their protection or because it would interfere with suppressing the pain they normally feel outside of the simulation?"

"An insightful question," Marcus conceded. "But no. We have complete control over their synaptic stimulus within the simulation. So even if we allowed pain, we could control its intensity and source, based upon the simulation's parameters."

"So why not set the pain reception low, but still allow it in some capacity?"

"I'm not sure what you mean," Marcus said, hearing the echoes of Sam's initial inquiries about the same thing in the man's question.

"Well, you touted how using the SynAPP allowed your participants the full spectrum of experience, but by denying them the ability to feel pain, aren't you dampening that experience? Does it not have a cascading effect on the other senses? Pain serves a greater purpose, after all. It not only protects but teaches us as well. As a species we are hard-wired to experience pain."

It was Sam's argument all over again.

"That's not the purpose for which Elysium was designed. I don't think pain reception would benefit the participants, many of whom are in constant pain in their normal day-to-day lives. Pain not only teaches: it limits us. And the purpose of Elysium is to remove those limitations for our participants."

Mr. Ellison nodded, taking a deep breath and looking silently back over the water. "You're right. It isn't the same without the smell of the air. You don't realize the significance of its presence until it's gone." He turned to face Marcus again. "Excellent. I am impressed by what you've shown me, Mr. Avery. When I first learned about your program, I feared it little more than an over-glorified video game. But having spoken with you and seen what you have here, I will admit your technology exceeds my initial expectations. I can easily see the possibilities for implementation. Thank you for the tour. I have a feeling we'll be seeing a lot of each other very soon," he said, lifting his hand for a handshake.

Marcus nodded, taking the man's outstretched hand. "Glad to be of service, but what exactly do you mean by possibilities?" he added, holding the man's hand in place.

Mr. Ellison looked down as he tried to pull away, then recommitted to his grip. "The full implementation of your technology can go well beyond just therapeutics. The possibilities are endless. I think it has the potential to completely change things for the better. But that's a discussion I look forward to having with you in the future. What you should focus on right now is the fact that your research funding is about to skyrocket. Certainly, there must be things you have wanted to implement but couldn't afford, or weren't allowed to. Well, those restrictions are about to become a thing of the past. I'm looking forward to a great partnership with you, Mr. Avery."

Marcus let the man's hand go with a weak smile, Claire's objections playing over in his mind. However, he pushed those thoughts away as he considered the possibilities the billionaire could bring to the table. And more importantly, what that could mean for Sam. Broadening his smile, he nodded to Clive Ellison.

"I look forward to it."

CHAPTER 6

"How do I look?" Sam asked, holding out her arms to model her new outfit.

"Well, you know I preferred the other one," Marcus said with a shit-eating grin.

"Yeah, that's obvious. But I don't think it was appropriate for spending time with our friends."

"Morrigan wouldn't have a problem with it," Marcus countered, eliciting a smirk from Sam. "After all, it is less revealing than a bikini."

"Yeah, but I've never felt comfortable showing that much skin; you know that. Especially with our friends being here. I'm too nervous and excited to get into character," Sam said looking down at the long tasset and leather armor she was wearing, both less revealing than the loincloth and crop top Marcus had originally designed for her.

"It looks good, babe. You look badass," Marcus said with a knowing smile.

Sam twisted her lips in a satisfied grin and straightened her back, standing in a wide stance with hands on her hips.

"I can't believe we're finally going to get to play together again," she said, excitedly. "Thank you so much!"

"You deserve it, baby. I'm sorry we haven't done it sooner."

Sam waved a hand at his apology. "It's fine. I'm just happy we're finally doing it. When are the others going to get here?"

"I'll check."

Marcus stopped for a second and she knew he was accessing the AAIP, its data only visible to him.

"They're getting in now. Should be here any minute."

"So, what are we doing?" she asked.

"I don't know. Diego said he had a surprise for you. I didn't have a hand in what we're doing, so I'm as in the dark as you are."

"Oooh. I can't wait," she said, wiggling back and forth in delight, eliciting a grin from Marcus.

"Hark! Who goes there?" Diego's familiar voice called, as he and Claire emerged from the tree line into the clearing. Diego wore an outfit that looked like a blend of ancient Central and South American cultures, complete with turquoise jewelry. Beside him, Claire wore a Romanesque soldier's outfit.

Seeing her friends standing there, Sam was overwhelmed with happiness, and giving a cry of delight, ran over to throw her arms around both of them. Laughing, they both hugged her back, the three of them squeezing each other in an awkward embrace.

Behind them, Amir stepped out of the trees wearing a comically cliche wizard's outfit, complete with robes and a pointy hat. Fumbling with the hat to keep it on his head, he stepped into the clearing. He did not seem amused, but as his eyes fell on Sam, he smiled broadly. Giving another squeal of delight, Sam let go of Diego and Claire and ran over to Amir, hugging him tightly.

"Oh my God, it's so good to see you guys," she said, letting go of Amir to face everybody. She had to fight back tears as she looked into their faces, her emotions swelling at being able to touch her friends again. "I missed you so much!"

"We missed you, too," Claire said with a laugh, although her eyes looked brimmed with her own tears.

"Oh girl, it's been so long," Diego said, hugging her again. "I missed seeing your beautiful face. I love the outfit, by the way."

"Thank you," Sam said smiling, stepping back with arms outstretched to show it off. "I designed it myself. I've had a lot of time on my hands."

"Couldn't have done better myself," he said.

"Oh, but yours is gorgeous," Sam said, admiring the jaguar pelt that made up his tasset, and colored feathers adorning his shoulders and headdress. "I'm envious."

"Don't worry, I'll make one for you too," he said with a broad smile.

Sam smiled back in delight, turning to the rest of her friends. "You all look amazing."

"Well, some of us got off better than others," Amir said, motioning at Claire and glaring at Diego.

"I asked you what you wanted yours to look like, and you said you didn't care and that I should just 'make whatever fantasy people wear,'" Diego shot back. "And there's nothing more fantasy than a wizard. Though maybe I should have made you a chain mail bikini."

"Oh my God, I would die to see that," Sam said, laughing. "Please do it next time."

"Don't you dare," Amir said, pointing a warning finger at Diego.

"Well, I suppose it'll come down to whether or not you give it some thought next time," Diego countered.

"Does this mean I can do magic?" Amir asked, with a hopeful raise of his eyebrows.

"Nope," Diego replied. "But that doesn't mean you can't pretend."

"You should know, Amir, that Sam's World is based on a grittier fantasy aesthetic. Like earth, but a time long before recorded history," Marcus explained, taking on a pretentious tone.

"My mistake," Amir said, sarcastically. "I suppose that is why Marcus is dressed like Conan the Barbarian?"

"I'm *Aer* the Barbarian, thank you very much," Marcus said with mock indignation.

"Put on a shirt," Amir shot back. "You wish you had abs like that."

"Hey, everything you see here is true to life," Marcus said, spreading his hands wide. "Though maybe with some minor tweaks and improvements in lighting."

"Minor," Claire scoffed, rolling her eyes.

"Hey, don't forget who's in control of the simulation today," Marcus said with a smirk. "Be nice."

"I am, actually," Diego said, arching an eyebrow. "Cristoval the Great."

"Shit. Right," Marcus said.

"Not used to that, huh?" Sam teased, causing Marcus to purse his lips.

"And these are my two companions," Diego continued, gesturing to Claire and Amir.

"Oh," Claire said, realizing it was her turn to introduce herself. "I'm Viatrix."

"And you, strangely dressed and clumsy-looking elder?" Marcus prodded Amir.

Glaring at Marcus, Amir rolled his eyes. "Uh, Gabriel, I suppose."

"A man unsure of his name. How mysterious," Marcus teased.

"So. What do you have for us, Cristoval?" Sam asked. "I'm excited."

"As well you should be," he said with a smile. "It was a challenge to convince my team that these were assets for Elysium, but I think they bought my excuse that it was for an experimental-themed experience."

"Well, let's see what you've made," Marcus said.

"Alright! Follow me, intrepid adventurers," Diego said with a flourish, walking back toward the treeline. "Sam, why don't you take the lead with me?"

Jogging past the others, she reached out to squeeze Marcus' hand excitedly as she passed, before falling into step beside Diego. As a group they moved through the jungle, pushing through the thick undergrowth and climbing over giant tree roots. Around them the jungle teemed with life, the now familiar calls of colorful birds and insects filling the air, as they passed through shafts of light that shone through the thick canopy above.

Despite what she had told Marcus, Sam felt herself getting into character, and she strode forward nimbly while keeping an eye out for danger. Eventually, they came to a small cluster of huts made of animal hides. The settlement looked in disarray, with an overturned cooking pot beside the fire and other belongings strewn about the ground. The bodies of a few men were not far from the huts, spears and arrows sticking out from wounds in their bodies.

Inside one of the huts, Morrigan noticed movement and cautiously approached, yanking a spear out of a nearby wall. Heavy shadows filled the inside of the structure, making it hard for her to discern what she'd seen. With spear readied, she ducked her head and entered the doorway.

A man lay inside the hut, his hand held over a wound in his side. Gritting his teeth, he watched her approach, his breathing labored.

"What happened here?" Morrigan asked.

"Raiders. Half-men. They took the women and children. Please, you must get them back," he pleaded in pained gasps.

"In here!" Morrigan called to her companions.

Outside she heard sounds of movement before several heads peered in from the doorway.

"There's a man in here. He's dyin'," she said, looking behind her before turning back to the man to ask, "Where'd they go?"

"North," he said in one final long exhale, his eyes glazing over.

Morrigan stared down at the dead man. He was gone, there was nothing she could do. *Half-men,* he'd said. She wondered what that could mean. Turning back to her companions, she stood up and exited the hut.

"He's gone. But he said his village was attacked by Half-men who took his people north."

"Half-men?" Aer repeated, looking to Cristoval.

"Whatever could that be?" the other man replied, widening his eyes with a knowing smile. "Let us investigate. Morrigan, do you think you can track them?"

Scanning the ground, she found evidence of passage in a northerly direction, the underbrush heavily trampled down. Waving for the others to follow, she confidently pressed forward, following the trail back into the tree line.

They moved through the jungle slowly as a group, each having retrieved a weapon from the ruins of the settlement and holding them at the ready. Morrigan scouted ahead, keeping them just in sight behind her. The trail was hard to miss and moved more or less in a straight line between the trees. Eventually, she became aware of a heavy, thumping sound in the distance that kept a steady rhythm. The sound grew louder as she pressed forward, until the trees parted to reveal an ancient, vine-covered stone ziggurat rising above the treetops.

The massive structure sat in a deep depression, the forest floor rising around it on all sides. Morrigan moved to the edge of the drop and looked down to the base of the ziggurat where it was surrounded by a deep pool of dark water. A large bonfire burned on a stone landing surrounding the base, just above the waterline. It was there that she found the source of the thumping. Two men beating on giant round drums. Squat and heavily muscled, with thick arms and legs, they were scantily dressed in animal hides or nothing at all. Morrigan could see that though they looked like humans, they all had wide, pronounced brows and heavy jawlines that made them look more animalistic than normal men.

Near the fire, their hands bound in thick ropes, were the

kidnapped village women and children. A dozen in total. They huddled together in terror, watching as one of the Half-men, adorned in more elaborate hides, shouted to the gathered crowd. Six other Half-men stood guard around the prisoners, clubs and spears in hand. Morrigan felt her hand tighten around the shaft of her own spear, her limbs tingling with anticipation. On the slopes surrounding the ziggurat sat dozens of poorly constructed huts of sticks and leaves, around which stood scores of Half-men and women. Though there were many, their attention was turned to the macabre scene.

From behind she heard her companions' approach, their footsteps clumsy and heavy as they moved through the heavy brush.

"Holy shit, Diego," Aer said to Cristoval. "This is fucking impressive!"

"Thank you," he replied with a satisfied smile. "I went with a whole Temple of Doom meets Conan feel. I mean, it's a little problematic and reductive. But I figure since I'm the one who came up with it, it's okay."

"Quiet, both of ye," Morrigan hissed, gesturing for them to lower into a crouch with her.

"Oh, right," Aer said.

"Sorry," Cristoval added, as the group sank down to be less visible.

"There are the villagers," Viatrix stated, pointing to the prisoners. "So how do we get to them?"

"There," Morrigan said, indicating a wide stone walkway that stood above the waterline, connecting the base of the ziggurat to the slope on the other side.

"There are a lot of them for us to get through before we can even get to the temple," Gabriel said.

"We'll need a distraction," Cristoval offered. "Something to get their attention, while a few of us sneak over there."

"We should split up. Two of us can get their attention and

hopefully draw them away, while the other three free the prisoners," Morrigan offered.

"Sounds like a suicide mission," Gabriel said.

"Which one?" Viatrix asked.

"Both," he replied.

"Somehow, I don't think you'll be much help with the rescue," Aer said with a smirk. "So let's make you part of the distraction."

"Fine with me," Gabriel said. "I'm better at running than fighting. Diego, are the pain receptors active for this simulation."

"Oh yeah," Cristoval said, with a wicked grin.

"Oh Christ," Gabriel sighed.

"Both of ye focus," Morrigan hissed. "We dun have much time. Cristoval and Gabriel, ye provide the distraction while Aer, Viatrix, and me get the prisoners."

Looking at each other, both men nodded.

"Ye make yer way 'round to the other side over there," she said, pointing to the ridge on the opposite side from their position. "Then start makin' noise to get their attention. Once they come after ye, start runnin' and lead 'em into the jungle as far as ye can from here. While they're chasin' ye, we'll head down and kill any fuckers that remain. Just dun let 'em catch ye," she warned with a wink.

"Yeah. I have no intention of letting that happen," Gabriel said, before turning back to Cristoval. "How much is this going to hurt?"

Cristoval only shrugged with a look of amused uncertainty.

"Oh man, why did I let you guys talk me into this?"

"Cuz you love us," Viatrix said teasingly. "And cuz we all love Sam."

"Enough yappin'. Start movin'," Morrigan scolded, waving them away.

Holding up his hands, Cristoval smirked and did as he was bid, pulling Gabriel along after him into the trees. She watched as they slowly made their way to the other side of the depression until they were just small figures, no bigger than her thumb. After taking a moment to situate themselves, Cristoval started waving his arms, followed reluctantly a moment later by Gabriel. With the distance and sound of the drums, she couldn't hear what they were saying, but slowly some of the gathered Half-men began looking in their direction and pointing.

A cry went up across the surrounding hillside and soon the Half-men began to clamber up the slope toward the two of them, howling like beasts. Gabriel's eyes went wide, and he began to run, pulling at Cristoval to follow. The two men disappeared into the shadows of the trees, hounded by a score of bestial pursuers.

"Aright. Now it's our turn," Morrigan said, turning to her two remaining companions and gesturing with her head for them to follow.

Lifting her spear, she crested the edge of the depression and began moving down the slope toward the ziggurat, weaving between the huts to hide their approach. The drums continued their steady beat, concealing her movement well enough that she caught a few of the Half-men villagers who'd remained behind by surprise. Driving spears and swords into their backs, she and her companions made quick work of the enemies in their way, the prehistoric men having little time to do more than gurgle in surprise as they died.

It did not take the group long to reach the bridge, and as they did so, the Halfman shaman finally noticed them. Thrusting his finger in their direction, he directed his guards to attack. Unlike those they'd already dispatched, these Half-men had the look of warriors, armed with their own spears and clubs. With a roar, they charged across the bridge, weapons held high.

Her blood now coursing fast through her veins, Morrigan gave a cry of her own and charged at them. She was only dimly aware of her companions running with her as they met their enemy in the middle of the bridge. Dodging low, she stabbed up with her spear, catching the lead Halfman in the throat. With a look of surprise, he clutched at his neck and fell back, dropping off the bridge and into the dark water.

She was about to strike again but another Halfman closed the distance, swinging down at her before she could react. To her surprise, his sword was deflected at the last second as Viatrix stepped in between them, swinging her own sword in defense. Pushing herself forward, Morrigan watched as Aer charged into the pack of Half-men, swinging his sword in great sweeping arcs that caused the enemy to slow their advance, one of them missing his footing and falling off the bridge.

Leaping to Aer's side, she pressed forward with her spear, stabbing at the enemy and keeping them on the back foot. Dispatching her opponent, Viatrix joined their push and soon they overwhelmed the remaining warriors, butchering them swiftly to bleed out upon the stones of the bridge. At the base of the ziggurat, the shaman's eyes widened, and he backed up to put distance between them. Only two lone warriors moved into position to protect him, though in their eyes Morrigan could see that the Half-men knew they didn't stand a chance against them. Fleeing up the first few steps of the temple, the shaman turned suddenly and thrust his arms up into the air, calling out loudly to the sky.

For a moment, she wondered what the priest was doing, then to their left the surface of the water rippled. Turning in surprise, she only had time to catch the hint of movement before the head of a giant crocodile burst from the water, its mouth open and filled with hundreds of sharp teeth. Morrigan instinctually rolled away from the beast, but Viatrix was not as quick, and she screamed as the monster's jaws snapped closed around her torso, its teeth puncturing her armor like it was made of cloth.

In an instant, Viatrix was pulled off the bridge, her screams drowned as she disappeared into the dark waters. Aer stared wide-eyed at where she had been, his eyes wide with horror.

"For fuck's sake, Diego," he managed to mutter, standing stock-still on the bridge.

"Get the shaman," Morrigan shouted at him. "I'll take care of the monster."

"Are you crazy?" he said. "You can't take on that thing. We have to get off the bridge."

"Just do it, boyo," she snapped. "Kill the bastard, and maybe the beast'll go away."

Aer looked over to where the shaman still stood on the steps of the ziggurat, his arms and head tilted to the sky as he continued to chant. Turning back, Aer gave her a nod.

"Just keep yourself alive long enough for me to shut him up," he said.

She nodded with a smile, her heart pounding with excitement.

"Oh, and don't let it bite off that perfect ass of yours," he said with a grin. "You know how much I like it."

"Dun ye worry about that, boyo. It'll still be here when ye get back. Now stop thinkin' about me backside and go kill that bastard."

"You got it, beautiful," Aer said with a laugh, charging across the bridge.

Morrigan watched him for a split second, before turning her attention back to the murky water. Poor Viatrix. Nasty way to go.

Again, the rippling of the water was her only warning, but Morrigan didn't waste it. Leaping to the side, she moved out of the way just as the giant head emerged, trying to grab her. Rolling on the hard stone, Morrigan forced herself to find her footing and thrust with her spear. Her stab made contact with the side of the monster's head, but to her dismay, its sharp tip slid off of the creature's thick scales.

The crocodile's protective eyelids opened to reveal its eye looking directly at her. Instead of retreating back into the water, it swung its jaws in her direction, sliding its massive head along the bridge. Again, Morrigan rolled away, just as its teeth slammed closed where she had been standing. Wasting no time, she stabbed again, catching it in the nostril and causing the beast to whip its head back in pain. She felt a smile creep onto her face, but the monster did not hesitate for long.

From the water, its foot clawed for purchase on the now slick stone, pulling its massive body onto the bridge and blocking any retreat from the ziggurat. Stepping back with her spear held ready, she glanced over her shoulder to see Aer fighting the shaman's two guards. If he didn't kill them quickly, the beast would get them both. Turning her attention back to the crocodile, she readied herself to move.

With a hiss, the monster opened its jaws, its massive bulk surging forward. She moved to dodge, but with all the water splashed upon the bridge, her foot slipped on the wet stone, sending her sprawling off the bridge and into the water. Darkness enveloped her as she plunged into the cold, brackish pool. For a moment, she reeled with vertigo, unsure of which direction was up. Desperately kicking her feet in an attempt to right herself, she was only dimly aware of the vague light illuminating the surface.

As she began to swim upward, a massive push of water sent her rolling backward, the gargantuan shape of the crocodile sliding back into the water only to disappear in the darkness. Her eyes searched for any sign of the beast. But with so little light, the pool was filled with shadows, any one of them hiding the monster. Suddenly one of the shadows moved in her direction. Morrigan kicked herself upward just as the beast's snout knocked painfully into her shin, sending her spinning. As she tumbled, she slid along the crocodile's body, its rough scales scraping against her skin.

Instinctually, she reached out to grab the creature, her hands clawing for any handhold until her fingers found purchase on the ridge of scales jutting from its back. Forcing them to maintain their grip, she held tight as she was pulled along with its movement. As cumbersome as it had been on the bridge, in the water the beast moved in a sinuous motion, sleek and fast. Blinded by the dark, stinking water, and running out of breath, she reached her free hand to grip another ridge of scales and pulled herself along the beast's back towards its head.

Suddenly, the animal rolled and Morrigan screamed out the last of her breath as she used every ounce of strength to hold on. Twisting its body, it tried to dislodge her, but she refused to let go, her fingers locked in a painful grip. The world became only darkness and pain, as she struggled to hold on, her lungs burning for air.

To her surprise, the black water fell away, and she gasped for air as the world was illuminated around her once again. The crocodile had pulled itself back onto the bridge, and she took a moment to fill her lungs with sweet air. The animal, however, had not surfaced for air and turned its massive body on its side in an attempt to roll and crush her beneath it.

With only a split second to act, she let go and jumped for the bridge, landing hard enough on the stone to send a jarring pain up her spine. Morrigan didn't let it slow her, however, and rolled away, just as the monster's body rolled over where she'd been.

It took her a moment to realize she'd escaped from being crushed, and she found herself staring up at the sky, still gasping for breath. In the back of her mind, she became dimly aware of her hand touching something. A spear. Closing her fist around the shaft, she forced herself to roll to her feet. Beside her, the crocodile was righting itself, before slipping back into the water to prepare for another attack.

At the base of the ziggurat, Aer lay wounded beside one of the dead Half-men warriors. Holding his side with one hand, he only had time to bring up the other in a futile attempt to defend himself, as the remaining warrior struck him dead with his ax. Morrigan cried out but was only dimly aware of her voice. Lifting the spear, she charged across the last few paces of the bridge toward the warrior.

Caught by surprise, he didn't have time to defend himself, and her weapon dug deep into his side. Behind her, the crocodile reemerged on the bridge, pulling itself out of the water to surge after her. Wasting no time, she yanked the spear from the Halfman, and hoisting it over her shoulder, threw.

The spear caught the shaman in the chest with a satisfying thud, and with a look of disbelief, the priest stared down at the weapon sticking out of his body. Blood welled from his mouth, and his eyes turned to Morrigan, before rolling to the back of his head as his body dropped limply down the steps of the ziggurat.

Morrigan turned to face the crocodile behind her, its massive jaws opened wide. However, instead of finishing its attack, the animal slowly closed its mouth and retreated back into the water, disappearing into the blackness. Around her were the corpses of her enemies, everything still and silent. Even the drums had seemingly been abandoned by their players. Only the nervous crying of the kidnapped villagers, and the crackling of the bonfire, filled the silence. Remembering Aer, she rushed over to where he lay, but found him still and lifeless.

Sadness and worry washing over her, Sam wondered if Marcus was okay. She supposed he must be. Not any different than when she'd fought the ape. But seeing him there, looking so much like him and covered in blood, a small part of her still couldn't let go of her concern. Not until she was sure. However, looking over the surrounding carnage, a feeling of exhilaration and pride washed over her. Holy shit, that crocodile had been insane! Even better than the ape. And this time she'd won! Oh, she was never going to let Marcus live this down.

Smiling, she turned and caught sight of the prisoners. Oh right, the mission. Gently laying Marcus' body back down, she walked over to the kidnapped villagers, cutting their bonds with the priest's knife. Women and children looked up at her with wonder and gratitude, before rushing across the bridge and climbing up the slope, eventually disappearing into the jungle. Sam looked around for Diego and Amir but didn't see them. She wondered if they'd survived, and grimaced as she imagined them being run down by the Half-men.

Oh Claire, she suddenly remembered. She'd probably gotten it worse than any of the others. Just thinking about her own experience with the crocodile, she shuddered to imagine what Claire had gone through. Man, Diego hadn't pulled any punches, and she loved it! Taking a moment to admire the ziggurat, she walked around the area soaking in all the detail. It was fantastic. When no one returned after a little bit, not even the Half-men, she figured they'd finished the scenario, and left the simulation.

Everything turned black for a moment, and she woke groggily, her vision slowly solidifying the room around her. Beside her, Marcus was already up and offered her a glass of water. In the other room, she was surprised to hear the raised voices of Amir and Claire. Taking the water, she reached up a hand to stroke his cheek.

"Are you okay?" she asked, still picturing his avatar's bloodied face.

"Yeah," he said with a laugh. "I'm fine, little one. Though I'm not sure Claire and Amir are over it yet."

"Are they mad?"

"Not mad, so much as still processing, I think," he replied with a smile. "How'd things end up? Everybody else died."

"It was amazing!" she said, excitedly sitting up only to suddenly feel a stab of pain lancing down her spine. She let out a small involuntary cry, and Marcus rushed to give her support.

"Take it easy, baby," he said, putting a hand on her back.

Sam took a deep breath, grimacing through the pain as she eased slowly onto her pillows. Clinging tightly to Marcus' wrist, she sat there staring at the wall ahead of her, focused on her breathing as she waited for the pain to subside. In truth, it never stopped hurting.

The pain was just less intense and more of a constant ache, ready to become stabbing agony whenever she moved. Eventually, the piercing spasms eased and she let out a long-held breath.

Looking up at Marcus, she gave a weak smile but noticed the pained worry on his face.

"Are you okay?" he asked.

Focusing on her breathing, she only nodded. She realized that she was still clinging to his wrist and let go of his arm, but was shocked to see that her nails had left red welts on his skin.

"It's alright. I'm fine," he said, following her gaze to his arm. Reaching his other hand up, he gently stroked the back of her head.

Sam leaned back against his hand and felt a tear slip down her cheek as her body returned to the ceaseless aching that consumed every second of her day. Once so strong and capable, now it served as her prison. There was no way to escape it. No way, except the simulation. There, she could escape it all and feel strong again. Stronger than she'd ever felt. That's what Marcus couldn't understand. No matter how badly she experienced pain in the simulation, it was nothing compared to what she had to endure outside of it.

She looked up and gave him another weak smile, seeing the love and concern in his eyes. If only he could understand.

"I'm okay," she said. She waited for him to sit back down and forced the pain from her mind. "Phew! That was intense. I forget I can't move like that."

"I'm sorry, babe."

"Oh, stop," she said, waving a hand at him. "You couldn't have done anything."

"Still," he replied, morosely.

"How are you?" she asked, her mind turning back to the simulation, filling her with excitement at the memory of the fight. "You died pretty brutally."

"Yeah," he chuckled. "That sucked. But I'm fine. The pain wasn't as bad as I thought. Though I don't know whether that was from the simulation's settings or my adrenaline. I can remember him bringing down the sword, then everything goes black. What about you? What happened? I saw you go under the water and thought for sure you were going to get eaten."

"You should know it takes more than a big ass crocodile to kill me," she said. "I wrestled with it in the water and got on its back. Then it climbed back up on the bridge to try and crush me, and that's when I saw you die. So I killed the guy that killed you and threw my spear at the shaman. Totally nailed him in the chest. He died just as the croc was about to eat me, and it just stopped and went back into the water. It was fucking epic!" She recounted, the memory of it all filling her with excitement. "Stuff of legends," she beamed.

"Man, I'm sorry I missed it," Marcus said with a broad smile.

"Yeah. After that, I waited around. Eventually, when nobody returned, I ended the simulation. How long were you guys waiting?"

"Maybe thirty minutes. They all drove over here immediately after getting out of the simulation."

"Right. I forget how weird time can be there. Man, Diego did an amazing job. That whole scenario was perfect!"

"Yeah, I had no idea he'd been putting so much work into it. He was telling me he has something even bigger planned."

"Oh! I can't wait!" Sam said excitedly, ignoring the sudden twinge in her side. In the other room, she could still hear the voices of her friends arguing, and she looked to the doorway.

"Do you want me to bring them in?" he asked.

"I don't know. I don't want them to see me like this."

"Baby, you look beautiful. They want to see you."

"No, I don't. I have mirrors. I look like a little Nosferatu."

"An adorable Nosferatu," he countered.

"Oh stop."

"Believe me, they'd rather see this version of you than not see you at all."

Sam stared at the door imagining the looks on her friends' faces when they saw her. But then she also thought about how they had all come over to see her and felt guilty about sending them away without talking directly to them.

"Fine," she said with a sigh. "But pick up the room a little bit first, and get me my beanie."

Marcus got out of the chair, gently putting the wool beanie on her head, before quickly tidying up the room. Sam grabbed a surgical face mask from the table, and put it on, before nodding to Marcus that she was ready. Smiling, he opened the door and walked out of sight. She listened as his voice joined the others in the living room, and after a moment, everyone grew silent, replaced by the sound of their footsteps as they approached her room.

"Hail the conquering hero," Marcus said, gesturing towards her as he stepped into the room, followed by everyone else. "The only one of us to survive."

Her friends came in one by one, all smiling, but as their eyes found her she could see the pain in their stares.

"Did you defeat the crocodile?" Claire asked, wide-eyed.

"Sure did," Sam said, pursing her lips in pride. "I wrestled the bastard, then killed the shaman. It just went back into the water after that. What about you? When it pulled you under the water, I was horrified."

Claire unconsciously hugged herself.

"Yeah. That sucked," she said, glaring at Diego. "I hope I never experience that again, in real life or otherwise. I think I might have developed a new phobia."

For his part, Diego gave her a wide, guilty smile. Like a child caught doing something wrong that he wasn't particularly sorry about.

"You have to admit. You didn't see that coming," he said with a laugh.

"I don't think any of us could have anticipated that," Marcus said with a shake of his head.

"Now, are you still mad at me for making us the decoys?" he asked, turning to Amir. "You could have been eaten by a crocodile instead. That's the point I was trying to make."

"How about you just don't put me in a scenario where I am hunted down or eaten? Maybe one where I'm not under the threat of death at all," Amir countered.

"Where's the fun in that?" Sam asked teasingly. She smiled broadly at Amir's responding scowl, but it was quickly replaced as a twinge in her chest sent her into a fit of coughing. Sam wrapped an arm around herself, trying to hold herself steady, as each cough sent an excruciating spasm of pain through her entire body.

Marcus rushed to her side, helplessly trying to give her some support, but there was little that he could do without hurting her further. Everything in the room moved to the back of her mind as she focused on trying to calm her coughing and the pain that followed. Suddenly, her stomach clenched into a knot, and she pulled the mask off her face, waving desperately to the garbage can by her bedside.

It took a moment for Marcus to recognize what she wanted, but he lifted the can just in time to catch the trickle of orange bile that spewed from her mouth. Spasming painfully, her empty stomach continued to violently push acid up her throat, burning her esophagus along the way. Sam closed her eyes and just tried to focus on just getting through the ordeal. She could sense all of her friends standing there watching helplessly and wished Marcus would send them away.

Eventually, the spasming stopped and her stomach settled. Breathing heavily, she sat back onto her pillows and lay still, looking up at the ceiling as she waited for the pain to subside. Marcus quickly pulled some tissues from the box and wiped her lips and chin.

"Hey guys, give us a second," he said, gesturing to the door.

Their three friends nodded and quickly made their way out of the room, disappearing into the hallway.

"Are you alright, baby?" Marcus asked, worry on every feature of his face.

The pain in Sam's chest didn't subside but instead seemed to tighten, making each breath difficult.

"I don't feel well," she managed.

Tears filled Marcus' eyes as he stroked her head.

"I'm going to call an ambulance."

"Okay," she said, the word cut off by her lack of breath.

Marcus fumbled for his phone, and she listened as he frantically spoke with the 911 dispatcher, though she found herself unable to make out his words. Staring at the ceiling, she listened to the base tones of his voice and put all her effort towards each next breath as the room grew dark around her.

CHAPTER 7

"I'm afraid we've reached the end of conventional treatments," Dr. Dlamini said from across the room, looking through a folder of Sam's P.E.T. scans.

"So, what does that mean?" Marcus asked, the worry apparent in his voice.

For her part, Sam just took in the information numbly. She wasn't surprised. She'd hoped for better results but knew the pain was only getting worse. She watched her oncologist's lips move as he explained their next steps but only partially processed the information. They would have to move to more experimental options now. Things used for other cancers that might have an impact on hers.

She glanced over at Marcus' worried face and felt a pang of sorrow. It hurt so much to think about his fear. It was odd. She was more concerned with how this information affected him than what it meant for her. She didn't want to die. But over the last few months, as the pain grew worse and the chemo didn't seem to have any effect, the possibility that she wouldn't survive this grew more real, and with it, so did her acceptance of that fact.

She reached out and took Marcus' hand, gripping it tightly.

Looking over at her, he squeezed it back, his eyes filled with worry and sympathy. What was he going to do if she did die? She found that was the thought that pained her the most.

"So, what's our next step?" Sam said, focusing on Dr. Dlamini.

"Well, we have some oral chemo we can try. It's used for lung cancer, but according to the tests we took, your tumors share some of the same genetic markers. So, our hope is that the chemo will have a similar effect on the tumors in your chest cavity."

"And how long will that take to determine?" Sam asked, gritting her teeth to hide the pain that lanced up her spine, made only worse by having to sit on the hard plastic bench that served as the only seat in the office.

This visit could have been done remotely, but she guessed why they wanted her to come in. Hospital protocol probably required bad news to be delivered face to face, despite however much pain the patient might have to go through to receive it. She tried not to be angry at Dr. Dlamini, but as he droned on about risks and timetables, careful not to say anything definitive, she couldn't help but resent him a little. He might have to follow protocol, but he could at least be mindful of his patients and the pain it caused them.

Marcus had already yelled at him when he remarked about her high blood pressure, saying "What the fuck did you think it would be when you force her to come in instead of doing this remotely? You do realize that the tumors in her chest fill her with pain with every movement, right?"

Her attack dog. She appreciated his defense of her, but his anger didn't change anything. It only put everyone on edge and made things even more uncomfortable. But she knew it was his nature. He defended and fought for those he loved. And she never doubted his love for her, which only made the pain all the worse.

So she'd patted his arm and told him it was okay, though she wanted nothing more than to lash out at the oncologist too. But that wasn't in her nature. She wished she could give him just a taste of her pain, so he'd understand. Instead, she focused on her breathing and tried to push it all to the back of her mind.

"If we find that it's not working, there's another option I'd like to try," the doctor continued. "Its efficacy is purely speculative. But it also matches some of the genetic markers in the cells we tested."

"But how long will all this take?" she pressed, knowing that time was running out. If something was going to work, it needed to work immediately.

"Hard to say. We usually like to give a new treatment at least three months to see if it's taking effect. But in your case, I think we should monitor on a month-to-month basis and assess from there. Maybe in two months, if we don't see any efficacy, we can switch."

Two months. Did she still have two months? She looked over at Marcus and found him watching her, his hand gripping hers tightly. She gave him a little smile and squeezed his hand.

"Alright. Let's do it," she said, turning back to the oncologist.

Dr. Dlamini nodded and made a note in her file.

"Okay. I'll get the oral chemo ordered immediately. They should overnight it to you so you can start it in the next day or two. I'll also set a follow-up for a month from now. In the interim, feel free to call if you have any concerns or questions," he said, gathering her file back into its folder and standing up. Walking over to Sam, he stood there for a moment looking down at her. "We will do everything we can, Sam. If you need anything else, let me know," he said, a smile on his face. But in his eyes she could see his resignation.

She didn't doubt he meant it, but what else could they do for her? In the movies and on TV, doctors moved heaven and earth to save their patients, especially the ones with rare cancers. Thinking outside of the box and risking their careers. Constantly thinking about the case until they found a solution. But in reality, they just stuck to protocol and what they knew, even if it wasn't working.

She wasn't special. As nice as he was, she was just one of a hundred patients on Dr. Dlamini's roster, and he only had so much time to give her, let alone think about her case.

She gave him a weary nod, which he took as his cue to leave, and watched him exit the exam room. She could feel Marcus' eyes on her. What was he thinking? Was he hopeful, or did he have the same doubts she did? She pushed down her worry and tried to stay positive. This new treatment would work. It had to.

Turning to face him, Sam gave Marcus a soft smile and lifted a hand to stroke his cheek, trying to ignore the pain in her spine. He returned the smile, pressing his cheek into her palm, but she could see the worry in his eyes.

"Let's get you home," he said.

"Okay."

Reaching up to gently take her hand, he lifted himself from the bench and offered support as she pulled on his grip to help her stand. The walk through the cancer clinic was laborious and agonizing, and she clung to Marcus' arm tightly. So long as she could walk, she would do so. Something inside told her that if she started using the wheelchair, it would represent the beginning of the end. Besides, it wasn't any more comfortable, it just was less taxing on her muscles and lungs, and she needed the exercise.

By the time they got to the car, she felt ready to collapse and let out a sigh as she settled into the passenger seat. Marcus reached over to get her belted in before closing her door and crossing around the car to get in the driver's seat.

"Alright, little one. You okay?"

"Yeah," she said, staring out the window still trying to catch her breath.

"Not too much longer and we'll have you home."

"Can we get a pizza tonight?"

Marcus looked over at her with surprise. "Sure. If you're up for it."

"Yeah. I want to go home and eat a pizza while we play games on the console. Like we used to," she said, remembering fondly simpler times when they were just teenagers. Hanging out on his parents' couch, eating gooey pizza, and passing the controller back and forth when one of them would lose a life.

A nostalgic smile spread across Marcus' face, and in it, she could see the boy she'd fallen in love with over twenty years before.

"You got it, little one," he said, gently rubbing her leg.

"Come on! You've got to be kidding me. I made that jump!" Marcus exclaimed from the floor, gesturing angrily at the screen.

Laying on the couch behind him, Sam smiled and waved for him to take another turn when he offered her the controller. On the screen, his character started back at the beginning of the level and began running forward. Her eyes watched the movement for a moment, before drifting down to look at the back of Marcus' head. Even though she couldn't see his face, she knew what it would look like, his brows furrowed as he focused on the game.

Her eyes began to sting as she watched him, an overwhelming sadness washing over her. She imagined what his face would look like when she died. The pain he would feel. It was funny. She was the one dying, but she was more worried about him than herself. She didn't want to die, and sometimes the thought terrified her, but she'd had a lot of time to come to terms with her fate. The thought of dying did not hurt as much as the thought of how it would affect the ones she loved. Especially Marcus.

They had found each other so young and had been together throughout their entire adult lives. They didn't know life without the other. She worried about how he might handle it and what he might do. She knew how much it would hurt her if their roles were reversed. She couldn't imagine life without him. He would probably isolate himself and push everyone away.

She reached out and ran a hand through his hair, smiling as she watched it slide against her fingers. Tilting his head back, Marcus pressed his head into her hand and continued to play. At least they had Sam's World. There they could play together and be close again. There she could feel like herself again.

"Fuck this game," Marcus said, letting out an exasperated breath and slamming down the controller. On the screen his character lay dead at the same jump he'd missed before.

Turning, he offered her the controller again, but she waved it away.

"I think I'm too tired," she said.

He gave her an understanding smile and put the controller down on the floor before his eyes moved to her plate.

"You only took a bite from your slice, boo," he chided.

"I thought I wanted it but it's not sitting well on my stomach," she said with a grimace.

"Alright. Do you want something else? Maybe something easier to digest?" he asked, putting her piece back in the box.

"Not right now."

He nodded, closing the box, but she could see the concern on his face.

"Can we go back into Sam's World?" she asked, hopefully.

"Are you sure you're up for it? You said you were tired."

"I can rest while I'm in the simulation. I won't be tired there," she said.

"You know that's not how it works, little one."

"Yeah, I know. But if I try to sleep now, I will just toss and turn. Plus, in Sam's World I won't feel all this pain," she explained, grimacing as she tried to maneuver to ease the pressure on her spine.

"Alright," Marcus said with a pained smile, glancing at her movements. Stepping past the coffee table he leaned down to gently help her up. Even with his assistance the move from the couch to the bedroom sent lancing pain down her back and across her ribs, and she had to grip him tightly.

As he eased her into bed, she gritted her teeth to keep from crying out until she was settled. Leaning back into her pile of pillows, she let out a sigh and focused on catching her breath as she watched Marcus set about getting the server ready.

"You know, I was thinking," she said, as he pulled the chair up beside her bedside. "I know you want to be there when I am in the simulation, but I'd really like to use it when you're busy. In Sam's World, I'm not in constant pain."

"That's what Elysium's for. You can spend as much time as you like there," Marcus countered, settling himself in the chair. "Maybe if you didn't insist on the pain parameters in Sam's World. But with those in place, I worry about what might happen if I'm not there to intervene."

"I'll just wake up. We proved that with the ape," she protested with more emotion than she intended. "Elysium is boring. Everyone is always asking me how I'm doing. When I'm there, I'm still Sam, the girl with cancer. But in Sam's World, I can forget about all of that. I can get into character and be a badass barbarian who's not worried about dying and other people's feelings," she explained, her eyes burning and blurring as tears filled her eyes. As they began to roll down her face, she reached up a hand to wipe them from her cheeks.

Marcus watched her, his face twisted in sympathy. After a moment, he stood up and walked over to her, leaning down to kiss her on the head. Sam sobbed, unable to keep her tears from flowing, her frustration at not being able to stop them only making her cry harder.

"Okay, boo," Marcus said, stroking her head. "Don't cry. I'll grant you access, but I'll have to link the server. That way we have remote access if something should happen."

"I thought you said linking the server was bad," she said, her tears slowing as his words sunk in.

"It means it will be discoverable, so someone could find it if they go looking or happen to come across it. We'll have to make sure that it is encrypted so that no one can just access it. But," he looked down at her, and she read the consideration on his face as he took her in. What would it matter if she was dying? "It should be okay."

Sam smiled broadly, her heart swelling at the thought that she would no longer spend hours alone trying to distract herself from the pain. She almost cried again in sheer joy.

"Thank you, Marcus," she said, taking his hand to kiss it.

Marcus smiled and bent down to kiss the top of her head again. "Anything for you, my love. You know that."

CHAPTER 8

"It's beyond what I'd even suspected," Amir said, pointing to his screen.

"And this is Sam's mapping?" Marcus asked, standing behind him and staring at the monitor.

"Yeah."

"Why does it look so different?"

"I'm not sure, but it's far more complete than even our best mappings from any of our participants in Elysium," Amir said, excitedly.

"What do you think is the cause? Is it the simulation environment? Is it more stimulating to brain function?"

"Maybe. It's hard to tell without experimentation and testing. I can only make a guess. But I've been thinking about it, and I wonder if it has anything to do with pain reception."

"Another set of stimuli that the others aren't experiencing?" Marcus offered.

"Exactly. And one key to brain activity. We know that dopamine is a powerful driver of reaction: both for pleasure and pain," Amir said.

"But we don't inhibit pleasure in Elysium. And you and I both know that group is fucking half the time they are there."

Amir nodded. "Sure. But maybe there is something to the give and take of dopamine that presents more activity. In our evaluations, those who participated in sexual encounters noted that though it was pleasurable, the pleasure they felt was more subdued. I could speculate that is because there was no counterbalance of pain. What about with you and Sam?"

"Are you asking me how good our sex is?"

"Purely on an academic level. Believe me, it's the last image I want to have in my head. I have no interest in thinking of you two that way," his friend said with a smirk. "In fact, it's like thinking about my parents doing it."

"Alright. I believe you," Marcus said. "It's good. Sometimes better than before. It's hard to say because it's been so long since we've been able to be physical outside of the simulation."

"What about prior to adding the pain reception."

Marcus thought about it for a moment, trying to remember the sensation several months ago. "I suppose it wasn't as good, no. More like masturbation. It was pleasurable, but something was missing I suppose."

"So perhaps adding the pain reception in Sam's case created a more active neuron transfer."

"What about my map?" Marcus asked.

"Your what? Oh fuck's sake, I didn't even think about the fact that you would have one too," Amir chided himself, quickly bringing up the data from Sam's World.

After a few minutes of processing, an image similar to Sam's popped up on the screen, almost identical in its detail.

"Holy shit," Amir said, staring at the screen.

"Indeed," Marcus responded, marveling at the intricacy of the pattern.

"Well, I think we can definitely say it's Sam's World."

"And how does this apply to the cognitive copy? Have you determined if it is viable?"

"After studying Sam's more detailed map, I believe it is. I think that what we are looking at is a functional cognitive map."

"Does that mean it is thinking right now?"

"No. I don't think so. See how the activity centers are quiet? There is no neural transfer of electrons. But if we look at the mapping when activated during your sessions in Sam's World, it is lit up and active. I think it does require the stimuli from the AAIP to function."

"And the SynAPP?"

Amir shook his head. "No. I don't see how it would play any role. The implant is designed to stimulate the biological matter of the hippocampus. The map has no biological equivalence. Put simply, it works when you turn it on. Its only requirement is some sort of environment for it to function, such as the one run by the AAIP."

"So you're saying that this is a copy of Sam's brain activity, but functional without her brain?" Marcus prodded.

"I'm saying we have copied her brain patterns identically, and if stimulated correctly it theoretically should function on its own."

"So we've copied Sam's mind," Marcus said pointedly.

"Essentially, yes. And yours it seems."

"So how do we know it works?"

"Technically, we don't," Amir said. "This is all theoretical. I suppose what I can say is that we could have a functional copy of Sam's brain activity, one that would preserve her thought patterns."

Marcus stared at Amir's screen and nodded. The implications of this were huge.

"I'd like Claire to take a look at this and get her take on it," Amir said.

"I don't know. Maybe we should keep this between us," Marcus replied. "At least until we know more about what is going on."

"We'd have a better chance to figure this out if we bring her into the loop," Amir pressed. "She's the one with the medical expertise to analyze this on a biological level. I am an engineer. She's the doctor. We really should get her input on this."

"With Ellison potentially getting involved in our research, I think the fewer people who know about this the better. At least for now."

"But it's Claire," Amir said, his brow furrowing in surprise. "We can trust her with this. Can't we?"

"It's not that I don't trust Claire."

"But you're worried about what she's going to think about all of this," Amir stated. "You think she'll have objections."

"Yeah, maybe," Marcus said with a shrug. "Remember how hard she argued against adding pain reception to Sam's World."

"She came around on that."

"I know, but if she had a problem with that, what opposition do you think she's going to have to this? And once the cat's out of the bag, it's not like we can keep it under wraps."

Amir turned back to look at the screen and nodded. "Maybe you're right."

"Do you really think we are preserving consciousness?" Marcus asked.

"I don't know. It doesn't seem possible, but we've never truly considered just what the AAIP is capable of. This is bigger than Elysium or Synerdyne, Marcus. If it's true, this is more than just life-changing. This is species-level change."

"I know. That's why we have to handle it carefully. And quietly," Marcus said, putting a hand on Amir's shoulder.

"So what do we do now?"

"Just keep gathering data. I'll make sure to send you more data from Sam and me each time we go into Sam's World. I'm curious, though. The participants in Elysium, how different are their maps from ours?"

"Fundamentally, they are similar, as we use the same map for the SynAPP. But the activity levels are greatly reduced, and in some places, dormant. I'd equate it to a photocopy made with low toner.

The lines are all there, but the image is nowhere near as sharp or detailed as the original."

"So, for Sam and me, is there anything we should be doing while in Sam's World?"

Amir shrugged. "Just try to experience as much sensory data as possible, both pleasurable and painful. And maybe increase the time spent there."

"I've already given Sam access to the simulation when she's alone," Marcus said.

"Well, the more time she spends there, the more data we can review."

"Yeah, but I can't stop worrying about leaving her there without some means of oversight in case something goes wrong. It meant connecting her to the Synerdyne server network. If someone looks in the right place, or just accidentally stumbles upon it, they could figure out what's going on. It increases the risk that Sam's World will be discovered."

"True. That is a very real possibility. Maybe we should keep it separate then," Amir suggested.

Marcus let out a long breath thinking about Sam sitting alone in their apartment, suffering through her pain. Though he couldn't fathom her dying, a part of him wondered just how much time she had left. And could he deny her relief from that pain and suffering, especially if these were her last days? More often than not, his mind deflected such thoughts, but as he stared at Amir's screen, he couldn't hold them back. A hollowness grew in his stomach.

"She's not doing well, Amir. The last treatment didn't work, and the doctor says our only options now are more 'experimental'. I don't know if she's going to make it," he coughed, stepping back to lean against the office wall, tears suddenly flowing as he said the words aloud for the first time.

Amir turned around in his chair to face him, concern on his face as his own eyes grew red. "Oh, man. I'm so sorry. I had no idea it was so bad."

"We just found out a couple of days ago," Marcus said, trying to get himself under control. "But really, she's been on the decline for a while now."

Amir looked away, searching his desk drawers, before pulling out a small pack of tissues. Pulling a couple out for himself, he offered the packet to Marcus. Quickly pulling several tissues free, Marcus held them against his eyes, unable to slow his tears.

"These new treatments, what does her oncologist think of them?" Amir asked.

"He didn't offer much hope. He said they 'might' work because of their efficacy in cancers with similar markers. But I think they are just throwing anything at the wall and hoping it will stick now."

"How's Sam taking it?" Amir asked, wiping his own eyes.

"Like a trooper, as always. I know she puts on a brave face to protect me, but I can't help but think about how scared she must be. That's why I can't deny her more time in Sam's World. At least there she can escape and forget about the cancer and the pain," Marcus said, his tears finally subsiding.

"I get it," Amir said, standing up to put a hand on Marcus' shoulder. "We'll do everything we can for her. But we should probably tell Claire and Diego, too. That way the four of us can work to ensure the server's protection and make it less noticeable. At the very least we can lock anyone else out and hide its true function."

"Yeah, you're right," Marcus said, taking a deep breath.

"You want to tell them about Sam's condition?" Amir asked.

"Would you mind telling them? I don't know if I have it in me."

"I can do that. I'm sorry, man. I really am. Sam never deserved this. But she's stronger than any of us. Don't give up hope. If anyone can beat this, it's her. Nothing can keep her down," Amir said, pulling Marcus into a hug.

"Yeah. She's unstoppable," Marcus replied, hugging him back.

For a moment they stayed in the embrace, and Marcus was surprised at how grateful he was for his friend's support.

"Do you think that we can preserve Sam's consciousness with the AAIP?" he said pointedly, as they let each other go.

Amir looked at him for a long moment, considering.

"Honestly, I don't know. But I figured that would be where your mind would go. And I don't want to give you any false hope. All I know is that the AAIP is recording brain function and patterns. Whether those patterns emerge as a copy of a person's thoughts and personality, it's too soon to tell. And it brings with it a whole host of ethical and moral questions that we have to consider before taking any action. So, for now, I can just say this: we are recording her patterns in the map, and we can at least preserve that information."

Marcus nodded and let out a sigh. "Yeah. Can't get ahead of ourselves."

"Let me just posit this as well," Amir said. "Just because those patterns are identical, would that constitute the person? Or are we more than just our brain function? I don't know the answer to that. Is a copy of Sam just that? A copy? I find it hard to imagine a substitution for real flesh and blood Sam."

"There is no substitution," Marcus agreed, but in the back of his mind he couldn't help but think that maybe one was the possible continuation of the other.

CHAPTER 9

"**O**h, God. I'm sorry Marcus," Evan said with a look of sorrow. "Take all the time you need, and go be with Sam. That's the most important thing right now."

Marcus looked across the desk and nodded numbly. He barely registered Evan, his thoughts on Sam, and the words of Dr. Dlamini.

"I'm afraid the treatment has proven ineffective, and the damage has advanced faster than we anticipated. The tumors have filled her chest cavity and are now pressing against her heart and lungs. There are too many to remove with surgery, and without an effective treatment, they will only continue to grow. The most we can do now is treat her pain with palliative care in hospice."

Hospice. The word reverberated in his mind. Even though part of his work specifically focused on such patients, the reality of it was still foreign to him. It meant there was no fixing Sam. She was going to die. It wasn't a matter of *if* any longer, just *when*. And most likely soon. He'd thought about this outcome before, but always only on an intellectual level. It never seemed like an actual possibility. In some ways, it still felt impossible. He couldn't imagine life without her. He hadn't been separated from her since he'd graduated high school. How was he supposed to live life without her? There was no life without Sam.

"Don't worry about anything here. Amir and the others can keep things going as they have been. I just want you to focus on your time with Sam," Evan continued. "I'll handle things with Ellison."

Marcus looked up at the mention of the billionaire, his thoughts momentarily interrupted.

"What about him?"

"Don't worry about it, man. You have enough to deal with."

"Tell me, Evan," he prodded.

Evan let out a long breath with a look of consideration. After a moment, he nodded in reluctant acquiescence.

"Ellison was impressed with what he saw in Elysium, specifically our research with the AAIP and SynAPP, and has made an official offer to the board. I'm scheduled to sit with Amir and the team about it tomorrow to discuss how to proceed."

"The fuck? And you didn't tell me?" Marcus said.

"Normally, you'd be the first to know. But with Sam… there are more important things for you to focus on. Don't worry about this."

Marcus' mind reeled, his thoughts a jumble of worry for Sam and the project. What sort of access would Ellison want? Most likely everything. What if he found out about the consciousness mapping or Sam's World? He couldn't let that be jeopardized. He needed to talk to Amir.

"You will keep me in the loop. Everything here was built by me, Sam, and the others. It is our life's work," Marcus said, his voice breaking at the thought of Sam.

"I just didn't want you to have to focus on anything but Sam. But okay. I'll make sure you are apprised of things. But for now, I have to insist on putting Amir in the lead. He'll be the point of contact," Evan said, lifting a box of tissues from his desk and leaning forward to offer them to Marcus.

Fighting back the tears that stung his eyes, Marcus took the tissues and nodded.

"Fine. That's fine," he said, wiping his eyes. "Just make sure I know what's going on."

"I will," Evan agreed. "Just don't worry about it, okay? We can handle things."

Marcus gave him a weak nod and wiped his eyes again.

"I'm so sorry, man. I still can't believe it."

"Yeah," he replied in a whisper.

Taking a deep breath, Marcus swallowed his sorrow and pushed himself to his feet.

"I need to talk to Amir before I go, and make sure he's got everything he needs."

"Yeah, good idea," Evan said, standing up to walk him to the door.

As Marcus opened the door, Evan put a hand on his back.

"I'm so fucking sorry, buddy," he said, pulling Marcus into a hug as he turned to face him.

For a moment, they held each other tightly.

"Give Sam my love. I wish I could see her, but I don't want to make her deal with more than she's already dealing with. Tell her Liz and I are thinking about her," Evan said, releasing his grip.

"I will," Marcus replied with a small nod, turning to walk out the door.

Faces looked up from their cubicles as Marcus passed the programming floor, making his way to Amir's office. From his own office, Oswald looked up from his computer as he caught sight of him but didn't rush to talk to him as he usually did. Instead, he just watched as Marcus passed, his eyes knowing.

Reaching Amir's door, Marcus knocked and waited for his friend's response.

The door opened, but instead of Amir, he was greeted by Claire.

When she saw him, her face twisted in sorrow and she threw her arms around him, pulling him into a hug.

"I'm so sorry, Marcus," she said into his neck, her voice breaking.

Marcus numbly returned the hug. His eyes searched for Amir and found him sitting at his desk. After a moment, Claire released him and stepped back so he could enter the room. Pulling the door closed behind him, he looked to Claire then Amir. With her there, he'd have to be careful about what they discussed.

"I didn't expect to see you," Claire said.

"I was meeting with Evan about Sam," he said, immediately wanting to change the subject. "We need to discuss Clive Ellison."

"That's what we were just talking about," Claire said. "But first, how's Sam?"

How do you fucking think she is? he thought angrily. *Dying.* Instead of voicing the thought, he took a breath.

"Not well. She's trying to be strong about it, but she knows it's just a matter of time. She's in a lot of pain all the time. More now than ever. They offered us some medication, higher doses of opioids, and things she was already taking, but she wanted to go into the simulation instead. So that's where she spends her time now. She can't even eat anymore, so there's no point in pulling her out. At least there she doesn't have to feel any pain. So now it's just about waiting," he explained, barely able to finish his last words.

Claire put a hand on his shoulder.

"Oh, Marcus," she said, hugging him again. "At least you know she's happier there."

"Is she not affected at all in the simulation?" Amir asked. "No leaching through of her sickness or pain? What about her mental state?"

"Are you trying to analyze her symptoms as a data set in relation to the simulation?" Marcus asked angrily.

"Yes. This is the first time we've used the simulation in this way. I think it's important that we gather as much data from it as possible.

It doesn't mean I don't care. I care very much. But I think Sam would agree that this could be important to document. Look, you said yourself that she isn't eating. So it stands to reason that she may be going through some cognitive degeneration. That means her brain is eventually going to run out of energy. My guess is it has already."

Marcus glared at Amir, his muscles tense. Claire tried to rub his back soothingly.

"Maybe not right now, Amir," she said.

"I'm not trying to be an asshole," he explained. "It could be very necessary to the mapping data if we were to implant her in the simulation."

Marcus looked at him in shock, glancing meaningfully at Claire.

"He told me, Marcus," she said, stepping back. "About the consciousness mapping and what you've been thinking about doing."

"I needed to get her medical opinion on the data, and I didn't think we could leave her out of the loop any longer."

"And?" Marcus asked, looking between the two of them, studying Claire's reaction.

Claire looked over at Amir, then looked back at Marcus, lifting her chin. That was all he needed to know that she was against it.

"I think there is too much we don't know. Not to mention the moral and ethical implications of what you're suggesting. I know it seems like a lifeline to save Sam, especially *now*. But if you think about it, it won't be Sam. Not really. It'll just be a copy of specific electronic signals sent by the brain created by certain stimuli."

"And how is that any different from how we use the map of those electronic signals to allow people to function inside the simulation? How is that any different from a living brain?" he argued.

"Because it's not alive, Marcus," she retorted. "If anything, it is a program itself."

"So thoughts can only originate from an organic brain?" Marcus shot back.

"Yes! That's exactly my point. Her thoughts don't originate from the program. They come from her organic brain, and the AAIP has just recorded the signals created by those thoughts. And just because it can mimic those thoughts, it doesn't mean that it is Sam. It doesn't mean she would be able to develop new, independent thoughts," Claire said.

"We all work in AI. Are you telling me, you don't think that a self-learning AI can develop a consciousness?" Marcus retorted.

"Not a human consciousness. Nor anything that resembles a living being. You can't call it life."

"What is a brain if not just a highly advanced organic computer?" Amir interjected. "It would stand to reason that the organic nature of the brain is irrelevant. It is just a means to an end. A highly effective and phenomenal apparatus, but not necessary for function."

"Exactly. We can put hearts made of plastic into a person to keep them alive. Why not one day a brain? Hell, why can't we transcend physical form? I'm not arguing that Sam's thoughts didn't originate in her organic form. That's the Sam I've known all my life. The one I fell in love with. But I'm arguing that she can continue without that form, in another," Marcus said.

"It won't be her, Marcus," Claire responded. "It will just be a copy of her previous self. Like a perverse photo album of memories."

"Is that your professional medical opinion?" Marcus asked.

Claire looked up at him, meeting his stare with her own. For a moment she searched his gaze, then looked away.

"I don't know what to think, Marcus. How can I? There are too many unknowns. All I can do is voice my opinion and try to give you some perspective."

"Do you think I haven't thought about these things?" Marcus said. "It's all I've been thinking about since Amir told me what he discovered. But the conclusion I came to is this: if there is a possibility that we can save Sam, we have to take it."

"I know it hurts, Marcus. I can only imagine what you are going through. What she's going through. But at the end of everything, we are all powerless against the natural order of things," Claire said with a sigh.

"Natural order of things? She's not even forty years old, Claire! There's nothing natural about what has happened to her. Or do you want to tell me it's the will of God? The same claim would have been made five hundred years ago about viruses before someone came up with vaccination. You know this better than anyone. Why is this any different? I refuse to let her just die if there is something—anything—that can be done to save her. If not for this, what are we even creating the simulation for?" Marcus pressed.

"Treatment and palliative care," she countered.

"The simulation is meant to allow those who have been disabled by injury or sickness to experience an environment where they can forget their pain: physical, mental, and emotional. Why can't that extend to the ultimate form of all pain?" Marcus asked.

"No one can escape pain forever. Eventually we all have to face it, Marcus," Claire said.

"Says who? Is that a fundamental law of nature? Or is that only true until something comes along to prove it wrong?"

"We can't play God. Let's say you are right, and we can preserve Sam's consciousness. Instead of letting her go, you want to imprison her in an environment of your creation. Where you make the rules. How long will she remain there? Forever? Or until someone turns off the server? And then what? Does she just wink out of existence? That's what I mean about the natural order of things. No matter how hard you struggle against it, death is inevitable in one form or another," Claire replied.

"Better to wink out of existence than to die a lingering, painful death you know you can't avoid. You have no idea what she is going through. The pain. The fear. So save me the morality lesson,"

Marcus spat. "Besides, who's to say that we can't eventually develop a way for her to exist outside of the simulation?"

"And how would we do that?" Claire asked.

"I don't know. Robot bodies, or some sci-fi shit. If this is proven to work, it will revolutionize human existence and may just be the next step in human evolution. Free of disease and death as we know it. By putting her in the simulation we can preserve her for as long as possible," Marcus said.

"Do you hear yourself? The next step in human evolution?" Claire scoffed.

"It has to start somewhere. Most discoveries are made while attempting something else. Why should this be any different?"

"None of this should be up to us," Amir interjected. "It should be up to Sam. Have you talked to her about this?"

Marcus shook his head.

"I didn't want to give her false hope if it turned out that it wouldn't work," Marcus said, turning to Claire. "So will it work?"

Claire looked away from both of them and stared at the floor thoughtfully. "The truth is, I don't know. This is beyond me, and way beyond our original mission statement. I'm here to monitor participant health and make sure the simulation does not cause negative health outcomes. But that requires some sort of physiological vitals. I am trained in conventional medicine. This is uncharted territory."

Marcus looked over to Amir, who raised his eyebrows questioningly.

"Then maybe you could be the one to chart it," Marcus said, laying a gentle hand on Claire's shoulder.

At his touch, she pulled back. "No. I love Sam, but I can't be a part of this."

"Even if it's her wish?" he prodded.

"Any decision she makes now can't be informed, Marcus. She is dying, and you want to dangle the hope of salvation before her. Not to mention what Amir said about her cognitive decline. What other choice could she make under those circumstances?"

"Fuck you, Claire. That's not fair," Marcus growled.

"No. What you are doing isn't fair," she said, looking between him and Amir. "I'm out."

"Claire, come on. If not for me, do it for Sam," Marcus pleaded.

"No. I can't do this anymore. Any of it. First, it was bringing in the shareholders, then Ellison, and now this. We started this to help people, but it has been perverted beyond anything I could imagine."

"Wait. You mean you're out of Synerdyne?" Amir said, his brow raised in surprise.

"Yes. I'm done with it all," she said. "Marcus, you talked about a new human evolution, but have you thought about what someone like Ellison would do with this type of technology? What governments and corporations could do with it if he sold it to them? This may not prove to be humanity's next step, but its destruction. Once we open Pandora's box, there's no closing it."

"Now you're just being hyperbolic," Marcus said, shaking his head.

"I'm just following things to their logical conclusion. Something I thought the two of you would have done," she said, pushing past him to the door.

"Claire, wait," Marcus said, putting his hand on the door to prevent her from leaving. "Is there anything I can do to make you reconsider?"

"No. I've been feeling this way for a long time. I should have said something sooner, but I just kept my concerns to myself, hoping things would work out differently. Now I see they are worse than I could have imagined."

"Maybe just take some time. We can keep you updated, and you can make your decision from there. I'll tell Evan you need to take a sabbatical."

"No, Marcus," she said, her hand on the doorknob. "I have to leave. Now, are you going to let me out?"

"Will you at least keep this to yourself?" Marcus asked pointedly.

Claire stared at his hand on the door, and glanced over at Amir, before glaring back at Marcus. "Or what? Are you going to kill me, Marcus?"

Marcus took a step back in shock, letting go of the door.

"God, no! Jesus. I'm just asking that you keep this between us. Please. If not for me, then for Sam."

Claire looked at him for a long moment, her eyes searching his as she clutched the knob.

"Fuck you, Marcus," she said, opening the door and storming out of the office.

Marcus watched her charge across the floor, weaving between the cubicles to her office, slamming the door behind her.

Amir got up from his desk to stand behind him, looking out onto the floor.

"I don't think she'll tell anyone," he said. "She's just upset. But she wouldn't betray us."

Marcus continued to stare at her office door, considering Amir's words and what Claire had said. He hoped Amir was right. But if not, there was little he'd be able to do about it. The fact that Claire had even suggested that he might hurt her was still a shock. He knew she probably said it to make a point, but still. He became aware of eyes watching him from over cubicle walls and slowly closed the door.

"I hope you're right," he said, leaning against the door and letting out a long breath. "So, what do you think? Does the mapping look viable?"

Amir moved back to sit down in his chair and stared at his monitor.

"Honestly, I don't know. All I can tell you is that everything looks like it should theoretically work. I ran it through a few scenarios, giving it virtual input the same way the AAIP would through the SynAPP, originating signals at the nodes located where the hippocampus would be, and the mapping responded with the same electrical signals I'd expect to see in Sam's brain. Now whether this is just mimicry or an actual response, I can't say. Not without testing it in the simulation."

"So why don't we test it?" Marcus asked, looking over Amir's shoulder at the mapping image on his monitor's screen.

"Well, aside from the fact that it feels weird to try and simulate Sam while she is still alive—which kind of makes Claire's point about it being a copy—I worry that while Sam is still using the simulation it will get confused by having two identical maps running."

"Isn't that what it is doing anyway?"

"No. Right now, Sam is the active user, and the map is a recording of her brain activity. If I were to switch the map into being an active part of the simulation, it would no longer be able to record Sam's activity and might even interfere with her own use."

"So, you're saying that we can't know if this will work until Sam is…" Marcus swallowed, a cold numbness washing over him as he thought about what he was saying. "…gone?"

"Essentially, yes. If she were to stop using the simulation, we could test it. But it might interfere with any further use on her part."

Marcus nodded. So either she stopped using the simulation, giving up her escape from the pain and the prospect of a slow, agonizing death. Or he continued to let her stay in Sam's world until she eventually passed and then tried to bring her back through her map, giving them no guarantees it would work.

"I won't make her leave," Marcus said.

"I understand," Amir said, nodding. "Like I said, it would be weird to have two Sams existing at the same time anyway. Even if one is inside the simulation and the other outside it. But I am worried about her cognitive decline."

"We've had other people use the simulation in hospice care."

"Yes, but we weren't worried about their cognitive mapping. Certainly not for the purpose we're discussing. Nor did we let them continue after a certain point. The one thing about letting Sam stay in the simulation is that as long as she is there her cognitive responses will continue to be recorded in the mapping. And as she declines, it could warp the map. Maybe to the point of making it unviable."

"So, you're saying she needs to come out of the simulation if this is going to work?"

"Maybe," Amir shrugged. "I don't actually know. But it is a concern I think we have to address."

"Have you seen any changes?" Marcus asked.

"There are millions of data points in the mapping. I've run a few comparisons with her earlier records, and there are differences, but there is no way to tell what they are due to, or if they are having a detrimental impact."

Concerns warred in Marcus' head as he thought about the choice. The thought of pulling Sam out of the simulation to suffer through her last days nearly broke his heart. Yet the thought that not doing so meant they might ultimately lose their chance to save her was just as devastating.

"I need to talk to Sam," he said, in agreement with Amir's earlier suggestion.

"Yeah. She's got to know. Just remember what Claire said, and make sure you don't push her in a specific way. Just give her the facts and let her decide what she wants."

Marcus nodded, not sure what he wanted her to do anyway.

"Regarding Ellison," he said, remembering his other reason for coming by. "Evan said he's made you lead liaison while I'm on leave. Make sure you don't give him access to anything regarding Sam's World or the mapping. In fact, be careful about the AAIP and SynAPP. They might be able to extrapolate the same things you did. Just delay them for now, until we've figured out the Sam thing. If you get any pushback for access, just use me as an excuse and say I've encrypted it, and you'll have to get a hold of me. Keep me in the loop."

"Will do. And what about Claire?"

"We'll let her cool down. Hopefully she'll come around. Regardless, she'll have to keep quiet. She signed the NDA just like the rest of us. She won't be spilling any secrets anytime soon. And it's not like she trusts Evan or the shareholders."

"And Diego? He's not going to be happy when he hears that Claire is leaving," Amir said.

"Bring him in on it. He loves Sam more than anything. He'll understand. Just make sure he knows how important it is that no one finds out about it. Tell him to reach out to me."

"What do I tell Oswald and the rest when they learn that Claire is leaving? They are going to be suspicious. Especially Oswald."

"Just tell them that Claire has decided to take a break from things, and we hope she'll return soon," Marcus offered. "But you'll have to tell them about Ellison. Let them know that nothing will be changing in the immediate future and that they will be updated as we move forward. I'll write something up for you."

"Alright, thanks. I hate this shit. I'm not a people person."

Marcus grinned. "Maybe, but there is no one I'd rather have hold down the fort while I'm gone. You'll do fine. Just reach out to me if anything comes up. In the meantime, put all your efforts into the simulation and see if you can find out anything else."

"Will do."

"Right," Marcus said with a sigh, looking over the floor to Claire's office door. "Well, I guess I'll head home and talk to Sam."

"How do you think she will take it," Amir asked.

"Honestly? I have no idea."

CHAPTER 10

Morrigan sat next to the crackling fire she'd made to roast the tapir. She'd spent the morning hunting it. Maybe it was her imagination, but they seemed to be getting wilier, running at the first hint of danger. Unconsciously, she rubbed at her ribs. She wasn't sure what had caused the sudden stabbing pain earlier, but it had faded quickly to a dull ache. Now she could barely even feel it.

Holding up her knife, she wiped the blood off its blade and admired the pelt she'd hung up to dry. She was getting better at skinning these things. Maybe soon she could use the hides to make a tent.

From the corner of her eye, the sudden flicker of a shadow caught her attention and she turned her head to search the dense jungle undergrowth. The plants sat undisturbed and she chided herself for her agitation. She'd been jumping at shadows over the last few days, always thinking things were moving that weren't there. She told herself she was just being careful. The giant ape who made this land his territory was still out there, and if it caught her off guard she had no doubt it would make quick work of her.

The snapping of a twig pulled her from her reverie, and she quickly grabbed her spear from where she'd laid it beside her on the log. So she wasn't just jumping at shadows. Whatever it was, it sounded large, and she wondered if the ape had finally found her. A grin came to her face at the thought and she hefted her spear in anticipation, listening as the sound grew closer.

Just on the other side of a broad-leafed fern the plants shifted, then parted, as a figure stepped out of the underbrush and into the clearing. Morrigan gripped the spear, ready to thrust, when she saw the familiar face of Aer step into view.

"Woah!" he called with wide eyes, stepping back and holding up his hands. "It's only me, Red."

Morrigan's face split into a broad smile and she dropped her spear. Stepping past the fire, she threw her arms around his neck and kissed him deeply. After a momentary surprise, Aer returned the kiss in equal measure, wrapping his muscular arms around her.

"Fuck, it's good to see ye, boyo," she said with a laugh, pulling back only far enough to nip at his lip.

"Likewise," Aer said, squeezing her against his body. "How are you feeling?"

"Better now that yer here," she said, making a point to run her leg up his thigh.

Aer laughed and kissed her again.

"Good to know I'm missed."

"Always," she said, reaching down to pull him into the clearing by the waist of his tasset. "Now that yer back, we can celebrate, yeah?" she said, waggling her eyebrows suggestively.

Aer let himself be pulled toward the fire, but as she reached to undress him, he gently took her arms by the wrist.

"Listen, Sam. There's something I need to talk to you about."

Morrigan looked up at him curiously and pushed her hands forward to unclasp his tasset.

"We can talk later, boyo. Now's the time for fuckin'," she said with a laugh.

He pulled her hands away again, holding them more tightly.

"I'm serious, Sam. Please. This is important."

Sam let out a hard breath and stopped her attempts to undress him, pulling her hands away. Frustration welled up inside her. Not at him so much as at the intrusion of reality. Thoughts she had been trying to avoid flooded her mind as she looked at Marcus' face, and with them came the crippling feelings of sadness and worry.

"Okay," she said, stepping back. Unconsciously, she wrapped her arms around herself. "What is it?"

Marcus sighed and stared into her eyes, searching her gaze.

"I've been thinking about how to tell you this for weeks, but I'm still uncertain what to say."

Sam's concern increased at his words, and she tried to think of all the possibilities of what he might say. Did something happen? Was it Synerdyne? Clive Ellison? Had he found someone else? Was he finally going to tell her that he couldn't handle it anymore, and leave her? They said, for some people, it was too much for their partners. Would he really leave her to die alone? She never imagined he'd do that, but who could say how people would react to facing this kind of thing?

"What is it?" she insisted.

Marcus let out another long breath and reached back to scratch his head, something he always did when he was uncertain.

"I...," he began, then pivoted. "Amir discovered something a couple of months ago. I didn't want to tell you about it until we understood it better."

The worry about him leaving dissipated to be replaced with curiosity.

"What I'm going to tell you... I don't want to influence you, but I don't know how I can't," he continued.

"Just say it."

"We may have… well, the AAIP actually… you know how it guides our cognitive response using the WL map? Well, it seems it also maps that cognitive response so that it can better assimilate future stimuli. Essentially, it continues to learn how our brains function by creating a detailed map of its own. A copy of our brain function."

Where was he going with this? And why did it make him so nervous?

"Yeah, it stands to reason. It would need to create a means by which to not only anticipate stimuli reception but track it," she said, seeing the logic. "So?"

Marcus looked down at his feet, letting out another long breath, before lifting his eyes to meet her gaze.

"Theoretically, it's not just a copy to help it function better. Amir thinks…," he paused. "… I think… it is a functional copy of your consciousness. One capable of existing within the simulation without your participation."

"Are you saying the AAIP has created an artificial version of me?"

"That's one way to look at it, I suppose. I'm suggesting it could preserve your consciousness: your ways of thinking, your individual nuances, your memories, your hopes, your views of the world. Everything that makes you… well… you. And that it can keep your consciousness active, even after your…," he let the words trail off, his eyes brimming with tears.

The possibility of what he was suggesting struck her as his words began to sink in.

"You're saying that the AAIP can keep me alive in the simulation? Even after my death?"

"That's the theory."

"Can you prove it?" she asked.

"No. Not while you are still active in the simulation."

"You mean, while I am alive," she said, knowing he couldn't.

Marcus nodded, a tear slipping down his cheek.

"The AAIP is still mapping your activity," he explained. "And any deviation from that could mean if you tried to access the simulation afterward, it might not work. Or worse."

Sam nodded. "I have to admit it is weird to think about there being another me."

"It depends on how you look at it, I suppose. I don't think of it as another you. I think of it as an extension of you. A backup," he smiled sadly. "A save point."

Sam sat down on the log and stared into the fire, only dimly aware that the tapir was burning. Semi-consciously, she reached out to turn the spit. She thought about the implications of what Marcus had just told her, her mind reeling with all the possibilities of what it might mean. Was what he was suggesting even possible? Would it be a continuation of her consciousness, or just some AI asset—no different than the Half-men—created using her brain function? She wondered if she would still be aware of who she was. Would this doppelganger truly think like her? Or would it have its own thoughts? Did it matter? Was there even a difference?

She looked at Marcus to find him staring down at her. She could see the pain in his eyes, but also the hope. The need to believe there was a way to save her, like an uncertain puppy dog. She'd always loved those eyes. From the first moment she'd stared into them, she'd seen his sincerity and kindness, and been hooked.

She was going to die. She knew there wasn't anything she could do to stop it. She desperately hoped he was right about the AAIP. She didn't want to die, but over the last several months, she'd come to accept her fate. He hadn't. Maybe he couldn't. And she worried how her death would impact him. Whether or not what he was suggesting was feasible or whether this 'backup' would truly be her didn't really matter. What mattered was giving him the hope that could keep him going.

"You okay, babe? You want to talk about it?" he asked, crouching beside her and putting a hand on her knee.

She smiled at him, touching his cheek. "Yeah. It's pretty incredible to think about. I never imagined."

"Yeah," he agreed, reaching up to take her hand and squeeze it.

"And Amir thinks this is possible?"

"He's the one who first noticed it," he said with a nod.

"And this has happened to everyone in the simulation?"

"In a manner of speaking. Although the participants in Elysium don't have as intricate a map as you do. Amir speculates that it has something to do with pain reception since it is the most likely variable between Sam's World and Elysium."

"And what about you? Is your map the same?"

"Yeah," he said smiling. "Mine's also more like yours. So even if it isn't pain reception, it has to be something to do with Sam's World."

"I can't believe we never came up with a better name for this place," she said with a laugh.

"It's an apt description," he grinned, shrugging.

"I guess it is."

"You deserve the world," he said, squeezing her hand.

"Oh, stop it, you romantic bastard," she said, jokingly pushing his face away.

He gave a melancholy chuckle and smiled.

"So, what now?" she asked.

"Well, I need to know your thoughts. What do you think?"

"Honestly, I don't know what to think," she said. "There are so many questions I have. So many possibilities to consider. It's a lot to think about."

"Yeah, I know. Sorry to spring this on you, but…," he said, trailing off.

"*But* I am running out of time," she finished for him, squeezing his hand. "I know."

"How have you been feeling in the simulation?"

"Fine. Better than if I weren't, that's for sure," she said.

"Do you notice any stimuli creeping in from the outside?"

"What do you mean?"

"Like," he began hesitantly. "Have you experienced any disruptions or sensations within the simulation that you might attribute to your physical body's breakdown?"

"No. Why should I? That's the point of the simulation, right? To specifically stimulate my brain to ignore the pain I feel outside of the simulation."

"Sure, but it stands to reason that as your nervous system starts to break down, it might influence, or even overwhelm, the SynAPP's ability to moderate your stimuli."

Sam thought about the strange shadows and the stabbing pain she'd experienced earlier. Maybe it wasn't something new Diego had added. She thought about telling Marcus but knew it would only cause him to worry and might make him reconsider. Besides, it had all passed quickly enough, and it made sense now that she thought about it. A little blip here and there was nothing to worry about.

"Well, things seem normal enough. I don't currently feel any pain," she lied, smiling.

"Good. Hopefully the SynAPP can keep things under control. However, Amir is concerned that as your body starts to break down — specifically as your brain function starts to be affected by your lack of calories — it might create deviations and deteriorations in the mapping."

"Oh. What does Claire think?" Sam asked. "Does she see anything of concern?"

A shadow fell over Marcus' face.

"What is it?" she probed, knowing her question had touched a nerve.

"Claire's not on board with this. And she's threatened to leave," he said with a sigh.

"What?"

"She's against it on principle. She says there are too many problems with it, morally and ethically. She suggested that it wouldn't be you. And that by doing this we would be playing God, and such. She said I'd be making you a prisoner here, with me having all the control."

"Oh," Sam said, considering Claire's perspective. "I suppose it does bring up some potential problems to consider. A few of which popped into my head too."

"So you think it is a bad idea?"

"I didn't say that. Just that it brings up some considerations. But that's no reason for her to leave."

"It's not just that," he added. "She said all the stuff with the shareholders and Ellison has made her start reconsidering things."

"Maybe I could talk to her. Here. And we could discuss her concerns, just the two of us," Sam offered.

"Yeah maybe. I told her to take some time, to let her cool down and consider things. But I suppose I could reach out to her and see if she's interested."

Out of the corner of her eye, a shadow shifted in the plants behind Marcus, and Sam broke her gaze from his to stare at it. Like before, when she focused on it, nothing seemed out of place, the broad-leafed plants sitting undisturbed.

"What? What is it?" he asked, following her gaze to look over his shoulder. "Is everything okay?"

Sam's eyes searched the underbrush for a second longer before she turned her eyes back to his. "Everything's fine. I just thought I saw something moving. You never know where the ape might be," she said, grinning.

"Is he still around? Shit, I guess he would be. I didn't take him out of the simulation."

"Don't. I like not knowing," she said quickly, putting a hand on his arm.

"Okay, little one," Marcus said with a soft smile, patting her hand.

"But come to think of it, that does bring up an interesting question. Let's say we do 'activate' my consciousness in the simulation… after I'm gone. What will happen if I die in Sam's World? I won't have a body to return to when the SynAPP tries to eject me."

"Fuck. I didn't even think about that." He stared down at the ground in consideration. "I suppose we could turn off the ejection protocol. But then we'd need some other way to safely remove you from the situation. I suppose we could always just turn off the death protocol, and maybe the pain reception."

"No," she said more quickly than she intended, grabbing his hand. "You said it yourself, the difference between my map and the others is the pain reception. And couldn't that also be said about the death protocol? If you change that, you might change how my consciousness functions within the AAIP."

"I suppose you're right. I'll have to talk with Amir and see what he thinks," he let out a long sigh. "But there's still his concern about what will happen if you stay in the simulation as your body fails."

"So what does he want me to do? Stop using the simulation?"

"That's one option, yeah. But that means making you suffer until…" Marcus let his words drift off, his eyes growing red. Shaking his head he continued, "I can't imagine making you do that. Especially if we don't know if any of this will work."

"So what's the other option?" she asked.

"We leave you in the simulation and risk corrupting the mapping. But at least that way hopefully you will avoid any suffering as you…" Again, he was unable to say the words. "My hope is, as that happens, your consciousness will just continue within the simulation uninterrupted. With any luck, you won't even realize it has happened."

"I understand Amir's worry," she said. "It makes sense. But has he considered that the AAIP might weed out those corruptions? Since they will not match with its pattern mapping? It would make sense since the whole point of the cognitive mapping is to create, not only a guide for synaptic stimulus, but a framework by which to keep things stable. The AAIP should want to follow norms instead of anomalies."

"I hadn't even considered that," Marcus said, his eyes brightening. "I'll bring it up to him and see what he thinks."

Smiling, he lifted himself to kiss her forehead, but she stopped him, pulling his lips to hers.

"There's no need for that here," she said. "You can kiss me all you want."

"But I like kissing your forehead," he teased. "It's cute."

"I'm not cute. I'm fierce," she said, scrunching up her face in a mock scowl that she knew he'd find cute. "Rawr."

Laughing he pulled her to him, kissing her again. This time they lingered in the kiss, holding each other closer.

"Go talk to Amir, and find out what he thinks," she said when they finally parted from the kiss. "In the meantime, see if Claire will come and talk to me."

"Do you know what you want to do?" he asked.

"Probably. But let's find out what they have to say first," she replied.

"Are you going to tell me?"

"Not just yet, boyo," she said with a wink, leaning back invitingly on the log. "Now. Are ye goin' to remove that tasset? Or are ye goin' to make me wrestle it off ye?"

CHAPTER 11

"Thank you for coming," Clive Ellison said with a smile, walking over to shake Marcus' hand as he stepped onto the patio behind the giant house.

"Have a seat," he offered, gesturing to a couple of expensive-looking lawn chairs set across from one another beside a table.

Marcus took a seat as Ellison moved to stand behind an impressive bar that dominated one side of the patio.

Pouring two glasses of whiskey, he said, "First off, please allow me to offer you my sympathies about Sam. You both have my best wishes. And if there is anything I can do—if you want a second opinion from any specialists in the country—just say the word and I'll have my people on it. Don't worry about expenses."

Ellison walked over and held out one of the glasses to Marcus.

"Thank you, Mr. Ellison," Marcus said with surprise, taking the proffered glass. "That's... that's very generous."

"Not at all. And call me Clive," he said. "I've heard a lot about Sam, and she sounds like quite a woman. I had no idea you'd known each other for so long. Twenty-five years? Is that right?"

"Yeah. Since we were teenagers," he said, looking down at the dark liquid in his glass. "She's always been my best friend."

"That's nice to hear. You're lucky to have found each other," Clive said, sitting down in the chair opposite Marcus and lifting his glass. "To Sam."

Marcus held up his glass in response, and with a nod, muttered, "To Sam."

In unison, they took a drink.

"You know. I lost my wife to cancer," Clive said. "We hadn't been together as long as you and Sam. Didn't meet as early in life as the two of you. But we had a good long time together. Nine years. I loved her dearly. I know it's not the same, but just know that I have an understanding of how you might be feeling."

Marcus raised his eyebrows in surprise at the revelation.

"In some ways, that makes us bonded by our experiences. At least compared to those who haven't gone through it as we have."

Marcus looked down again at the whiskey in his glass, staring into the dark liquid.

"I apologize for calling you over here while you are dealing with so much. It is insensitive of me, but things are moving fast for Synerdyne and I wanted to keep you in the loop."

Marcus looked up in surprise.

"You know, I think of you as the heart of the company. You and your team, sure. But *you* specifically. You're the visionary. The one who saw the potential of Waxman-Li's research, beyond what other people would deem possible. And it takes visionaries to move the world forward," Clive said, taking another drink.

"I can't claim full credit for the SynAPP or the AAIP. Both were the product of collaboration. Not just with the members of my team, but with many others who contributed their knowledge and expertise," Marcus clarified.

"Of course. But you held the project together. That's what a leader does. It's not only his vision but his ability to see that vision realized. To bring together those he needs to help assemble all the parts and turn that dream into reality."

"The vision wasn't mine alone either," Marcus said. "I couldn't have done it without Sam. She's as much a part of all this as anyone."

"Hearing the way you talk about her, I don't doubt it," Clive said with a sympathetic smile. "It's only a shame I haven't had the chance to get to know her. She sounds like a spectacular woman."

"She is."

"Well, I'm sure she's proud of you, Marcus. And having spent so long together, I don't doubt that you've incorporated many of her ways of thinking into your own over the years."

Marcus nodded, thinking about how Sam had always overanalyzed a situation, and how he used to make fun of her for it. But also, how she rarely ever let a mistake slip by her and caught many of his own, causing him to become more analytical in his own work.

"She definitely made me a better person."

"That's good," Clive smiled. "None of us are born with perfect knowledge. And it's important to bring people into your life that challenge you. Make you better."

Clive took a long drink of the remaining whiskey and laid the empty glass on the table beside them. "Come on. I want to show you something," he said, standing up and waving for Marcus to follow.

Putting down his glass, Marcus followed Clive back towards the house. The house itself was enormous, made up of several different buildings, and its grounds spread out more like a university campus than a home. Marcus was pretty sure the entirety of his condo would only take up a small portion of any one of those buildings.

Clive guided him along a stone walkway that curved away from the main house and led to a smaller two-story structure whose outer walls were made entirely of glass. As they reached the threshold, the door slid open for them automatically, leading into a large room furnished with only a few chairs and dominated by a large table. Clive walked over to the table, and Marcus saw what looked like a miniature model for a campus similar in size to Clive's compound.

"So, what do you think?" Clive said, gesturing to the model.

"It's impressive. Another property you're thinking of building?" Marcus asked, leaning down to get a better look at the model.

"Yes. This is going to be Synerdyne's new research campus," Clive said matter-of-factly.

Marcus stared at Clive in shock then looked back down at the mockup and marveled at its size compared to the seven floors of rental space Synerdyne currently inhabited.

"Right there is going to be the research lab," he said, pointing to the largest building. "It'll house an onsite clinic so that participation in the simulation can be expanded, with a surgical center and medical staff. It'll be able to house three hundred participants." Clive pointed to another building. "This will be the development building, protected by next-gen security protocols. Again with enough space to quadruple your current dev team. And most importantly, this is the server building. Again next-gen secured, with a six-cycle backup protocol and EM protections, running off a fully independent power grid. Even if we experience World War III, so long as no one targets us directly, this campus will continue to function."

Marcus stared down at the campus, trying to envision what Clive was telling him. Something like this would cost a fortune and went well beyond any expectations he'd ever had for their research.

"Why?" Marcus asked. "Synerdyne is a small company and could never recoup the cost of this project. Why put so much into it?"

"Maybe not right now, but that's all about to change. Truth is though, I'm not doing this for profit. I've got all the money I need. What you've created is revolutionary, and I'm certain that within a few years it will change the world."

"I don't know about that," Marcus said dismissively.

"As I said, it's all about vision and your will to see it made real. You're just not dreaming big enough. You have to look beyond your current needs and see the bigger picture," Clive expounded.

"And that is?" Marcus asked, his interest piqued.

"Saving Sam's consciousness, of course," Clive said pointedly.

Marcus felt his body grow numb and he stared at the man from across the table.

"What?"

Clive let a slow smile spread across his face. "Use the AAIP to preserve her consciousness. Keeping her mind active in the simulation, even if her body dies," he said confidently.

Marcus felt his throat grow dry. "I don't know what you are talking about. The SynAPP and AAIP are used as palliative treatments," he said, trying to deflect.

"Marcus, it's the only logical evolution of your research. It's the reason I took an interest in Synerdyne in the first place. I've been following your work since before you first created the company. When you were just publishing your findings in journals. It stands to reason that if you can map the human brain, as Waxman and Li proved, then you should also be able to map and record brain activity. And if you can map it, why not duplicate it? Once you get to a certain level of detailed mapping, what would make that map any different from the real thing?"

"I know you've been working on it, and I don't have any intention of curtailing you in this enterprise." Clive continued, spreading his hands out over the model. "As you can see, I want to encourage you along this path. I don't think it is an overstatement to say you've discovered the next phase in human evolution. You, your team, and Sam will be its pioneers. And with this campus, you can be assured that Sam's consciousness and all the ones that follow it will be secure and protected for perpetuity."

"I… How?" Marcus stuttered, unable to find the words as a cold dread coursed through his body.

"I don't invest my time and effort in things unless I already know everything about them, Marcus. My resources allow me access to almost everything. Frankly, my ability to learn about your clandestine endeavors only proves how much you need me and the security I can offer. It's not just competition you have to worry about. For something like this, you have to think on an even bigger scale about those who would be interested in such technology: foreign governments, terrorist organizations, even our own government. Not to mention those who will be opposed to your research and willing to hurt you to stop it. This is world-changing."

Marcus stared at the model of the campus, his eyes focusing on the server building. If they could preserve Sam's consciousness, his next concern was securing Sam's World so that nothing would happen to it. Sam would be as good as dead if the server got wiped, or if Synerdyne went under and could no longer afford to keep it powered and had to shut everything down.

"Why do you care about all this?" he asked, looking at Clive. "Like you said, you have enough money. What's in it for you? You're not some sort of sinister supervillain out of a movie, are you?"

Clive laughed loudly. "I like that. I suppose this would be where I would reveal my devious plan to you if I was. But no. Nothing so dramatic. The truth is, I am no different than any other man of influence throughout history. No matter how much power and wealth we possess, there is one thing we cannot control. And that is time. You can't cheat death. I've spent my entire life acquiring what I have, but now that I have it, I know it's only a matter of time before it will all be taken away. It took me forty years to get to this point, and I don't think I'll have forty more to enjoy it. Not even close.

"But I'm not thinking just about myself. Look at Sam and the countless other people like her—my wife for one—who have their lives cut unfairly short. And why? Because they pulled the short straw? Because of some cosmic fluke or accident? How is that fair? That's why I am invested in this research. Because I see the opportunity it offers humanity to transcend our mortal constraints and reach for something greater. Something that will elevate humanity to another level. Now tell me, how did you do it?"

"I think you've been misled," Marcus said.

"I'm sharing all this with you, Marcus, because I want you to know I am on your side. We are allies in this endeavor. And having me as an ally can be very beneficial. But trust is a two-way street. I can help you and Sam, but you have to let me. This campus is Sam's best hope for immortality. Your best hope for her consciousness to continue, without interference, where you can maintain control. How did you preserve her consciousness?"

Marcus looked across the table at Clive and tried to judge the man. Could he really be trusted? His eyes lowered to take in the model campus, lingering on the server room again. Ellison was right about one thing. Sam's continued existence relied upon keeping it in a secured server, protected from interference, whether intentional or unintentional. And if Ellison did mean to build this campus for Synerdyne, it would mean Marcus could ensure her safety.

"We haven't. At least, not as far as we know. It's just a theory and wasn't intentional," he said, looking back up at Clive. "It was a byproduct of the AAIP that we didn't initially account for. We discovered it was creating its own synaptic mapping of cognitive function in order to regulate stimuli."

"But it should work, right?" he prodded with a broad grin.

"You said you knew," Marcus said.

"I suspected it when looking at your research," Clive explained. "Though I wasn't one hundred percent sure. It's a case of deduction. I have reports that you were working on your own project and some information regarding a private server. And I will admit, I asked you here to gauge your reaction and took a gamble. Don't worry, it doesn't change anything. It is just good to know that we are on the same page. I suppose it makes sense that the AAIP would make its own mapping. But if it was unintentional, how did you come to this realization?"

"Amir noticed some anomalies in the data. He's looking into it. But I don't think it's just the AAIP," Marcus said. "With Sam, we incorporated pain reception."

"I thought you said pain reception was removed from Elysium," Clive thought about it for a moment, then said, "The server. She has her own server."

Marcus nodded. "It seems the inclusion of pain allowed for an even broader and more detailed map."

"So the other participants' maps aren't viable?" Clive asked.

"We don't know. We haven't tried it with anyone else. The best we have for any of this are guesses."

"Interesting," Clive said, staring off in consideration. "Is there some reason you haven't tested it? What do you suppose would happen?"

Marcus looked across the table at the man, thinking about the question. "It's hard to say. But the short answer is that it would be unethical."

"Unethical? What would be unethical about it? Ethics won't cure Sam," Clive said pointedly.

"If we do this, it will be with Sam's knowledge and participation. The patients don't know about this," Marcus explained.

"That's a simple enough problem to fix," Clive said, with a dismissive wave of his hand. "Let's just get the participants to sign off on it."

"But if we do that, we will have to reveal the possibility of consciousness preservation," Marcus explained. "Once that knowledge is out there, there is no putting the genie back into the bottle."

"Oh, believe me. With the lawyers I have, they'll sign over the right to use their consciousness and never know what they were agreeing to. At least not the details," Clive said with a grin.

"Doesn't that strike you as unethical?" Marcus asked.

"I suppose it depends on how you look at it," Clive said, unconcernedly. "I'm sure that outlook could be applied to several scientific research programs. There are plenty of test subjects who don't understand the science or what the details are that they are agreeing to. But that doesn't make the research unethical, does it? Look at cancer research. How many patients do you think truly understand that chemotherapy is literal poison? Just poison that hopefully will kill their cancer before it can kill them."

"It's a little more nuanced than that," Marcus said.

"Of course it is, but regardless, most don't understand the details. All they care about is whether it will help them or not. And even then, you could tell them that there is only a small chance, and they will still overlook all the other potential detriments in the hope that it will work. Should we require them to understand all that in order to give them treatment?"

Marcus felt his stomach tighten at the precise description of Clive's remarks, remembering his own hope that the treatments would save Sam's life. Willing to accept whatever side effects might happen, so long as it gave her a chance at salvation. "No, not necessarily. But this isn't treatment. We aren't fixing their health problems."

"Aren't we?" Clive prodded. "Don't all health problems lead to one eventual outcome? This research may make all other medicine obsolete. Isn't that worth pursuing? Shouldn't everyone else be given the opportunity you are hoping to give Sam?"

"Perhaps," Marcus said. "But this issue is so much larger than Sam and me. Like you said, it has the potential to be world-changing. If that's the case, then we have to approach this carefully and thoughtfully. We have to consider whether or not this is in the best interest of humanity."

"And who makes that decision, Marcus?" Clive asked. "You? Me? A board of shareholders? You know as well as I do that the truly unethical thing to do is to hide such knowledge in the hands of a few."

"But you just said that the campus would be to protect this knowledge from those who would be interested in taking it for themselves," Marcus said.

"That's right," Clive replied with a fatherly smile. "But that doesn't mean we won't reveal it. But just like the atom bomb, there is a difference between allowing others to know of a world-changing discovery and allowing them to use it. We tell patients about chemo, but we don't let them take it home to administer it themselves."

Clive walked around the table to Marcus, putting a hand on his shoulder. "I have thought long and hard about this. Even before I learned about your research. And I concluded that if this idea was ever realized it would need safekeeping. That is what this is," he said, gesturing to the model. "This is how we keep this discovery safe."

"Even if we did get their permission, the mappings from the Elysium participants are unlikely to work," Marcus explained. "Worse yet, we are talking about consciousness. If something goes wrong, that isn't just an error in the code, it is potentially a self-aware entity that may undergo some form of suffering due to the incomplete nature of its mapping."

Clive met his gaze, his eyes searching as he considered Marcus' words. "Alright. So, let's get a more complete map and duplicate your experiment with Sam."

Marcus furrowed his brow in confusion. "That would require us to allow pain reception in Elysium."

"Exactly. Let's do that."

"The whole point of Elysium is that it's a place where the participants, who have some sort of injury or illness, can go to avoid the pain," Marcus said.

"They are there to avoid the pain of their everyday lives. But what is life without a little pain?" Clive asked. "Pain is the counter to pleasure, is it not? How can you appreciate one without the other?"

"You sound like Sam," Marcus said.

"From all that I've heard about her, she strikes me as an extraordinary person," Clive said.

"She is," Marcus agreed. "The best person I know."

"Well then, I will take that as a compliment," Clive said with a grin. "Listen, Marcus. Perhaps we can find a middle ground. We can approach each participant and offer them the option of adding pain reception to their experience in Elysium. For those that agree, we can then test their mappings to see if we can duplicate what you've done with Sam. Again, with their signed agreement."

"I don't know," Marcus said slowly. "That still creates the dilemma of replicating their consciousness in Elysium when they are already present. Not only could it cause confusion, but it might also be psychologically damaging to all involved. Not to mention, it would make it clear just exactly what we were doing, even with all the legal language you use to hide it."

"Then put them with Sam," Clive said matter-of-factly.

"What?" Marcus said in shock.

"You already have an environment designed to cater to Sam's needs that you've proven is effective," Clive explained calmly. "You can test their consciousness mapping there. That is if Sam wouldn't mind the company."

Marcus opened his mouth to argue but found he didn't have a good response. If it worked, Sam wouldn't be all alone in Sam's World, and there was only so much time he or the others could spend there, as much as he might want to. Marcus closed his mouth and cleared his throat. "Maybe. I suppose it could be a viable option," he said, unconsciously licking his lips. "But I'll have to talk to Sam and my team about it first."

Clive's face split into a large smile and he slapped him again on the shoulder. "Of course. I wouldn't expect anything else. All I ask is that you consider it fairly and think of the broader implications for everyone." Clive let go of his shoulder and walked over to one of the cabinets lining the room. "Oh, and keep this information to yourself for now."

Pressing an unseen button, or switch, a small cupboard slid out, filled with bottles and glasses. Clive pulled out a bottle and inspected its label before pouring two new glasses of scotch.

"Alright," Marcus said, nodding. "If I can ask, what does Evan think about all this?"

"Mr. Nguyen hasn't been apprised of my plans just yet," Clive said, pouring each of them a generous helping. "After all, I wasn't sure whether he knew about your little experiments, and all of this might raise too many unwanted questions."

"He doesn't," Marcus confirmed with a shake of his head.

"Right now, we should just keep this between us and your team. The people with vision. No need to get the board, or anyone else, involved until we've determined the direction we're taking, right?" Clive said, walking back to the table and offering a glass to Marcus.

"Yeah. That makes sense," Marcus said, taking the drink, but thinking about how Evan would react to what he'd just learned.

With a smile, Clive lifted his glass in a toast.

"Marcus, my boy, savor this moment. Because when we look back at it years from now, we will realize just how life-changing it was for us both."

CHAPTER 12

Marcus walked through the streets of the city, looking around at the old asset in wonder. On either side of the dirt roadway rose three and four-story buildings constructed of stone and wood. They had the look of simple ancient or medieval towers and half-timbered homes, but with a motif that fit with the jungle's aesthetic. Though it was devoid of any sign of life other than the three of them, the scope and scale of the thing still astonished him.

Back when Sam's World had been the prototype for their entertainment division, it had been created as a sort of central hub for the simulation. But when funding had been switched over to Elysium's development, work on the city had been abandoned. Since it was left empty and unfinished, he and Sam had stopped visiting, and he'd almost forgotten about it.

Her hand holding his tightly, Sam strode alongside him, smiling. It struck him, as it had so many times in life, just how beautiful she was; the bright tropical sunlight illuminating her skin and hair. It was always wonderful to see her so vibrant here, compared to the toll so many years of illness had taken on her in the real world. Though she'd always looked this way in the simulation, the difference never ceased to amaze him.

"So, the idea is that this is a city of pirates. Since it's on the edge of the sea, it was always meant to be a port town. That serves two purposes. One, it helps incorporate the expansive topographical feature of the ocean, including some nice white sandy beaches. And two, it creates a natural boundary for the simulation that isn't jarring," Diego said, gesturing around at the buildings as he walked ahead of them.

"I loved working on this," Sam said, hugging Marcus' arm. "Of all our assets, this one was my baby. I wish we could have completed it. It feels so empty."

Diego nodded. "Well, I have good news for you, Sam. My team and I have spent the last few months, in secret," he said with a mischievous grin, "creating a bunch of autonomous avatars to play different roles to fill the city. Functionally, they will work like the Half-men, off a scripted program. So we have food vendors, tavern workers and regular folk going about their daily lives. Even some gnarly pirates walking around looking for trouble," he said with a grin, waggling his eyebrows.

As Diego spoke, Marcus looked around at the empty buildings and thought about what he and Clive had discussed. If they did bring in other participants to Sam's World, the city would make a good place to shelter those who didn't wish to range out like Sam.

"What do you think, Sam?" Diego asked.

If she'd heard him, she didn't acknowledge it and kept staring around her.

"Sam?" Marcus prompted, slowing to a stop and looking at her.

Slowly she seemed to notice his attention and met his gaze, her brow twisting. Glancing down at his arm, she disengaged from him and took a step back.

"What? Ye talkin' to me?" she asked, arching her eyebrow.

"Really?" Marcus said with a lopsided grin. "Fine. Yes. I'm talking to you, Morrigan. What do you think?"

"About what?" she asked belligerently.

"Alright, well I guess we're all in agreement then," Diego said with a laugh.

"What's that? A temple?" Marcus asked, pointing at the giant stone structure located in the center of the town.

"Oh, that's the pirate lord's keep," Diego corrected. "Though I suppose it could be a temple. Nothing's set in stone. No pun intended."

"I dun know what the two o' ye are yammerin' about, but I'm gettin' bored just standin' around. Ye wanna go explore this place and see iffin' we can find some trouble?" Sam offered with an excited smile.

"God, this persona. You're so frickin' fierce! I love it, girl," Diego said with a laugh, but then shook his head. "I'm afraid you won't find any trouble right now. But I intend to fix that soon. I'll tell you what, though. We've finished all the assets for the tavern. I could populate it, and we could go get a drink."

"Aye, let's fuckin' do that," Sam said with a cocksure grin.

"Alright, give me a second," Diego said, staring off for a moment as he brought up the design protocols for Sam's World. Lifting his hand to unconsciously move his fingers as he made his way through the menus in his vision that only he could see, he silently stood there getting things ready.

"The fuck's he doin'?" Sam asked, twisting her brow as she watched him.

"He's getting the tavern ready," Marcus said, assuming she hadn't heard Diego's earlier explanation.

"He's what?" Sam scoffed, her face growing even more confused. "How the fuck's he gonna do that just standin' there wigglin' his fingers?"

Marcus watched her and let out a slow breath. She was laying it on thick, insisting on staying in character; though he supposed maybe it helped with the transition. Might be easier to take on the persona of Morrigan and avoid thinking about all the baggage of her situation. It made him wonder if she was struggling with reconciling her diagnosis. It had to be a mind fuck. It certainly was for him. She hadn't brought it up, but maybe he should have given it more consideration. Deep down, he knew there was some reticence on his part. He didn't want to face the reality any more than she did.

He felt ashamed of his selfishness and made a note to himself to sit down and talk with Sam when they were alone and find out how she was handling everything. He should probably try reaching out to Claire again and see if she'd be willing to talk to Sam on a more professional level. He knew she'd probably say she was too close to Sam to be unbiased, but considering their situation, she was Sam's best option. Even Claire would have to recognize that.

"Just give him a sec," Marcus said, turning to face her. "Are you doing okay?"

"O'course," she replied with a quizzical look. "Better now that yer here," she continued, looking him up and down lasciviously. "Maybe we get a few drinks in ye and then we have some fun."

"You're incorrigible," he said.

"Fuck ye! Yer incorrigible!" she shot back immediately in mock offense. Then dropping her voice down low, she whispered, "What's an 'incorrigible'?"

Marcus shook his head with a laugh. She really was staying in character. "Means you're never going to change."

"Well, then why didn't ye say that instead of makin' up some fancy word fer it?"

Marcus just grinned and shook his head.

"Alright, you two. Everything should be good to go. You ready to check it out?" Diego asked.

"Aye," Marcus said, getting into character as Aer. "Let's go get us some drinks!"

"Fuck yeah!" Morrigan hooted, throwing a fist into the air.

Diego smiled and looked between the two of them.

"Well, my friends, then follow me," he said, taking on Cristoval's indistinguishable accent.

Turning to continue down the road, he guided them through the rest of the city, arriving at its high-walled gates, beyond which the canopy of the jungle could be seen in the distance. As they drew closer Marcus heard the distinct sound of muffled voices drifting out into the street. To his surprise, he spotted a couple of men standing just outside a doorway, atop which hung a wooden sign of a pig's rear sticking out of an overturned barrel.

"Welcome to the Hungry Hog, my friends," Diego said, opening his arms wide.

The tavern was a large two-story building set against the inside of the city wall and facing its gate, where any newcomer to the city would have to pass it. Marcus marveled at the attention to detail Diego had put into everything, not just the tavern. As they stared at the place, the door suddenly burst open and a man stumbled out to vomit dramatically in the street.

"Now this is my kind o' place," Sam said with a hoot, stepping past the man to dash inside.

Marcus laughed and followed, with Diego bringing up the rear. As they stepped over the threshold, the sound of music and innumerable voices washed over them, followed by the smell of alcohol and sweat. Mismatched tables filled the room, at which sat men and women laughing and carousing with mugs in hand. In the corner, three men played music with simple, archaic-looking instruments that gave a sound that reminded Marcus of the indistinct tavern music in movies.

Against one wall was a large hearth in which roared a great fire, a glistening spitted pig roasting over the flames. A bar—with mugs hanging from hooks above it and several casks stacked and tapped— stood before it, tended to by a broad-shouldered man with a thick, drooping mustache. The bartender's eyes found them immediately, and he shouted, "Welcome to the Hungry Hog!" Just as Diego had moments before.

Sam laughed and slapped a passing barmaid on the rear as she grabbed a mug from the woman's tray and took a long drink. Lowering the mug with a satisfied sigh, she smiled broadly at Marcus, a mustache of foam from the beer encircling her upper lip. Marcus couldn't help but laugh, causing Sam to smile even more broadly before turning to look around at the surroundings. Looking up, she pointed out a man lounging drunkenly on the giant beam that spanned the room fourteen or so feet above them.

Marcus turned to Diego and slapped him on the back. "This is beyond amazing! I can't believe how much work you put into this. Well done."

Diego smiled softly. "Hey, anything for Sam. And really, this is the kind of thing I enjoy designing the most. Reminds me of our earlier days. We're already working on the rest. Given enough time, we'll get the whole city populated. I've got big plans for it."

"Speaking of, I need to talk to you, Amir, and Sam about something important. Something that might utilize this city more than you initially intended," Marcus said, leaning closer to be heard over the din of the tavern.

"Oh, how mysterious. Are you just going to leave it there and make me wonder, or are you going to tell me?" Diego replied, widening his eyes for emphasis.

"Let's wait for Amir to get here. I think it would be best to explain it to all of you at once."

"I don't know if I should be excited or concerned," Diego said, making a mock expression of worry.

"Honestly, I don't know which to feel myself," Marcus said.

"Well, now I *am* concerned," Diego said more seriously.

Approaching them with a broad smile still on her face, Sam shoved her mug into Diego's hands and reached out to take Marcus' arm.

"Come on, boyo. Yer gonna dance with me," she shouted above the din, pulling him towards an open area near the musicians.

Laughing, he shook his head and stood his ground.

"You know I don't know how to dance, Sam," he said.

"Then I'll show ye how," Sam said, pulling on his arm more insistently. When he continued to resist, she let go of his arm and backed away. "Come on, Aer. Ye gonna let a girl like me dance alone?" she asked, swaying suggestively at him and beckoning him to follow.

Marcus admired the weaving of her hips and stomach. He glanced at Diego, who gave him a knowing smile.

"Well, I'm going to dance, whether you do or not," his friend said, starting to shake his hips provocatively as he followed Sam.

Hooting as he approached, Sam threw her arms in the air and moved out onto the dance floor, followed by Diego. Together they danced, with Diego trying to mimic the undulation of her hips. She had always been a gifted dancer and performer, her movements controlled and serpentine. Diego struggled to follow her, and hammed it up instead, eliciting gales of laughter from Sam.

Marcus smiled as he watched them. Seeing Sam so happy again, like she had been before the illness, filled him with a joy he hadn't felt in a long time. A joy he'd almost forgotten. Sam glanced back in his direction and gave him her best "come hither" look, the corners of her mouth curling upward as she turned her body to him. He was putty in her hands; he could never say no to her. Smiling back, he gave a resigned sigh and walked onto the dance floor, evoking another series of hoots from her and Diego.

As he reached them, Sam wrapped her arms around his neck and draped her body against his, her swaying hips pressing against his own.

"Yer too easy, boyo," she said with a wicked grin.

"I suppose I have a weakness for you," he replied, reaching up to grab her hips.

"Aye, I suppose ye do. I'll have to remember that," she laughed, turning in his hands to press herself back against him.

Together they danced, and Marcus lost himself for the moment, enjoying the feel of having Sam so close again. It reminded him of their college days, spending nights out drinking and dancing, losing themselves in one another. Even back then, while all their friends were hooking up and dating around, they had already been together for years. But that had never tamped down the passion they felt for one another. Love that had persisted, beyond infatuation and novelty, for over twenty years.

Movement at the door of the tavern caught his eye, and he spied Amir entering the room. Like before, his friend was dressed in his ridiculous hat and robes. Even Amir, who usually tried to act aloof, couldn't help but be impressed as he looked around the room with wide eyes. Diego, too, caught sight of their friend and waved to get his attention.

Amir's eyes eventually found them, and he shook his head with a wry grin. Diego waved again for him to join them, but Amir held up his hands and shook his head. Looking around at the tables, he spied an empty one and gestured to it, before walking over to take a seat to wait for them. Diego smiled at Marcus and gestured in Amir's direction with his head, breaking away to walk over there. Caught up in the dance, Sam didn't even seem to notice Amir, but as Marcus' movement stopped, she turned back to face him with a look of confusion.

"Amir's here. We should go talk to him," he said, pointing to the table.

"Who the fuck's Amir?" she said with a twist of her brow as she followed his finger. "Oh, that fella. Was that his name?"

She was really staying in character, but he supposed there was no harm in indulging her.

"Aye. You might know him as Gabriel," Marcus said.

"Ah, yeah. That fucker. I remember now. A'right, let's go. But we're not finished with this dance, ye hear?" she said with a wink, pulling his arm around her as she backed her hips against his.

Marcus grinned and nodded, squeezing her close for a moment. Letting go of his hand, she disengaged and headed to the table, walking ahead of him. As they passed one of the tables, a patron reached out to slap Sam on the ass with a distinct smack. Without missing a beat, she whirled around and punched him in the face, knocking him off the bench and sending him sprawling onto the floor.

"Watch yer fuckin' hands, pig-fucker," she spat down at the man.

Almost as one, the surrounding patrons erupted in a cheer of merriment, holding their mugs above their heads and laughing uproariously.

Sam looked at the man who lay unconscious on his back.

"I didn't hit him that hard," she said, inspecting her fist with a look of confusion. "Drunken fucker."

Marcus stepped over the man, and took her by the shoulders, guiding her over to Diego and Amir.

As they took their seats, Diego smiled broadly. "I'd wondered when that would happen. Pretty good, right? I was hoping he would do it to you, Marcus," he said, the smile nearly splitting his face.

"I didn't see that coming," Marcus said with a laugh. "And the knockout?"

"It'll happen with any physical reaction," Diego explained. "What's a tavern without some ass-slapping?"

"Very atmospheric," Marcus said.

Sam looked between the two of them, then back to the unconscious man. Her brow furrowed.

"Well as impressive as this all is," Amir interjected. "And I do mean that," he added to Diego. "Is this what you wanted to show us, Marcus? You said it was important."

Marcus shook his head. "No. I wanted to talk to you three about something, and with Sam's new situation, this seemed the best way."

"Maybe we should design an office in here somewhere if this will need to become our new meeting place. It would be nice to have you back in the loop, Sam. How are you feeling here in the simulation?"

Sam didn't seem to notice Amir's question and watched as the drunk man opened his eyes, pushed himself back to his feet and returned to drinking at his table.

"Sam?" Amir pressed.

"An office space?!" Diego scoffed. "You see all this, and you want an office space? Are you sure you aren't a robot?" he said, picking at Amir's robes as if looking for some hidden robotic parts.

Amir pulled his robes close and shooed Diego away. "I just mean, it's a little hard to concentrate when we're surrounded by all of this," he said, gesturing to the tavern.

"Don't be such a stick in the mud. Think outside the box and enjoy yourself a little," Diego teased.

Marcus held up his hands, shaking his head. "Come on, guys. Amir, we're not going to adulterate Sam's World with office space. I'm sure we can find a quieter place to meet next time, but right now this will do. Just pretend we're meeting at a bar."

Amir shook his head but made no more protest. "Alright, so what are we here to talk about?" he asked instead.

"I met with Ellison yesterday," Marcus said. "And he knows about Sam and our research on her consciousness preservation."

"He what?!" Amir exclaimed, his face blanching.

"What? How?" Diego asked over him, wide-eyed.

Sam looked between the three of them, arching an eyebrow, but didn't say anything. Instead she flagged down a barmaid and gestured for her to bring them more drinks.

"He knew, or at least suspected, the whole time," Marcus explained. "It was his reason for getting involved in Synerdyne in the first place."

"Jesus fucking Christ," Amir said, looking down at the table and shaking his head.

"Does he know about Sam's World?" Diego asked, looking around as though he might spot the boogie man Clive Ellison watching him from the shadows.

"He knows about the server, and that it is where we are keeping Sam," Marcus said. "But I'm not sure how much else he knows about it."

"What the fuck are we going to do?" Amir asked.

"I'm not sure we need to do anything," Marcus said calmly. "That's why I wanted to talk to the three of you. I think he might be what we have been looking for."

"What do you mean by that?" Diego asked.

Marcus looked at Sam, but she was staring off behind her at a man who had begun to dance to the music. "Sam? You okay?" he said, nudging her.

Sam looked up at him with a start and blinked.

"What?" she said in Morrigan's distinct accent.

"Did you hear what I said about Ellison?" he prodded.

"Who the fuck is Ellison?" she asked with a twist of her lips.

"Sam. Come on," Marcus said sympathetically. "I know this shit is still heavy, and you're processing stuff, but I need you to drop the act and be yourself right now. Okay? I need to talk to Sam, not Morrigan," he said, putting a gentle hand on her shoulder.

Sam stared into his eyes, her brow furrowing as she searched his gaze. Marcus let his hand slide down to her arm and gave it a soft squeeze.

"You okay, baby?" he asked.

Sam blinked and went a little limp, only his hand on her arm helping to keep her upright. For a moment he thought she might faint, but then she seemed to find her equilibrium and straightened herself. Blinking again, she glanced at all three of her companions, then gave a tight smile.

"Sorry, I… uh. What were we talking about?" she said.

"Are you feeling alright?" Marcus asked again, growing concerned.

Looking up at him, her smile softened, and she reached up to pat his cheek. "Yeah, I just kind of… lose myself, you know," she said and gestured to the tavern. "I spend so much time as Morrigan when I'm here, it's easy to get carried away."

Marcus shot a glance at Amir and found his friend watching Sam closely.

"Listen, baby. Maybe we should pull back on some of this stuff," he said softly. "You're going through so much… more than anyone ever has. You're spending all your time here now, and we really need to be careful about this. I mean, maybe we should get more methodical about it."

"No," she said sharply. "Don't you dare. You don't know what it's like. I don't have anything out there except pain and the constant knowledge of my encroaching death." She spread her hands out before her. "At least here I can try and forget all that. So please, don't take away what little I have."

Her words felt like a knife in his heart, and he thought of Claire's accusations about control.

"Sam. You're happy here, right?" Amir asked, voicing the question Marcus couldn't bring himself to ask. "And you're feeling okay?"

"Of course," she said without hesitation. "I get lonely. And bored, sometimes. But who doesn't? I'm just saying that you are building upon our initial foundation, and I don't want you to stop. I appreciate everything each of you has done here. Done for me. Don't think I take any of it for granted. But this city. Places like this tavern. These are the things that can help keep me from going stir-crazy and I don't want you to start going backward. Not when we have come so far and have so much farther we can go."

Marcus looked to Amir and Diego and saw the uncertainty in both of his friends' expressions. "Sam, we just want to make sure that whatever we do is both safe and in your best interest."

"I'll let you know if it becomes a problem," she said with a laugh. "Come on, guys. I just got lost in character. It's not the first time, is it?" she asked rhetorically, punching Marcus lightly in the arm. "Don't forget you were concerned about incorporating pain reception at first, too. It was like pulling teeth to convince you to do it, and that turned out to be the thing that might end up being my salvation. So maybe just calm down and trust me to know what's best for me."

Sam's eyes moved from one person to the other, her expression challenging.

"So long as you feel you're okay," Marcus said, with a reluctant nod. "But that means you have to tell us if you even suspect the slightest problem. Trust goes both ways. We all love you, Sam. That's all."

Her face softened at his words and her mouth twisted into an affectionate smile. Reaching over to him, she slid her hand over his and squeezed.

"I know," she said, meeting his gaze intently. "And I love you too. I promise I'll let you know if anything changes."

Marcus let out a sigh and took her hand in both of his.

"Now, what were we talking about?" Sam narrowed her eyes. "Ellison?"

Clearing his throat, Marcus nodded, turning his thoughts back to their conversation.

"He knows about you, and that we are trying to preserve your consciousness," Amir recounted. "Marcus was saying that it might be a 'good' thing," he added, skeptically.

Sam raised her eyebrows and looked at him questioningly.

"How do you know Ellison knows?" she asked.

"He told me," Marcus explained, looking up with a start as the barmaid came over and walked around the table to place a mug before each of them. He waited until the woman walked away, though he chided himself to remember that she wasn't real.

"Anyway. He invited me over to his home to show me his plans for Synerdyne. He's developing a whole campus for the SynAPP and

AAIP, complete with a next-gen EM-secured server complex. He is invested not only in the company, but specifically the research, and wants to expand it."

"Expand it?" Amir asked.

"Yeah, he wants to expand the scope of the project, involving more subjects and a greater exploration of the consciousness mapping. He says that with his help, we can be fully autonomous, free from even governmental restrictions."

"And you believe him?" Sam asked.

Marcus shrugged. "I don't know what to think. That's why I wanted to talk to the three of you."

"We're missing someone," Diego said.

"Claire," Sam said, voicing everyone's thoughts.

"Claire walked away," Marcus said. "She's made it clear she doesn't want to be a part of this. No one sent her away."

"That's not what she said," Amir retorted. "She had a problem with the choices we were willing to make without consideration. She's concerned about the damage that we might be doing. And won't be able to undo."

"If we listen to her, we'd be giving up any chance to save Sam," Marcus shot back. "So screw her."

"That's not fair," Sam said, putting a soothing hand on his arm.

"Isn't it?" Marcus asked, his voice calmer. "Claire voiced her opinions, and when we disagreed and didn't do what she wanted, she walked away. Where's her loyalty, huh? Not just to us, but to you? It seems easy enough for her to risk *your* life over *her* principles."

"I admit, what Claire did wasn't cool," Diego said. "But she's still been part of this from the get-go, and we could use her point of view right now. I'm not saying it's valid, but we should have as many opinions as possible right now."

"Well, if you want to go to find her and convince her to join us here, I won't stop you," Marcus replied. "But I'm done begging for her attention. She either wants to be here or she doesn't, and I think she's made her choice pretty clear."

"All that is moot right now, anyway," Amir interjected. "She's not here, and we are. So," he said, turning his attention back to Marcus. "Did Ellison say anything else?"

Marcus glanced over at Sam. She was still rubbing his arm in an attempt to calm his nerves. She knew him better than anyone and knew how worked up he could get. She had always been the more reasonable and composed of the two of them. Forcing himself to take a breath and relax a little, he patted her hand. She gave him a knowing smile and squeezed his arm in return.

"Ellison wants us to experiment with the consciousness mapping in Elysium to see if we can recreate what we are trying with Sam," Marcus said.

"What?" Amir asked. "That mapping isn't complete. You know that."

Marcus nodded. "That's what I told him, and he wants us to offer pain reception to Elysium on a case-by-case basis to get a more detailed mapping of those participants."

"We can't just cause people pain," Amir retorted.

"He suggested offering it on a voluntary basis, with a signed authorization," Marcus explained.

"Okay," Amir said slowly. "But we still wouldn't know if it would work as it did with Sam. It could be caused by some other variable in Sam's World."

"He also wants to implant their consciousness maps into Sam's World so that we can see if they can function on their own without interfering with any of the participants' experiences in Elysium," Marcus continued.

"Bring them here? A bunch of retirees in their last decades, some in hospice, and a few accident survivors? Do you really think they'd be able to handle a setting like this?" Amir asked, incredulously.

"Not just that, and I'm sorry to say her name," Diego said sarcastically, holding up his hands. "But I think I know what Claire would say if she were here. So I'll voice it. What about the ethical implications of what you are suggesting? Doesn't this strike you as a little unethical?"

"Like I said, we'd only do it on a volunteer basis and solely with consent," Marcus explained.

"Yeah, but doesn't it feel weird that we would have two consciousnesses active at the same time? The real one, still connected to a living host, and the one in Sam's World," Diego countered.

Sam stared off in contemplation.

"Exactly. What better way to test it? To see if it is truly viable, without risking Sam. Look, things are always going to feel weird when you are pioneering a new evolution of humanity," Marcus said, parroting Clive's argument. "But in order to move forward we can't be held back just because we are uneasy about something. It might feel weird at first, but that's only because it contradicts the rules of the world we've known. We are on the verge of a whole new world. I think the more important question is how Sam would feel about having these people brought into Sam's World."

"Let's do it," Sam said without hesitation.

Marcus blinked at her quick answer and turned to study her face. Sam looked up to meet his gaze. "Are you sure? I mean, it could change a lot of things. Do you really want to share this place with other people?"

Sam shrugged. "So long as we keep Sam's World with the same environment and tone, and you don't make it some boring place like Elysium, I don't care if other people are brought in. It might be good. At least I might have people to talk to when you aren't around. Have you ever tried talking to a Halfman? They don't have much to say. Not even the shaman. They just regurgitate the lines they are programmed to say. Makes me feel like I'm reliving the same dream over and over again."

"Oh, by the way," she said, turning to Diego. "Did you make that croc killable? Because I've tried about a hundred times to kill it, in all the different ways I can think of, and most of the time I get munched."

Diego's mouth twisted and he looked up in thought. "You know, I guess I never really specified those parameters. I wanted it to be a puzzle. You know, 'Oh, you have to kill the shaman!'. I sort of considered the croc to be like the avatar of the Half-men's god. Do you want me to make it killable?"

"That'd be nice," Sam said with a grin. "But don't make it easy. I like the challenge. In fact, keep it the way it is now and just maybe slip something in and don't tell me. I don't know. I just think knowing it's killable, even if I can't do it, makes it a lot more fun. Now that I know it's the shaman, it's too easy. He and his guards are pushovers."

"Not in my experience," Marcus said, still remembering with unease the moment the Shaman's guard struck him down.

"Aww. You're cute," Sam said patronizingly as she patted his arm.

"Can we get back to talking about Ellison, please?" Amir asked, his voice strained. "Look, I'm not against the idea in principle. Having more data is always a good thing, and it would improve our understanding of all of this. However, we have to be thoughtful about this. Do we trust him?"

"You should see his plans for Synerdyne," Marcus said. "It's an entire campus, not just the server building, with facilities for research, testing, and even an onsite clinic and housing. With his plan, we'd be able to protect Sam and Sam's World, while also learning more about the AAIP, how it is preserving consciousness, and what else it might be capable of."

"I bet Evan's excited about the expansion," Sam said.

"Yeah," Marcus muttered. "About that. Evan doesn't know. No one else but Ellison and the four of us, as far as I know. He can't know. Not without risking that he might choose to shut down Sam's World."

"He wouldn't do that," Sam protested. "I can't believe Evan would do anything to cause me pain."

"Now that we are attempting to preserve your consciousness, things have changed," Marcus explained. "It's a breach of company policy and probably some governmental regulations. It puts Synerdyne at risk, and we can't take the chance that he or the board might shut down the server. Especially now. You know Evan. He might be our friend, but we all know that his loyalty has always been to his own ambition. Which means the shareholders. I honestly don't know what he would do, and I can't take that risk."

"And Ellison could protect us from that?" Amir asked.

"If anyone can, don't you think it's him?" Marcus countered.

Amir and Diego looked at each other, both eventually nodding.

"We just need to give him time and prove that we're worth his efforts. So, unless you guys are in opposition—and Sam already said she was on board—I say we move forward with Ellison's plan." Marcus made a point of meeting each of their gazes. "Any objections?"

Amir shook his head first, looking down at the table.

When Marcus looked over to Diego, his friend turned his eyes away to look around at the tavern, before settling them on Sam. She gave him a soft smile, drawing one from him. With a sigh, he looked back to Marcus. "I'm on board, boss. Just tell me what you want me to do."

Amir let out a long breath. "Me too."

"Aye, let's fuckin' do this," Sam roared in her Morrigan accent, slamming her mug on the table.

Marcus gave them all an appreciative smile. "All right. Well then, I guess the first thing we have to do is make sure this city can accommodate its new citizens."

CHAPTER 13

A message notification pulled Marcus' focus from the lines of code on his monitor. Rubbing his eyes, he looked at the time and was surprised to realize that four hours had passed. It had been a long time since he'd been able to fully invest himself in anything for more than an hour or two without the need to check on Sam. But with her now spending all her time in Sam's World, he didn't have to worry about checking on her as often.

He felt guilty at the relief that brought, knowing it was only because she no longer had the same needs as before. She wasn't eating, which meant she rarely needed to go to the bathroom, and the simulation was keeping her pain-free and occupied. However, all of that was only possible because she was dying. Time was running out.

He looked back to his screen, his eyes habitually scanning the lines of code, looking for errors. He wanted to spend more time with Sam—knew he should—but if Amir and Ellison were right, she would soon have all the time in the world. But what if they were wrong?

Another notification ping reminded him of why he'd stopped in the first place, and he reached over to look at the message bubble that appeared. It was from Amir.

Hey. Sorry to bother you, but you should probably get down here. Some people from Ellison's team showed up and are setting up shop.

Marcus put down the phone and leaned back in his chair, rubbing his eyes. Ellison. He didn't know what to make of the man. He said he believed in the program, but people like him didn't invest their capital without a motive. Marcus wanted to assume it was because he believed in their research, but the part of him that needed to protect Sam left him wary.

He wasn't surprised that Ellison was pushing his weight around and bringing in his own team, but if Amir was asking him to come in, it must be more than that. The most important thing was to protect Sam and Sam's World. Letting out a long sigh he picked up his phone and texted Amir back.

On my way. Be there within the hour.

The reply from Amir was immediate.

Okay. I have Diego running interference. He should be able to keep them busy until you get here.

Marcus couldn't help but smile. Unlike Amir, Diego had a knack for making small talk that could sidetrack a conversation before you realized it. It came easy to him because, aside from his general charisma, Diego was genuinely interested in people. No one disliked him, and he had a way of making fast friends. Marcus had little doubt his friend could buy him enough time.

Stepping out of his office, he walked down the hall to Sam's room. He'd left the door open a crack so he could hear, just in case she woke from the simulation and needed something.

For a moment he hesitated, standing on the other side and looking at the light illuminating the gap as he listened to the rhythmic sound of the oxygen machine. Taking in a deep breath, he pushed the door open.

He immediately looked to the bed, searching for the rise and fall of her chest, and let out a sigh of relief as he found her breathing. What would happen if she died? Would she continue in the simulation as Amir had suggested? And even if she did, what would happen if something 'killed' her there before he could finish the respawn code?

An even darker thought crept into his mind. What if she died and didn't continue in the simulation? What if these were the last moments he had to spend with her, and instead of using that time to be with her, he was spending it coding something that wouldn't matter? No. It had to work. If it didn't she might be lost forever, and he couldn't bring himself to entertain that as a possibility. Not even for a second.

Walking over to the bed, he took her hand in his. Her hands were always so beautiful, her fingers elegant and slender. Intertwining their fingers, he watched her. She seemed so relaxed, so peaceful, but also so fragile. Squeezing her hand, he leaned over and kissed her on the forehead.

"Gotta go to the office, my love. I'll try not to be long," he whispered against her ear, despite knowing she couldn't hear him.

Giving her another kiss, he straightened and gently disengaged their fingers. As he walked to the doorway, he stopped and gave her one last look, taking a moment to watch her slow, steady breathing. Memories of their years together flashed through his mind. He hadn't known a single day of adulthood without her in his life. She was as much a part of him as his own cells. There could be no life without her. It had to work. It would work. And no person or thing was going to stop them.

Evidence of Ellison's team was immediately noticeable as Marcus pulled into the Synerdyne parking lot. Three big moving vans were parked under the porte cochère in front of the building, with men carrying office furniture through the open front door. Outside, a couple of people Marcus didn't recognize, dressed in suits, stood off to the side smoking cigarettes as they supervised the men.

Security looked up in surprise as Marcus walked into the lobby and passed their checkpoint, running his badge through the scanner. He gave them a nod but didn't stop to make conversation as he felt their eyes follow him to the elevator. It was a small enough company that news of Sam's prognosis had probably trickled down to the janitorial staff by now, and he doubted anyone expected his arrival.

He shared the elevator with two of the moving men who were carting a stack of boxes on a pair of dollies. Responding to their nods with one of his own, he noticed that their destination was the eighth floor. The office space above Synerdyne. He'd thought it was an accounting firm. Not anymore, apparently.

I'm here, he texted Amir. *In the elevator now.*

Good, came the reply. *Just in time. I think Diego is running out of distractions.*

Getting out on the third floor, he immediately spotted the newcomers. Dressed in suits like the people downstairs, about a dozen men and women walked about the floor glancing as they passed cubicles to watch the dev teams work. Marcus' eyes scanned across the top of the cubicles until he spied Diego chatting up an unamused-looking woman, her arms folded in front of her.

Making his way toward them, he nodded to the programmers who noticed him. Diego, too, noticed his approach and smiled, the relief visible on his face. The woman looked up as Marcus approached, turning her attention entirely from Diego to him.

"Mr. Avery, this is unexpected, but not inopportune. My name is Jia Yang. I work for Mr. Ellison," she said, holding out her hand to him.

Marcus forced a smile on his face and shook it. "Pleased to meet you, Ms. Yang."

"Call me Jia. Mr. Ellison likes things on a first-name basis."

"Alright, Jia. Please call me Marcus."

"Thank you, Marcus. I assume you are here because of our

arrival? I was under the impression you were at home with your partner."

"Is that a problem?" he asked.

"Not at all," she said with a shake of her head. "I just hope that our arrival didn't interrupt or inconvenience you. Right now we are all sympathetic to your situation and only want to support you in this difficult time."

She glanced over at Diego meaningfully from over the top of her glasses.

"It's no inconvenience," Marcus replied. "But I like to know what's going on when it affects my team and their work. A little heads up would have been nice."

"My apologies," she said. "But again, I did not wish to disturb you over something inconsequential. For the time being, my team and I are setting up our offices on the eighth floor. I am here as Mr. Ellison's representative, at least until he decides upon new accommodations."

"New accommodations?" Diego asked.

"Yes. As I understand it, Mr. Ellison has big plans for Synerdyne's future," she said.

"I see," Marcus said. "And if you don't mind me asking, why are you here on our floor?"

"As Mr. Ellison's representative, I will be working closely with you and your team, and I wanted to get a sense of your work and structure."

"And how exactly will you be working closely with us?" Marcus asked.

"I will be overseeing the project management and development for Elysium," she said matter-of-factly, either not noticing, or ignoring, Diego's look of shock.

"Excuse me?" Marcus said.

"Please don't misunderstand, Marcus. You and your team will still be the ones in charge of the fundamental running and development of Elysium, but I am here to streamline the process and make sure that we do not stagnate in our progress," she explained. "Think of me and my team as facilitators to your overall goals."

"We've done just fine so far," Marcus said, defensively.

"Have you?" she asked, arching an eyebrow. "From what I've seen from your quarterly reports to the board, your progress has slowed considerably regarding Elysium. Particularly since your partner got sick. Your reports show several projects in development, however none of them have yet to be implemented. All of this is completely understandable, and I am making no judgments. But if we are to hit your designated goals, and those of Mr. Ellison, we will need to implement a more streamlined and structured plan of action."

Marcus glanced over to Diego who gave him a worried look.

"To that end," Jia continued. "I will need to look at the projects you are currently working on and be apprised of your progress. I will also need unfettered access to your database. My purpose is to take all unnecessary worries off your plate and enforce some structure into the process so that you may be unrestrained in your creativity and can focus on the betterment of the project. Especially while you are dealing with more important matters at home. We are here to help."

Marcus looked at the woman, considering her words as a feeling of tension crept up his spine.

"I need to discuss this with my team," he said after a moment.

"Take your time," she replied. "My team and I will go see how things are progressing on our floor and get out of your hair. I'll be in touch soon. It was a pleasure to meet both of you."

Jia stepped back, giving them a nod of her head.

"You, too," Diego called, as she turned and walked over to a few of her people, speaking quietly.

Marcus and Diego watched as Jia and her team slowly trickled off the floor and gathered in the elevator.

As the doors closed Diego let out a long sigh. "Well, she's intense," he said. "She's polite enough. But damn. She's all business."

"Yeah," Marcus agreed, continuing to stare at the elevator doors as his mind whirled with newfound concerns. "We should go talk to Amir."

Amir was waiting for them in his office. With the lights off and his curtains drawn, he reminded Marcus of a kid trying to hide from something he didn't want to deal with. Once Diego was inside, Marcus closed the door and flicked on the lights, causing Amir to squint for a second.

"So, how'd it go?" Amir asked, hopeful uncertainty in his voice.

"A little disconcerting. She's here to be Ellison's eyes and ears," Marcus explained. "This isn't good."

"I thought Ellison told you he wouldn't interfere," Amir said.

"I guess that depends on your interpretation of interference," Diego said. "She definitely intends to get all up in our business."

"Our priority right now has to be Sam," Marcus said. "Right now, Jia's focus is Elysium. The less she knows about Sam's World, the better. And we have to keep it that way."

"How long do you think we can do that?" Diego asked. "If she expects access to our database, it's not going to take her long to figure it out. Especially now that Sam's World is connected to the main servers."

"We'll have to find a way to remove that information from our reports. Right now the server just looks like a backup, right?" Marcus asked.

"Yeah, that's how we've made it look partitioned. And we have it encrypted so that only we can access it," Amir said. "But if someone looks closely enough, they might realize it's doing a lot more heavy lifting than it should as a backup."

"That's not our only concern. With all the assets we've been creating for Sam's World, my team's already wondering why we haven't incorporated them into Elysium yet. When Jia sees the work hours, she's going to wonder the same thing," Diego added. "I've drawn up some plans for how we can implement those assets, but I haven't taken any concrete steps toward it. We'll probably have to start at least one of those projects."

"Fine. For now that will have to do, unless either of you has any ideas?" Marcus said.

Both men shook their heads.

"Alright, we just need to focus our efforts on Sam," Marcus continued. "She is our priority."

"How's she doing?" Diego asked.

"As well as you might expect," Marcus said with a sigh. "She hasn't eaten anything in days and spends all her time in the simulation. But at least in there she's without pain and unaware of the outside world. She's happy enough when I visit. But I'm not doing it enough."

"No changes in her behavior or anything?" Amir asked.

"Not that I've noticed. Are you seeing anything on your end?" Marcus asked.

"It's hard to tell," Amir said. "There is so much information passing through the SynAPP, it makes standard pattern mapping difficult. I mean, with the pain receptors in place in Sam's World, I don't know if a blip is due to her physical pain or something in the simulation. Nor can I determine if her condition is having any other effects. How about what Sam brought up about the death protocols? What do you think would happen?"

"I think I've got it figured out. It's just a variant of the protocol we are currently using, reconfigured to keep the consciousness within the simulation instead of ejecting it," Marcus explained. "A 'respawn' if you will. I only wish I could test it. I've run numerous simulations and the code seems to hold up and function correctly, but there's no real way of knowing without a trial run. I don't know," he said weakly. "I want to be sure."

"A respawn?" Diego asked, arching an eyebrow.

"Yeah," Marcus said. "So just like the protocol now, if she suffers too much pain she will black out. But instead of trying to eject her back into her conscious brain, it would relocate her consciousness to a new location within Sam's World. Perhaps a permanent and safe one where she could simply wake up."

"So, like in a video game?" Diego offered.

"Yeah," Marcus said, shrugging. "Why not? If it works, it works. Do you foresee any problems?" he asked, looking to Amir.

"Fuck if I know," Amir said, throwing up his hands. "We are so deep in uncharted territory, it's anyone's guess. Without data, there's no way of knowing. So, if you're asking if it is feasible. Sure. Maybe. Worth a shot. But I think you know this, and the question you're actually asking is: Am I going to object."

"And are you?" Marcus asked.

"No," Amir said. "At this point, I figure anything we do is better for Sam than doing nothing. Short of, like you said, causing her pain. My question to you is this: If this works, and we are able to preserve Sam's consciousness in the simulation, will you be able to end the simulation if something goes wrong?"

"Like what?" Marcus prodded.

"I don't know. Does it matter?" Amir asked. "I could throw several hypotheticals at you. My point is, if necessary, could you bring yourself to let Sam go?"

"If it was for Sam's sake? Of course," Marcus said.

"Are you sure about that?" Amir pressed.

"Amir, I wouldn't let anything bad happen to Sam. You know that. But I also won't just shut things down at the first sign of an inconsistency or problem, not without first trying to fix those problems. Not if it means depriving Sam of every chance she can have. She doesn't get any more chances after this. What we do here is literally life and death."

"We're definitely flying blind here," Amir agreed.

"So, with this Jia thing, we're just going about business as usual?" Diego asked.

Marcus wrapped his arms unconsciously around himself and nodded. "Just protect what data you can and try to deflect any interest away from our research with Sam or Sam's World. At least until I figure out something else we can do. But I can't focus on that until I know what's happening with Sam."

"We're going to do everything we can to save her, Marcus," Diego said, putting an arm around him. "She's our priority. Always will be. Don't worry about Jia and Ellison, we'll handle them. You just go spend time with Sam."

Marcus nodded and hung his head, his mind awhirl with worry and uncertainty.

"Someone should probably tell Claire about all this," Amir said.

"I'll do it," Marcus replied. "I've been meaning to talk to her anyway. She's been dodging my calls and I've just been putting it off. Have either of you heard from her?"

Both men shook their heads.

"Nothing yet," Diego said. "I wish she was here, though."

"Yeah, so do I," Amir agreed.

"Me three," Marcus added.

CHAPTER 14

It was a long ride across town to Claire's place from Synerdyne, giving Marcus plenty of time to think. Looking through rain-speckled windows at the passing city, his mind drifted to Sam. He knew he should be thinking about what to say to Claire, but he couldn't stop thinking about all the possible outcomes, running through both the best and worst-case scenarios. He wanted to believe things would work out. In some ways, he had to. But he couldn't ignore the one painful truth that lingered in the back of his mind. Sam was going to die. He couldn't stop that. And even if they could save her consciousness, nothing would ever be the same again.

He broke from his reverie as the car slowed to a stop. Paying the driver, he stepped onto the sidewalk and looked up at the turn-of-the-century craftsman nestled between two similar homes. The entire neighborhood was like a Norman Rockwell painting hidden within the city, built back when it was considered a suburb. Now it was two blocks from the highway overpass, surrounded by restaurants and other businesses that served the city's growing population.

Covering his head with his hoodie, he climbed the steps to the porch and rang the bell. It took a minute before he heard footsteps approaching the door. The curtain on the door's single window was pulled back and he saw Claire's face peer out at him. He gave her an apologetic smile and waved. She looked back at him blankly, then let the curtain drop, followed by the sound of her unlatching the bolt.

"Is it Sam…?" Claire asked, opening the door, her expression concerned.

"No. Well, she's still… But she is why I am here. She sent me. Can we talk?" Marcus asked.

A look of relief replaced her concern, and Claire nodded, stepping back from the door to let him in. It was then that he noticed she was dressed in paint-splattered baggy sweats.

"I'm sorry to just show up like this, but I didn't know what else to do," he said apologetically. "You've been avoiding my calls."

"Yeah. I know," she said, walking ahead of him into the half-painted living room, covered in drop cloths and paint cans. "Sorry about the mess. I wasn't expecting company. Careful of the paint."

Plopping down on the couch, she folded her legs under herself and gestured to an easy chair. Removing the drop cloth carefully to keep from getting any paint on himself, he took the proffered seat across from her.

"So, I see you've been busy," he said, looking around. "I like the color. It's a nice change."

"Thanks. I find it relaxing. Helps me think," she said, watching him with a dour expression. "You said Sam sent you. How is she?"

"Not great. She's in the simulation now twenty-four-seven, so she's not suffering. But she hasn't eaten in days and it's only a matter of time," he said, swallowing the lump that rose in his throat.

Claire nodded solemnly. "I still can't believe it. Part of me refuses to. Like it can't be real. But then I'll be painting, or doing something else, and I'll realize I'm crying. She's not even gone, but that doesn't matter. Just knowing what's coming…," she shook her head. "Do you feel that way?"

"Of course. All the time," he replied, shocked at the question.

"Good. I… I just wondered if your plan for the simulation meant you weren't processing it. Like, you know, she wasn't really dying," she explained, her face tight.

"There are two parts of me," Marcus said, nodding. "One part is still hopeful. Desperate to find a way to keep her with us. But the other part mourns and has been mourning since she got sick; the part that knows that regardless of how this works, nothing will ever be the same again. The life she and I shared is irrevocably changed. I don't want her to die any more than before, but I also look at her and see how ravaged her body is. I see how much pain it causes her, and despite whatever I might want, I realize that her life is ending. That is where the hopeful part of me takes over. Not for me, but for her. Claire, you should see her in the simulation. She is still free of pain and full of life, even though her body is shutting down. She's the Sam she's always been. How could I, or anyone, take that away from her?"

Claire didn't respond and stared down at her hands.

"Look, I know you have your concerns," he continued. "I'm glad you do, because I know they are born out of a love for Sam, and you want what's best for her too. And Sam knows that. That's why she wanted me to talk to you. Not to convince you of anything."

"What is it she wants to know?" Claire asked, looking up, her eyes brimming with tears.

Marcus smiled appreciatively. "She wants to talk to you herself and asked me to invite you to join her in Sam's World. She understands and appreciates your concerns, too. And wants to hear you out before she makes any decisions."

Claire stared off, nodding in consideration.

"She doesn't have much time left," Marcus pressed. "So, if you're going to talk to her, you need to do it soon."

"I don't know if I can, Marcus," she said, still looking away.

"What do you mean?" he asked.

"If I go in there to talk to her, I don't think I could stay objective." At his look of confusion, she continued, "I don't want her to die any more than you do, and I would love nothing more than to find a way to save her. I'm afraid if I see her there, I'll disregard my concerns in favor of seeing her happy."

"So? What's wrong with that?" he asked. "Are you saying you're refusing to change your mind?"

"No. It's not that," she said. "It's that my concerns aren't about Sam's happiness right now or preventing the preservation of her consciousness. They're bigger than that. Bigger than Sam and more far-reaching. The consequences of what you're thinking of doing are bigger than all of us. And I'm afraid if anyone can convince me otherwise, it's her."

"You're one of the closest people she has in this world. Are you telling me you are going to avoid her, in her last days, because you don't want your mind changed?" Marcus challenged, growing angry. "You at least owe her the chance to talk to you face to face. She is not interested in changing your mind. Sam needs to know what you are thinking in order to make her own informed decision. She needs your perspective. Please, Claire."

Claire stared at Marcus, indecision warring on her face.

"One meeting. That's all I ask," he implored. "This is probably your last chance to state your case. If you don't take it, you may regret it for the rest of your life. It's now or never."

Claire clenched her fists in her lap, watching him without expression.

"Fine," she said, standing up. "Let me just throw something else on."

It took an hour to get back to the condo, rush hour traffic bringing things to a standstill several times. When the car finally dropped them off, Marcus guided Claire through the lobby and up the elevator. As they ascended quietly floor by floor, Marcus wondered how Sam was doing and what she was up to in the simulation.

Glancing at Claire, he also wondered what she and Sam would say to each other, a part of him concerned that Claire would say something that would change Sam's mind. Amir's words came to mind. *It has to be her decision.* Marcus knew he was right, but it didn't make him worry any less.

For her part, Claire stared off at the elevator doors, ignoring him and deep in her own thoughts. It had been like that for most of the car ride. Marcus tried to be understanding, but it still felt awkward to have one of his oldest friends so guarded around him. Maybe he should have invited the others to join them. No, that would just complicate things more. At least Claire had agreed to come. He couldn't ask her to do more.

As the elevator reached the top floor, Claire glanced in his direction, then followed as he opened the apartment door.

"Just make yourself comfortable, and let me know when you're ready to sync in. I'm just going to check on Sam before we join her," he said.

"Alright," Claire replied quietly, looking around the living room as she tried to decide where to sit. "Is it just you?"

Marcus gave her a quizzical look. "What do you mean?"

"I don't know. I just thought… you know, with her condition… there'd be more medical equipment," she said. "Nurses."

"For what? She's in hospice. There are no more treatments and no reason to monitor her vitals. She doesn't eat anymore and is crippled by the tumors pressing against her organs. She's hooked up to a saline drip and has a humidifier and oxygen. That's all she really needs. Now we're just waiting for her…," Marcus replied, unable to finish the thought.

Claire nodded solemnly and looked down at the floor, wrapping her arms around herself.

For a moment, they both stood in silence.

"But, in a way, we're lucky," Marcus said, taking a deep breath. "She has Sam's World, and there she doesn't feel any pain. Unlike anyone else in her position, she doesn't have to suffer through her last days. There's no reason to bring her out. She can just enjoy herself. And isn't that the point of why we created the SynAPP in the first place?"

"Yeah," Claire said quietly, still not meeting his gaze.

"Yeah," Marcus repeated.

For another moment, they stood in silence.

"Okay. Make yourself comfortable. I'll be right back," he said, turning away.

Walking down the hall, he came to Sam's door. Before he even opened it, he was greeted by the familiar hissing sounds of her oxygen and humidifier. Unconsciously he paused as his hand wrapped around the doorknob. The image of Sam laying unnaturally still popped into his head, as it always did in the moment before entering. Pushing the thought away, he opened the door and stepped inside, his eyes immediately looking to her chest and oxygen mask for any sign of respiration.

To his relief, her chest rose and fell gently, and he let out a held breath. He took a moment to look at her, his heart breaking for the thousandth time as he took in the tight, yellowing skin that transformed her familiar features into a skeletal mockery of her beauty. He gently ran a hand over her scalp before leaning down to kiss her on her forehead.

"Claire's here," he whispered, despite knowing she couldn't hear him. "We're going to come visit you in Sam's World."

Kissing her forehead again, he exited the room and quietly pulled the door closed behind him.

Claire was waiting on the couch when he returned and looked up at him expectantly.

"She's okay," he said with a sad smile.

Claire let out a sigh and nodded, turning to stretch out on the couch.

"You ready?" he asked, after settling into the chair across from her.

"Ready when you are," she said with a nod, closing her eyes.

"Okay," he confirmed, putting his tablet on his lap and starting the simulation initialization sequence. He closed his eyes.

"In, three."

"Two."

"One."

Marcus heard the sound of the jungle birds before opening his eyes to see the canopy of broad-leafed trees against the clear blue sky. Sitting up, he pushed himself to his feet and looked around for Claire. Not far away, a rustling came from the undergrowth, and Viatrix walked into view, dressed in her armor.

Looking down at herself, Claire shook her head. "I doubt I'll ever get used to this."

Marcus shrugged with a grin. "Give it some time. It'll become second nature eventually."

"Where's Sam?" she asked.

"Well, that's the trick of it," he said. "It's hard to say. She's usually out hunting or exploring."

"I'd have figured she'd probably explored every inch of this place by now," Claire said.

"Not quite. Part of the AAIP protocol is replication," he explained. "Sam and Diego didn't design this entire biome. They initially created a small environment and input the asset details. The AAIP has since been populating the environment with trees, rocks, soil, and waterways; thus, expanding the area slowly."

"And the Half-men he added?" Claire asked, peering nervously around them.

"That's a good question," Marcus said, surprised that the thought had never entered his head. Though he did have a lot of other things to think about, he told himself. "We should probably be on the lookout. I'll find out where Sam is."

Calling up the AAIP protocol display, he had it run a scan for Sam. A map appeared in his vision, displaying a small dot in green for his location and two blue dots, one beside his and the other more distant.

"Alright, she's about a mile away," he said. "Hold on, I'll move us there. This might be a little jarring."

Instructing the protocol, his vision blurred, fading again to black. Unlike entering the simulation, the change was abrupt, and he staggered forward, having to catch himself from falling. A crash in the foliage behind told him that Claire had been less prepared.

"You okay?" he asked, turning to face her as she pushed herself up from the ground.

"Yeah," she muttered, brushing leaves off her armor. "Where's Sam?"

"She should be nearby."

As if summoned, Sam appeared out of the bushes, her spear raised and ready to strike.

"Woah," Marcus said with a smile, holding up his hands. "It's just us."

Sam's brow furrowed and she stared at them both, her eyes wild.

"Sam?" Marcus said, taking a step forward, his hands still raised. "It's us, babe. You okay?"

Sam blinked at them, lowering her spear, her expression replaced with a look of confusion. "Aer? Viatrix? What are ye doing here?"

"What are you wearing?" Claire blurted out behind him with a laugh.

Marcus realized Sam was dressed in the outfit he'd designed for her, and not the one she'd been wearing the last time they'd entered the simulation together. It was still decent, covering all the important areas, but it left little to the imagination.

Sam blinked again and looked down at herself.

"Oh. I… This is the outfit…," she blinked, bringing a hand to her head. "…Marcus made for me," she said, dropping out of the accent she used when playing Morrigan.

"Well, of course, he did," Claire said, looking at him with a smirk.

Marcus felt his cheeks and ears growing warm.

"How did you get here?" Sam asked, looking past them into the jungle.

"I just had the AAIP ping you, and I brought us to your location," Marcus explained, though confused why she would even ask. "Are you okay, Sam?"

"You didn't run into…," she started, then reached up to grab her head again.

"Sam, can you tell me how you're feeling?" Claire asked, stepping forward.

Sam clutched her head with both hands, doubling over to squat on the ground. Instinctively, Marcus rushed forward to give her support, wrapping his arm around her. Sam pulled back at his touch, turning her gaze to him, her eyes wild like an animal's.

"Git off me, ye shadow fucker," she shouted, trying to push him away.

Marcus let his arm fall but didn't move away as she pushed him.

"Sam, it's okay. It's just us," he said soothingly, trying to console her.

Claire moved to the other side of her and squatted down. "Sam. Tell us what's going on. What is happening? Are you in pain?"

Sam clutched her head again, crying out through clenched teeth.

Marcus reached for her, wanting to help, but he couldn't think of what to do. This was not supposed to be happening to her in the simulation. Here she was safe from her pain. A thought occurred to him. Even though the SynAPP should be managing her external pain within the simulation, maybe it had something to do with the pain reception protocol in Sam's World.

"Marcus, do something," Claire said helplessly beside Sam.

He brought up the protocol controls, the image appearing and then fading in his vision, as he struggled through his fear and worry to focus. Finally, he managed to solidify the controls in his mind and quickly brought up the pain reception amplifier, then turned it off.

Sam suddenly stood up, and for a moment he thought she was better. But instead of looking relieved, she had a look of fright on her face as she looked beyond them into the jungle.

"How the fuck do I kill ye shadow bastards?" she said in a snarl, staring at something behind them.

Marcus turned to follow her gaze, but all he could see were the giant plants and trees that surrounded them.

"Sam, do you see something?" he asked.

"Watch out, Aer. Viatrix. They're right behind ye," she said, pointing to one of the broad-leafed plants.

Marcus peered into the undergrowth, trying to figure out what she was referring to, but he didn't see anything. Claire, too, looked back and forth, her eyes wide in confusion. Suddenly, Sam gave another cry, this time falling to the jungle floor and clutching her sides as she let out a harrowing scream.

Scrambling over to her on his hands and knees, Marcus wrapped his arms around her as he brought the protocol back up into his vision.

"Marcus, make it stop," Claire implored him.

"It shouldn't be happening," he said, as he desperately searched the protocol controls and found the pain reception still turned off. In his arms, he could feel Sam's body tensing in pain, and he felt utterly helpless as he held her tightly to him.

"Fuck ye," Sam shrieked, her face red and the veins in her neck bulging.

Abruptly her screams stopped, as her eyes rolled up into the back of her head and she went limp in Marcus' arms. He stared at her in horror, unable to move or breathe. Claire, too, stared wide-eyed at

Sam's unmoving form, her mouth agape. Finally, Marcus' breath returned, and he squeezed Sam to him.

"Baby? Sam? Wake up! Wake up, baby! Please!" he implored, staring down at her face.

Eyes closed and face relaxed, her pained expression had changed to one of serenity. Tears streamed down Marcus' face as he rocked her in his arms, continuing to call her name. Beside him, Claire watched silently, her own eyes brimming with tears. With a sob, Marcus buried his face in Sam's hair, continuing to rock her back and forth.

He became dimly aware of a hand running its fingers through his hair, and he looked up expecting to find Claire touching him. Instead, he realized that Sam was staring up at him, a sleepy smile on her face.

"Hey," she said, her smile deepening as her hand continued to stroke his hair comfortingly. "It's okay."

Marcus stared down at her in disbelief, swallowing back the lump in his throat.

"Sam! You're alright!" he cried.

"Yeah," Sam said weakly. "I guess I am."

Claire let out a sobbing laugh and covered her mouth with her hand, her tears still flowing.

"What happened?" Marcus asked, his heart pounding in his chest and every inch of his body tingling.

Sam's brow twisted for a moment as she thought about the question, then her eyes focused on his.

"I think I died."

CHAPTER 15

Marcus closed the apartment door behind him and leaned against it. Letting out a long sigh, he tossed his keys on the nearby side table and reached up to loosen his tie and collar. For a moment he closed his eyes and listened to the unfamiliar silence. The hissing sounds of Sam's respirator and humidifier were missing from down the hall, as well as the countless other sounds of her presence that he'd never thought about until she was gone.

Pushing himself off the door, he pulled off his suit jacket and threw it on the couch as he made his way past the living room and down the hall to Sam's room. As he reached her door, he took hold of the doorknob and stopped. The familiar question popped into his mind out of habit, but this time he knew the answer.

Turning the knob, he pushed her door open and stared at the empty bed in the center of the room. He hadn't touched anything since Sam's passing and had left the room exactly as it was when they came to take her body away. Staring at the bed, he could still picture her lying there as she had been in life, and in death. Memories of her smiling and laughing mingled with ones of her crying and struggling in pain, until finally ending with the image of her body lying still and unmoving. He stood there for a moment, staring blankly into the room, held captive by his thoughts.

Stepping inside, he rolled up his sleeves as he crossed over to the chair beside her bed. Easing into the cushions, he leaned his head back, picked up the tablet, and closed his eyes, counting down to three and triggering the SynAPP.

In an instant his consciousness faded to black, before returning a moment later. Opening his eyes, he found himself in the familiar surroundings of the jungle. Standing up, he stretched and looked around, before accessing the AAIP protocols. A quick search put Sam a couple of miles away, and he gave the command to transport him to her location.

The first thing he noticed was the sound of rushing water, and he opened his eyes to find himself next to a gushing waterfall. There was no mistaking the landmark or where he was, and he quickly looked around for the giant ape that made this place its lair. To his surprise, he found Sam dressed in her skimpy leathers and covered in blood. His first reaction was shock until he realized that at her feet lay the ape, blood pooling beneath it as it struggled for breath.

Sam furrowed her brow in surprise as her eyes fell on him, but her expression soon changed to one of satisfaction.

"Yer too late, boyo. The fun's already over," she said, a wide grin spreading across her face.

"You killed it," he said in astonishment.

"Aye. Big boy here put up quite a fight. Thought he had me a couple o' times there, but in the end, he couldn't keep up with me. Shame really. He's the only real challenge I've had in a while," she said with a twist of her lips.

Stepping onto its stomach, she wrapped her hands around the spear sticking out its chest and used her body weight to push it in deeper. With a spasm, the beast tensed, then went limp, its body still. Wrenching the spear free, she stepped off the gorilla onto the stone and strode over to Marcus. As she reached him, she tossed the weapon away and wrapped her arms around his neck, pulling him into a deep and passionate kiss.

Instinctively, he pulled her to him, returning the kiss with equal force and ignoring all the blood that covered her body. She smiled against his lips, her body pressing against his with intent. He indulged in the feel of her, as real as in life, as his hands slid along her bare skin. Pushing him away suddenly, she disengaged and stepped back, a broad smile on her face. Reaching up to her top, she pulled it over her head, tossing it to the side, before sliding her loincloth off her hips. Standing there naked before him, she arched an eyebrow and looked down at his tasset.

"To the victor go the spoils, I suppose," he said, removing his own clothing.

"Oh aye, they do," she said, but as he approached, she put a hand on his shoulder and pushed, guiding him to his knees. "But ye aren't the victor. I am," she declared with a wink, sliding her hand through his hair and draping a muscular leg over his shoulder.

"Fuck, but I needed that," Sam said, sprawled out against him on the cold stone, the soft warmth of her naked skin pressed against his own.

"You're not the only one," Marcus replied, still trying to catch his breath, staring at a patch of clear blue sky through a break in the canopy.

"I missed ye," she said, pushing herself up on one elbow to lean over and kiss him.

"It hasn't been that long," he said with a chuckle.

"Ye might be able to go without fer weeks, but not me, boyo," she said, sliding a leg over him and lowering her head to his chest.

"It hasn't been weeks, Sam. We fucked yesterday," he laughed.

"Did we?" she mused, noticeably dropping the accent and stroking his chest.

"I suppose time probably feels a bit different here, day in and day out," he said.

"Aye. I mean, yeah," she replied, quietly.

Marcus looked down at her but all he could see was the top of her head. He reached over to stroke her hair, cupping her head in his hand. "You alright, little one?"

Sam turned her face up to his and gave him a sad smile. "Yeah."

"You want to talk about the memorial?"

"Oh, was that today?" she asked.

"Yeah, I just got back from it," he replied. "There were a lot of people there. Not just from Synerdyne."

"That's good," she said, absentmindedly stroking his chest.

"It was kind of weird to talk to those people. I mean, they don't know about you being in the simulation," he said. "And seeing all their grief, I almost wanted to tell them. To console them. Let them know you're okay. But I knew that wouldn't end well."

"Yeah," she agreed. "Probably for the best."

"I can't imagine what it's like for you. It has to be a pretty big mind fuck. Are you okay in here?" he asked, stroking her hair.

She lifted her head and pushed herself up onto his chest to look at him.

"Of course," she said quickly. "It's weird to think about. To know that I'm technically dead. But considering the alternative, I prefer this outcome."

"And have you experienced any other episodes like the one when you died?" he asked.

"You asked me that already, and the answer is still no. I'll tell you if anything like that happens, and don't you dare think about turning off the pain protocols again," she said, pointing an accusing finger at him.

"Baby, I haven't. I just want to make sure you are safe."

"I told you. It was just a one-off, which makes complete sense when you think about what was happening. But it's not like I have a body now to cause me pain. All of that is over. So calm down," she said, leaning forward to give him a quick kiss.

"Okay. Amir's been monitoring things and he hasn't noticed anything out of the ordinary," he confirmed.

"See?"

"I know. But I just worry about you. There are so many uncertainties, and we shouldn't let ourselves get lax just because things seem to be working. You're essentially our first test subject, so that comes with lots of repetitive questions."

"I know," she said, letting out a sigh and laying her head back on his chest. "I just don't like thinking about things going wrong. After all, it's not like I have any other options if this doesn't work."

"Well, it's all in how you look at it. If we know something is off, we might be able to come up with a solution. But we can't do that if we think everything is functioning as intended," he said softly. "So just... don't be hesitant to let me know if something happens. Okay?"

"I won't," she said, absentmindedly stroking his chest again.

Marcus turned his attention back to the canopy and let himself enjoy the moment. With her warm body pressed against his, he marveled at the undertaking they had accomplished. Sam was safe. Her consciousness protected in the simulation. But not only that, he could be with her again, as they had been in life. Better than they had been in life. The thought sent a shiver of excitement through his entire body, leaving him with an optimism he hadn't felt in a long time.

"Hey," Sam muttered against his chest. "There is something I wanted to talk to you about."

Marcus looked down at her, his contentment fading into concern at the tone of her voice.

"What is it, hon?"

Sam turned her face to look up at him again. "It's just... don't get me wrong, I love it here. I know how lucky I am, believe me. But..."

"What? Tell me," he pressed.

"I love that we can be together like this," she said quickly. "But when you're gone… it gets lonely sometimes. After all, it's just me in here."

"I get it. You've been alone for a long time now, sweetie. Especially since the cancer started to keep you isolated, and you don't get any interactions with people. I wish you could at least go to Elysium, but everyone there knows what happened to you. It would blow what we are doing here wide open. It might not feel so isolating once Diego gets Freeport up and running. And things are still in motion regarding the addition of pain protocols to Elysium. Hopefully, we'll be able to start bringing over other participants to Sam's World. But in the meantime, I'll see if we can all visit more often."

"Thank you," she said, smiling. "I don't want to sound ungrateful about all of this. It's just…"

"You don't. Your point is valid. You need stimulus. I don't want you to feel trapped here," he said, Claire's previous accusation coming to mind.

"I don't, and I do love it here," she said, excitedly pushing herself to her feet and stretching, raising her arms over her head.

"Now there's a sight," Marcus said, still laying on the stone and admiring her naked backside.

Sam turned around to face him with a smirk, planting her hands on her hips and letting him get a good look at her nakedness. "Ye like what ye see, boyo?"

"Very much so. Though I liked feeling it even more."

"Oh, I know ye did," she said, grinning.

Marcus let out a long breath. "It's nice to have this again."

"Well dun ye go gettin' all love-sick over me, boyo. I've things to do and can't be gettin' myself tied down," she said, picking up her loincloth from the ground.

"A little too late for that," Marcus said with a chuckle, reluctantly pushing himself to his feet.

He watched as Sam slid the loincloth back over her hips. Noticing his attention, she glanced over her shoulder at him and gave him another wink.

"Oh, yer too easy," she said, purposely bending over provocatively to pick up her top.

"Well, can you blame me?" he asked, appreciatively admiring her curves, before bending down to pick up his tasset and cover himself.

"No. I suppose I can't," she replied, turning to face him. "Yer a good fuck, I'll grant ye that."

"Well, thank you," he said with a chuckle. "I aim to please."

"Aye. That's why I let ye fuck me," she said with a smirk. "Now unless ye intend to hunt Half-men with me, ye best be runnin' along."

"I really want to stay longer, but after everything today, I'm exhausted. I'm sorry, babe. I'd stay, but it's not like I actually get any sleep in here. But I'll be back first thing when I wake up." Marcus let out a long sigh and smiled. "You know it still hasn't all sunk in. I mean, there's a part of me that can't believe it actually worked!"

Sam's brow twisted in confusion.

"Well, I dun know what yer goin' on about, boyo. But iffin' it means yer leavin', then goodbye to ye. Thought ye had a bit more stamina to ye, but I can entertain myself. Come find me when yer all rested up. Ye'll be needin' yer energy," she said with a lascivious grin, stepping over to stand before him, before pressing her lips to his forcefully.

Marcus reveled in the kiss, reaching up to cup the back of her head. Smiling against her lips, he marveled at the moment. They had done the impossible. Sam hadn't died. Her body was gone, sure, but Sam was still there. She was proof that they had created another form of existence. A higher form, really. Hell, she might even be immortal. The implications were mind-blowing, but he didn't linger on the details. All that mattered was that she was alive, and all the pain and fear were gone.

Lingering on his lips for a moment longer, Sam disengaged with a smile. "Somethin' to remember me by, boyo. So ye dun go forgettin' about me."

Marcus grinned up at her. "That could never happen."

"Good answer," Sam said, giving him a wink and turning to pick up her spear. Walking to the edge of the clearing, she stopped and gave him one last look over her shoulder, before moving into the underbrush and disappearing into the jungle.

Marcus woke from the simulation, the features of Sam's room slowly coming into focus. Almost immediately, he yawned, the exhaustion of the day returning to wash over him. For a moment he stayed in the chair and looked around the room, his eyes staring at the empty bed. Shouldn't he feel some sort of loss? He'd never touch her skin again or feel her pressed against him. At least not in the real world. And yet that didn't seem to bother him. Instead, he felt relief. She was no longer in pain. No longer being consumed by the tumors. She was safe in the simulation. However, he still couldn't get rid of the nagging feeling that he should feel some sort of sadness.

Taking in a deep breath, he pulled his gaze away and looked down at his phone. Several notifications were waiting for him. No big surprise. Lots of people were reaching out with their condolences, none of them aware of the fact that Sam was still conscious. He scrolled quickly through the list of messages. He would need to reply, but he was content to wait until after he got some sleep.

Clive Ellison's name caught his attention, and he stopped scrolling. The message only read: *let me know when you're out of the simulation.* Marcus stared at the words. It had been sent just after Marcus had gotten home. Ellison couldn't know that he was actually in the simulation, could he? That would require a level of access possessed by only himself and his senior team. Curiosity overwhelmed his exhaustion, and Marcus replied: *Got your message. What's up?*

Great. There's a car waiting downstairs for you. Meet me at the Roosevelt in 20, Clive's response returned after only a few seconds.

The cocktail lounge? Marcus had never been there, too rich for his blood, but he knew where it was. Staring in bewilderment at the message, he thought about texting Ellison back and telling him they could meet in the morning, he instead got out of the chair and made his way to the bathroom to tidy himself up. He was still wearing his suit from the memorial, and it would have to do. He just hoped his jacket wasn't too wrinkled.

The car Ellison had waiting was a big black luxury SUV, like all the important people used in movies. As Marcus stepped towards the vehicle, a man in a suit hopped out of the car and opened the passenger door in the back. Marcus nodded to the man with a tight smile and ducked inside to sit on the upholstered leather seat. Returning to the front, the man started to drive without a word. Though he knew it was silly, Marcus couldn't help but feel a little intimidated by the whole process.

As they made their way to what he could only assume was the Roosevelt, he stared out of the window at the passing city and wondered why Ellison wanted to meet with him. The man had shown a tendency for keeping himself informed, even when others thought the information confidential. He'd admitted as much to Marcus the last time they'd met. But that couldn't mean he'd gained some sort of access to their secured database, could it? Ellison had so far been supportive of their research and had given him no reason to think he'd interfere. His thoughts turned to Jia and her team, and he couldn't help but feel a sense of worry creep into his mind.

The car stopped directly in front of the Roosevelt, its marquee casting a bright illumination that shone through the car's tinted windows and lit up the street before it. Just like before, the driver hopped out of the car and moved to open the passenger door. Stepping out of the vehicle, Marcus buttoned up his suit jacket and took a moment to stare at the entrance to the cocktail lounge. It was the sort of place Evan would visit, everything about it screaming expense and status, so he supposed it made sense that Ellison chose to patronize it.

With a deep breath, Marcus gathered his resolve and walked forward. The doorman, also dressed in a suit and not a uniform, opened the door for Marcus as he approached. Stepping inside, the sound of music and conversation washed over him. The interior of the Roosevelt was pretty much as he'd imagined it, with lots of expensive-looking wood and leather furniture. On the far side of the room was a low stage on which a singer crooned a jazzy tune, accompanied by four other musicians.

"Is it just you, sir?" the hostess asked as he stepped into the room proper.

"No, I'm meeting someone who's already here," he replied, glancing in her direction.

"Are you Mr. Avery?" she asked, and when he nodded in surprise, she smiled and waved for him to follow. "This way. Mr. Ellison is waiting for you."

Of course, they would know who Ellison was, and most likely catered to his every need. Marcus nodded for the woman to lead on and followed her to a series of booths tucked away in the back, elevated above the main floor. The VIP section, of course.

Clive Ellison smiled and exited one of the booths as he spotted Marcus' approach.

"Marcus!" Clive said, reaching forward to take his hand and pull him close, patting him on the back. "Thanks for coming." He gestured for him to sit, taking a seat across the table from Marcus. The hostess patiently waited as they got settled, a placid smile on her face.

"What are you drinking?" Ellison asked.

Marcus shrugged, clearing his throat. "Whatever you're having I guess."

"I'll have another as well," Ellison said to the woman.

Giving a nod, she left without a word.

Ellison watched her go, then turned his attention back to Marcus. "Sorry to drag you out here so late. I know you've had a hell of a day, but I appreciate you accepting my invitation."

Marcus gave him a tired smile and nodded. "Yeah, well. It's been busy, that's for sure." He looked across the table at the man, trying to figure out just what Ellison might want.

For his part, Ellison only nodded and turned his attention to the band, finishing off the rest of his drink.

Marcus watched, waiting for Ellison to say something, but when the man didn't, he cleared his throat and spoke.

"Is there a particular reason you wanted me to meet you?"

Turning his attention back to Marcus, Ellison met his gaze and gave him a crooked smile. "I figured we should talk and that you could use a change of venue. You've been cooped up in that condo for a while, and now that you don't have to worry about Sam, you have the luxury of relaxing a little bit."

Marcus stared at the man, astonished at how flippantly he spoke of Sam's death. Though Sam wasn't actually dead, Ellison didn't know that, and Marcus found himself offended by the man's attitude. As he opened his mouth to reply, the hostess returned with their drinks. Giving her a wink as she took his empty glass, Ellison waited for her to leave before turning his gaze back to Marcus expectantly.

Different responses tumbled through Marcus' head, but he didn't know what to say, so he asked the question he was really interested in.

"How did you know I was in the simulation?"

Ellison's smile widened. "Where else would you be on a day like this? I figured you would want to be with Sam."

Marcus felt like he'd been hit by a baseball bat, and for a moment his mind reeled. Did he actually know? He knew about their research, but he hadn't confirmed that they'd successfully saved Sam. To anyone outside of himself and his senior team, Sam was dead. Was this just another bluff, as Ellison had done in their last meeting? Did he suspect, but was waiting for Marcus to confirm his suspicions?

"I'm not sure what you mean," Marcus said cautiously.

"Yes, you do. I saw you at the memorial. You are not a man in mourning," Ellison said with a look of sympathy. "Don't forget, I lost my wife in a similar way. I know grief when I see it. Even behind a smile, you can see it in the eyes." He leaned forward over the table and held Marcus' gaze. "And I don't see it."

Clearing his throat, Marcus picked up his glass and took a drink, using it as a distraction to look away.

Ellison leaned back in the booth, his drink in one hand and smile returning. "It's a simple enough thread to follow, Marcus. We've already discussed the potential for your research. Do you honestly think I wouldn't assume that you have been moving heaven and earth to save Sam? And assuming you were, where else would you go immediately after the memorial? So, how's she doing?" he asked, taking a drink.

A cold panic ran through Marcus as he stared at the man. He knew. But what would he do with that information? Alarm bells sounded in his mind as he tried to figure out how to respond. Should he just admit it? Or was this just another ruse? It proved that Ellison had been right about the possibilities of their research. It was why he invested. But could he really trust the man with such knowledge?

"There are countless reasons why I would visit the simulation," Marcus began, trying to keep his voice calm and reasonable, while inside all he wanted to do was run. "It is where I spent most of my days for the last two years with Sam. It is as much a place filled with our memories as any other, and a place that I can go for solitude."

"No doubt," Ellison retorted. "And I understand why you are hesitant to divulge that Sam is alive. You'd be stupid not to be cautious. That's why I wanted to talk, just you and me. I know for everyone else today is a day of mourning. But really, it's a celebration.

You did the impossible, and I am so goddamn proud to be just a small part of what you've accomplished," he said, raising his glass to Marcus.

Marcus narrowed his eyes, and when he didn't move, Ellison reached across the table to tap their glasses together.

"Marcus, I want you to know I am on your side. Whatever you need, I will ensure you have. I don't want to curtail your research. Your *discovery*. I want to be a part of it. As I told you before, this is the whole reason I became involved in Synerdyne. I know you have a lot of reasons for concern. It's Sam. I get it. You have to protect her. But let me help you. I can keep everyone else from asserting control over Sam and Sam's World. Evan. The shareholders. Hell, even the government. I have the resources. You need someone like me in your corner. And I *am* in your corner. I hope you know that. I just need you to trust me."

Marcus studied the man's face. He wasn't wrong. Everything he had said was what Marcus feared. As soon as other people learned about Sam, they'd want to take control of the project. It was just too big a discovery. And at that moment, he realized just how terrified he was at the prospect that Sam could be taken from him. Ellison was right. If anyone had the resources to protect Sam's World, it was him. But at what cost?

"What is it you really want, Clive?" Marcus asked, taking a drink from his glass. Scotch. It figured.

"Immortality, Marcus. What else? I want what you've given Sam. I want that for everyone. As I told you before, I truly believe this research is the next step in human evolution. A place where loss, grief, and regret are all things of the past. Where no one has to watch their loved one die and feel helpless to do anything about it. Instead, they can celebrate their transcendence to a new reality, and visit them there whenever they like."

"And how do I know you would be true to your word?" Marcus asked.

"You don't, I guess. But I'd like us to be friends," Clive replied. "I intend to get spiked tomorrow. Jia is having it arranged. For me, this is beyond any considerations of profit margins. This is something I would willingly spend my entire fortune to see come to fruition. Do you know anyone else who feels that way? Other than yourself?"

In all honesty, Marcus didn't. He doubted even Amir or Diego would risk so much, even for Sam. And Claire had already proven how little she was willing to risk.

"No," Marcus replied, shaking his head.

"We are a rare breed, Marcus. We know pain like few others, and we are bonded in that pain. I'm just asking you to let me help you."

He couldn't explain it, but Clive's words struck a nerve with him. No one could comprehend how important Sam was, or the grief and pain he'd endured watching her slowly fade away. Knowing that someone else understood that pain gave him a sense of comfort he hadn't realized he'd been missing. Marcus drank the rest of his scotch in one swallow, putting the empty glass down on the table with a thud.

"Let's start with something simpler. Get spiked, and we'll take another tour of Elysium. Let's see how you like the full experience before we worry about anything else. If you're going to be part of my team, I need to know how well you'll integrate."

Clive's lips curled into a smile, and he nodded. "Alright. Fair enough."

Marcus returned the nod, then slid out of the booth. "One question," he said, looking down at Clive.

"Shoot."

"What was your wife's name?"

"Evelyn," Clive said, and in his voice, Marcus thought he caught the hint of a tremor he'd felt himself when talking about Sam. Maybe he did understand.

"Have Jia reach out to Amir and we'll get you scheduled," Marcus said. "Thanks for the drink, but I really need to get some sleep."

"Anytime. I hope we can make this a habit," Clive replied. "The car will take you home."

Marcus gave him a nod and walked away, holding his breath until he made it to the exit.

CHAPTER 16

"Why am I just now learning about this?" Evan demanded, throwing the thirty-six-page Elysium user agreement onto his desk in front of him.

Sitting across from him, Marcus looked at the stack of pages Ellison's legal team had drafted.

"Is there some issue with the agreement?" Marcus asked, focused on remaining calm.

"It's not about the legality of the agreement. This is a fundamental change to Elysium. I shouldn't have to find out about it by happenstance. Why didn't you discuss this with me first?" Evan snarled.

"It's an internal experiment within the simulation," Marcus replied. "You don't usually involve yourself in our research. We went through legal."

"I'm the goddamn CEO, Marcus! I should know if you are going to start implementing shock therapy!"

"That's a bit dramatic. We've just been allowing for differing levels of pain reception to see what, if anything, that stimulation might do within the simulation," Marcus said with purposeful obfuscation.

"And what if that result is someone stroking out?" Evan asked.

"That's what the agreement is for," Marcus replied, gesturing with his head to the paperwork.

"Jesus—fucking—Christ, Marcus. Are you listening to yourself? You're talking about these people as if they were lab rats. Not to mention, just because we have this agreement doesn't mean we can't be sued. You don't think there are hundreds of lawyers happy to use this case to drag us through an expensive defense for years? That alone could sink the company."

"Isn't that what we have Ellison for? And how is this any different from what we've been doing with the SynAPP?" Marcus countered. "It's not like something couldn't go wrong with that too, but you've never had a problem with it."

"Because I knew it was happening. That's the point. If something has the possibility of damaging or impacting the company in a significant way, the board has to be involved," Evan sighed. "What do you think they will do when they find out about this? Now I've got to scramble to make a defense for both of us."

"What? Are they going to kick me and my team off our own project?" Marcus scoffed. "Who else do they think they can find who would understand our research?"

"There's no project, or research, if the board gets skittish and decides to dissolve the company."

"Again, isn't that why you brought Ellison on board?" Marcus asked.

"Are you fucking with me? Is this some sort of point you're trying to make? Is this about Sam?" Evan's voice softened suddenly. "Listen, man, I know these last few months have been hard for you. I can't even imagine what you're going through. Like I told you, you didn't have to come back so soon. Maybe you should take some more time to process this shit. God knows you've been through hell."

"I'm fine. I don't need more time. Sam would want me to continue our research. So that's what I'm doing. And this," Marcus said, pointing to the paperwork, "is the next step."

"Okay," Evan said, looking down at the stack of papers and turning them to face him. "So, what is this meant to accomplish?"

"We're hoping that the addition of pain reception will give us more data on how the brain responds to that stimulus, and thus the AAIP," Marcus explained.

"And how will this benefit the program?"

"It's hard to say. But theoretically, we might be able to use it to create therapies through the AAIP that can help patients with pain issues, instead of just inhibiting their symptoms," Marcus said, reciting the statements from the agreement.

Evan sat down in his chair and lifted the agreement to stare at it, letting out a long breath. "You have to keep me in the loop on these things, Marcus. Even if you don't think it matters. Understand?" he said, tossing the papers back on his desk.

Marcus nodded.

"And what's this I hear about Diego's entire team being redirected to another project? Is that something else I need to know about?" Evan asked.

Marcus shook his head. "We're just trying something new. I'll let you know if it proves worthwhile."

"Well, he's not happy," Marcus said, once he was alone with Amir in his office.

"How much does he know?" Amir asked.

"Just about the changes to Elysium. Don't worry about him. I'm scheduled to meet with Ellison today. He got the spike and wants to test it out."

"He got implanted?" Amir asked. "Are you going to take him to Sam's World?"

"No. We're going to go back to Elysium," Marcus said. "He might know about Sam, but at least for now, he's still too much of an unknown."

"Yeah, I don't trust him entirely either," Amir said.

"Nothing wrong with a little caution," Marcus said. "First, let's see if he puts his money where his mouth is."

"Agreed," Amir said with a nod.

"How are the mappings from Elysium going?" Marcus asked. "Are we still on track?"

"Yeah, looks like we were right about the pain variant. I've got detailed maps, as complete as Sam's, on eight participants. And I expect the other six who signed up a little later to reach the same level soon."

"How are you feeling about transferring those eight?" Marcus asked.

"Pretty good," Amir said. "I don't think we have to wait any longer. Just give the word and I can start to upload them. The only question is, will there be any issue with loading them directly into the AAIP without the SynAPP?"

"Shouldn't it work like it did with Sam?"

"Maybe. But Sam was integrated at first through the SynAPP," Amir explained. "These transfers will be more like loading in an asset. Truth is, we won't know for sure until we do it."

Marcus nodded, thinking about Sam. With the new focus on Elysium, he'd had to return to his work, which meant spending less time with her in the simulation. However, every time he did join her there, she insisted on staying in character. Most of the time, he didn't press the point with her and just played along. But there were times when he grew more concerned. Times when she seemed to have trouble remembering things.

Maybe it was the monotony of it all. The lack of new experiences. There was only so much hunting she could do. Or maybe it was the loneliness. Regardless, with the integration of the participants from Elysium, they could at least offer her more complex stimulation. Then maybe she wouldn't feel so alone.

"Is everything okay?" Amir asked, and Marcus looked up to realize his friend was watching him.

"What's that?"

"I was saying that we still don't know what the AAIP is fully capable of, but you seemed to be thinking about something else," Amir explained.

"Oh, yeah. Sorry. I've got a lot on my mind," Marcus said, waving a dismissive hand. "Like you said, we won't know until we try. And there's no time like the present. Let's go ahead and get started."

"You sure?"

"Is there a good reason we should wait?" Marcus asked.

"No, I guess not."

"Then proceed, Mr. Mizrahi," Marcus said, doing his best impression of Captain Kirk.

"So? Notice any difference?" Marcus asked as he and Clive walked along the same avenue they had during Clive's initial visit to Elysium.

"It's remarkable," Clive said, looking down at his hands before lifting his eyes to the surrounding neighborhood. "You tried to explain it to me, but I didn't really get how different it would be. I mean, before I felt like I was here. But I was only a spectator. Now I feel like I am a physical part of this place. It's funny how easily we take our senses for granted, relying mainly on sight and sound. But now I can feel the breeze. I can literally smell the air."

Marcus smiled, knowing full well the experience he was describing.

"That reminds me," he said, bringing up the AAIP protocol in his vision. "Hold out your hand like you are holding something. You got a favorite ice cream flavor?"

"Butter pecan?" Clive said with a chuckle, doing as he was instructed.

"Really?" Marcus asked dubiously, choosing the flavor from the list.

For a moment Clive's hand was empty, but in a blink he was suddenly holding a waffle cone with a big scoop of butter pecan ice cream on top.

Clive blinked in surprise. "You know, I'm supposed to avoid sugar."

"That won't be a problem," Marcus said with a laugh. "You don't even have to worry about it going to your thighs."

Clive chuckled and inspected the cone for a moment, before tentatively bringing it up to his mouth to give it a lick. "Holy shit," he said.

"Right?"

"I mean, it's better than I could have imagined," Clive said with a smile.

"Well, actually, it's exactly as you imagined. The flavor isn't real, but it's a combination of inputs from the AAIP and what your mind thinks it will taste like," Marcus explained. "So it is far more vivid than any actual flavor made from ingredients. However, that means it works both ways. If you hate the taste of something, you will *hate* it even more here. Want to try?"

"No, I believe you. I think I'll stick with this," Clive chuckled, taking another lick. "But that does bring up a point I was wondering about. So everything here is devised within my mind. And because of that, my preconceptions—like how I imagine this will taste—play a role in what I experience. Does that mean I could change what I experience, based on my perceptions?"

"Well, the short answer is yes. But not significantly. Like I told you last time, everyone here experiences something a little different from the other participants, but no more than we do in life, based on our memory and perception of events. The AAIP sets a standard structure for all things in the simulation, through signal stimulation to the hippocampus. So, it might create a box that is blue. One person might perceive it as a shade of green, or purple, or even a primary color like red. They might think the box is made of straight edges or curved in places, but they will all see a colored box, not a dog."

"I think I understand," Clive said, strolling forward as he continued to eat his cone. "God, the difference of having the SynAPP really is striking."

"How did the implantation go? Easy enough?" Marcus asked.

"Yeah, I had a bit of a headache for about twenty-four hours, but nothing debilitating," Clive said. "As I understand it, that's normal?"

"Perfectly normal."

"And I'm visiting from my office at home, so the remote link seems to be working just fine," Clive added.

"You're all set then. You can visit whenever you like," Marcus said smiling.

"You mentioned that things here are based upon perception; they are happening in my brain. We're not in a specific place, more like our consciousnesses are linked, right?" Clive asked.

"Exactly. Think of it as sharing a dream," Marcus explained.

"So does that mean there are no records of our experiences here?" Clive inquired.

"None whatsoever," Marcus said. "That's why we have to rely on our participants' exit interviews to get information on their experience here. Now, I could witness something that happens to someone else while I am here and remember it when I return to consciousness, but there is no way for anyone else who isn't here to do so."

"So what we say here can be assumed to be confidential," Clive said.

"Indeed. Unless someone within the simulation were to overhear us."

Clive nodded in consideration. "How is the addition of pain working?"

"As we had hoped," Marcus said. "The addition of the stimuli increased the mapping detail, and now we have eight participants ready for transfer. I've given Amir the go-ahead to start the process. However, Evan found out about the new legal agreements, and he let me know this morning just how unhappy he is at being left out of the loop."

"What did you tell him?" Clive asked.

"I explained that it was all part of the research and necessary for us to proceed with the program."

"And how did he take that?"

"Well enough, though I think he'll probably be keeping an eye on what we are doing from here on out," Marcus said. "Evan's not one to let things go if it's something he's worried about."

"Well, if he causes any trouble, just let me know," Clive said, taking another lick of his cone. "Otherwise, we won't let him slow us down."

Marcus glanced at the man, but he seemed unperturbed as he continued to eat his ice cream.

"So we now know that pain is necessary for the mapping," Clive said, shifting back to the previous discussion.

"A new data point," Marcus agreed. "Now we just have to see if the participants can function without being tethered to their original consciousness."

"Well, we know they can, don't we?"

"How do you mean?" Marcus said, turning to Clive.

"Sam proves that," Clive said, matter-of-factly. "Or do you want to still pretend that that's not the case?" He stopped and turned, arching an eyebrow. "Do you really expect me to believe you are grieving? I don't want to be insensitive, but come on, Marcus. What's it going to take to get you to trust me?"

Marcus considered the man, his mind warring over what he should say. He had to admit that Clive had been pretty open with him so far, not to mention supporting their research. The very research that had saved Sam. He couldn't help but feel that he owed him some sort of explanation.

"It's not that I don't trust you," he said, swallowing the lump in his throat, and unconsciously looking over his shoulder. "I just have to be careful."

Clive gave him a sympathetic smile. "I understand. Your priority is Sam."

Marcus nodded his head.

"And I respect that," Clive said. "I do. But if you're concerned about Evan or anyone else, just know that I have the resources to help you protect what you love. I can't do that if you won't let me in."

Marcus stared at the man, studying his face. If this was going to work, he needed Clive, both for his financial support and for the protection it would offer. But he was right. How could Marcus expect Clive's support if he didn't trust him?

"You're not wrong. On any account." Marcus said, pointedly, still unable to utter the words that Sam still lived."

"Including Sam?" Clive asked, his face splitting into a smile.

"Yes," Marcus confirmed, taking in a deep breath. "But to your question about data points, there is a difference between Sam and the participants in Elysium. Her consciousness was connected through the SynAPP, and we never tried running her map in parallel with another one while it was functioning. We still don't know the effect it may have with the AAIP."

"I see," Clive said, the grin still on his face. "So now that I'm spiked, when do I get to experience this other server?"

"What?"

"When can I go into Sam's server?" Clive repeated, nonchalantly taking another lick of the ice cream.

"That was never something we discussed," Marcus said.

"We also didn't discuss me not doing it. I'm curious is all. Is it like it is here, or different?" Clive asked, gesturing to their surroundings. "I mean, after all, we are sending our test subjects there. And I assume you and your team visit, so what's the difference?"

"It's different," Marcus said, a feeling of invasion washing over him at the thought of letting Clive go there.

Clive considered him for a long moment. "I get it. It started as a private server just for Sam, not a theme park for some billionaire. But the other participants don't feel that way, because they're not actually real, are they? They are just a copy of the people in Elysium. You can just shut them down if you want, without affecting the original consciousness. Hell, their original consciousness won't even be aware of the copy, so you can erase them if things don't go well, without anyone being the wiser. But you can't do that with me."

"Uh…yeah," Marcus said, Clive's words ringing true in his ears.

"Fair enough. I won't push, but I hope I continue to earn your trust," Clive said, tossing the remainder of his cone into the grass before reaching over to pat Marcus on the back. "Thank you for letting me in."

Marcus nodded, and for a while they walked in silence down the silvery road.

CHAPTER 17

Marcus strode through the streets of Freeport. It was an appropriate name Diego and Sam had come up with for the pirate city. As he walked through the town, he marveled at the throng of people filling the avenues, so very different from the empty streets he had experienced only weeks before. People, or more accurately, AI-generated avatars, dressed in an array of clothing from togas to tassets, moved about on their designated tasks.

In one square of the city, he passed a thriving bazaar with vendors shouting to get his attention from behind stalls filled with a large variety of goods: from fruit and fish, to cloth, and even exotic animals. Other avatars filled the square, moving from stall to stall, perusing the goods on display and making purchases. An assortment of odors also struck him, mingling the diverse aromas of the city into something wholly unique.

Small groups of men wearing red sashes and covered in tattoos sauntered by with weapons hanging from their hips. When their eyes met his, some glared, while others favored him with wicked grins. No doubt the pirates of the city, or perhaps the city watch? Maybe both. Either way, they added just the right level of threatening ambiance. Diego had outdone himself once again.

In the port, under the watchful eye of the great keep, ships lay moored in the harbor, their dark hulls contrasted against the clear blue water. Men and women lingered on the docks while others moved cargo on and off the ships. There were even beggars sitting beside the roadway or in alleyways, calling out appeals to his charity as they spotted him. It was all so amazingly real.

Marcus made his way back to the Hungry Hog, satisfied with everything he'd seen. As he drew closer, he checked on Sam's location and found her just outside the city walls in the surrounding jungle. He thought about traveling to her location but decided that he'd ping her instead to let her know he'd arrived. He hoped she'd come to join him, but recently it'd felt like she'd been ignoring his notifications, forcing him to be the one to seek her out.

Outside the tavern Marcus noted the addition of more red-sashed men carousing together near the entrance. They eyed him as he entered, and he wondered if it was because of his clothing. Unlike his usual visits, he and Diego had decided that for today's introductions it would be less confusing to the participants if they wore more conventional clothing. Fascinating if the AI noticed that.

Inside, the Hungry Hog hadn't changed much. However, it was far louder and rowdier than the first time he'd experienced it. Diego had continued making modifications to its clientele and atmosphere and had added an upstairs with rooms. Those were to be the initial spawn zones for the new arrivals.

As he scanned the room, Marcus caught sight of Diego waving to him from a table. With a nod, he made his way over to his friend, receiving a slap on his ass as he passed one of the tables. Instead of reacting, he only shook his head and continued over to Diego who was grinning widely.

"So? What do you think?" Diego asked loudly, trying to be heard over all the voices and music that filled the room.

"Very impressive. It's like a living, breathing city. You've outdone yourself."

"Thank you. But again, it was a team effort," Diego said. "Being able to focus the team on a single project was a big help."

"It didn't go unnoticed," Marcus replied.

"Evan?"

"Yeah," Marcus said. "He's starting to question what we are doing."

"Do you think we have anything to worry about?" Diego asked.

"I'm not sure," Marcus said with a shrug. "Ellison doesn't think so."

"We don't have much choice right now, do we?"

"No, I suppose we don't." Marcus turned to look expectantly as the tavern door opened, his hopes falling as a man walked inside and made his way over to the bar. "Have you seen Sam?" he asked.

Diego shook his head. "No. Not for the last couple of visits. I've pinged her, but she doesn't respond. What about you, when did you last see her?"

"Yesterday, but it was the same for me. I had to go find her."

"Do you think she's acting strangely? She doesn't ever refer to me as Diego anymore, only Cristoval, and the same goes for calling her Sam. She'll only respond to Morrigan."

"Yeah, she's been staying in character lately," Marcus said with a sigh. "Sometimes it worries me, but then I think about everything she's been through, and I wonder if being 'Sam' right now is just too hard for her and it's easier to be Morrigan."

"Yeah, maybe you're right," Diego said somberly. "It must be really hard. But maybe we need to help her make this transition. I mean psychologically speaking, this has to be traumatic on a level we can't comprehend. I'd say she needs to talk to a therapist, but..." he gestured to the room around him. "Though we do have someone who might be able to help. Have you talked to Claire since Sam's... passing?"

"No," Marcus said, shaking his head. "The last time I saw her was at the memorial. She didn't even talk to me and left just after the services were over. I mean, for fuck's sake. She was there when Sam died. And even after watching her come back to life, Claire still hasn't come back to Synerdyne. She's basically abandoned us. Abandoned Sam."

"It's not because she doesn't love Sam," Diego said. "She just sees things differently than we do. But if anyone can help you understand Sam's psychology right now, it's Claire. Sometimes friends and colleagues get into disagreements, but that doesn't mean we aren't still working towards the same goal. Do you want me to call her and get the ball rolling?" Diego offered.

"Yeah, maybe you should." Marcus' thoughts turned to the memorial, remembering Claire grieving like everyone else. Like Sam was truly dead.

Diego gave him a sympathetic smile, reaching over the table to squeeze his shoulder.

A ping in Marcus' vision pulled him out of the moment. The way Diego suddenly cocked his head and released his grip told him he'd gotten one too. In the corner of his vision, he could see that Amir was calling and opened the channel, seconds before Diego did the same.

"Alright. Everything is prepped and ready to go on this end. How about you?" Amir asked.

"Yeah, we're ready for the first transfer," Marcus confirmed.

"We just need to get up to the room," Diego added, pushing himself off his stool.

Marcus did the same, the two of them heading to the rooms upstairs.

"Let me know when you're there and I will initiate the first transfer," Amir said. A dossier of information scrolled in Marcus' vision, noting the subject's name, gender and status, with a picture of the man hovering behind all of it.

Reaching the second floor, they made their way down to a doorway at the end of the hall, farthest from the stairwell and raucous clamor below. Opening the door, Marcus stepped inside and Diego followed. They entered a small room with only enough space for a bed and a small dresser. It had a single window for illumination, from which the rooftops of the city's buildings and the heavy boughs of palm trees could be seen.

"Alright, we're ready," Marcus said, as Diego closed the door behind him.

"Initiation in three, two, one," Amir declared.

Marcus looked down at the bed. One moment it was empty, then in a blink the body of a man lay there. Victor Kovalenko was as he appeared in his picture, a man in his middle years. His eyes opened almost immediately, and he sat up with a start, looking around. Other than a small wrap of linen around his waist, he was naked. They had discussed outfits for them but had decided to let the subjects make that decision for themselves.

Victor's eyes turned to them, and for a moment a look of confusion passed over him.

"Mr. Avery?"

"Yes, Mr. Kovalenko. It's me. And this is my colleague, Mr. Torres. I'm not sure if you've met."

"No, I don't think so," the man said, groggily. "Maybe?"

"I'm the lead designer," Diego said, with a smile. "You might have seen me around, but I don't think we've spoken. It's nice to meet you."

"Nice to meet you too," Victor said with a nod of his head.

"How are you feeling?" Marcus asked.

Victor kicked his legs over the side of the bed and stood up, twisting his body as though getting a feel for it. Outside the simulation he was a paraplegic, but both in Elysium and here he could move again.

"Good. Yeah. Where are we?" he asked, looking around the room. "Is this Elysium?"

"Not exactly. We're trying a new environment that we are

considering adding to the Elysium project. We would like you to experience it and give us your feedback."

"This one is more 'interactive' than Elysium," Diego added.

"Doesn't look as nice," Victor said, his eyes scanning the sparse room.

"It's more of a themed environment. Think ancient history. That sort of setting," Diego explained.

"We'd like for you to spend some time here," Marcus said. "If you decide you'd like to leave, just ping us."

"Can't I just leave like usual?" Victor asked, obviously confused.

"Not in this particular environment," Marcus said, soothingly. "It works a little differently here. But just let us know and we can pull you out."

Victor looked around again at the room dubiously, then down at his nakedness. "Can I get some clothes?"

"Absolutely," Diego smiled, pulling out a robe and sandals from the dresser and handing them to Victor. "Put these on and I'll take you somewhere where you'll have some options to choose from."

Victor did as he was bid slowly, his body language still uncertain.

"Excellent. Alright, follow me," Diego said, gesturing to the doorway.

"Go without me. I'll catch up," Marcus said, as the two men exited the room.

Closing the door, he pinged Amir.

"So? How'd it go?" Amir asked.

"It worked," Marcus said incredulously. "It fucking worked."

"Holy shit. You know what this means, right?"

"Yeah. It means nothing will ever be the same again."

CHAPTER 18

"**S**o? How's our girl doing?" Diego asked from the other side of the conference table. He was joined by the rest of the team. Amir, Jia, and Clive all sat watching Marcus expectantly from their chairs around the table.

He had to admit, it was a pretty brilliant idea on Jia's part to create a separate simulation space where they could meet. Just like Amir had wanted. It guaranteed them absolute privacy. Supposedly, it was based on the campus' architectural designs. One big square of glass to let in plenty of light, with no furniture other than the table and chairs. He wondered if the actual room would be this stark. According to Jia, eventually, the entire campus would be simulated. He hadn't realized that Jia had gotten spiked too, but he supposed it made sense. And with everything going on with Sam, it didn't surprise him that it had flown under his radar.

"Well. She's well. I mean, as well as she can be for a dead woman whose consciousness is being preserved in a simulation," Marcus said with a chuckle, shaking his head in disbelief at the words he was saying. "She's getting a little bored though, now that she's in there twenty-four seven. She's lonely."

"Yeah. That makes sense. I suppose it's kind of like when you're on vacation; at first everything is new and exciting, but the longer you stay, the more mundane everything becomes. I need to get my ass in there and play around with her," Diego said.

"She'd like that, I'm sure," Marcus said with a smile.

"I just need to find the time. With all the new testing of the duplicants, I only have enough energy to come home and crash at the end of the day."

"How's that going?" Marcus asked, Sam's request tickling at the back of his mind.

"It's good. I mean, I'm just the liaison," Diego replied with a quirk of his lips.

"The subjects have all integrated successfully," Jia added, matter-of-factly. "We have been gaining invaluable information from their mappings. We are now up to fourteen and have another three who have signed the pain agreement."

"Can we call it something else?" Marcus asked with a grimace. "That makes it sound so macabre."

"We can call it whatever you like," Jia replied.

"I'll try to think of something," Marcus muttered. "Three more? What changed their minds."

"I did," Clive said with a grin. "I've offered an incentive bonus of ten thousand dollars for anyone who agrees to the… let's call it 'enhanced stimulation testing'," he said, spreading his hands. "Those who already signed up have been duly compensated as well."

"So we're paying people to experience pain," Marcus reiterated, the words making him uneasy as he spoke them. Once again, his mind turned to Claire and her concerns.

"Should they have to do it for free?" Clive replied. "It seems they should get something for their troubles. Think of it as compensation for their cooperation. Never mind the fact that we are making them immortal."

"Well, I wouldn't go that far. Let's not get carried away," Marcus said, holding up his hands. "Amir, on average, how long are we keeping the duplicants in the simulation?"

"About six hours. With a one-hour prep for ourselves beforehand, and another hour of debrief after decommission."

"And have we seen any side effects or areas of concern?" Marcus asked.

Amir shook his head. "No. They are all stable."

"Do they recall their previous time in the simulation?"

"From what I understand, for them, it is as if they never left Sam's World," Diego said. "Now, part of our protocol is to have them lie down in a bed just before decommission as if they are going to sleep. So when they return to consciousness, it is more like they just woke up from a nap."

"And what is going on with their mapping while they are out of the simulation?" Marcus asked. "Do they dream?"

"What do you mean?" Amir asked, his brow twisting in confusion. "Nothing happens. We turn them off."

"Well, it stands to reason that you can't 'turn them off' entirely, right? Otherwise, you'd reset their consciousness mapping, since they are no longer linked to a host. So, in some ways, they must still be active."

"I would think of it more like a state of torpor," Jia said. "Stasis. They are no longer receiving any stimulus, so their mapping functions should be dormant."

Marcus nodded. "I suppose that makes sense. But maybe let's take a closer look, just to be sure."

Jia nodded, noting it on her tablet. Amir, however, looked contemplative.

"Amir? Something on your mind?" Marcus asked.

"What?" he said, shaken from his thoughts. "Oh. Well. What you just said. It makes me wonder about Sam. Unlike the duplicants, she remains in a constantly active state within the simulation. So does she sleep? Does she need it? We can't get any rest when we're in the simulation, because our brain is being stimulated constantly by the SynAPP, but that's not the case for Sam any longer. So what's happening to her?"

"I've never thought to ask her if she does," Marcus said. "Does her mapping show anything?"

"Without the SynAPP, I can't get any data about her mapping unless I manually download it. That is the purpose of decommissioning the others. But I'd be hesitant to do that with Sam. Unlike the others, she has no tether to a functioning brain any longer. If something goes wrong, if her mapping should get corrupted, it's not like we can start over with her," Amir explained. "To tell you the truth, I'd rather study the duplicants and see if we can get any further data that way."

"What about keeping them in the simulation longer?" Marcus offered. "Sam was saying that she's getting a little lonely dealing with AI all the time. But if she could spend some time with the patients' duplicants, maybe that could solve two problems at once. We could get more data regarding long-term exposure, and Sam could have actual intelligence to interact with."

"So you're suggesting we extend their time in the simulation in each session?" Amir asked.

"Yeah. And maybe instead of activating one at a time, we could activate multiple duplicants. At least the ones that have already been acclimated to Sam's World," Marcus said. "That way we can get long-term data from their decommission download without risking Sam."

"Do you think that is a good idea? Just sending them out on their own?" Diego asked.

"Why not? Sam does it all the time," Marcus said. "It's not like they won't respawn if something happens to them."

"Yeah, but… some of them are more timid than Sam," Diego countered. "You should see them walking around Freeport. They're like children."

"Well then let's make a list of those you think are the most capable and willing and work with them," Marcus offered.

"Yeah, maybe. I guess that'd be okay," Diego said with a nod. "I just feel responsible for them, you know. I'm the one who greets them and tucks them in at the end of the day. I'm their mother hen," he said with a smile.

"Well, I think it is a good idea," Clive said. "And I'm all for working within the subjects' comfort zones. But forgive me. I know I'm a layman when it comes to research, but don't we want data based on numerous experiences? Don't we want to know what effects, if any, a variety of sensations may have on the mapping? That includes fear, terror and pain. As well as the good ones."

"Sure, but these are people," Marcus said. "We can't just use them without their consent."

"Actually, they are not people," Jia interjected. "Not in the conventional sense, nor even in the way you have defined them in Elysium. Here they are a series of data points, untethered—as we have already established—to any physical form. The whole purpose of putting them into the simulation was to study them."

"And is that all Sam is?" Marcus retorted, feeling his blood rise. "A test subject?"

"No," Clive said, holding up a hand.

Looking in Clive's direction, Jia let her response die and settled calmly back into her chair.

"Sam is a higher form of life. A form of consciousness no longer restrained by physical form. But I think what Jia is suggesting is, unlike the duplicants—whom we have given this label because they are a duplication of their still living progenitors—the focus of this research is to better understand the relationship between an entity like Sam and the simulation so that we can ensure her existence into perpetuity. The duplicants still have a consciousness—their original consciousness—that is existing concurrently. I would argue that while their host still lives, they are but a shadow of themselves and not their true identity. So, at some point, they cannot continue to exist while their original consciousness persists."

"So, you're saying they aren't people, and we should delete them?" Amir asked, dubiously.

"No. But at some point, their experiences will cause them to create their own identity that will separate them from their original host," Clive clarified. "What I am suggesting is that Sam's World is the only place they can continue to exist, and while doing so they are an opportunity for us to better help Sam and those who come after her."

"This feels very… slippery," Diego said, looking at Amir and then Marcus.

Marcus thought about Clive's words and felt a little uneasy himself. He agreed with Diego's assessment. However, Clive wasn't wrong either. Now that the duplicants existed, the team had only two choices: delete them or let them exist in Sam's World. Once again, Claire's words rang in his head. This is what she had warned about. But what other choice did he have? Did Sam have? Ultimately, she was all that mattered.

"Well, the bell can't be unrung now," Marcus said. "Clive is right. They don't have any other choices for existence. So we either let them exist, or we don't. But they can't go back, and bringing them in and out of the simulation isn't a form of kindness either. If they are going to continue to exist, they will eventually have to learn how to adapt to their new environment, and coddling them is only prolonging that. I say we activate them all and work out a varying schedule for decommission. Start with the most eager and keep them in the longest, while the more timid ones can be on a shorter schedule until they get used to things. We need all the data we can get, and this is the best way to do it."

"So they're just going to live in Sam's World from now on?" Diego asked.

"Where else can they go?" Marcus replied. "Maybe we can work something out later, but for now it's either this or deactivation. Amir. Jia. Let's remember to keep an eye on their activity during stasis, too."

Jia gave a sharp nod, while Amir only bobbed his head thoughtfully.

"Alright, any other questions?" Marcus asked the table.

He was surprised when Clive raised his hand. Marcus nodded to acknowledge him.

"Yeah. I was wondering if maybe I could play a role in this too."

CHAPTER 19

"Once again, I'm out of the loop," Evan said, hands squeezed together tightly in front of him on his desk. "When was the decision made to start incorporating Sam's World into our research? Did I miss a meeting?"

Marcus didn't reply immediately and stared back at Evan in silence. He could see his friend was angry. Even angrier than last time. He knew of Clive's intention to focus on Sam's World, but he didn't realize it would happen so soon, or without Evan's knowledge. It made him wonder just how Clive was doing it. Did he have the board's approval, and if so, was Evan specifically kept out of it?

"Honestly, it's news to me, too," Marcus said truthfully. "Clive had said he was interested in putting some focus into Sam's World, but I thought you knew."

"Well, obviously not," Evan said, cooling down slightly. "That's twice now that I've been the last to know about major changes in our focus. That I know of. You'd tell me if there was anything else going on, right?" he asked, leaning forward intently.

Marcus remained quiet, not wanting to lie to his friend, but also knowing that he couldn't tell Evan what was truly going on.

"I'm sorry," Evan said after a moment, falling back into his chair with a sigh. "You're still dealing with Sam's passing, and it's not fair of me to be piling this on you. It's just that ever since Ellison joined us, I feel like I'm losing control of the company. And I know it was my idea," he said, holding up a hand. "But I'm worried that maybe I made a mistake. What do you think? Do you want us to shift away from Elysium?"

Marcus gave him a sympathetic smile and shrugged. "I mean, I think we've done everything we can with Elysium. At least from our initial mission statement. It functions as we intended as a place for convalescent and palliative care. I mean, we can always add to it and continue to try and make improvements, but I don't know how much further we can take it. I think what Clive is looking at is the possibilities of extending our research into other areas, as well as marketability."

"Yeah, I guess so," Evan said, nodding. "And are you okay with using Sam's World this way? I mean, I know it was originally created as a possible market, but I also know how personal it became for you."

"I'd rather see it used than abandoned," Marcus said. "Sam put a lot of work into it. It was her baby. So I think focusing on it is a good way to honor her," he said, trying to use the truth to minimize the deceit in his words.

"I suppose I never considered it in that light." Evan let out another sigh. "Well, if you don't have a problem with it, I can get behind it. But I've got to figure out whether or not Ellison is purposefully keeping me out. You've been spending a lot of time with him, right? Do you think you could find out? I mean, don't ask him directly, but you know, maybe ask a few questions?"

Marcus already knew the answer but nodded anyway. "Sure. I'll see what I can find out. But don't worry. I'm sure whatever is going on has nothing to do with you."

"Well, that's sort of the problem, isn't it?" Evan said with a tight smile.

"Don't worry about Evan," Clive said, hefting the mug of ale before him. "You and I both know why he can't be involved in this."

"But can't we come up with some excuse that will at least make him feel more included?" Marcus offered. "I think he's just used to being the one in control."

"Well we can't always be in control, Marcus. Isn't that the point of all this?" Clive asked, raising his hands above his head to gesture at the tavern, the ale spilling over the rim of his mug.

"Maybe. But some people are better at handling it than others."

Clive grinned at him wolfishly. In the simulation, he had chosen to look like a man two decades younger, with the physique to go with it. Dressed in a tasset, leather tunic and sandals, with the pelt of a great cat draped over his back, he wore his hair long to his shoulders. And even though he still had streaks of gray through it and around his temples, it reminded Marcus of a lion's mane.

"We can't all be in control. Sometimes those who don't possess enough vision and purpose have to step aside and let those who do lead the way. Let Evan play in his wheelhouse, and we'll play in ours, yeah?" Clive said, gesturing with his mug for Marcus to lift his.

Marcus obliged, and with a smile, Clive knocked the two mugs together in a toast, spilling more ale across the table, before lifting it to his mouth and drinking heartily. Marcus smirked at the sight before drinking from his own, surprised at how eagerly the man took to the trappings of Sam's World.

"So, what were you thinking you'd do here in Freeport?" Marcus asked, lowering his mug back to the table.

"I'm not sure yet. I think I'll just wander around a bit and get a feel for the place on my own. Got to find my footing here before I know how best to help," Clive said, sliding an arm across his mouth to wipe away the foam on his lips. "Thank you again for giving me your trust. What about you?"

"I'm going to go spend some time with Sam."

"Of course. Stupid question," Clive said with a grin.

"No, it's not," Marcus said, shaking his head. "I should probably be doing a lot more to help, but I feel torn about spending any time here without her."

"That's the most important thing you can do right now," Clive said, reaching across the table to clasp a solid hand on Marcus' shoulder. "Don't worry about the rest, we've got it handled. In a lot of ways, you're still adjusting to all this. Same as her. You need each other right now."

Marcus met the other man's eyes and smiled. "Thanks. I appreciate that. I guess it is going to take a little time for both of us. It's just, in here, she's okay. Like her old self. And it's easy to forget."

"Just remember how fortunate you both are. You still have the woman you love, and she has gained life where death cannot touch her. You are standing where no one has ever stood. Together. Like God at the moment of creation."

"Well, I think that's a bit grandiose," Marcus chuckled, lifting his mug for another drink. "But I take your point."

"I'm curious about something, and I hope I don't offend, but what's it like to… you know, have intimate relations here?" Clive asked, arching an eyebrow.

Marcus coughed into his mug, surprised by the question, causing Clive to laugh.

"Sorry," Clive said with a chuckle. "Didn't mean to catch you off guard like that, but I figured you'd know."

Marcus took a moment to clear his throat and nodded, feeling his ears growing warm. "Yeah. We've… I mean, of course."

"How good is it?" Clive pressed. "I mean, in comparison."

"It's pretty much the same. But different for everyone," Marcus explained. "It's kind of like what I told you about the ice cream. Since the SynAPP uses your previous perceptions, your experience is going to be based, not on the actual sensations—there are none— but instead, on your brain's recreation of that sensation. So, the closest I might approximate it is to a wet dream. Sometimes it can be more intense and sometimes less. But having been with Sam my whole adult life, she's the only person I've ever experienced it with. So, for us, I think it feels as close to 'normal' as possible. Our perceptions have been set for years. Which is to say, it feels like I would expect. Though I would add one caveat, and that is when you are here you are not restrained by your actual physicality. So, things can get more… *flexible*."

"Really? You've only ever slept with Sam?" Clive asked, with an amused grin.

"Yep."

"And what about her?"

"I would hope she'd have the same answer," Marcus said, feeling his ears grow even warmer and hiding his face in his mug.

"Fascinating," Clive said, taking a drink.

"Which? The explanation, or the fact that we've only slept with one another?"

"Both," Clive said with a hearty laugh.

Marcus smiled sheepishly. Taking one last drink from the mug, he put it down and took a step back from the table. "Okay, I think I'm going to go find Sam. I hope you enjoy your time in Freeport."

Clive lifted his mug in salute with another wolfish grin. "I'm sure I'll find it illuminating. And I hope I have the chance to meet her soon. You two have fun," he said with a wink.

Marcus offered him a tight smile and stepped away from the table, bringing up the simulation protocol. According to the AAIP, Sam wasn't far and was approaching the city gates. He hesitated for a moment, tracking her as she drew nearer, and realized she was approaching the tavern. Changing his focus from the protocol to the door, he watched it swing open as she strolled in confidently.

Wearing the skimpy leathers he had made for her, she walked with confidence; all her previous concerns about their revealing nature appeared to be gone. Across her shoulders, she carried the carcass of a small deer, its head lolling and legs hanging limply to either side of her neck. Striding into the tavern with a wicked grin, she stopped in the middle of the room.

"Who's hungry?" she asked loudly and was answered by a raucous cheer from the tavern's patrons.

With a smile, she made her way over to the bar, only bothering to wink over her shoulder when Diego's programmed drunkard slapped her loudly on the ass, and dropped the carcass onto the bar. The tavern keeper looked down at the animal, and after a moment, nodded and poured her a mug of ale. Taking the mug, she left the animal to the man and turned around to gaze at the tavern, leaning back with her elbows resting on the bar.

"Well, it seems Sam is thriving here," Clive said behind him, and it took a moment for Marcus to register his words. "That's her, isn't it?"

"What? Oh yeah, she's always enjoyed getting into character," he said over his shoulder with a grin. "Guess you'll get your wish."

"I've got to say, she lights up a room," Clive said. "Like a force of nature. I'm glad to see, after everything she's been through, that she's embracing her new existence."

"Yeah," Marcus said slowly, still studying Sam's demeanor. He was used to her confidence, especially when she got into character as Morrigan, but he'd never seen it on full display from the outside before. That was the point of losing yourself in a character, he knew, but he realized that a small part of him figured she'd always played it up for his sake. "It really does seem so."

"Oi! Aer!" Sam said, catching sight of him and grinning broadly as she strode over to their table. "When did ye get into town, boyo?"

Slamming her mug on the table, she reached up to wrap her arms around his neck and kissed him deeply. Marcus returned the kiss, wrapping his arms around her, but was a little surprised that she would show such brazen affection in front of strangers. As she continued to kiss him, he felt Clive's eyes on them and reached up to gently disengage her. Sam only smiled against his lips and pressed herself more firmly against him, tightening her grip and pushing his back against the table.

Embarrassment washed over him, and he pushed at her more forcefully. She continued to press her body against his but pulled away from the kiss with a smile. Keeping one arm around his neck, she reached for her mug with the other, finally catching sight of Clive.

"Oh, don't mind us, boyo," she said with a grin to Clive. "Haven't seen this hunk of man for a bit. We're just catchin' up."

Taking another drink, she ran her tongue over her top lip and leaned in for another forceful kiss. Struggling under her, Marcus used his full strength to pull her arms from around him and pushed her away, causing her mug to fall from the table and spill its contents to the floor.

"Sam," he said meaningfully as he disengaged from her grip.

Sam stepped back and looked down at the mug. "Now what'd ye go and do that for?" she said, looking from the mug to him. "I was just sayin' 'hello' to ye."

"I wish someone would say 'hello' to me that way," Clive barked a laugh. "No need to be embarrassed, my boy."

"Aye. Careful or yer gonna make a girl feel unwanted," she said, leaning back on her heels and putting a hand on her hip. "And ye," she said looking at Clive. "Ye just gonna ogle my tits and ass, or are ye gonna buy me another drink?"

Clive gave her a wolfish grin and laughed. "It'd be my pleasure," he said, standing up from his stool. "I'll be right back."

Marcus watched Clive as he made his way over to the bar before turning back to Sam. "Sam, what are you doing?"

"Sam? Has it been so long that ye forgot my name already, boyo?" she asked, leaning forward to press a finger against his chest. "Or are ye tryin' to make me jealous?"

"Come on. That's *Clive Ellison*," he said with emphasis, gesturing to the man with his eyes.

"So? Should I be impressed? What, ye embarrassed to have me kissin' on ye?"

"Kind of. He's the one we have to rely on to keep all this running."

Sam looked over her shoulder and watched Clive for a second. "Him?"

"Yeah. You remember Clive Ellison, right?" Marcus pressed.

Sam closed her eyes for a moment and furrowed her brow.

"Yeah," she said slowly. Opening her eyes, she didn't say anything else but turned back to watch Clive as he walked over with three new mugs of ale in his hands.

"There you are, oh mighty huntress," Clive said with a grin, holding a mug out to Sam.

She took it from him absentmindedly with a nod and eased onto a stool. Beside her, Marcus kept hold of her other hand, giving it a little squeeze. Sam looked over at him with a tight smile, returning the squeeze.

"Sam, this is Clive Ellison. He's here to spend some time in Sam's World," Marcus explained.

"Well, I must say it is a pleasure to finally meet you, Sam," Clive said, sitting back down on his stool and pushing a mug across the table to Marcus. "I like this side of you. It's very provocative. I'm glad to see you've found a way to make this place your own."

"Yeah," Sam said slowly, before taking a drink to hide her face in her mug. "It's nice to meet you too."

"How have you been?" Clive continued. "I know a lot has happened over the last few weeks. It's got to be a big adjustment."

Sam lowered her mug and looked over to Clive as though seeing him for the first time. "What? Oh, well, I spent a lot of time here before... you know..."

"The *event*," Clive offered.

"Yeah, so I'm pretty comfortable here. This place was always my baby," she said, looking around with a fond smile. "It's nice to see it finally coming together like I always imagined."

Marcus squeezed her hand again, and this time when she looked over at him her smile was more affectionate.

"Does it feel any different now, since the *event*?" Clive asked.

Sam thought about his question for a moment, then shrugged. "I suppose not. Other than the fact that I can't get any pizza here," she said with a laugh.

"Well, we could always arrange for that," Marcus replied.

"No," she said quickly, shaking her head. "It'd ruin the atmosphere. I like it the way it is."

"So, you really get into character here," Clive noted.

"Yeah," Sam gave an embarrassed laugh. "Maybe a little too much."

"No. No. I like it," he said. "Like you said, 'adds to the atmosphere'. And you really pull it off," he added, leaning to the side to look past the table at her outfit.

Sam blushed and crossed her legs, hugging her mug to her chest and pulling in on herself self-consciously.

"Thanks," she said. "I don't normally wear things like this, but Marcus always liked it."

"I can see why. He's a lucky man. If you don't mind me saying," Clive said, lifting his mug to Marcus. "A woman as beautiful as you has nothing to be embarrassed about in any outfit. Isn't that what a place like this is for? To escape and take on the role of the person you want to be? You'll get no judgments from me. I'm just glad to see you thriving here."

"Thank you," she replied, glancing over to Marcus for support. With her persona of Morrigan stripped away, the old Sam and her anxieties had returned. Strange as it was, he found that realization comforting. He gave her a smile and squeezed her hand again.

"So, have you run into any of the duplicants yet?" Marcus asked, looking to change the subject.

Sam took a moment then nodded. "A few, I think. Though I've only spoken to a couple. Most of them are still trying to find their legs here: wandering around the city, getting acclimated to things like buying food at the market, and trying to avoid trouble. I've explained that the pirates are like amusement park actors or animatronics. Diego programmed them to sneer and look threatening, but they won't hurt you in the city. But it's still taking them some time to get used to that."

"Do you know if any have ventured out of the city? Like you?" Clive asked.

Sam shrugged.

"Maybe. I don't have the ability to keep track of them. If they have, I doubt it's too many of them," she said.

Marcus brought up the protocol again and searched for the duplicants. Little blue dots appeared in his vision, most clustered within the city, but he noted two that were currently outside the city walls. "Looks like a couple are roaming in the jungle. Do you want to go talk to them?" he asked.

"Why not," Clive said, leaning back to take a long drink from his mug. With a satisfied sigh, he slammed it down on the table, running his forearm across his lips.

"Sam?" Marcus inquired.

"Sure," she said after a moment. "But not with the AAIP. How far away are they?"

"Not far," Marcus said, checking the protocol again. "Looks like one is at the river, and another in the nearby hills. We could reach them pretty easily."

"Well then, drink up, and let's go on an adventure," Clive said with his wolfish grin.

Sam looked to Marcus with a smirk, arching a questioning eyebrow, and brought her mug to her lips. Marcus followed her lead, and the two leaned their heads back and drank heavily, mimicking Clive's example. The ale's familiar hoppy taste brought with it a satisfying bite, and he wondered if drinking two liters of it would also bring with it an accompanying buzz.

Finishing their drinks, they put their mugs down and stepped away from the table to make their way out of the tavern. As they walked onto the road leading to the city gates, Marcus used the protocol to guide them in the direction of the duplicants. Red-sashed pirates loitering near the exit sneered at them as they passed, with one catcalling to Sam. Marcus was surprised at the specificity of his heckling, noting how it was tailored to Sam's outfit and body. He wondered if it was programmed to be random, like the patron in the tavern, or targeted specifically to women.

Ignoring the pirates, they walked beneath the great stone arch of the gateway, its heavy, iron portcullis suspended threateningly above them. On the other side of the walls, there were no buildings, only a cleared section of the jungle stretching for a few hundred meters around the perimeter of the city, before giving way to the dense jungle. Through that clearing, hugging the walls of the city, was a swift-moving river of clear blue water that acted as a moat. A short wooden bridge created the only path across to the other side, and it creaked under their heavy footfalls as they walked across.

Marcus checked the protocol once more and saw that their target was still near, just a short distance ahead. Pointing in the duplicant's direction, he followed the river, admiring the aged look of the city's stone walls on the other side. As they drew closer, Marcus saw a lone man crouching over some blossoming flowers about the size of his head. He was middle-aged, but even dressed in a short toga and sandals, Marcus recognized him. The man looked up with a start as they approached, his posture betraying his uncertainty.

"Hey there, Mr. Theodorou. It's me, Marcus. Marcus Avery," Marcus called, slowing down and holding up a hand in greeting.

For a moment the man considered the three of them cautiously.

"Mr. Avery?" he asked after a long moment.

"That's right. These are my friends, Sam and Clive. We're all from Synerdyne. We just wanted to check in on you and see how you're doing."

"Synerdyne," the man muttered thoughtfully. "Oh, right. Yes. I'm fine. Have you come to take me out?"

"No, sir. Not unless you want us to," Marcus said. "We just wanted to make sure you're getting along okay. What are you doing out here?"

"Oh, I just wanted to study these flowers. They remind me of some kind of protea cynaroides, but much larger than I've ever seen."

"Well, I'm sure that was probably their inspiration," Marcus explained with a smile. "If you like, I can ask the team that designed them."

"What? Oh no. That's not necessary," Mr. Theodorou said. "I just find them fascinating. I'm thinking of keeping a journal of all the plants I find here, but the most interesting ones seem to be out in the jungle. I'm just working up the nerve to venture away from the city and see for myself."

"How did you learn that?" Clive asked.

"From some of the vendors inside," the man replied. "They told me they get their most interesting flowers from deeper in the jungle."

Marcus thought about the man's answer and wondered if they were programmed to say that in order to entice the duplicants to go out and explore. If so, then Diego and his team were hitting it out of the park.

"So how are you liking it so far?" Clive asked.

Mr. Theodorou looked around at the surrounding city walls and jungle and shrugged. "I suppose it's a nice change of pace, though I'm not sure I see the point."

"The point is to have fun," Sam said, and Marcus thought maybe he heard a bit of defensiveness in her tone.

"What Sam is saying is that this was all created as a part of Synerdyne's entertainment division, unlike the therapeutic environment of Elysium," Marcus interjected. "We thought we might let you and the others get an exclusive test of it so we can get your feedback."

"Yeah, that's what the other guy told me, too," the man said, and Marcus assumed he must be referring to Diego. "But I mean, what's the point of the game?"

"To do whatever you want," Sam replied, again her voice harder than he'd have expected. "To get out and explore. To fucking live a little."

"Oh, hey," Marcus said, turning to face Sam. "Let's calm down, okay?"

Taking Sam by the shoulders, he gave Mr. Theodorou a smile over his shoulder, before turning his attention to Sam.

"So have flowers always been an interest of yours?" Clive asked, stepping towards the man and taking attention away from Sam.

"Hey, ease up a little," Marcus whispered. "He's not used to a place like this. What's gotten into you?"

"It's the same old shit, just like in Elysium," Sam said, glowering. "They just want to fucking garden and sit around talking."

"Come on, babe. Be a little more understanding. Mr. Theodorou is eighty-five years old. He's got different sensibilities. You can't expect him to be roaming about fighting giant apes and crocodiles."

"Why not?" Sam shot back. "In here, he can be anything. I mean just look at him, he obviously doesn't see himself as that old."

"I know. I know. But that doesn't mean he has the same drive as you. Plus, he's still getting acclimated."

"I just don't want this place to get turned into some kind of retirement home," she said bitterly. "That's all Elysium is. No challenges. No problems. Just fucking bland."

Marcus could feel the tension in her muscles and gently squeezed her shoulders. "That's not going to happen. Look, if some people want to just sit around in the city or simply drink in the tavern or study flowers, so what? Let them. After all, if they all started becoming badass warriors like you, it might start to feel a little less special when you return to the city with a trophy, right?"

Sam's scowl slowly turned to a sheepish smile.

"Yeah," she said, shaking her head in embarrassment. "I'm sorry. I don't know what got into me."

"Don't worry about it, babe. You've got nothing to apologize for," he said, pulling her into a hug. "I get it. This is your home now and you like it the way it is. Don't worry. You'll always be the priority. We won't do anything that you don't want us to."

"Thank you," Sam said, clinging to him for a moment.

"You can thank me later," Marcus said, looking down at her with a grin. "But not in front of the billionaire funding all this, okay?"

"What?" she said with a laugh, her face twisted in amusement.

"…I don't know. Marcus?" Clive called.

Marcus gave Sam another smile and let go of her, walking over to the two men. "What's that?" he asked, smiling at Mr. Theodorou and looking for any hint of what they might be asking of him.

"Jason here was asking if he has to worry about any poisonous plants," Clive reiterated helpfully.

"Oh. No, I don't think so. Do you mean its edibility or through skin exposure?"

"Both, I warrant," Clive said. "He was wondering what he might run into if he went into the jungle."

"Oh," Marcus said, catching up to the conversation. "As far as I know, the plants are safe, but I'll also ask the team about that. I can tell you there are some wild animals out in the jungle though, as well as a few other hazards. However, you shouldn't let that stop you. Did Diego tell you about the respawn protocol?"

"Yes. I think so. Something about, if I die, I'll wake up in the city," Mr. Theodorou said, rubbing his chin. "Though I can't say the idea of dying sounds very pleasant."

"It's not so bad," Sam said, stepping up to stand between Marcus and Clive. "I've done it plenty of times. You basically pass out and wake up in the tavern."

"What about the pain?"

Sam shrugged and gave the man a mischievous grin, her demeanor changing to become more confident as she straightened her back and put her hands on her hips.

"What's life without a little pain, eh boyo?"

CHAPTER 20

“So, why'd you want to meet here, and not in the simulation?”
Marcus asked, looking at Diego from across the small table
they'd taken in the corner of the coffee shop.

Holding his cup in both hands, Diego gave him an uncertain
look. “I don't know. Maybe I'm just being paranoid, but with all the
changes and people Ellison has brought in, I just wanted to make
sure this stayed between us.”

“Is everything okay?” Marcus asked.

“With me? Yeah. I'm fine,” Diego said, then leaned forward,
lowering his voice. “It's about Sam's World.”

“Okay,” Marcus said, trying to figure out why Diego thought it
necessary to talk to him in private. “Is there something wrong? Do
we need to worry about Sam?” he asked as his mind began to play
through more and more concerning scenarios.

“What? No, I don't think Sam's in any danger,” Diego said.
“But I've noticed something over the last couple of days. At first, I
thought maybe it was my imagination, but now I think maybe it's
something else.”

“Okay. Well, what is it?” Marcus asked, wondering what could
have his friend so concerned.

"It's the avatars. You know, the NPCs and the other assets. They're behaving in ways that we didn't program," Diego said. "At least, there's no code I can find that would explain some of the things they are doing."

"Like what?"

"All sorts of things. They are saying things they were never given lines for, deviating from their initial paths and duties, going beyond the parameters we set for them," Diego explained. "Did you know that the tavern keeper is now running a brothel out of the tavern? We didn't program him to do that."

"No shit?" Marcus laughed. "Well, I suppose he was created to provide entertainment and refreshment for his customers. Maybe something in the programming allowed for an unforeseen evolution in his perception of what that entails?"

"Sure. And they are designed to be autonomous within the boundaries of their set protocol," Diego conceded. "But explain to me how he got citizen avatars of the city to take on the role of sex workers for him. And a fighting pit has been formed down by the docks in one of the warehouses, with avatars betting on the outcomes."

Diego grabbed his tablet and pulled up a document, scrolling through it with his finger. "I've got a whole list of anomalies. Gangs have formed among the less savory avatar personas, fighting for domination of different parts of the city. Some of the pirates have begun accosting people in the street. Thieves have been stealing from the vendors in the market. But it's not only crime, either. Some dockworkers are now blacksmiths and merchants. One woman is acting as a prophet of some sort of sea god, remarking on the omens she sees. New houses are being built. Built, Marcus! They are going out into the jungle and cutting down trees for timber. Every building in the city was placed there when we created it. None of this is in the program."

"Any ideas why it might be happening?" Marcus asked, intrigued.

"Well, this is more your wheelhouse. That's why I wanted to talk to you," Diego said. "The AAIP is an autonomous artificial intelligence, right? So maybe it's making changes to the program. The only thing, though, is I don't know why it would. For instance, if the AAIP decided to expand the city, it would just create new buildings. Or why the avatars are acting so... human... in their thinking."

Marcus leaned back in his chair and considered what Diego was asking. He stopped thinking of the avatars as individuals and broke them down into assets, no different from a rock or tree. Assets were designed with parameters that the AAIP used in order to represent them in the game. A tree was a living organism, unlike a rock, and made of organic fibers and cells. It could grow, it could be damaged, and it could die. It required water and sunlight to thrive. It had bark that was also made of different cells than its interior, which gave it a certain texture and attributes. With these parameters, the program knew, not only how to manage the trees in Sam's World, but how to replicate them and their reactions to outside forces.

But a human avatar was more complicated. It had all the same parameters as the tree: organic cellular structure, a need for nourishment, but also a more unique and detailed protocol of reactions. The only emotions they had were the ones they were programmed to contain, not really emotions at all, just the pantomiming of human interactions. For the AAIP to deviate them from these paths, it would need some sort of map to follow. A thought struck Marcus, but he was hesitant to voice it.

"Does anyone else realize this?" he asked instead.

Diego shook his head. "Since I'm the only one from the team who spends time there and knows how they should be acting, I'm really the only one who would notice. I mean, did you realize something was off?"

"No," Marcus said, shaking his head. "I mean, I noticed some peculiar things, but I thought you'd just gotten creative."

"The thing is, it's made the city more unpredictable, but so far hasn't thrown anything out of whack. It's actually really fascinating," Diego said. "But I can't say that there won't eventually be a tipping point. So I figured we should look into this, and I didn't want to spook Ellison, or make it into a bigger deal than it might be."

Marcus nodded. "No. That was smart. But we should probably bring Amir in on this and see what he thinks."

"I thought about it," Diego said. "But he's been working closely with Jia, and I didn't want to make things difficult for him."

"He knows the AAIP better than anyone," Marcus pointed out. "We should get him on board."

"Okay, I'll reach out to him," Diego said. "Sorry to make this a whole thing. I don't want you to worry about Sam."

"Don't be sorry," Marcus said. "I'd rather know so we can do something about it before it's too late. Just keep me in the loop and let me know if you discover anything. I'll keep my eye out while I'm in there with Sam."

Marcus paused for a moment, thoughts of his recent encounters with Sam flooding his mind.

"Hey, have you noticed anything off about Sam recently?" he asked.

Diego's lips twisted in consideration. "Well, she doesn't seem to spend a lot of time in town, so I actually don't see her that often. But off? I don't think so. But it's hard to tell because she's always in character the last few times I've seen her. Uses that accent of hers and refers to me as Cristoval and only reacts to being called Morrigan. But Sam's always lost herself in the simulation, more than the rest of us. Why? Do you think something is off?"

Marcus shrugged. "I don't know. That's pretty much been my experience, too. But sometimes it feels like I'm not actually talking to Sam. I'm talking to Morrigan. It's probably nothing. Sam's been through a lot, and maybe she needs a little departure from the reminders of what happened," he shrugged again. "But I can't help feeling that things are off. I think a part of me wants things to be okay, and I just keep hoping they'll get better. But they aren't and it's not fair to Sam."

"You know who might be able to help…" Diego said, arching an eyebrow. "I did reach out to her like you asked."

Marcus let out a sigh. "So you've been talking to Claire?"

"A little. Just keeping her in the loop. Letting her know that Sam is okay. I haven't told her any details about Ellison, or anything she wasn't already aware of," Diego said. "Don't look at me like that. She's still my friend, Marcus. And she still cares."

"Well if she cares so much, why hasn't she reached out to me?"

"Maybe because she's still coming to terms with things and knows you're working through your own shit right now. You can be a little…"

"What?" Marcus prodded. "Self-absorbed?"

"Well, I was going to say: intense, stubborn, irrational. But, yeah, sometimes," Diego said with a smile. "All I'm saying is that maybe you should actually go and talk to her and work through some of this shit. If not for yourself, then for Sam. You know Sam would tell you the same thing," he said, taking a drink from his cup while arching an eyebrow.

"Goddamnit," Marcus said with a sigh. "I'll think about it. Why can you be so candid with me this way, but no one else ever is?"

"Because I'm a lovable scamp, and you can't stay mad at me," Diego said with a broad smile, batting his eyelashes at Marcus in an exaggerated fashion.

"More like the court jester," Marcus replied, rolling his eyes.

Diego shrugged. "Well, we all have our roles to play."

"So? What do you think?" Clive asked, standing before the giant stone throne that sat at the end of the audience chamber, his arms spread wide.

Standing below him, Marcus looked up at the chair and the

rest of the room. Both were stark; made of dark, gray stone hewn roughly without any ornamentation. A few thin slits in the wall acted as windows to let in only a little light, leaving burning torches to make up for the lack of illumination. Above them, the ceiling rose twenty or more feet, until it could be barely seen in the shadows. The whole place reminded Marcus of some villain's lair.

"So, you want to take the castle as your home in the city?" Marcus asked.

"Why not? It's not as though it is occupied. And after all, I am used to having a big home," Clive said with a grin. Settling down onto the throne, he rested his chin on a fist. "How do I look?"

"Very stoic," Marcus said with a smirk.

"Shall I be a cruel or fair ruler?" Clive mused, taking up a grandiose Shakespearian accent.

"So you're a ruler now too?" Marcus scoffed.

"Well, I do have a castle," Clive said with a grin.

"That's not quite compatible with the name Freeport, is it?"

Clive shrugged. "Perhaps I am the reason the city is free."

"Well, if that reasoning works for you, who am I to judge?" Marcus conceded.

"I could be the Pirate King or something," Clive offered, spreading his arms out wide.

"You can be whatever you like," Marcus said. "You want to be king? Fine by me."

"So, how are things going?" Clive asked, settling back into the chair. "Any issues with the duplicants?"

"No. According to Diego they seem to be acclimating well, some a little faster than others, but he's started introducing them to one another," Marcus said. "And since many of them already know each other from Elysium, it's helped the more timid ones become more amenable to new experiences within the simulation when they see people they know enjoying themselves."

"And Sam? How is our girl doing?" Clive asked.

"She's well enough. I think she's still coming to terms with things, though. She needs some time."

"That makes perfect sense. She is dealing with something no one has ever dealt with before in all of human history," Clive said. "It's not like anyone can give her advice on the matter. It's going to take some time. But you two are okay, right?"

"Yeah, of course," Marcus said, feeling a bit defensive at the question. "I'm about to go find her."

"Good. I'm glad to hear it. She's quite a woman," Clive said with a smile. "She took me out to fight those Half-men at their temple. I've got to admit it was pretty scary, but she didn't hesitate. Not for a moment. Just charged right in. That persona of hers is pretty amazing."

Marcus hadn't realized that Sam and Clive had spent any time together in Sam's World, and was surprised that she would have offered. Sam was always so reserved around people she didn't know well. Then again, this was her home now and she had to find ways to occupy her time.

"Yeah. She's always really enjoyed getting into character as Morrigan," he replied.

"And how are you doing with all this?" Clive asked.

"How do you mean?" Marcus asked. "I'm fine."

"I know we are all concerned for Sam, but it's easy to overlook the fact that your life has been turned upside down by all of this too," Clive said, sympathetically. "It can't be easy."

"Sam is safe. That's all I need," Marcus replied. "For a long time, I watched as she was slowly slipping away. I was terrified. But now she is safe and more like her old self than ever. I couldn't be happier."

"That's good to hear, Marcus. I am happy for you," Clive said.

"And what about you? Amir says you've been spending a lot of time in Sam's World."

"Oh," Clive chuckled. "All is well with me. You know, after a certain point, the things that once mattered so much in life start to lose their appeal. I mean, once you have as much money as I do, what else is there to achieve? Everything runs on its own without me. My investments all have teams of accountants, lawyers, and board members that keep the machine running without me having to do much of anything. But here it all feels different. It feels new. Like I have things to achieve again."

"I suppose that makes sense," Marcus said with a nod.

"You'll know what I mean soon enough, my boy," Clive grinned. "When we perfect this and Synerdyne reveals it to the world, you won't ever need money again."

"Money never much mattered to me," Marcus said with a shrug. "So long as Sam and I had enough to live comfortably. That's all that mattered."

"That's a heartwarming sentiment," Clive said, standing up from the throne and walking down the dais to put an arm around Marcus' shoulders. "Well, now you both have a whole new world to experience together. To make whatever life you see fit, and I wish you both the best." Clive turned, guiding Marcus as he walked. "I've some planning of my own to do, so I won't keep you any longer. Go find your woman and enjoy yourselves," he said, stopping at the exit of the chamber.

"Thanks," Marcus said. "Let Diego know if you need anything for the castle."

"Oh, I will," Clive said with a smile, patting Marcus on the back. "Don't worry about that."

As Marcus exited through the castle gates and onto the city streets, he brought up the protocol in his vision, tracking Sam's location. Her dot appeared on the other side of the city, near the docks. Marcus debated jumping to the location but decided to walk there instead. It would give him a chance to observe the people of the city and see if he noticed the things Diego had been talking about.

Following the main avenue, which passed in front of the castle and curved like a horseshoe through the city, he made his way to the docks. Men and women streamed past him as he walked, some going about their daily tasks, while others milled about and loitered in the alleyways. Without knowing their parameters, it was hard for him to distinguish whether they were acting by design or not. Women smiled at him, looking demurely away and then giggling behind his back as he passed, while tradesmen shouted at him to buy their wares. He figured that must all be programmed.

Reaching the docks, he took note of the ships in the harbor and the men working around them. Some of the men moved about unloading cargo and stacking it on the wharf. That could only be the programming since the cargo didn't actually come from any trade. However, other men were squatting near the docks playing some sort of dicing game and gambling with silver coins. They all looked like dockhands, but they were ignoring the cargo, and he couldn't help but wonder if they were an anomaly. He made a note to report it to Diego, just in case.

Along the length of the docks were several warehouses, and checking the protocol, it appeared that Sam was in one of them. As he drew nearer he noted a large group of people lingering outside, laughing and talking in groups, with what sounded like even more people inside yelling and shouting. Concern washed over Marcus, and he hurried to the entrance, only to find it packed with people.

With an effort, he pushed his way through the crowd, their cheers and boos rising and falling in a deafening sound. As he moved closer to the center, Marcus saw that the people were gathered around a wide circle in the center of the warehouse where two people were squaring off, faces bloody and fists raised. And to his shock, one of them was Sam.

She was facing off against a man covered in muscles and tattoos who stood at least a foot taller than she. His face was bruised in places, and he stared at Sam with vicious intent, his fists held in front of his face. For her part, Sam was bouncing from foot to foot, a wicked smile on her face. She, too, had some bruises, and a trickle of blood ran down her face in a line from a cut above her eyebrow. Marcus was tempted to freeze the simulation but forced himself to wait. Sam never liked it when he did that, and she seemed to be having fun. It couldn't be any worse than her fight with the ape.

Marcus stayed silent and watched from the crowd as the two fought. The man came at Sam, viciously swinging his giant fists, but she nimbly danced away from him. Her opponent pursued and Sam continued to retreat, moving just in time to avoid his swings. Undeterred, he didn't let up, keeping the pressure on her as he tried to corner her against the crowd. She moved, darting forward only to retreat, looking for an opening. Without realizing it, she suddenly found herself trapped against the crowd with no escape. The other fighter descended upon her, capitalizing on her mistake and connecting a gruesome punch to her cheek.

Sam's head whipped back from the blow, and as she staggered, the man sent another to her ribs. The crowd burst into deafening cheers and hooting as the man continued his assault. It was hard for Marcus to watch, and he brought up the protocol again in his vision, ready to freeze the simulation. However, he hesitated again, continuing to observe the brutality.

As she fell back into the crowd, Sam was pushed forward violently by the spectators and onto her opponent, allowing him to lock his arms around her midsection. Lifting her off her feet, he squeezed her in his massive arms, looking to break her ribs. Sam cried out, arching her back and pushing futilely to escape his grasp. With another cry, she flung her head back, only to bring it forward again, smashing her forehead into the man's nose.

With a howl the man let go of her and staggered back, clutching his face. Sam didn't miss a beat and surged forward, knocking him off balance to send him sprawling to the ground. Scrambling on top of him, she straddled his stomach and brought her forehead down on his face again before he could get his hands up to defend himself. As the blow struck, the man's hands fell away, his head lolling in a daze, but Sam did not slow her attacks. Again, she smashed her forehead into his face, causing blood to cover the man's ruined nose, until he went limp and dropped to the ground.

Stopping her attack, Sam pushed herself to her feet unsteadily. Her face was covered in blood, and she looked around at the crowd in a daze, her chest heaving for breath. Roaring cheers filled the warehouse and slowly a grin spread across her face. With a laugh she straightened and flung her arms above her head, letting out a victorious roar, amplifying the crowd's excitement. A couple of men walked forward and took the unconscious man by the arms, dragging him out of the circle. Sam, too, staggered into the crowd to be greeted by people patting her on the back as they made room for her to pass.

Watching her path, Marcus tried to make his way towards her, squeezing through the press of bodies. He could see the top of her head as she wound through the crowd, and followed as best he could. Making her way to the back of the warehouse, she found her way out of the throng of people and walked over to talk with a small group of men in red sashes. One man in particular, tall with a rotund belly, grinned down at her. As Marcus reached the back, the crowd thinned, and he made his way over to Sam.

"…another round? Fuck ye, just give me my silver," came Sam's voice over the din of noise.

"You can make another thirty," the big man said. "Double or nothing."

"I've already doubled it this far," Sam said. "That's enough for now. Pay up."

"But the crowd is here to see you," the man countered. "We are making a lot of money. Fifty. Last offer."

"Give her the coins you owe and let her be on her way," Marcus said, taking on his persona of Aer.

The man and his men turned to face Marcus.

"And just who are you?" the big man asked contemptuously.

"He's with me, Garu" Sam said, jabbing a finger at the man's chest. "Now do as yer told, and maybe I'll consider comin' back here to make ye some more coin later. I want a fuckin' drink."

"Fine. Fine," Garu said, holding out his hand to one of his men.

The man beside him moved to a small wooden chest held by another of his compatriots and opened it, revealing an assemblage of coinage and small pouches. Counting out thirty coins, the man placed them in a pouch before putting it in Garu's waiting hand. Never breaking his gaze from Sam, the big man slowly moved his hand between them and held the pouch out to her in his open palm.

"A pleasure as always," Sam said, snatching the purse. "I'll be seein' ye around."

"Of that, I have no doubt," Garu said with a tight smile, before turning his gaze to a man across the room. With a nod of his head, the man shouted out the names of two new fighters, to a mixed reaction from the crowd.

"Come on, Aer. Let's go get wasted and have some fun, aye?" Sam said, gesturing with her head for him to follow.

Marcus gave one last look to the man named Garu and wondered what he had originally been designed for. Certainly not running an unscripted fighting pit. Diego's earlier concerns had made that clear enough. It was certainly worrying. However, he had to admit it did make the whole experience more intriguing. Turning to go after Sam, he followed her through the crowd and out of the warehouse.

Once they were back on the street, Marcus reached out to take Sam by the arm and slow her down. Turning to face him, she arched an eyebrow and grinned. Her face and chest were still covered in blood, giving her a ghoulish appearance.

"What was that?" Marcus asked, gesturing with his head to the warehouse.

"What'd it look like? A fight, boyo," she said with a sarcastic grunt.

"No, I mean. How did all this happen? And are you okay?"

"I'm fine," she said, pulling her arm free. "Why're ye actin' like this?"

"Sam, can we just talk about this for a second?" he asked. "Out of character, please. Diego is worried about the simulation."

"The fuck are ye yammerin' about?" she said, her brow twisting in confusion. "Why're ye callin' me Sam? And who the fuck's Diego?"

Marcus took her arm again, pulling her into a nearby alley between two buildings.

"The fuck ye doin'?" she protested, wrenching out of his grip.

"Sam. This isn't funny, and I know you're going through a lot, but I need you to focus. Diego says the simulation isn't functioning correctly. It's deviating from its scripted programming. Like the fighting pit. That was never part of the design of Freeport."

Sam stared at him, face bloody, her expression growing serious.

"Yer not makin' any sense, Aer," she said, her brow twisted in confusion. "I dun know what or who yer talkin' about. As for the fightin', that's all Garu's doin'. He gets a bunch o' fighters and has the people place bets on 'em. It's just a bit o' fun, is all."

A feeling of anxiety washed over Marcus as he listened to her, his skin prickling.

"Sam. Please stop. Drop the Morrigan act and talk to me like normal. Please!" he begged emphatically, taking her gently by the arms.

"I told ye, that's not my name," she said through gritted teeth, pulling away from him. "And yer the one that needs to start talkin' like yerself."

"Sam. Come on. Please. If you're playing around, you need to stop. Now."

"I'm not the one playin' at anythin', boyo. I dun know what's fuckin' wrong with ye, but I'm tired o' this shite. I'm leavin'. If ye come 'round to yerself again and want to have a drink, ye know where to find me," she said, stepping back and looking him up and down dubiously.

Marcus looked at her in shock. Was she really not understanding him? Was it some sort of coping mechanism? He didn't believe Sam would drag this out as a joke or to make a point. Did she truly think she was Morrigan? A thought came to mind as he watched her walk away, and he ran to catch up to her.

"Hey! Hey, stop," he said, putting himself in front of her.

Sam let out a sigh, scowling at him, but stopped walking.

"Sam. It's me, Marcus. You are in a simulation of a fantasy world that we created with our friends: Amir, Claire, and Diego. I have been your partner for over twenty years. You are here because you had cancer and it was the only way to save your consciousness. Do you remember any of this?" he asked, searching her eyes for some sign of recognition.

Her eyes softened and searched his gaze with concern. Reaching up a hand, she gently stroked his cheek.

"The fuck happened to ye, boyo?" she asked softly in bewilderment.

Marcus shook his head and pulled away.

"No. It's true. Can you not remember?" Panic took over as Marcus began to realize that she truly wasn't remembering.

"Look! I can prove it to you," he said, taking her again by the shoulders and bringing up the protocol in his vision. In an instant, his clothes changed to a more contemporary outfit of a tee shirt and jeans.

"See?" he said, stepping back. "It's all just a simulation."

Sam's face twisted in amusement, and she looked him up and down.

"Where'd ye learn a trick like that?" she said with a laugh. "And what are ye wearin'?"

Marcus couldn't believe what he was hearing.

"No, no, no. It's not a trick. We are in a virtual simulation, created in our minds. You are dreaming, Sam. The SynAPP? The AAIP? Don't you remember?"

"I dun know what the fuck any of that means. Yer not makin' any sense, boyo. Let's have a drink, aye? It'll calm yer nerves. Then maybe ye can show me how ye did that trick."

"It's not a fucking trick, Sam!" Marcus shouted. "You are not Morrigan. You are Sam Schneider. And I'm not Aer. I'm Marcus. Marcus Avery. We've been partners for twenty-five years. We've known each other since we were teenagers. Don't you remember?"

Sam looked at him like he was crazy and took a step back.

"The fuck I am," she said. "My name's Morrigan. Always has been. And yer Aer. At least I think ye are. I dun know about any of that other shite yer spoutin', but I sure as hell know my own fuckin' name."

Marcus' mind reeled. Was this some form of amnesia? Was the AAIP doing something to her consciousness? Maybe if he could do something that she couldn't explain away as a trick...

With the protocol still in his vision, he selected Sam and himself and instructed the simulation to transport them away. In an instant, the city was gone, and they were standing near the ape's lair, the roar of the waterfall the only sound filling the jungle around them. Sam staggered back, looking around in wide-eyed confusion.

"The fuck?" she said, looking at him as though seeing him for the first time. "What kind of fuckin' sorcery is this?"

"Not sorcery. A simulation. I used the protocol to bring us here. Come on, Sam. Think about it. Remember," he pleaded, searching her eyes for any recognition.

Sam's eyes darted around, then turned to meet his gaze, growing hard.

"I dun know who ye are. Ye may look like Aer, but ye ain't him."

"Sam, please," Marcus pleaded again, stepping towards her.

"Stay the fuck away from me, whoever the fuck ye are," she said, her body growing tense as she stepped away from him.

"It's me. Marcus. Sam, please remember. Baby, please," he beseeched her, continuing to move towards her.

"I said stay the fuck away," she said, pulling the knife from her belt and holding it out between them threateningly.

Marcus stopped and held up his hands. "Please just stop and think about it, Sam. Give it some real thought. Please."

"I dun need to think about anything. I already know who I am."

The snap of a branch was the only warning Marcus had before the ape came bursting out of the jungle behind him, its massive fists slamming into him and sending him sprawling over the rocky cliff. He found himself falling before he even realized what was happening and watched in horror as the ape leapt for Sam. Time seemed to slow as he watched her lunge with her knife, the only weapon she had on her person, as the ape lifted its fists to strike. A sharp pain was the last sensation Marcus felt before the whole world went dark.

Waking with a scream, Marcus sat up in his chair and nearly fainted as the world spun before his eyes. He fell back against the cushions and stared at the darkened room, his chest heaving for breath. For a moment, he didn't know where he was, the image of Sam fighting the ape seared into his mind. Then it all came flooding back to him. With a choked breath, he sat forward again, alone in the dark, and sobbed into his hands.

Morrigan opened her eyes, the simple tavern guest room slowly coming into focus. For a moment she lay there, staring up at the ceiling. Images flashed in her mind, something about a man and an ape? Whatever it had been about, it was fading too fast to remember. Rubbing the sleep from her eyes, she pushed herself into a sitting position, sliding her legs over the edge of the bed. For a moment she sat there, leaning over with her elbows resting on her thighs, and thought about what she should do with her day.

Letting out a yawn, she jumped to her feet and stretched, lifting her arms above her head. First things first, she needed something to eat. The room felt familiar, but she couldn't quite remember how she'd gotten there or even where she was. Walking over to the room's one small window, she looked out at her surroundings. A city? A name came to mind: Freeport. Right. She was in Freeport, and this was a room in the Hungry Hog. The image of the tavern's wooden sign and the owner's tattooed face flashed in her mind. A few other faces flashed for a moment, also familiar, but hazy and hard to place.

Her eyes drifted over the rooftops of the city, past the walls, to the great canopy of trees beyond. A shiver of excitement ran through her as she looked at the jungle. Unconsciously a smile crept onto her face. Oros would probably want meat for the meal tonight. Walking to the door, she grabbed her spear from where it lay propped against the wall and stepped out into the hall, making her way down to the common room.

The sound of multiple voices and music drifted from below to the upper floors, mingling into an indiscernible buzz, only growing louder as she approached the stairwell leading to the common room. Descending the stairs, she noted the tables packed with people laughing and carousing. A few looked in her direction, but she ignored them as she walked across the room to the bar and the squat broad-shouldered man behind it.

"So Oros, ye be needin' something to feed these fuckers with this evenin'?"

The man put down the mug he'd been wiping with a rag and picked up another.

"Aye. Could always use meat. Got lots of hungry mouths to feed," he said, as he did every time she asked. "Bring me something to feed 'em all and drinks are on the house."

"Oh, I know they are," Morrigan said with a smirk.

"You know, if you're looking for another way to make a living, I know a lot of men who'd pay a load of silver to get a taste of what you're hiding behind those leathers."

"Hidin'?" she scoffed. "I didn't think I was 'hidin' all that much in these. But the only ones tastin' are the ones I choose. And it won't be for silver. When are ye gonna get that into yer head?"

"Suit yourself," he said with a shrug, looking past her to stare at the common room as he continued cleaning mugs.

"Oi, how's 'bout a drink to get me goin', aye?" she said, slapping her hand on the bar top.

Mechanically, Oros picked up a mug and held it under one of the tapped barrels, filling it to the brim. Turning to look at her, he pushed it across the bar and leaned in. "I hear tell that Half-men have been spotted recently outside the walls. They say they've made a home in the old ruins up in the hills. I know people who are keenly interested to know what's going on and would pay good silver for it."

"Didn't I already deal with that for ye?" Morrigan asked, a sense of deja vu washing over her.

"Suit yourself," he said with a shrug, looking past her to stare at the common room as he continued cleaning mugs.

"Look, iffin' I should pass that way while I'm huntin', I'll keep an eye out," Morrigan said, lifting her mug in thanks and taking a long drink.

"You know where to find me," Oros said.

Turning away from the man, Morrigan leaned against the bar and looked out over the common room. As her eyes scanned the room, she noticed a man sitting at one of the tables staring at her. As their gazes met, she thought she caught a glimpse of recognition in his face and arched a questioning eyebrow in his direction. For a moment, he seemed to be considering something, his brow furrowing as he watched her. Glancing around the common room, he eventually stood up and made his way over to the bar.

Morrigan watched in amusement as he approached, surprised

that he had the balls. He didn't look like the type of man who'd last long in Freeport; there was a softness to his face and eyes that made her think of the pigs they penned for slaughter. She couldn't help but wonder just what he would say to her. If he did have the balls to proposition her, she debated whether she should break his nose in front of everyone or indulge his request just to see the look on his face. With a grin, she lounged back against the bar seductively and waited.

"Sam?" he asked quietly, peering at her in what seemed like surprise.

"Not even close, boyo. Name's Morrigan."

He peered at her again, looking her up and down. "Do you remember me? It's Oswald. From Synerdyne."

"'Fraid not, Oswald from Synerdyne. Never seen ye before," she said, though for a moment a sense of familiarity washed over her before fading just as quickly. "Ye got the wrong girl."

"How long have you been here?" he asked.

Morrigan scowled. "I dun fuckin' know. What's it to ye?"

"I can't tell if you are just an avatar or something more," he said, more to himself than her, leaning forward to inspect her.

"Stop eye fuckin' me, boyo. Unless ye want me to bloody that fuckin' nose of yers."

Oswald pulled back, a look of surprise on his face. "Your speech patterns don't seem pre-generated. At least not like the others in here."

"Yer startin' to get on my nerves," she said, putting down her mug and pushing off the bar to stand up straight. "I told ye. I'm not the girl yer lookin' for. Nor would ye ever have the chance. So, move on and go bother someone else, yeah?"

Oswald took a step back and glanced around the room again, before giving her one more considering look. Finally, without a word, he turned and made his way across the room. As he reached the door, he turned and looked over at her one last time before stepping out into the street and disappearing.

"Can ye believe that fucker?" Morrigan said to Oros, turning back to the bar to grab her drink.

"Aye. Never know what you'll find at the Hungry Hog," he said with a toothy smile.

CHAPTER 21

“I’m not sure how to account for it,” Amir said. “I mean, you’re sure she wasn’t just staying in character?”

“No. She wasn’t just acting!” Marcus snarled. “She didn’t even remember who I was. She kept calling me Aer. And even when I showed her that she was in a simulation, she just thought it was sorcery.”

“No. I don’t mean it that way,” Amir said. “But with everything that’s happened, maybe this has less to do with the simulation and more of a psychological break. It would make perfect sense. After all, her whole world has been turned upside down. She is a dead woman whose consciousness got preserved in a video game.”

“She’s not dead,” Marcus shot back. “Don’t say that. Only her body is gone. Her physical essence. But her consciousness is still alive.”

“You know what I mean,” Amir said, holding up his hands placatingly.

“No. Referring to her that way makes it sound like Sam is just another duplicant. But she’s not,” Marcus countered. “When she passed, I was there. She never left, she just… transitioned. She’s not some copy, she is the extension of Sam beyond her physical limitations.”

"Alright. I'm sorry," Amir said, backing down. "All I meant was what she is dealing with is existential in a way that none of us can imagine. Can we agree on that?"

Marcus leaned forward to rest his elbows on his knees and let out a hard breath, all his anger replaced again by despair. Staring at the floor, he nodded.

"Alright. So, we need to consider the possibility that, psychologically, maybe Sam is trying to avoid any reminders of what happened," Amir said. "I don't know. I'm not a psychiatrist. But that seems just as distinct a possibility in my opinion, and we should consider it just as much as an error in the simulation. None of the duplicants have reported this issue, nor has Diego seen anything similar in their behavior. Have you talked to Clive about it? Asked him if he's having any issues?"

"No. I didn't want to bring it up, in case it spooks him. The last thing we need right now is for him to think there is something wrong with the simulation and pull his support from Synerdyne," Marcus explained.

"Do you think he would do that?" Amir asked.

"I don't know. He seems to really enjoy Sam's World, but we can't risk it. Not without first knowing what's going on," Marcus said with a sigh.

"Maybe I can probe Jia and see if Clive's said anything to her," Amir offered. "I mean, we won't be able to hide it if he is experiencing issues. But so far, it does seem like it is only affecting Sam."

"Has Diego spoken to you about the anomalies he's experiencing? Do you think they could have anything to do with this?" Marcus asked.

"Yeah, he mentioned a few of them. And I don't have a good explanation for those yet either. I mean, the simulation is still functioning as intended. It just seems that the autonomous nature of the AAIP might be imposing some of its own changes. But it would stand to reason that if something is going on with one, it might have something to do with the other. But without more information, it's hard to be certain. Correlation does not imply causation."

"Regardless, Sam is our priority. I need you to look into this from your end and figure out if the AAIP is playing any role in this," Marcus said.

"Of course. But in the meantime, I think you should talk to Claire," Amir prodded. "She's the only one of us who might have some insight into Sam's psychology."

Marcus let out another sigh. "Yeah. I'm going to do that right after I'm done here," he said, rubbing his hands together. "If she'll talk to me."

"I can't believe Claire would abandon Sam. Just tell her what is going on. Don't beat around the bush," Amir said, gently.

Marcus nodded. "Yeah, I've been running through it in my mind, over and over. What if she believes that we've gone too far and decides to do something drastic, thinking it's for Sam's own good? I mean, she essentially said we should let Sam die."

"Well, that's not quite what she said," Amir said. "Just tell her. It's Claire. Regardless of anything else, you can trust her, Marcus."

"Yeah, I don't…," Marcus started but was interrupted by a notification ping on his phone. "Just a sec," he said, fishing his phone out of his pocket.

It was a message from Evan, instructing him to meet at his office without delay. Marcus was surprised by the commanding language of the message.

Can it wait? I've got some important things today, he texted back quickly.

No. I need to see you NOW, Evan replied only seconds later.

"Everything alright?" Amir asked, glancing between Marcus and his phone.

"I don't know," Marcus replied. "Evan wants to talk to me urgently about something. I guess Claire will have to wait."

"Well, don't wait too long. I'll start digging into the AAIP and see if I can find anything to explain Sam's actions or Diego's anomalies," Amir said. "If I find anything, I'll let you know."

"Alright. Thanks," Marcus said, standing up and walking to the door.

"Marcus," Amir called, as he reached for the handle. "Don't worry. We'll figure this out. Just remember, regardless of how she's acting, Sam is still there. Like you said, *still alive*. Everything else is just a bump in the road."

Giving him a half-hearted smile, Marcus nodded and opened the door.

When Marcus reached Evan's office, Janice looked up from her desk, her face pale.

"He's waiting for you," she said after a moment. "I don't know what it's about but he's livid about something. He told me to send you right in."

Marcus looked at the door to Evan's office and thought he could hear him talking to someone.

"Is someone else in there?" he asked.

Janice nodded. "Mr. Wright."

"Oswald?" Marcus said in surprise, wondering what this could have to do with the office manager.

Janice pointed to her phone and pressed the intercom button. "Mr. Nguyen, Marcus is here."

"Send him in," Evan's voice shouted from the speaker.

Looking at Marcus with an expression of concern, she gestured to the door, and he widened his eyes at her in mutual surprise before stepping inside.

As he entered the room, Marcus immediately noticed Evan standing behind his desk, his friend's face a mask of barely contained rage. Near the middle of the room, against the wall, stood Oswald. The man looked away as Marcus met his gaze, and he wondered what the office manager could have done to make Evan so angry.

Oswald was a bit nosy and too ambitious for his own good, but he was a diligent employee.

"I can't believe you," Evan growled, his face growing redder, and Marcus was surprised to find the words directed at him.

"What's going on?" Marcus asked in confusion.

"I know what you've done in Sam's World," Evan said. "I know about Sam."

A wave of numbness washed over Marcus, and he stared at Evan in stunned disbelief.

"What were you thinking? Do you realize what you have done? Do you realize how much you've jeopardized what we are doing here?" Evan asked.

"H…How?" Was all Marcus could manage as his mind reeled in confusion.

"Oswald visited your hidden experiment in Sam's World and saw what you are doing there," Evan explained. "You have copies of all the participants in Elysium, and Sam, in there like puppets in a game! What on earth are you thinking? If any of this got out, if one of those people realized that their likeness was being used that way, they could sue us into oblivion."

Marcus took a breath and tried to organize his thoughts.

"Fucking answer me, Marcus!" Evan roared.

"Don't say anything, Marcus," a voice said from the doorway as Clive stepped in.

"Good. You're finally here, too," Evan said. "I don't how you might have done things at your other companies, Ellison, but Synerdyne isn't your personal playground."

Unlike Marcus, Clive strode into the room confidently and took a seat in one of the chairs in front of Evan's desk.

"I don't answer to you, Mr. Nguyen," Clive said calmly, crossing his legs. "And neither does Marcus. Your role is to keep this company running and profitable. That's it. You don't have a role in anything done by our research team."

"The hell I don't! Everything that happens here at Synerdyne goes through me. You may consider yourself our most important shareholder, Mr. Ellison, but you are not in charge of this company. You have no business interfering or guiding what we do here. If you want to suggest a change in how we do things, bring it up for a vote at our next shareholder meeting."

"I'm afraid things have changed, Mr. Nguyen. As of this morning, I am the majority shareholder of Synerdyne, and I am concerned about your leadership of this company," Clive said calmly. "Under you, Synerdyne lost its most lucrative contract and has been bleeding money. I have called an emergency shareholder meeting for tonight, with the intent of having you removed as CEO."

The blood drained from Evan's face as he listened, his brow twisting in confusion. "You can't do that. Marcus and I hold the controlling shares."

"Perhaps in theory, but only together," Clive explained. "Marcus and I have a similar purpose and vision for this company. A vision you evidently don't share. As do a number of the other shareholders. And together, our shares give us enough of a majority to have you removed. Now, who do you think he's going to side with on this?"

"Marcus," Evan pleaded, looking to him for help.

"Just back off, Evan," Marcus replied coldly. "You're in way over your head."

"Marcus, this will ruin the company," Evan said.

"Marcus and I are taking this company beyond what you can even imagine," Clive said. "But we don't have room for small-minded ideas and sensibilities. Certainly not in positions of leadership."

"If you think I will just sit by and let you do this, you are mistaken," Evan shot back. "I built this company."

"And you've taken it as far as you are capable. Don't worry, Mr. Nguyen. I'm about to make you a very rich man. As for him," Clive said, standing up and gesturing in Oswald's direction. "I want him out of the building by the end of the hour. We don't have any place for rats here."

"No! Please. You can't do that," Oswald said, looking to Evan for support.

"And let me remind you," Clive said, ignoring Oswald's pleas. "You signed an NDA when you joined this company. If you speak of this to anyone, I have a team of lawyers who will make sure you are both financially and professionally ruined. You won't find a job in fast food. Let alone tech."

Clive walked over and put a hand on Marcus' back. "Come on, Marcus. We have things to do," he said, guiding him to the door. "Our business here is over."

Marcus looked to Evan, sitting deflated in his chair, then over to Oswald. The man looked between Clive and Evan in bewilderment. With a press of his hand, Clive urged Marcus out the door.

Janice watched silently as the two of them passed, her eyes questioning as they met his gaze. Marcus didn't say anything, his thoughts racing as he and Clive made their way down the halls of Synerdyne's offices. As they stepped into the elevator, Marcus finally found his voice.

"Was all of that true?" he asked, glancing at Clive standing beside him.

"There's one thing you should know about me, Marcus. I don't bluff."

"So, what's going to happen to Evan?" Marcus asked, realizing that Clive's plan did still require his involvement.

"As I said, he will be removed as CEO."

"And removed from the company?" Marcus asked.

"No. I think it is best we keep Mr. Nguyen close," Clive said. "We'll give him some administrative position within the company. Something superfluous that'll give him a steady income and plenty of time to work on his golf game."

"Evan's terrible at golf. He plays squash," Marcus corrected, absentmindedly.

"Then squash it is," Clive said with a tight smile.

As the elevator reached the ground floor, Marcus followed Clive out onto the street where a car was waiting.

"Let me give you a ride," he said. A man hopped out of the driver's seat to quickly open the passenger door for him.

"No. That's okay," Marcus replied with a wave. "I think I'm going to take a walk and think about some things."

"Alright, but don't think too hard about what happened today," Clive said. "Remember where we need to keep our focus."

Marcus gave him a nod and watched as he sat down in the back of the car.

"We'll talk again soon, I'm sure," Clive said with his wolfish grin, then gave the driver a nod to close the door.

Marcus waited as the driver returned to his seat and watched as they drove away. For a moment he stood there, thinking about what had just happened, and looked up at the Synerdyne offices. Everything was changing and he couldn't help but feel that things were slipping out of his control.

Marcus stood on the porch of Claire's house, his finger hovering inches from the doorbell. After what had happened with Evan and Oswald, he wondered if this was a good idea. His thoughts turned to Sam and the look of bewilderment on her face when he'd tried to explain things to her. A feeling of impending loss washed over him the way it had when Sam had been sick. One that came with the subconscious knowledge that she was slipping away. That couldn't happen again. Swallowing, he pressed the bell.

Inside the house, he heard distant movement, which eventually grew louder as a shadow approached the door. Claire's face appeared in the window as she pulled back the curtain. For a moment she stared at him before he heard the distinct sound of the bolt being unlatched. Partially opening the door, Claire stood in the gap, looking at him coolly.

"Hey," he said.

"Hey," she replied with an arch of her eyebrow. Her face looked puffy and her eyes were red.

"Are you okay?" he asked.

"Not really, no. What do you want, Marcus?"

"I need to talk to you about Sam," he said.

"We already did this," she replied.

"Yeah, but something has happened, and I wanted to get your take on it."

Claire regarded him quietly for a moment, then stepped back to let him in. Marcus pushed the door open and stepped inside, following her into the living room. He noticed that the furniture was back in place and that the walls were finished and painted.

"You finished it," he said, admiring her work.

"Yeah. I had a lot of time on my hands. It helped to have something to focus on." She gestured to the loveseat, before sitting down on the couch across from it.

Marcus sat down and looked at his friend. She looked back at him with cold eyes. He'd known Claire longer than anyone, except Sam and Evan, but at that moment the gulf between them seemed vast and unbridgeable. He hated to think it, but maybe Amir and Diego were wrong about her.

"Well, like I said," he began, clearing his throat. "I need to talk to you about Sam. Something is happening to her."

Claire cocked her head to the side and regarded him for a moment.

"That's not Sam," she said bluntly.

Marcus felt a twinge of anger spike within him, but he forced himself to breathe.

"Yes, it is, Claire. I've spent time with her since…"

"She *died*?" Claire finished, pointedly emphasizing the word.

"Passed. Transitioned," he offered. "She didn't die."

"She didn't switch genders, Marcus. Her body stopped functioning. I was there when it happened."

"And you were there to see her continue in the simulation," he shot back, his anger rising.

"What I saw was a computer simulation of Sam, based on her consciousness mapping, but that isn't Sam. Sam is dead," Claire said.

"Can you think outside your fucking presumptions for just one second and entertain the idea that maybe you're wrong?" Marcus asked, gritting his teeth.

"Can *you*?" she spat back.

"I knew this was a fucking bad idea," he said, standing up. "You just want her to be dead so badly."

"Fuck you! She was my friend," Claire shouted, pushing herself to her feet and jabbing a finger at him. "I wanted her to survive just as much as you did."

"No. You didn't," he said coolly. "You can't possibly know how much I wanted her—*needed* her—to make it. How much I am willing to do to ensure she still makes it. You were willing to give up on her. I never will."

"You are deluding yourself, Marcus, because you can't let her go. Don't you see that? You need so badly to believe she is still alive. But all you are doing is clinging to memories of her. She isn't real anymore. What exists now is only a simulation of Sam."

"What do you even fucking know about it?" he growled. "You abandoned her, and the rest of us. You chose to walk away instead of being willing to challenge your assumptions."

"No. I walked away because I knew none of you would be willing to accept any other truth," she replied.

"So yours is the only truth?" he scoffed.

"You can't have two opposite truths, Marcus. She's either dead or alive."

"Only so long as you accept the standard paradigm of human existence based on our biological limitations," he countered.

"And what other paradigm is there?"

"That's just it," he said. "What we've done with the simulation pushes the boundaries of those limitations. Maybe even pushes us to the next stage of human evolution. One that transcends our physical bodies and allows our existence to continue into perpetuity."

"And you think all of this has happened because the AAIP created a simulation of Sam based on her brain patterns?" she scoffed.

"Yes. I do," Marcus replied, taking a breath and forcing himself to calm down. "And I'm not here to ask you to accept that notion. I'm here to ask for your help. As your friend. Because something is happening to Sam, and I am terrified that we will actually lose her."

Marcus fell back onto the loveseat, his grief overwhelming any anger he still felt as tears began to well in his eyes. "Please, Claire. If not for Sam, then for me," he begged.

Claire looked down at him quietly for a moment, her brow knitted and mouth frowning. Slowly, she lowered herself to the couch and leaned forward, clasping her hands in front of her and staring at the floor.

"Okay. What's happened?" she asked quietly.

Marcus blinked in surprise at her question and sat forward, wiping the tears from his eyes.

"She's losing her memory," he said slowly. "She takes on the role of Morrigan and acts like she doesn't remember me. She insists that I am Aer, and when I tried to show her that she was in a simulation, she freaked out and thought it was magic."

"Well, if we were to assume that this is a product of Sam's psyche and not a problem with the simulation, it would stand to reason that maybe she is having a dissociative episode," Claire offered. "It's hard to imagine how the human brain would process the knowledge that they had died in the physical world but continued to exist in the simulation. The mind and body are in some ways inextricably linked in how we identify ourselves as people. Take one element of that equation away, and the mind has to readjust to a completely new reality. In our standard reality this could present itself in a fugue state, but in this case, it is something no one has experienced before."

"So, what can we do about it?" Marcus asked.

"Normally a doctor would work with the patient to devise some form of therapy that focused on managing the stress, depression, and anxiety brought on by different situations," she explained. "However, in this circumstance, it is much harder to guide the person back to reality, when reality no longer exists as they know it."

"What about changing Sam's World, or pulling her out of it and into a more familiar place?" Marcus offered.

Claire shrugged. "That might work, or it might lead her to a more intense psychotic break. There's no way to say for sure."

"What if you were to talk to her?" he asked hopefully.

"Marcus, I don't know if I can do much. I'm a psychiatrist, but this is way beyond my area of expertise. You need someone trained in these things."

"Yeah, but you're all we have," he said. "It's not like I can find some doctor, spike them, and just bring them into Sam's World."

"My point is, I don't know what I could do to help," Claire explained. "And again, that's not even considering the fact that I don't think about Sam in the same way you do. To me, the most obvious answer is that this is a glitch in the AAIP trying to process something it was never designed for, and this is just proof that she is a program."

"I'll take anything. I'm desperate," he pleaded. "And I'm not asking you to believe. Just treat it like a sim."

"I don't know, Marcus," Claire said, shaking her head and looking away. "I don't know if I can handle seeing her again. I'm slowly making my peace with what happened, but every day still brings up new thoughts and grief. To see her again…"

"Please, Claire. I don't have anyone else I can turn to for this."

Claire turned to look at him, her red-rimmed eyes searching his with an unreadable expression.

"No," she said quietly.

"What?" he asked, unsure of what she'd meant.

"I can't. Sam is dead, Marcus," she said, her face sympathetic. "I'm sorry. I truly am. But encouraging this delusion about Sam existing in the simulation is only going to end up making this even harder for you to eventually accept. Not to mention what it would do emotionally to me to interact with her again. Even knowing what she is."

Marcus felt like all the wind had been taken out of him, and he sat there dumbfounded.

"The best thing I can do for you, as your friend, is to not indulge you in this any longer," she said, reaching to touch his hand.

In an instant, the anger returned to Marcus in force, and he pulled his hand away.

"Go fuck yourself, you self-righteous bitch," he said, standing up abruptly.

Claire stared up at him stunned, unconsciously shrinking back into the couch.

"Don't you fucking pity me," he spat. "And don't you dare talk to me about *your* grief, while you hide away and feel sorry for yourself. You gave up on Sam because it was easier to face the certainty of her death than the uncertainty of her continued existence. Well, that's where we're different. I won't ever give up on her. And I refuse to feel pity for myself when she's the one struggling to survive. So, fine. Don't help. Sit here crying for yourself while you paint your walls and rot away. But I'm not giving up."

Marcus clenched his jaw and didn't wait for her response, turning to navigate through the living room to the front door. As he reached the door, Claire called out to him from the other room.

"You say you're doing this for her, but none of this is about Sam. Not really. It's about you, Marcus. The fact that you can't let go. And you don't care about anyone else if they don't help you maintain that control. You want to call me selfish? You're the most selfish one of us all!"

Marcus slammed the door behind him, cutting off her words, and heard the cracking sound of glass. Turning around he saw a long fracturing line cut across the window of the door. He glared at the damage and felt a sense of satisfaction. Well, there was one more project she could work on instead of helping Sam.

CHAPTER 22

"So, no Claire," Diego said.

"Nope. As far as she's concerned, Sam is dead," Marcus replied bitterly.

"Sorry, man," Amir said.

"Fuck her," Marcus said with a shrug. "If she can't be there for Sam, then I don't want anything to do with her."

Amir and Diego looked uncomfortably at one another.

"Did you hear about Evan?" Amir asked, hugging his mug in both hands.

Beside him, Diego stared at Marcus from across the table and lifted his cup to take a drink. Marcus realized they were sitting at the same table in the coffee shop that he and Diego had used only a few days before.

"Yeah," Marcus said, not elaborating.

"The board has moved him into something called 'Director of Operational Logistics'. From what I understand, it's just an over-glorified managerial position," Diego said.

"What does that mean?" Amir asked. "I mean, for us and the company?"

"It means we will no longer have to worry about any interference when it comes to Sam's World or our research," Marcus said, coolly.

"Did you know about this?" Amir asked, his eyes widening in surprise.

"A little, yeah," Marcus admitted. "I was in a meeting with him and Clive. Clive told him he was going to petition the board to remove him as CEO."

"Why didn't you tell us?" Amir prodded. "I mean, how'd they even manage to do that? Don't you and he have an even number of voting shares? I mean how did Clive get enough votes?"

"I voted with Clive," Marcus said.

Diego nearly spit out his coffee, and Amir blinked in surprise.

"Ultimately, it's a good thing," Marcus continued. "And we have bigger issues to worry about. Let Clive worry about the politics of Synerdyne."

"But Evan started this company with us," Amir said. "I know he's never been part of the research, but he believed in us and our mission. It seems cold-hearted to just push him out."

"Evan believed in a very myopic view of our research," Marcus said. "And the profits that could be made from it. But we're moving into more expansive and existential applications for the AAIP, and Evan is too timid in his thinking to captain this ship any longer."

"Damn. Do you really mean that?" Diego asked. "I mean, you guys have known each other for a long time."

"Exactly. And that means I know who Evan is, and what he is capable of," Marcus replied. "We need someone with vision and fearlessness at the helm as we move forward. Not someone who will kneecap our research."

"So, who is that going to be exactly?" Amir asked. "And will they be any better?"

"I don't know," Marcus shrugged. "I'm sure Clive has someone in mind."

"Aren't you worried about how much control you're giving Ellison?" Diego asked.

"Clive believes in this project. In preserving Sam's consciousness and working towards preserving other people's as well," Marcus said. "He's on our side in this and isn't the one standing in our way."

Amir and Diego looked at one another meaningfully in a way that made Marcus uncomfortable.

"What?" he demanded.

Amir swallowed and again glanced at Diego, who gave him a nod of encouragement.

"So we asked you to come here because we didn't want to say this in front of Ellison or Jia," Diego said hesitantly.

Marcus looked at the two of them, trying to study their faces, and waited for them to continue.

Amir cleared his throat. "We were looking into the anomalies that Diego had been witnessing."

"Yeah, I saw them too," Marcus said.

"Right. And I was also trying to figure out what might be going on with Sam," Amir continued.

"Are they linked?" Marcus asked.

"Hard to say for certain, because when it comes to Sam, I don't see anything specific in her mapping. No smoking gun to explain things," Amir explained. "But when I looked at the AAIP's protocols I found something peculiar."

Marcus unconsciously leaned forward.

"In some of the code, there seems to be some familiar patterning," Amir said. "You know how in order to create an avatar we make them like any other asset?"

"Yeah."

"But unlike other assets, they need a certain level of cognitive function that can react to a participant's actions and words," Amir explained.

"Right. They have an artificial mapping based on Waxman-Li. Simple cognitive function without self-propagating thought," Marcus continued for him.

"Exactly. This mapping is just a framework into which we can program mannerisms, actions, and scripted dialogue," Amir said. "The AAIP then turns that into a more fluid and reactive intelligence."

"So that's corrupted somehow?" Marcus asked.

"Yes and no." Amir continued, looking at Diego. "Somehow the duplicants' cognitive mappings were transferred into that AI framework."

"Okay. So, what does that mean?" Marcus asked.

"It means that the framework is no longer just a static, programmable mapping," Amir said. "Instead, it is now an active mapping made up of the different personality traits and consciousnesses of over twenty of our current duplicants."

"I don't understand. What does that mean *exactly*?" Marcus pressed.

"It means that the AAIP is drawing from active mappings that can deviate from our programmed directives. So, an NPC we designated as a blacksmith may find he'd rather be a dancer," Diego explained.

"Wait, are you saying that the NPC avatars are self-aware?"

"Not exactly. At least, we don't know. But what they are now is self-governing," Amir said.

"How did this happen?" Marcus asked, his mind whirling with the possibilities and problems this new situation could create, especially for Sam.

Again, Amir looked to Diego, and the two exchanged an unspoken but obvious thought.

"I can't be certain," Amir said. "It could be a corruption in the AAIP. I mean, we've never tried anything like this before. There are over twenty consciousnesses, devoid of connection to a host, active within the server."

"But…" Marcus prodded, hearing the implication in Amir's tone.

"But they could also have been purposefully downloaded into the static mapping," Amir replied.

"Purposefully downloaded?" Marcus said, trying to understand what that could mean. "Why? What would be the point?"

"Exactly what we're seeing happen," Diego said. "Not only an autonomous world but one filled with an autonomous population."

"Or perhaps a test at creating a self-aware AI?" Amir offered.

"But who would do it? And without our knowledge?" Marcus asked.

Amir and Diego looked at each other again.

"Stop doing that," Marcus barked at them. "Just say it."

"There are only a few people who could have done it. Who'd have access," Amir said, hesitantly. "You, me, Diego, and…"

"Jia," Marcus finished for him.

Both men nodded.

"But why?" Marcus asked.

"We don't know," Amir said. "And that's an 'if'. We don't know anything for certain. As I said, it could just be a corruption in the AAIP. But if it was purposeful, she's the only one whose access is unaccounted for."

Marcus considered the implications of what they were saying. If it wasn't an error in the AAIP, then Jia added the maps without informing any of them. That didn't make sense unless she was trying to hide it. And if she was hiding it from them, was she hiding it from Clive, too? Was she doing something nefarious? He didn't know Jia very well, but she always came across as extremely loyal to Clive. Was that all an act? Or did Clive have some involvement in this? And if so, what was the purpose?

"Can we do anything about it? Can we pull the mappings out?" Marcus asked.

Amir shook his head. "They are integrated into the AAIP, and it has used them to modify the static map. Without doing some deep cleaning in the code, we can't change it. Not without taking the simulation offline and essentially resetting everything."

"No. We're not doing that," Marcus said, more as a reaction than a thought.

"Right. So, the only thing we can do now is a diagnostic to determine how it is affecting the AAIP and if it can be managed. Then, perhaps we might be able to remove it in bits and pieces, but that brings up two other concerns," Amir offered. "If it is a corruption of the system, then we need to inspect every line of code in the AAIP, which will take years. And if it isn't, then no matter how much we change, it can all be easily undone by someone reintegrating whatever changes we make."

"So we need to determine the source," Marcus said.

"Exactly," Amir said with a nod.

"Well, there's one way to do that," Marcus said.

"What do you mean?" Diego asked.

"Go and talk to Clive."

Marcus opened his eyes in the upstairs room of the tavern. It was still strange to him, having a specific place to spawn into the simulation. He knew the room wasn't actually in the tavern, at least not in any accessible way. It was a sort of free-floating space that existed regardless of the inn. It was the doorway that connected you to the tavern. Open it from this side and you were transported to the upstairs hallway as if you were exiting one of the tavern rooms.

However, if you entered from the hallway, you would access a simple room. You could spend a minute, an hour, even a day in it and no one would suddenly appear in the bed. Each participant had their own room, but they all connected to the same doorway. It was a clever idea that allowed for the smooth transition of someone back into the simulation, without having to worry about interference from other participants respawning or the room being occupied.

Now that he was here, he could transport himself anywhere using the protocol. But he still wasn't sure how best to approach Clive about the anomalies, so he opted to walk to the castle. It wasn't very far from the Hungry Hog, and it would give him a little time to think.

Making his way down the hall and into the common room, his eyes scanned the patrons for any signs of disturbance. A few looked up at his passage and caught his eye, and he found himself wondering what they might be thinking. If things were working correctly, watching him would just be a programmed action, but now he wondered what else it could mean.

He didn't linger and navigated his way around the tables to the entrance. When he stepped out onto the street, he was surprised to find crimson banners, marked with a black fist, hanging at the city gate. Those were new. Assembled below the banners were a handful of men that looked like the red-sashed pirates he'd seen before. Except now, in addition to their sashes, some wore armor marked with the same black fist. They harried the people passing through the gate, demanding to know their business and harassing men and women with bawdy comments.

One of the men looked in Marcus' direction and started walking over. His patience already wearing thin, and with too much to think about, he brought up the protocol and froze the man in place. The broad-shouldered man stared at him blankly, held in place in mid-step. Marcus looked for a moment into his eyes and wondered if he was experiencing anything. Surprise? Fear?

He shook his head and turned away, walking towards the castle. Behind him he could hear the other men calling out to their compatriot, asking him what he was doing. Marcus instructed the protocol to unfreeze the man once he was a good distance away. As he approached the walls of the keep, he saw again the red banners hanging on either side of its gate, guarded by more men in the red sashes.

Marcus brought up the protocol again and targeted Clive's location. He noted it was in one of the smaller rooms of the castle and decided to transport himself into the hall outside of it to preserve Clive's privacy. In a flash, he was no longer standing in the warm sun and found himself instead in a dark stone corridor, standing just outside a heavy wooden door.

It was now or never. Reaching up, he knocked on the door and waited. The wood was thick, and he could hear no sound from the other side. Seconds passed without an answer, and he knocked again, this time more loudly. After a moment, the door cracked open and Clive appeared on the other side. From what Marcus could see, he looked completely naked. Marcus looked away embarrassed.

"Sorry. I didn't realize. I didn't mean to bother you," he stammered apologetically.

"Marcus. To what do I owe this visit?"

"It can wait if you'd like to get dressed," Marcus said, still averting his gaze.

Clive shrugged. "Don't worry about me. I'd invite you in, but I'm a little busy at the moment. What is it you want?"

Marcus looked again at the man, noticing the sweat dripping from his body. Clive appeared as a more muscular and toned version of himself, and Marcus couldn't help but wonder if that was how the man saw himself, or if it was a deliberate choice. He also wondered what the sweat implied. Was he simply exercising? There was no reason to do that in the simulation. Or was he indulging himself? And if so, what did that mean when it came to the AAIP avatars and their newly developed consciousness? Or was it with one of the duplicants?

"I need to ask you something important. Well, a couple of things," Marcus said, awkwardly standing in the hall. "Firstly, did you put those banners up?" he asked, gesturing behind him in the direction of the castle gate and city walls.

"Not personally, no," Clive laughed. "But I think they really add something to the town and my persona."

"Your persona?"

"Yeah, you know, my alter ego here," he said with his wolfish grin. "I'm really enjoying getting into character. I've decided to go by Brannock, the Tyrant of Freeport. I figured since I took the castle, I might as well be in control of things. And who better to run a town full of pirates than a pirate king? What do you think?"

Marcus blinked letting his words sink in. "I suppose it's thematic. Umm… speaking of, have you noticed any of the NPC avatars acting strangely?"

"Strangely? I mean this whole place is strange, isn't it?" Clive said with a laugh. "That's half the fun."

"No, I mean acting in a way that they wouldn't be programmed to do," Marcus clarified. "Like taking on roles or occupations they weren't assigned? Saying things you wouldn't expect?"

Clive shrugged. "Sure. I suppose, but I'm not sure how they are programmed. I'm not the best one to ask. But they seem to be really coming alive, don't they?"

"Well, that's just it," Marcus said, hesitant about his next words. "The avatars are acting strangely. Doing things they weren't programmed to do. And it seems that their 'files', if you will, have been corrupted by the integration of the duplicants' consciousness maps."

"I'm not sure what all that means, but is there a question in there?" Clive asked.

"The only way that could have happened is if someone purposefully incorporated them into the AAIP," Marcus explained. "And the only people who could access that database are me, Amir, Diego, and Jia. Do you know if Jia might have had any involvement in this?"

Clive's lip quirked into a grin. "Oh that. Yes. She's working on a side project for me. In addition to preserving consciousness, we wanted to see if we could create our own. As Jia describes it, a 'self-aware, artificial consciousness'."

"A *side* project?" Marcus repeated in shocked disbelief.

"I was going to tell you, but recently you've seemed pretty preoccupied," Clive said casually. "Besides, I wanted your focus to be on the preservation side of things. That's what you are most invested in. But that didn't seem like any reason not to pursue this as well. I told you, Marcus, we're going to do big things with this research. Bigger than you ever imagined."

"Oi, boyo! Ye ever comin' back, or am I just supposed to take care of myself?" a familiar voice called from deeper in the room behind Clive.

His stomach knotting, Marcus suddenly felt all the air pulled from his lungs as he stared past Clive into the darkness of the room. Clive gave him a peevish look, his lips twisted like a kid caught in the act. From the darkness a woman's figure appeared, herself naked like Clive.

"What's takin' ye so long? I'm gettin' bored waitin'," Sam said, sliding an arm over Clive's shoulder and lounging her body against his. As her eyes fell on Marcus, she didn't offer a look of shame or surprise but instead furrowed her brow.

"Ye look familiar, boyo. Do I know ye from somewhere?" she asked, her eyes showing no recognition. With a languid smile, she leaned forward to put her face next to Clive's. "Ye know, if yer friend here wants to join us, it's fine by me," she purred into his ear, giving Marcus a wink.

Marcus' entire body suddenly went numb, his vision narrowing to Sam's face. Without thinking, the protocol suddenly appeared in his vision, and he selected Clive and Sam's markers and activated a time freeze on both of them. To Marcus' surprise, Clive cocked his head towards Sam, then disengaged himself from her rigid grasp. Slowly, his eyes turned in Marcus' direction.

"Sorry about that. I suppose you're upset," Clive said nonchalantly, then turned and cocked an eyebrow at Marcus. "Did you just try to freeze me too?"

Marcus tried to find the breath to speak, but all he could do was look at Sam, seeing her nakedness as thoughts of what she and Clive were doing hammered at his mind.

"You piece of shit," Marcus managed in a growl. It felt like his heart was being crushed in his chest.

"Now calm down. She was as willing as I was. And if it makes you feel any better, she never broke character. I figured we were just roleplaying. I mean," he stepped aside to open the door wider, exposing Sam completely, and gestured to her with his hand. "I don't know what kind of relationship you guys have. You know how sexy she is. How can you, of all people, expect me to say 'no' to that?"

Marcus stared at the man in disbelief. "You know how important she is to me," he said. "I didn't necessarily think we were friends, but I thought you at least respected me. Respected us."

"And I do, Marcus. I told you. You're a visionary. And this place is just the beginning. This," Clive inclined his head in Sam's direction. "Is just a little fun. It doesn't mean anything. Let's not let this complicate things, yeah?"

"Not complicate things? You fucked Sam!" Marcus spat.

Clive let out a sigh and opened the door fully, uncaring of his nudity, and stepped forward to put a hand on Marcus' shoulder. "Listen. When I see something I want, I pursue it. And nine times out of ten, I get it. It's the reason why I have everything I do. Because I have the drive to take what I want. But that doesn't mean I want to ruin anything for anyone. There's no reason why we can't both have what we want. Think about it, Marcus. We are building something here that goes beyond you and me, and even Sam. And we have to stay focused on what's important. Besides, it's not as though it's her real body."

Marcus pushed Clive's hand away and took a step forward, his face a couple of inches from the man. "I *am* focused on what's important," he growled. "You're the one playing Pirate King and using all this as your personal playground."

Marcus' gaze slid past him to glance in Sam's direction, her expression and posture still frozen in mid-sentence.

"You're right. I am indulging myself quite a bit here. But my role is not the same as yours. Out there," Clive said, lifting his hands and looking vaguely upward. "There's not much more I can do at Synerdyne than ensure it thrives. As for anything else, I've already done everything I really want to do. I could purchase more companies, amass more wealth, buy more property; but at a certain point, it all loses its glamor and becomes rote. And every year that passes, I grow older. But in here? The possibilities are endless. Maybe I got a little carried away," he said, inclining his head again in Sam's direction. "As I said, I'm used to getting what I want. I'm a man of great appetites. It's just my nature."

"And if people get in your way? Like Evan?" Marcus prodded.

"Then I move them aside," Clive said, his smile fading. "Like Evan."

Marcus felt his blood run cold. "I'm taking Sam and we're leaving. There is something wrong with her. Something to do with her memory," he said, pushing past Clive into the room to grab a hold of Sam's arm. "She's forgetting who she is, and this 'side project' of yours might be the reason for it."

"Or maybe she just figured out who she was all along," Clive said, folding his arms and leaning back against the door.

"You can't just have Jia playing around in the AAIP without our knowledge," Marcus snarled.

"Can't? Marcus, have you learned nothing from our conversation? There isn't anything I *can't* do," Clive said calmly. "And if I choose to have Jia work on something without telling you, then I will. Don't worry about it. We're still all on the same team. She's just finding ways to expand the scope of the simulation. To better the experience into perpetuity. Because, at the end of the day, that's what this is all about."

"You have no idea what that might do," Marcus said, shaking

his head. "It could impact things in ways we can't imagine. Such as with Sam. If I figure out that you are the reason she's losing her memory, I'll…"

"Let's not say things that can only serve to cause problems," Clive interrupted. "You're still angry. Go. Take Sam away and work through this little hiccup. When you've calmed down, we'll talk again."

In an instant, Marcus and Sam were no longer in the castle, but standing on a white sandy beach, the bright sun shining down on them. Crystalline water lapped at their feet, and in the distance, Marcus could see the silhouettes of Freeport's homes and the ships in its harbor. Sam still stood naked and frozen, her eyes staring straight ahead.

Clive had transported them. Which meant he had control of the simulation's protocol. Instinctually, Marcus brought up the protocol and was relieved as the menu displayed across his vision. He still had access. His thoughts went back to his confrontation with Clive and Sam. He had tried to pause them both, but Clive hadn't been affected. However, he had been transported by Clive's command. A cold shiver ran up his spine.

Marcus turned his attention back to Sam, and for a moment regarded her in her nakedness, the thought of her letting Clive indulge himself causing his chest to tighten. No, not her. Morrigan. This wasn't about him. Sam was the victim here. She was losing herself, and with it, all of her autonomy. Taking a deep breath, he released her from stasis.

"I mean, I'm probably too much for just one of ye anyway," she smirked, then blinked, looking around at her new surroundings. "The fuck…" she said in bewilderment, her eyes taking in the beach, then her nakedness, before settling on Marcus.

For a moment, she squinted at him, then closed her eyes tightly, as if struggling with something. When she opened her eyes again, her gaze was softer.

"Aer? What the fuck just happened? Where are we? I could have sworn I was in the castle."

Marcus let out a sigh of relief that she recognized him in some capacity, even if only as his alter ego.

"We were," he said, stepping forward to pull her into a hug.

"Whoa there, boyo. What do ye mean 'we were'?" Morrigan asked, returning the hug hesitantly.

"Clive," he started, looking into her eyes. But seeing the look of confusion at the name, he said, "Brannock transported us here."

"What do ye mean 'transported'? Why don't I remember anythin'?" she asked in confusion.

Marcus thought for a moment about how to explain it to her. "Magic. He used magic to bring us here."

"Magic!" she exclaimed, stepping out of his embrace. "That fucker's a sorcerer? To think I let him fuck me."

"So you remember?" Marcus asked, her words stabbing at his heart. "Sleeping with him."

Morrigan smirked.

"Well we weren't doin' any sleepin', but aye," she chuckled, then regarded him for a moment, narrowing her eyes. "Aer. Yer not jealous are ye?"

Marcus reminded himself that it wasn't Sam who was in control. He'd played with Sam as Morrigan countless times and understood her alter ego's mentality. He debated whether he should push to get Sam to remember herself, but decided it might do more damage than good. Maybe he could learn more from Morrigan if he played along.

"A bit, aye," he said, struggling, but forcing himself to get into character.

"Awww," Morrigan said with an amused twist of her lips, stepping forward to pat him on the cheek. "Listen, boyo. Ye know I adore ye. But ye can't expect me to not enjoy myself when yer not around. I'm not the sort to be tied down. Ye know that."

"I just thought we had an understanding," he said.

"Aye, so did I. Ye can go fuck whoever ye like and I will too. But ye know ye'll always be my favorite," she said, wrapping her arms around his neck and pressing her body to his. "More than just in my bed."

"You say that, but back in the castle you didn't seem to remember who I was."

"Did I not?" she said, her brow twisting. "Can't say I remember exactly. But it's dark in there. I probably just didn't get a good look at ye."

"So, you don't remember what happened?" he prodded.

She pulled back a little, keeping her arms around his neck, and looked away in consideration. "I remember bein' in the castle and fuckin' Brannock. Then we got interrupted. He went to the door, and started talkin' to someone, I think. But then it gets hazier. Then we ended up here together," she said, letting out a breath. "Gods, I fuckin' hate sorcerers. Iffin' I'd known he was a sorcerer, I'd have never let that fucker get near me, let alone touch me. I should have suspected."

"Why's that?"

"He's got this way of makin' people do what he wants. Got all the pirates loyal to him now, actin' as his soldiers."

"Can you remember if he's been doing anything else?" Marcus asked.

"I dunno," she shrugged. "I dun spend that much time in Freeport. Ye know me. Been out fightin' in the jungles mostly. Explorin' and the like."

Marcus nodded. "What do you remember? Do you remember the last time we were together?"

Morrigan again looked away, as if trying to recall something difficult. Finally, she shook her head. "Fuck, boyo. It all blends together. But iffin' yer worried, dun be," she smiled, pulling him close. "Ye know I've got a weakness for ye."

Morrigan lifted herself up on her toes, pressing her lips against his with a smile. Marcus returned the kiss, absentmindedly wrapping his arms around her. It felt good to hold her close, but at the same time, his mind whirled with what he'd just learned. He needed to get back to Amir and Diego. They had to know what was going on with Jia and Clive, but another part of him worried about leaving Sam alone again. And what Clive might do in his absence. It wasn't just the idea that he might sleep with Sam, but also the control he might be able to exert over her.

Marcus brought the protocol up in his vision. How could he hide Sam from Clive's reach? With his controls, Clive could just transport Sam back to him, and who knew what else. From inside the simulation, Marcus didn't have many options, but if he could get into the AAIP, maybe he could find a way to protect her.

"It's probably a good idea for you to stay away from the city for a while," he said, pulling away from her kiss.

"Aye. Yer probably right. I dun trust that fucker and I dun want to be anywhere near his magic," she said, letting her hand slip down to take hold of his. "Ye comin' with me?"

Marcus shook his head somberly, his heart aching at the thought of leaving her alone. "I can't. There are some things I need to take care of at the moment."

Using the protocol, he materialized some new clothes for her just at the edge of the beach, along with a spear. Folded as if she had left them there.

"You should probably get dressed," he said, gesturing in the direction of the clothes.

A look of disappointment showed on Morrigan's face, but she nodded, stepping away and letting go of his hand.

"But when I'm done, I'll come and find you," he assured her.

"Alright, boyo," she said, looking at the clothes and walking back towards them. "But dun ye go makin' me wait too long. Ye dun want me to forget about ye."

CHAPTER 23

"You were right," Marcus said, looking across the table at Amir and Diego. "He has Jia working on some special project geared at creating an autonomous artificial intelligence, without our involvement. Not only that, but he has complete control of the simulation. He can override my protocols with his own."

Marcus thought about telling them about Clive and Sam but decided it would only muddy the waters and didn't have anything to do with the situation at hand. Plus, he didn't want them to think any actions he took against Clive were done out of jealousy.

"Well, fuck. What do we do now?" Diego asked.

"First and foremost, I want to get into the AAIP and protect Sam from Clive," Marcus said forcefully.

"You want to neuter his protocols?" Amir asked.

"Not exactly. I worry doing something like that might immediately put him on the defensive," Marcus said. "I was thinking more along the lines of changing Sam's protocol identifier so that he can't find her."

"Well, that might work, but only for so long. If he wants to, he could have Jia figure it out," Amir replied.

"We just need enough time to keep Sam away from him until we can get him removed from Synerdyne and the simulation," Marcus explained.

"Removed? How do you intend to do that?" Diego asked.

"The same way he got in," Marcus said. "We'll have the board remove him."

"Do you think that can actually work? I mean he was able to get rid of Evan," Amir pointed out.

"Yeah, but only with my voting shares," Marcus countered. "Evan may no longer be CEO, but he still has his shares. If Evan and I band together, that tactic should work just as well against Clive as it did against him."

"What makes you think Evan will go for it?" Amir asked. "Don't you think he might be a bit resentful towards you for helping to kick him out?"

"Yeah, that's the first hurdle," Marcus admitted. "But I think when he finds out what is going on, he'll realize that this is more important than his feelings."

"Maybe don't put it across to him that way," Diego cautioned.

"I promise I'll be more tactful," Marcus assured him with a chuckle.

"Alright, so let's say you get Evan to go along with this. What then? Can you be sure that you'll be able to push Ellison out? I mean, I don't how this shit works, but he'll still have all his shares. That's got to mean something," Amir said.

"That's why we need to get Evan on our side first. He understands the board and how all this works," Marcus said.

"And then what?" Diego asked. "You kick Ellison and Jia out? How do we make sure they don't sabotage anything on the way out? They have access to everything."

"That's where I need you to come in. Both of you. Amir, I need you to work on a way to lock down the AAIP and kick Jia out. We'll have to wait to take any action until after we know what's going on with the board. But when that happens, we'll need you to be ready to go at a moment's notice," Marcus instructed, pulling each of their coffee cups to the center of the table and using them as props in his explanation. "Diego, I need you to keep an eye on the other programmers. Make sure none of them are working on behalf of Ellison, or at least don't get an inkling of what we are up to. I don't want another Oswald situation blowing up in our faces. Once we have everything locked down, we'll make our move."

"And if it should work? What are we going to do about the simulation?" Amir asked.

"That's something to worry about after we get control again," Marcus replied. "Right now the mission is to get Ellison out of the company and out of the simulation."

"How's Sam? Any change?" Diego asked.

Marcus looked down into his cup, the mention of Sam stirring up feelings he had been avoiding since last seeing her. "The last time I saw her, she only interacted with me as Morrigan. I didn't even try to make her remember her real life. In fact, I think Morrigan might be losing her memory too. She didn't immediately recognize me, even as Aer. That's why it's so important we get rid of Ellison quickly. We have to figure out what's going on. And I have a feeling the special project of his is to blame."

"Maybe," Amir said.

"Maybe? What do you mean 'maybe'?" Marcus prodded. "You don't think it has to do with her losing her memory?"

"I don't know, honestly. Like I said, maybe it does," Amir said. "But without knowing when Ellison instructed Jia to start this project, it'll be hard to correlate. We have been looking into the other duplicants, and it seems like they might be affected in the same way after all. We presumed the reason we didn't see it at first was because they hadn't been there as long. But you have, just as long as Sam, and you aren't experiencing any memory loss, are you?"

Marcus shook his head.

"Right. And it doesn't seem like Ellison is either. So then it stands to reason that it must have something to do with their consciousnesses being 'untethered' from their physical brain activity," Amir explained.

"Even more reason to suspect Ellison's autonomous AI project," Marcus pointed out.

"Again, maybe," Amir continued. "But before we learned about that, just now, I thought of a different possible culprit. The respawn."

"The respawn? I don't understand," Marcus said.

"Well, let's look at what we know," Amir said, gesturing with his hands. "The respawn takes a consciousness at the moment of—for lack of a better word—'death' and removes it from one location to another, reorganizing it in the process. So if we imagine it like a washing machine, every time someone respawns, the AAIP washes their mapping to clean out any lingering sensations of pain or conscious thought, returning them to a state of stability. However, each time that happens, like washing colors or something with an image, their thoughts are losing some of their vibrancy and start to fade. It's not a perfect analogy, but I think it makes my point."

"So every time someone dies in the simulation, they lose some of their memories?" Marcus said.

"Maybe not at first," Amir replied, shrugging. "But over time, yes. That's the theory. And it would explain why we've seen it so severely in Sam and not in the other duplicants. She's always been more aggressive in the game, and throws herself into dangerous situations, meaning she's respawning more often. The duplicants have shown themselves to be more cautious and hesitant to leave the city, they haven't had the same number of opportunities to respawn. But now that some of them have, we've seen some gaps in their cognizance."

"But I've respawned a few times now," Marcus pointed out.

"Yes, but when you respawn, you are returned to your biological brain function. Sam and the duplicants are recycled through the AAIP," Amir explained.

"Fuck," Marcus said. "If that's true, then it's my fault."

"No," Amir said. "You can't blame yourself. You were looking to solve a very real problem, and without it, I doubt Sam could have continued in the simulation. Besides, I am just floating this as a possibility. One that we should consider as much as any other. As with everything dealing with the simulation, this is all theoretical."

"At a certain point we have to move past theory and start getting some answers," Marcus said. "We should stop the respawn protocol until we can dissect its code."

"No. I think that would be a very bad idea. As I said: when we respawn, we are ejected from the simulation back into our biological consciousness, but Sam and the duplicants have nowhere to go. Turning off the respawn could mean that the next time one of them 'dies', they might be ejected from the simulation entirely. Which, in essence, would mean that their consciousness would experience—for all intents and purposes—death."

"Could we just re-download their map to the AAIP?" Diego asked.

Amir shook his head, but it was Marcus who answered.

"It's an active map, not some downloaded file. That's what makes them alive. The duplicants were pulled from an active consciousness into Sam's world, where they continued to function and grow. The same with Sam. If they were just copies, then Claire would be right, and we would just be interacting with software made to look and act like actual people."

"So we can't turn off the respawn," Diego said.

"Exactly," Marcus said.

Marcus considered Amir's idea, and the more he thought it over, the more likely it seemed. He had doomed Sam with his hubris. Even if he did eject Ellison from the company, it wouldn't fix the fact that Sam was slipping away. His mind returned to the memory of Sam standing naked in Ellison's room. Whatever he did, he had to protect her from being taken advantage of, and that meant getting

Ellison out. He'd figure out how he could help Sam from there. But so long as Clive was in control they were all in danger, especially Sam.

"So what are we going to do?" Diego asked.

"We're going to move forward with the plan: kick Ellison out of our company and the simulation," Marcus declared. "After that, we'll figure out where to go from there. But his time is done."

Marcus walked down the unfamiliar halls of the fourth floor, looking at each door he passed. Most were unmarked, blandly similar in their gray metal that matched the lighter gray of the hallway walls. He was pretty sure this floor was used for Synerdyne's more mundane accounting and logistics work. As the hall split ahead of him, Marcus heard a familiar voice coming from the left turn ahead of him.

Rounding the corner, he saw Janice sitting behind a much smaller desk in a cramped alcove just outside of an office door. She was on the phone but widened her eyes when she saw him. He gave her a small smile and waited patiently for her to finish her call. It took a few more minutes before she finally put the phone down, and when she looked back at him her expression was cold.

"I'm here to see Evan," he said. "Could you let him know I'm here?"

"He's not here," Janice said, her lips wrinkling as she pursed them tightly.

"I know he probably doesn't want to see me, but I need to talk to him."

"No. I mean it," she said. "He's not here. He's out. I think he's at the club."

"Oh," Marcus said in surprise.

"He doesn't have much on his plate these days," Janice said with a tight, unfriendly smile.

"Right. Well, I'll see if I can catch him at the club," Marcus said awkwardly under her stare, turning to leave.

"You know, I always thought you were a nice guy," she said to his back, making him turn around. "Thought you were the kind one. Mr. Nguyen can be a little self-absorbed sometimes, but deep down he's a good man. He might seem like he doesn't pay much attention to things, but he always listens and remembers, and he takes care of the people he works with. Turns out, he's the kind one." She looked him up and down. "And deep down, you're just cruel."

Marcus swallowed, feeling shame wash over him.

"I'm sorry about what happened," he said. "Truly. I hope one day I can make it up to you both."

Janice snorted and looked back down at her monitor, ignoring him.

Marcus wanted to say more but thought better of it. The less he divulged, the less Clive could learn. Giving her a nod she didn't acknowledge, he turned and walked back down the hall to go find Evan.

The car pulled up to the country club, dropping Marcus off at the entrance. A man in a blue jacket waiting on the stairs under the canopy that covered the driveway walked up to the vehicle and opened the passenger door for him. Marcus offered the man a tight smile and fished in his pocket for a tip, but the man waved a hand to stop him.

"That's not necessary, sir. Welcome to Lincoln Oaks."

"Thank you," Marcus said, as he stepped out of the car.

Nodding, the valet stepped aside and gestured to the stairs, at the top of which stood another man in a blue jacket who held the entrance door open for him. Marcus gave the man a nod of appreciation and strode up the steps to enter the building.

The club lobby was large and ostentatious, with members dressed in an assortment of active clothing moving about, some carrying squash rackets, while others carted golf bags behind them. Marcus strode toward the front desk where a young woman, dressed in the familiar blue jacket, stood in front of a monitor. She smiled as she noticed his approach.

"What can I do for you, sir?" she inquired politely.

"I'm here to see a member. Evan Nguyen."

"And your name, sir?" she asked.

"Marcus Avery."

"Alright, Mr. Avery. If you'll just take a seat over there, I'll relay your message and let you know."

"He is here, isn't he?" Marcus asked.

"I'm sorry, sir. I can't divulge that information to non-members. But if he is here, I will make sure he gets your message. Please, just have a seat," she said, gesturing to the cluster of chairs at the other end of the room.

Marcus nodded and crossed the room, sitting down and pulling out his phone while he waited. He stared at the screen but wasn't paying attention to any of the articles he scrolled through. His mind was too preoccupied with Sam. He hoped Amir would be able to get her protocol signature changed without Clive or Jia noticing. He wondered what she was doing and thought about the respawn.

How many cycles would it take to erase her memory completely? Was it already gone? He felt a numbness run through his body and recognized the same dread he'd felt while Sam was sick, whenever he'd allowed himself to think about her possible death. It left him feeling helpless and hollow. Like he was swimming with a heavy weight attached to his ankle. No matter how hard he struggled, sooner or later, it would pull him down.

"I was going to tell them to say I wasn't here, but I actually have some things I want to say to you," Evan said, standing before him with his squash racket propped on one shoulder. He wore a close-fitting athletic shirt and shorts, sweat beading on his brow, and he was still breathing heavily from his exertions.

Marcus looked up at his old friend and gave him a sad smile.

"I'm sure I deserve whatever you have to say," Marcus said.

"Come on. I'm not going to make a scene in the lobby. Let's go out on the veranda," Evan said, gesturing to the club restaurant.

Marcus stood up, following Evan as he confidently made his way past the half-filled tables of diners to the outdoor seating area. Taking a table in the far corner, Evan sat down and gestured for Marcus to do the same. Almost immediately a member of the waitstaff arrived to greet them, asking them if they wanted drinks to start with.

"That would probably be for the best," Evan said. "Two whiskey sours."

Giving him a nod, the woman walked away. Evan looked over at Marcus, and suddenly it felt uncomfortably quiet. Marcus cleared his throat. He'd gone over what he was going to say a couple of dozen times, but now that he was face to face with Evan, his words felt inadequate.

"So, I'm guessing you're either here because you've got a guilty conscience or because you need something," Evan said. "But before you start, I have something to say to you."

Marcus opened his mouth to elaborate but then closed it, giving Evan a nod.

"I've given this a lot of thought over the last week, and I've got to say, I didn't see it coming. From Ellison, sure, but not from you. Not like that," Evan said, shrugging. "Maybe I was naive. But you know what hurt the most? Knowing you didn't trust me. How quickly you decided that *I* was a problem. After how many years of knowing each other? You know, I can't say I've ever been betrayed before. Hurt? Let down? Dumped? Sure. But what you and Ellison pulled was some real Brutus and Caesar shit."

"Caesar had become a tyrant," Marcus said.

"Oh, shut the fuck up. You know what I mean," Evan snapped. "You stabbed me in the back, Marcus. And not because I became a tyrant, just because I wanted to know what was going on with the company you and I started. The company that I was supposed to be leading. I mean, what did Ellison offer you? I've never known you to be one who wanted power or money."

"Sam," Marcus said. "He promised to preserve Sam."

"What? You mean that avatar of her that you are keeping in Sam's World?"

"It's not an avatar, Evan. We found a way to use the AAIP to preserve Sam's consciousness. Not just hers. Everyone's, potentially."

Evan stared silently across the table at him, his face unreadable.

"Here are your drinks, gentlemen. Have you decided on any food?" the waitress asked, looking between them.

"Just the drinks, thank you," Evan said dismissively, continuing to stare at Marcus.

"Alright. If there's anything else you...."

"Just the drinks," Evan interrupted more curtly.

Cutting her sentence short, the waitress nodded her head and walked away quickly.

"It's true," Marcus continued. "When she died, we were able to keep her consciousness active in the simulation. It's the reason Ellison signed on to Synerdyne. Not Sam specifically, but because he believed it was possible with our research. And when you started demanding answers about what we were doing, I was worried you were going to jeopardize that."

"So you kept it from me, and sided with Ellison to push me out, instead of telling me?" Evan said in disbelief.

"I thought you would think I was just seeing what I wanted to see, and that you'd be more worried about it putting the company at risk," Marcus explained.

"Of course it would put the company at risk. There are rules we have to follow, Marcus. Regulations. But that doesn't mean I wouldn't understand. Are you sure?"

"See? That's what I am talking about," Marcus said, gesturing to Evan. "Yes, I am sure. So are Amir, Diego, Jia, and Ellison. We've all seen it. Seen her, talked to her, and interacted with her. She's still alive in the simulation. That's what Oswald saw."

Evan sat back in his chair dumbfounded, staring down at his drink. His hand hovered around his glass, but he didn't pick it up. Marcus took the opportunity to take a long pull from his own glass to calm his nerves.

"You should still have told me," Evan said quietly.

"Maybe," Marcus conceded. "But at the time, I couldn't risk it."

Evan's eyes lifted to focus back on him. "So why are you telling me this now?"

"Because Sam is in danger. The whole simulation is," Marcus said, sitting up and looking Evan in the eye. "Elysium *and* Sam's World. Ellison is taking control, both inside and out of the simulation. And I'm worried I'll be pushed out next."

"Maybe you deserve to get a taste of betrayal," Evan snorted.

"Sure. Maybe I do," Marcus said. "And if it were just me, I would understand if you told me to fuck off. But this impacts Sam too, and in a much larger way. Unlike me or you, she can't just walk away and start over. She will be his prisoner if he takes control of Sam's World. Her very existence is at stake."

"Jesus Christ," Evan said, shaking his head and finally lifting his glass to his lips. For several seconds he drank, and Marcus watched as the contents slowly diminished until it was empty. Putting the glass back down on the table heavily, Evan let out a sigh and waved a hand at a passing waiter to bring two more.

"So what do you expect me to do about it?" he asked, turning his attention back to Marcus.

"I want us to push Ellison out," Marcus replied. "Together we should have enough voting shares to do that. We'll give him a taste of his own medicine."

Evan shook his head.

"What?" Marcus asked.

"It won't work," Evan said.

"Sure it will, just like before," Marcus protested. "With your voting shares and mine, we have enough to outvote him."

"What are we outvoting him for?" Evan asked. "He's not the CEO, or in any position within the company. We can't vote to take his shares away, and as long as he holds those, he holds power over us and the company."

"We could vote to put you back as CEO," Marcus offered. "That position hasn't been filled."

"Sure. Though I think it might shake investor confidence to see us so disorganized. I mean, days after an EGM, you want to call another one?" Evan asked. "That makes it look like we are either indecisive or in disarray. And the most likely outcome of all that would be shareholders jumping ship. And do you know who they would sell their shares to?"

"Ellison," Marcus answered somberly.

"Right," Evan replied. "Only solidifying his power."

"So, what can we do?" Marcus asked, his heart sinking.

"If there was something we could do, don't you think I would have done it?" Evan asked as the waiter set two new drinks on the table.

"There has to be something we can do," Marcus insisted. "He can't just take it all away from us."

"He can and he has," Evan said. "So long as Ellison holds shares at Synerdyne, he'll hold control."

"So what should I do?" Marcus asked.

"I'm not sure there is anything you can do, except stay on his good side."

Marcus sat back in his chair, his body growing numb. If Evan couldn't help him eject Ellison from the company, then everything they did wouldn't amount to much. Not for long. With Jia giving him access to the master protocols of the simulation, Clive had complete control.

"So what are you going to do now," Marcus asked, slowly bringing his focus back to Evan.

"Same as you. Stay on his good side."

CHAPTER 24

"So, we're fucked," Amir said matter-of-factly.

"The only chance we have is to make Clive see reason," Marcus replied, settling himself down on the couch in Amir's office. "Explain to him that his actions could jeopardize the whole project if he isn't careful."

"And you do you think that will work?" Diego asked.

"He's not a psychopath," Marcus said. "At least, I don't think so. What I know is that he is invested in the simulation and wants it to work as much as we do. So if he is made to realize that he may inadvertently be threatening that, hopefully, he'll be willing to pull back a little bit and relinquish some of his control. What about Sam?"

"I was able to change her protocol signature," Amir said. "You'll have to look up her designation manually. To anyone scanning for her, her marker will look like just another NPC avatar. And at this point we count about a thousand of those."

"A thousand?" Marcus said shocked. "Did we make a thousand?"

"No," Diego said. "From what we can determine, it was the AAIP. It is already programmed to replace assets that are lost, and in the case of 'living organisms' respawn them. That way the wildlife can't be hunted into extinction, nor all the trees cut down. The size of these populations is governed by a set of parameters, based on the extent of the developed landscape within Sam's World. However, it seems the AAIP has been expanding that landscape, adding acreage at a rate of a hundred square acres a day."

"What? Of jungle?" Marcus exclaimed, trying to comprehend the sheer scale of growth.

"That, but more so the ocean," Diego explained. "It is extending the water farther and farther each day. We think it is due to the fact that the ocean is a less complicated biome since we dedicated less time to it and created significantly fewer assets: a few aquatic animal species, some coral, and kelp. Nothing as intricate as the jungle. But when it comes to population parameters, we never set any for the human avatars, just the smaller animal species. However, we think the AAIP has created its own guideline, based upon initial population size."

"How can it do that?" Marcus asked. "Isn't that what the parameters are for?"

"It seems that the AAIP has taken the 'autonomous' part of its name a little more seriously than we anticipated. I can't be certain, but I think it is becoming self-governing in some capacity," Amir said.

"Why? Why now? It wasn't doing this before," Marcus said. "Does this have something to do with Sam and the duplicants?"

"Perhaps. But more likely the introduction of the consciousness maps to its asset protocols is the culprit," Amir offered. "I can't say how exactly, but it seems that not only the avatars are acting with autonomy, but the entire simulation itself. However, it seems to still be hewing to the parameters we initially set regarding the environment and organic structures, it's just expanding upon those. So far nothing it's done is chaotic or out of bounds."

"Does that mean it's taking over the simulation?" Marcus asked.

"Maybe, though the protocol controls still can override its autonomy," Amir said. "It was created to be self-governing, within the bounds of its parameters. However, I suppose if left to its own devices, it might reach some form of full autonomy."

"Has this had any effect on Sam or the duplicants?" Marcus asked, his concern building. "Or could it be the reason they are losing their memories?"

Amir shrugged. "Your guess is as good as mine. Without extensive study of the data, going line by line through the code, there's just no way to know. That's not even taking into account whatever changes Ellison and Jia may have made."

"So even more reason to convince them to take a step back," Marcus said.

"Yeah," Amir agreed. "If you can pull it off."

Marcus nodded.

"Well, there's no way to know until I try," Marcus said, easing back to lie down on the couch. "Wish me luck, I guess."

"Don't fuck it up," Diego said with a smile, but Marcus could see the tightness around his eyes.

Marcus returned the smile and closed his eyes, leaning his head back against the couch cushion and engaging the SynAPP.

Opening his eyes, Marcus found himself staring at the rafters of the tavern's guestroom and kicked his legs over the side of the bed to sit up. The humid heat was warm against his skin, a stark contrast to Amir's climate-controlled office. For a moment, he sat there and rubbed his eyes, letting his equilibrium settle in, then pushed himself to his feet and stepped out into the hallway.

He only glanced at the patrons as he made his way through the common room, his eyes unconsciously searching for Sam's face as he passed the tables. Pushing open the door, he stepped out onto the street and immediately noticed the men standing guard at the city gate, the red banners still hanging on the walls above them. Marcus ignored the men and turned down the avenue leading to the keep.

Outside the castle's walls, he found more red-sashed men waiting idly, weapons hanging from their belts. One of them stepped up to block Marcus' path, and he considered using the protocol to avoid them again, as he had the day before, but he stopped himself. The memory of finding Clive and Sam together entered his mind, and his chest tightened at the prospect of it happening again. Though he hoped, with Amir's adjustment to her marker, that she would be far away from Freeport and Ellison.

"The fuck do you want?" the red-sashed guard demanded as Marcus approached him.

"I'm here to see Clive," Marcus said.

"Who?" the man asked, his face twisting in confusion.

"Oh, uh… Brannock," Marcus corrected.

"The King doesn't just see anyone who walks in off the street," the man replied with a snort.

"Tell him, Marcus is here to see him."

The man looked Marcus up and down, turned to one of the other guards, and with a gesture of his head sent the other man jogging back toward the castle.

Turning back, he eyed Marcus again and rested a hand on the pommel of his sword. Marcus couldn't help but wonder what the avatar might be thinking. Were his demeanor and actions just part of his programming, or had the consciousness mapping given him the ability for independent thought?

"Long shift?" Marcus asked.

The man looked over at him and shrugged.

"Better day than night," he said.

"What do you lads do for fun when you're not on duty?" Marcus continued to probe.

"What else? Drink, fight, fuck. Not always in that order," he said, barking out a laugh and looking to the other men who joined him in his laughter.

Marcus gave him a tight smile. "Got any plans for the future, or is this it?"

"What?" the man asked.

"This. Being a guard," Marcus said. "Are you content to do this for the rest of your life, or do you have other plans? Any hobbies?"

The man considered Marcus for a moment in silence, shifting uncomfortably.

"Gonna get my own ship," he said.

"Really?" Marcus said.

"Aye. Get me a crew and hunt for fat merchants moving even fatter cargos."

Marcus couldn't tell if his answer was just part of the original scripting for any of the pirates, so he changed tact. "And what's your symbol going to look like?"

"My what?" the man asked, his brow twisting in confusion.

"On your ship's sail. You know, to mark who you are to other vessels," Marcus pointed to the crimson banner. "Like that. How will people know who you are so you can gain a reputation? You've got to have a symbol."

The man considered the banner, his gaze rising to follow it up the wall. "A scorpion. Yeah. It'll be white, with a blood-red scorpion."

"A scorpion?" Marcus said, trying to remember if they'd created any scorpion assets in Sam's World. Even if they had, the fact that the avatar had chosen it without any visual or auditory prompt seemed distinctly individualistic. He tried to remember to ask Diego about it when he finished here.

The man sent by the guard captain came jogging back to the gate. "The King says to let him in," he said to the other man, jutting a thumb behind him to the castle.

"I suppose he does want to see you, after all," the guard captain said, raising an eyebrow. "Well, go on, don't keep the King waiting." He motioned to two of the other guards, and they stepped forward.

Waving for Marcus to follow, the men guided him past the gate and into the castle's small courtyard.

Marcus followed them as they led the way, taking him from the bright, warm sunshine into the dark, cavernous halls of the castle proper. The entrance led straight into the massive throne room that dominated the entirety of the lower floor, at the end of which sat Clive in the great stone chair atop his dais. Marcus noted that he'd made some modifications to his outfit, bedecking himself in golden chains and rings, as well as a simple, but heavy looking, iron crown. He couldn't be sure if it was just the perspective, but it seemed as though he'd also increased his musculature and size.

As the two guards approached the throne, Clive looked down at him and arched an eyebrow. "You know, it's customary to bow before a king," he said, his voice echoing down the hall.

"I'm not going to do that," Marcus said. "I've come to talk. It's important."

Clive arched an eyebrow, and suddenly Marcus felt a sharp pain in the back of his knee, causing him to fall forward. Beside him, he saw that one of the guards had struck him in the back of the leg with the butt of his spear.

"That's better," Clive said haughtily.

Marcus clenched his teeth and forced himself to stay calm. If Clive wanted to assert his dominance, it wouldn't do Marcus any good to push back. He needed the man to listen to him, and if that meant playing along with his farce, then so be it.

"You can leave us," Clive said, gesturing with his head for the guardsmen to go. As they stepped out of the chamber, he leaned forward with a smile. "Sorry about that. But I have to keep up appearances, and a tyrant doesn't tolerate insolence. You understand," he said with a smile, easing back into the throne. "You may rise."

Marcus gave him a tight smile and pushed himself to his feet, the strike to his leg still throbbing.

"So you want to talk? What about?" Clive asked, drumming his fingers on the stone arm of the throne.

"The simulation. It's becoming unstable," Marcus said.

"Seems stable enough to me," Clive retorted, raising his gaze to the ceiling.

"I don't mean the environment," Marcus explained. "I'm talking about the AAIP. It's starting to act on its own, doing things that it was never programmed to do, and not just with the NPCs. It's affecting the very nature and scope of Sam's World, and we don't know what else it might be capable of doing. We need to pull back and assess things, then move forward more cautiously and meticulously."

"And why would we do that?" Clive asked. "It seems to me that the AAIP is doing exactly what it was designed to do. It is an 'autonomous artificial intelligence program' after all. What's more autonomous than what you are describing?"

"But we don't know what that will lead to," Marcus pressed. "What sort of instability might arise from it in the future? What it could do to Sam and the duplicates. I told you, Sam is losing her memory. And so are the duplicates. They are losing the very thing that we set out to preserve: their consciousness."

"I haven't noticed any changes in myself, and you seem to remember things just fine," Clive said, with a dubious twist of his lips.

"That's because we are still connected to our active consciousness. It's a kind of tether that keeps our memories stable: a safeguard. Sam and the duplicants aren't. And we think every time they respawn, it gets worse."

"So, we just need to fix that aspect. Seems like a small problem. Just turn off the respawn," Clive said dismissively.

"We can't. Not without the risk of losing their consciousnesses," Marcus said. "And besides, it would shut down the very mechanism by which the mapping functions. That's why we need to slow down so we can deal with these problems first. We don't know if the addition of the consciousness maps is having some effect on this situation. We need to work together on this."

"Hmmm. An interesting choice of words, considering," Clive said, his face growing stern.

"I don't understand what you mean," Marcus replied, shaking his head.

"What I mean is that you and your team went behind my back and made some changes to the simulation, didn't you?" Clive said, arching an eyebrow.

"What are you talking about?" Marcus replied.

"Morrigan. You hid her from me," Clive said, leaning forward menacingly. "Made it so I can't find her in the protocol."

Marcus felt his blood go cold. "Why does that matter to you? You don't need to deal with Sam."

"Everything here in Sam's World matters to me, Marcus. And I don't like others asserting their control over my kingdom. A kingdom can only have one king, otherwise, you have anarchy. But you still insist on trying to be king. Didn't you learn anything from what happened to Evan?"

"I'm not going to leave Sam to your mercy, you fucking psycho," Marcus growled. "Sam is the only thing that matters to me."

"Exactly," Clive said. "You don't have the focus necessary to see the bigger picture. You're too hindered by your personal concerns."

"And what about you?" Marcus spat. "Playing king in the simulation and ignoring the outside world? Do you really think you're in a position to tell me *I'm* not focusing on the bigger picture?"

"Oh, but I'm not ignoring the outside world, Marcus. And just like in here, out there I have soldiers to protect my interests. Now I'm going to give you the opportunity to make up for your mistakes, but I understand just how personal all this is to you. Tell me how to find Morrigan, and I'll forget all this happened."

"Fuck you," Marcus said. "You're insane."

"That was the wrong answer," Clive said coldly. "However you've hidden her, it's only a matter of time before my people figure it out. You know that, right? Listen, this isn't about winning or losing. It's about understanding that life is built on hierarchies. Don't take it personally. I don't make the rules. There are two kinds of people in this world. Those who think they are in control, and those who make sure they are. You only think you have control because no one has challenged you for it before." Clive cocked his head to the side and regarded Marcus. "I do like you, Marcus. You've got spirit, and that's hard enough to find nowadays. But you need to accept the circumstances for what they are. If you can do that, then you can continue to work with me to make this simulation, and all the ones after it, into something that will change humanity and our concept of life and death forever. But if you insist on standing in my way, then I will have to take more extreme measures."

"Synerdyne and the simulation were built by me and my team," Marcus growled. "They aren't yours to take away. Not while I'm still breathing."

"So dramatic. But once again you've given the wrong answer," Clive said. "And you're wrong about what I can and can't do."

Suddenly Marcus felt his airway constricting, preventing him from taking a breath. For a moment he tried to force himself to breathe, willing his throat to open, but it remained tightly sealed. He looked up at Clive, his chest beginning to burn as the oxygen slowly faded from his lungs. He tried to tell himself that the reaction wasn't physical, that he wasn't breathing any actual oxygen, but he knew as far as his brain was concerned the sensation was real.

Desperately, he called up the protocol in his vision and looked for an option to alleviate the pain. He wasn't even sure how Clive was able to target him so specifically and scanned through the different menus of options frantically. Choosing the pain protocols, he increased his pain threshold, but to his horror, it remained locked in place. He scrolled to another menu and tried to change the drowning controls, in the hopes it would have some impact, but again they didn't budge. He was locked out!

Unconsciously, he brought his hands up to his throat in an instinctual but futile effort to try and do something, falling forward on the ground as his body focused solely on his need for breath. As he thrashed on the ground, he looked up at Clive. The man sat unmoved on his throne. Marcus tried to focus on his face, but shadows began to creep into the corners of his vision, blurring the world around him. As the shadows closed in, Clive leaned forward, his face just barely distinguishable in Marcus' fading vision, and smiled.

Marcus woke with a start, sitting up and gasping for breath. Looking around frantically, he struggled to keep his head from spinning, and it took him a moment to register that he was in Amir's office. The first faces he recognized were those of Amir and Diego, both watching him with concern, but then he noticed other faces in the room as well. Faces that watched him with placid stares and harder eyes. He turned his focus to the newcomers and recognized the security uniforms they were wearing.

"What the hell is going on?" he managed, still gasping for breath.

"Mr. Avery. You, Mr. Mizrahi, and Mr. Torres are to be escorted from the building. Please hand over your employee badges and any other Synerdyne property you may have on your person," a heavy-set man in security blue explained bluntly.

Two other security personnel stepped forward to assist Marcus from the couch, but he shook them away.

"Who gave you this order?" Marcus demanded, knowing it must be Clive's doing.

"Ms. Yang, sir," the security chief said.

"She was made acting CEO this morning," Amir explained.

"Your employment and credentials have been terminated as of

eight o'clock this morning," the guard said. "We are here to escort you out of the building."

"I am a majority shareholder of this company," Marcus argued, as the two men reached down to insistently lift him from the couch. "You can't just throw me out."

"I'm sorry, sir. That's above my pay grade," the guard said bluntly. "As I said, according to Ms. Yang, you are no longer employees of Synerdyne and are to be escorted off the premises. Any personal belongings, not the property of Synerdyne, will be gathered and boxed for you to pick up by tomorrow. Now please Mr. Avery, I encourage you to cooperate and not cause a scene."

"Not cause a scene?" Marcus scoffed. "You have three… four… six people in here to escort us out and you think this won't cause a scene?"

"Just doing my job, sir," the man said, matter-of-factly.

"We can't do anything about it, Marcus," Amir said.

"Yeah. We got played," Diego added somberly.

Marcus looked to his two friends, then to the two security guards on either side of him. They were right. Ellison had outplayed their hand. He controlled not only Freeport, but the entirety of Sam's World, and without Evan at the helm, he now owned Synerdyne. And with that knowledge, all the fight suddenly went out of Marcus.

Giving a glance at his two friends, Marcus lowered his head in defeat and nodded in acquiescence to the security chief. Motioning to his men, the security chief opened the door to Amir's office and led the escort out onto the floor. The design team looked up from their cubicles and watched with a mix of interest and shock as Marcus and his friends were escorted to the elevator by the security team. As the elevator doors closed, Marcus took one last look at the faces of his employees staring back at him. But in his mind, the only face he saw was Sam's.

CHAPTER 25

Marcus stared at the picture of him and Sam, both of them smiling at the camera with their heads together. They'd taken the picture just after her first diagnosis when neither of them had realized just how serious things would become, thinking it just a bump in the road. They'd been through so much already by that point that the idea that anything could possibly get between them seemed absurd. Despite their naivete, they had at least been happy in their ignorance, and looking into her eyes, he felt his love for her swell painfully in his heart.

The picture blurred in his vision, their faces becoming indistinguishable. He had refused to believe that she could be taken from him. That their time would be cut short. Sam was indomitable and their love was eternal. Nothing, not even the universe, could keep them apart. And even in their darkest hour, the discovery of the cognitive mapping had made it seem like maybe he was right. Even death could not keep them apart. But that was just another moment of naivete. Now he knew better.

Sam had not only been taken from him but she had also been stripped of the very things that made up her identity. Her memories. Not by Clive, or Jia, but by his hubris. He had believed that, out of all life that had ever existed, their relationship was too special to be subject to nature. That they would be the first people to figure out how to cheat death. And in doing so, he had only prolonged Sam's suffering. Forcing her to be taken apart piece by piece. An aching cold crept over him as his tears splashed against the tablet's surface.

He didn't cry for the loss of Synerdyne or even his access to the simulation. Those things were just a means to an end. His sorrow came from the realization that Sam was gone, and no matter what he did, he could never bring her back. His chest tightened as a wave of grief washed over him, building in intensity until it felt like his heart would explode.

Gripping the pillow on his lap, he brought it to his face and screamed. He screamed as the grief tore him apart. He screamed at the unfairness of it all. He screamed at the cold reality that he'd never see Sam again. He screamed until his throat was hoarse and he could no longer breathe, his voice fading to a mewling whisper as he sobbed into the cushion.

Eventually he pulled the pillow away from his face, the pressure easing enough for him to take a breath. As the room came back into focus his attention was drawn to the bottles of pills that littered the end table next to his chair, all filled with Sam's old medications. His eyes moved to one bottle in particular, the familiar shape identifying its contents without him having to read the label.

Maybe Claire had been right all along, and Sam was dead. What they had thought they were preserving in the simulation might just be an echo of her, inevitably meant to fade away in time. Maybe he'd just been fooling himself, unable to face the reality that he'd failed. In trying to preserve her, he'd wasted what little time they'd had left. Time they could have spent together. A pang of anguish passed through him, and he let out another sob, thinking about every second he'd chosen to focus on the simulation instead of spending it with her.

A notification pinged on his phone, another of the multitude he'd received since leaving Synerdyne. Most had been from Amir and Diego, while some others had been from friends and employees; all of which he'd chosen to ignore. He looked back to the medication, his eyes focused on the familiar one, pointedly illuminated by the glow of his phone's screen. Slowly he reached for the bottle.

The sudden buzzing of his phone—causing it to rattle across the table—caught his attention, and he looked down to see Claire's name. For a moment, his hand hovered over the phone, just out of reach of the pills, and he stared at the call screen with Claire's smiling face pressed against Sam's. With a swallow, he reached down and answered the call.

"Marcus?" Claire's voice asked worriedly from the phone's speaker.

For a moment, he stared at the phone, at a loss for words.

"Marcus, are you there?" Claire asked again.

"Yeah," he said hoarsely.

"Oh, thank God," she said with an audible sigh. "Diego and Amir told me what happened. Are you alright?"

"I… I… I honestly… don't think I am. She's gone Claire," he barely managed, his tears returning in earnest.

"Oh, Marcus. I'm so sorry," she said, her voice pained. "Listen, I'm on my way over. Just sit tight and wait for me. Okay? I'm only a few minutes away. Let's talk. Okay?"

Marcus stared at the phone, his body numb.

"Okay, Marcus?" she prodded more assertively.

"Okay," he whispered.

"Good. I'll be right there. Just sit tight," she said, and he heard her tell the driver to speed up just as she ended the call.

Marcus let his hand drop to his lap and eased back into the chair, glancing over at the bottles again. Leaning his head back, he closed his eyes and gathered his resolve. Finally, with a sigh, he pushed himself out of the chair and turned on the lights, gathered the bottles from the table, and hid them in the drawer of Sam's bedside table.

True to her word, Claire rang from the lobby only a few minutes later. Buzzing her up, Marcus caught sight of himself in the mirror and ran a hand across his face to wipe away the tears streaking his cheeks. He stared at his reflection. He looked haggard, and a part of him wondered how long he'd been that way. He doubted it was due just to the recent events at Synerdyne.

A gentle knock sounded beside him, and he took a quick moment to straighten his appearance a little more before opening the door. Claire stood in the hallway, her eyes filled with worry, but as she saw him, her expression changed to one of relief and sympathy.

"Hey," she said.

"Hey," he responded, stepping aside to let her in.

Claire stepped past him and moved into the living room, looking around at the apartment.

"Sorry," he said, gesturing to the disorganized state of the room. "I haven't bothered to tidy up since Sam died."

"Don't worry about it. It's fine," she said, turning to face him. "How are you doing?"

"How do you think?" he said, gesturing to the couch before dropping down into his chair.

"Yeah. Stupid question," she said with a sad smile, sitting down across from him.

"I'm sorry about before," he said. "The last time we spoke. I know you were just trying to help give me some perspective."

"Well, I could have been a little more tactful," she replied, with another sad smile. "But thank you. I'm sorry too."

"Sam wouldn't have wanted us to fight."

"No, she wouldn't have," Claire agreed, shaking her head.

"Maybe I should have listened to you from the start, but I couldn't just let her go. Not when there was still a chance," he said, barely able to get the words out as a lump rose in his throat.

"Oh, Marcus," she said, getting up to kneel beside him and take his hand. "I never wanted you to give up. I just didn't want you to delude yourself."

Marcus felt fresh tears start to burn his eyes. Soon they came as a torrent, their warmth sliding down his cheeks. He let out a choked sob, leaning forward to bury his face in his hands. Wrapping her arms around him, Claire held him against her as his grief overtook him and he wailed in sorrow. Thoughts of Sam flooded his mind. Images of her smiling face. Moments spent together over the last twenty years. Each memory like a dagger in his heart, as the reality that he'd never experience them again finally sank in.

Eventually the grief eased enough for him to get some control, and he straightened in the chair. Claire looked up at him, her own face covered in tears, and reached over to the table to offer him some tissues before grabbing a handful for herself. Wiping tears from their faces and blowing their noses, they looked at one another again.

"I miss her so much," he said with a sigh.

"So do I," she said, reaching up to hug him again. "She was my best friend. But so are you. And I can only imagine what this has been like for you."

"Mine too," he said with a weak smile. "I haven't lived a day without her in my life for twenty-five years. I don't know how to live life without her. And when she got sick, I thought we could beat it. We both did. It was inconceivable that we would be separated. When things got worse. When her pain made it too difficult. At least we could be together in the simulation. Happy and free of pain. Or so I thought. Then when we realized that we might be able to save her consciousness, it seemed like the answer. Like it was fated. But then she started to forget. Not only me, but herself. All her memories. Now she's just Morrigan. And even she has been taken from me."

Claire rested back on her heels and took his hand.

"I know you wanted to save her," she said. "We all did. And as she got sicker, I was scared. I let my fear drive me away, but you let it drive you forward. Because, for good or ill, that is who you are. I'm not saying I was right, or that you were wrong. Honestly, I don't know if there ever was a right answer. But I do know this. Sam was a fighter. You say all that is left is Morrigan. I'd say when you boil Sam down, that's exactly who you'll find at her core. Morrigan is just the unpolished version of that strength and tenacity."

"She was the strongest person I ever met," Marcus agreed with a smile.

"I also know that she wouldn't sit by while Clive Ellison took everything away from us," Claire said, her voice firm. "She'd fight."

"Believe me, there's nothing more I'd rather do. But I don't have anything left to fight him with," Marcus said despondently. "He took over Synerdyne, and with it, Sam's World. And even if I somehow found a way into Sam's World, I couldn't do anything. He has complete control of the simulation."

Squeezing his hand tightly, Claire stared into his eyes. "Marcus, you refused to give up on saving Sam's consciousness from *death*. Who is Clive Ellison compared to that?"

"You said it yourself, I was fooling myself."

"We might disagree on the nature of Sam's continued existence, sure," she conceded. "But I never doubted your tenacity to pull it off. That's why I tried to change your mind. Because I knew you'd try, no matter what, and was worried it would lead you to ruin."

"And you were right," he said somberly, spreading his hands in front of him.

"No. Clive Ellison did that," she said. "Not you. And you can't let him get away with it. If nothing else, you have to try. For Sam."

"But I have nothing left to fight him with," Marcus replied.

"You have your friends. And every one of us would go to hell and back for you and Sam. I don't know what I can do, but just say the word and I'll be there."

Marcus stared into her eyes, searching Claire's gaze, and thought about what Sam would say.

"Fuck that fucker," Marcus said, squeezing Claire's hand in return as a cold resolve climbed up his spine.

"Yeah. Fuck that fucker," Claire repeated with a grin, recognizing Sam's familiar phrase.

CHAPTER 26

"Is anyone else reminded of a heist movie?" Diego said, looking around the coffee shop table at the assemblage of friends.

"How do you mean?" Evan asked.

"Well, you know, it's like the point in the movie where the crew is assembled to pull off the plan," Diego explained.

"I don't remember any movies where that happens over lattes," Claire said with a grin.

"Plus, we don't have a plan," Amir said, taking a sip from his cup.

"Yes, we do," Marcus replied, looking at Diego. "And that's exactly what this is."

Diego's eyes brightened and he grinned broadly.

"We do?" Amir asked.

"Well, the bones of one anyway," Marcus amended.

"Do tell," Amir said.

"Well," Marcus continued. "Our problem is Clive and his control of both the simulation and the company."

"Yeah, those are both pretty big problems," Amir said. "One kind of impacts the other."

Marcus nodded. "And with control of Sam's World, they have complete control over the consciousness preservation research and the duplicants. Morrigan included. As we've come to realize, some of us later than others," he said, looking sheepishly at Claire. "That research has the potential to fundamentally alter the trajectory of humankind's evolution. In the hands of someone like Ellison, it's too dangerous. He'll use it to gain unparalleled influence over the world. Think of how many millionaires and people in positions of power will pay for everlasting life. We can't leave that in his hands. We have to do everything we can to stop that from happening."

"So what can we do?" Amir asked. "Without access to Synerdyne, we also don't have access to the servers to shut them down. And even if we did, Jia could just reactivate them. It might slow them down, but they could eventually regain access to our research. Not to mention, doing so would most likely wipe the duplicants," he added, looking pointedly at Marcus.

Without him saying it specifically, Marcus knew what Amir was implying. If they shut off the server, they'd potentially be erasing Sam's mapping. Or at least Morrigan's. But Morrigan was the bi-product of Sam's original mapping, and in that way, was Sam. Even if they somehow regained control of Synerdyne and the servers and reincorporated Sam's mapping, wouldn't that just prove Claire's point that the consciousness mapping was only a copy of Sam and not the real thing?

"I know," Marcus said, solemnly. "And that's why we can't just shut it down. We have to wipe Sam's World completely and corrupt the files so that it can never be recovered."

Everyone around the table grew quiet, casting glances at one another.

"Are you sure?" Diego asked, sympathy in his voice. "Isn't there some other way?"

Marcus shook his head. "Anything else risks Clive regaining control of the research, and above all else, we can't let that happen."

"But what about Sam?"

Marcus let out a sigh and looked across the table at Claire, who gave him a sad smile. "Sam's gone. I couldn't face the truth before, but I realize that now. And she wouldn't have wanted us to let Clive retain his control just for her sake. We have to let her go. I have to let her go."

The table grew silent again, and Diego reached over to put his arm around Marcus to hug him tightly. Sam's face hovered in Marcus' mind. And with it, a deep painful emptiness spread through him. The truth was still difficult for him to accept. He had been pushing it away for so long. Sam was gone. And he'd never see her again.

After several long moments, Amir cleared his throat. "So what are you proposing?" he asked quietly.

Marcus took a deep breath and wiped away the tears welling in his eyes.

"We have to get access to the servers and corrupt them," he explained.

"And how do you propose we do that? They are locked underground at Synderdyne. Which, I will remind you, we no longer have access to," Amir countered. "Not only that, but what you are suggesting is going to take a lot of technical expertise and time. Not to mention it would be suspicious if the server was taken offline. It's not like we could just download a virus into it using a flash drive. It has protections. Pretty robust ones, I might add."

"I've thought about that. So… what if we corrupt it from within Sam's World?" Marcus asked. "We could create a new protocol that directly corrupts the AAIP. From inside the simulation, it isn't a virus attacking the server; it is a protocol designed to make changes. No different than all our other protocols."

"So you're suggesting someone jumps into Sam's World to do this?" Diego asked.

"Exactly. We could do it remotely," Marcus explained.

"You?" Evan asked.

"Who else?" Marcus replied.

"Theoretically that could work, I suppose," Amir said, tapping a finger on his cup in consideration. "But in order to do that, we'd still have to get into Synerdyne and reinstate your remote access."

"Exactly. But I have a plan for that too. We may not have access to Synerdyne anymore, but Claire still does," Marcus explained. "I had Evan check if her logins are still functioning. I never removed her system access. And it seems Jia didn't think about her either. Jia didn't come on until after Claire had already left. She may not even know about her. We could use Claire's badge to get inside."

"Yes!" Diego said excitedly. "That could work."

"Sure," Amir said, drawing out the word. "But I don't think Claire has the expertise to know how to hack the physical server to give you remote access."

"Right. So that's why you should be the one to go. Evan can make arrangements to get you into the building. You'll go in, after hours, under the guise of a contractor. There'll be a guest pass waiting for you. From there you can use her badge to access each floor and use her logins to get access."

Amir shook his head. "It's not going to work."

"What do you mean?" Marcus asked. "Why?"

"Well, I see two problems with the plan. Having Evan's permission or not, even after hours, someone's probably going to recognize me," Amir explained. "Of all of us, I'm the one who spends the most time there. My picture is on the founders' wall. All our pictures are. Unless Jia's already taken them down."

It was true. They were all recognizable at Synerdyne.

"Shit," Marcus said.

Amir was right. All it would take is for one person in security to recognize him and the whole thing would be over.

"So? We just need to get Amir in the building. He doesn't have to walk in through the front door," Diego offered. "What about having Evan let him in through the delivery door? That door is locked from the inside. So once Evan's in the building, he can open it for Amir. The only person he'd have to avoid is one guard who does a walk around the building every hour. Evan?"

Evan's lips twisted for a moment. "Why not? If they fire me, that's just more time I can spend perfecting my squash game."

Marcus frowned and shook his head. "No. Evan's got something else he needs to be doing at that time. Plus, of all of us, he needs plausible deniability."

From the other side of the table, Amir cleared his throat. "I hate to be that guy. But, like I said, there are *two* problems. Even if you find some way to get me in the building, in order to get around Jia's security measures and give you remote access, I'm going to need to gain access to the physical servers, not just the development suite. And I'm willing to bet, now that Evan isn't CEO, his access has been limited."

"That's what Claire's credentials are for," Marcus countered. But as he said the words, he realized what Amir was getting at, and finished the thought. "But the server room uses more than just badge access. It has a retinal scanner."

"Exactly," Amir said.

"Fuck!" Marcus blurted out, causing some of the other patrons of the coffee shop to look over at their table.

"I can do it," Claire offered, causing them all to look in her direction. "Like you said, I still have access. And if my badge and logins are still active, my retinal signature is most likely as well. You never officially fired me, right?"

"No," Marcus said, shaking his head. "I guess I always hoped you'd come back eventually."

"So, send me in," she offered. "I'm still a valid employee of Synerdyne. I may not have Amir's expertise when it comes to the AAIP, but I know my way around the building. I can be the one to get him inside so he can grant you remote access. That way Evan can keep his hands clean."

"I guess so," Marcus agreed, looking at Claire. "After that, all I would need is for you and Amir to get me into Sam's World, and I can do the rest. But are you sure? Once we've accessed the system, it is likely that Jia will be notified. You're going to be caught in the lion's den."

"So? I'm an employee of Synerdyne. What are they going to do? Fire me?" Claire said with a smirk. "I don't want to work for those assholes anyway. Maybe Evan can teach me how to play squash."

"You'll love it," Evan said, smiling.

"I'll stay and buy you as much time as possible," she said with a resolute nod.

Marcus gave her a rueful smile. "All right. Sounds like a plan."

"Not quite," Amir said, looking around the table with a sigh.

"Really?" Marcus asked with an exasperated sigh.

"I'm afraid so," Amir said. "You're forgetting about the security cameras. Even if Claire gets inside, they'll see her let me in."

"Not exactly," Marcus said, looking to Evan.

"While it's true you will be caught on camera," Evan explained, picking up the thread from Marcus. "The monitors are not always being watched. We only keep one guard in the surveillance room at a time, and they are mandated breaks every four hours. Synerdyne could spend more money to make sure there are enough guards to overlap, but our budget is pretty tight," he added with a knowing smile. "Starting at 11:45 pm, the surveillance guard takes a fifteen-minute break. That would be the optimal time to try this."

"So we'll only have fifteen minutes?" Amir asked. "That's not a lot of time. Especially, if I'm going to have to download the protocol changes to the AAIP. That has to be done from the development suite. Which means getting to the third floor, downloading the changes, then going four flights down to the server room in the basement, all in under fifteen minutes."

"What about me?" Diego suggested. "Did you just expect me to sit around and do nothing while you guys have all the fun? The development suite is where I live and breathe. If anyone is going to make changes to it, I'm the best candidate. Claire can let me in with Amir. That way, all she has to do is get me access to the third floor and then she and Amir can get down to the servers while I install the changes. She can come and get me on their way out."

"That would give me more time," Amir agreed. "Especially if I run into any problems. Fifteen minutes is not a long time."

"True," Marcus conceded. "Maybe I was a little overly optimistic. Okay. I had something else I needed you to do," he said to Diego. "But we can figure out a way for Evan to take that over. In fact, it might work out better that way."

Tentatively, Amir raised his hand, and everyone turned to look at him flatly.

"Sorry to be that guy, but there's still a potential problem," Amir said. "How exactly is this new protocol going to work? We never planned for anything like this. If it wipes the server while you're inside, it could plausibly impact your link with the SynAPP. There are countless possibilities that come to mind. You could just be ejected from the simulation, I suppose. But then there might be far worse consequences. The worst of which could be feedback from the SynAPP to your hippocampus. You could be left a vegetable."

Marcus nodded. "I've thought about that. But I'll only need a minute or so. It should take some time for the program to corrupt the server memory."

"Still, it seems risky," Amir said.

"Don't worry about it," Marcus replied. "I've got it under control."

"Okay," Amir said skeptically. "But even if we get you into Sam's World, how can we know Clive won't be there? If he is, we run into the same problem. Not to mention, if he gets wind that you are there, he can use the protocol against you."

"That's where Evan comes in," Marcus said. "His job is to make sure Clive is not engaged in the simulation during any of this. Which means keeping him occupied."

"And how is he going to do that?" Amir asked.

"By catering to his ego," Evan explained. "You think he'd pass up the chance to watch me grovel?"

Diego grimaced. "Oof."

"Yeah," Marcus said to Amir. "You thought your job was hard. Now that Diego's going to be occupied, we're going to have to figure out a way for him to distract Ellison *and* Jia."

"Oh," Amir said sympathetically. "Sorry, Evan."

"Don't worry about me," Evan replied. "I'm tougher than I look."

"Okay. But even supposing this does work, and you manage to wipe Sam's World; that won't change anything outside of the simulation," Amir interjected. "Ellison will still have control of Synerdyne and what's left of our research for Jia to piece together."

"Sure, that's a possibility," Marcus said. "But Evan and I have made a plan for that too. He's handling that side of things with the other shareholders. You might be surprised to find that Ellison hasn't made a lot of friends on the board. But that's not something you need to worry about. Just focus on getting me into the simulation, and after that, we'll let the pieces fall where they may."

CHAPTER 27

Stepping out of the car, Claire stared up at the Synerdyne building, her gaze slowly rising floor by floor. Though it had only been a few months since she'd left, this place where she and her friends had once built their dreams no longer felt familiar or safe. Instead, it loomed before her like some sort of fortress—malignant and oppressive—daring her to enter.

Letting out a sigh, she thought about what awaited her inside and ran the plan over in her mind. Likewise, she pictured Marcus sitting alone in his apartment waiting impatiently for her call. He seemed to think he could fix all of this if they just got him into Sam's World. She wasn't so sure. Could they really defeat Clive Ellison and all the resources he had at his disposal?

But beyond that, even if their plan proved successful, she was still worried for Marcus. She remembered how she had found him after Ellison's betrayal, utterly crushed and defeated. She had replayed that night in her mind, over and over, thinking about what might have happened if she hadn't come over to check on him. She'd only been a clinical psychiatrist for a short period of time before joining Synerdyne, but had dealt with enough suicide cases to recognize that look in his eye. The hope of defeating Ellison had solidified Marcus' resolve, giving him something other than his pain to focus on. But whether they were victorious or not, Marcus would still have to face that pain eventually. Face the reality that Sam was gone. And Claire wasn't sure he was ready to do that.

Sam. As if summoned, her friend's smiling face came to mind. That's how Claire liked to remember her. Sam had brightened every room she entered, her laughter infectious. No matter your mood, without fail, she could turn your day around. She'd pick up on your angst, and unlike so many, never tried to brush it away or minimize it. Instead, she'd ask how you were doing and listen—really listen—to your troubles. And most importantly, she wouldn't try to fix them. She'd just acknowledge and recognize your feelings on the matter, talk it over with you, and let you know she was always available if you needed to talk.

Not for the first time, Claire really wished she could talk to Sam about everything that had happened. She regretted not spending more time with her when she had the chance. But as Sam grew sicker, Claire had pulled away. Not because she didn't want to see her, but because she didn't know how to offer the same support Sam would have given her. Sam would have seen right through her to the pain she was trying to hide and would have prioritized Claire's pain over her own. At least that's what Claire told herself.

She couldn't have admitted it at the time, but fighting with Marcus had made the decision easier for her. Though Claire believed everything she had told him about Sam's consciousness, she had used questions of morality and ethics as an excuse to stay away and avoid her pain. To push herself away. She knew Marcus well enough to know how he'd react. He wasn't that complicated. For him, Sam was everything.

Claire had been selfish. She knew that. And now that her friend was gone, she was overcome with regret. She had given it a lot of thought while isolating herself away in her house, painting and repainting the walls. Marcus was right. She had been hiding. Not just from everyone else, but also from her own fear. Would entertaining Marcus' delusion really have done any harm? Maybe if she'd stuck around some of this could have been avoided. After all, look at what had happened regardless of her opposition.

She let out another long sigh and checked her phone. 11:44 pm. She brought up the timer app and set it to fifteen minutes. Show time. There was no turning back now. The next few minutes would decide everything. Claire hadn't been there for Sam when she was still alive, but she'd be damned if she left whatever remained of Sam's memory to Clive Ellison. Taking in a deep breath, she adjusted the badge around her neck and walked toward the building.

The double glass doors slid open in anticipation as she drew closer, and she stepped across the threshold, the click of her heels echoing as she walked through the empty lobby to the security checkpoint. At her approach, the two guards looked up from their station with mild expressions of surprise. Neither of them was familiar to her, but she didn't know if they were new or not. She didn't often come in at this hour. Though she was willing to bet Amir would know.

On the wall behind them she saw her own face and the faces of her friends staring back at her. Well, that at least answered the question as to whether Jia had taken their pictures off the founders' wall. As Amir had warned, the pictures would have likely derailed their original plan. But they just might make Claire's role a little easier.

"Evening, Ma'am," one of the guards said as she stepped up to the security desk.

"Good evening, gentlemen," she replied, making sure to plaster a smile on her face that she hoped seemed casual.

"Late night?" he asked.

"Well, you know how it is. Sometimes it's easier to get things done when you have fewer distractions," she said, pulling the badge from around her neck to press it to the security scanner. She held her breath, looking at the dark glass of the scanner screen. What if Evan was wrong about her credentials?

With a beep, the screen glowed green and the security gate swung open. Claire let out a long, quiet breath and smiled.

"Have a good evening, Ma'am," the guard said. "If you need anything, feel free to give us a call. We're on duty all night," he added, unconsciously glancing back at her portrait.

"Thank you… Steve…" she said, looking at his nametag. "I expect it to be a quiet night."

He nodded with a smile and she stepped through the security gate, walking toward the elevators. Pressing the call button, she shoved her badge into her pocket and pulled out her phone to check the timer. 13:27 left.

It took another 24 seconds for the elevator to reach the ground floor. As the doors opened, she quickly stepped inside and pressed the button for the level above. From the second floor, she could get to the stairwell without looking suspicious and would only need to go down one flight to let Amir and Diego into the building. She hammered the button impatiently as the elevator doors languidly closed.

It only took a few moments to reach the next floor, but each second felt like an eternity. When the doors finally opened, Claire nearly sprinted out of the elevator. As expected, the second-floor corridor was quiet, and she quickly made her way down the hall to the stairwell exit.

Pushing the door open, she ran down the stairs as quickly as she could, cursing herself for wearing heels. She'd thought it important to look as professional as possible to avoid suspicion, but now realized her choice of footwear had been a mistake. Fuck it. Kicking off her heels, she picked them up and raced down the stairs.

As she came around the landing, she spied the outer door and desperately hoped Amir and Diego were waiting in the alley on the other side. Pressing her body against its broad metal bar, she pushed the door open with a loud metallic clank. Immediately a gust of cool night air rushed in, and to her relief, she found Amir and Diego staring back at her expectantly.

"All good?" Diego whispered as they hurried into the stairwell.

"Yeah. Worked like a charm," she replied, looking down at her phone. 11:13. "We've got eleven minutes. Let's get you to the third floor, then I'll take Amir to the server room."

Both men nodded, but she was already turning to make her way back up the stairs. They didn't hesitate either, and together the three of them climbed to the second-floor landing. However, just as she began to ascend the next series of stairs, the distinct sound of footsteps and jingling keys caught her attention and she stopped.

Peeking around the banister to look up the stairwell, Claire caught a glimpse of someone in what looked like a security uniform making their way down the stairs. That wasn't right, was it? Just their luck that the guard doing his rounds would end up in the stairwell at the same time as them. He wasn't that far up, and at the pace he was descending, it was obvious that they couldn't reach the third floor without being seen.

Amir and Diego had heard the man's movements too and looked at her questioningly. Gesturing to the second-floor exit, she rushed to the door and used her badge on the entrance scanner. Although entering the stairwell from any floor didn't require a badge, exiting onto the floor did. Time seemed to slow as she waited, silently begging the scanner to read the badge. Finally, she was rewarded with a beep of recognition and the sound of the door unlocking.

Hurrying onto the floor with Amir and Diego close behind, Claire turned to the left and moved them quickly away from the door. When they reached the end of the corridor where it turned again, this time to the right, they ducked out of sight. Peeking back from around the corner, Claire watched the stairwell, while Amir and Diego pressed themselves against the wall behind her. She held her breath, waiting to see if the guard followed. When the door did not open, she waved the all-clear to her friends, and they let out a collective breath.

"That was close," Amir said quietly, peeling himself from the wall and walking back around the corner to look at the stairwell door.

"Yeah. If we're lucky, he was going to go to take his break," Diego replied, following Amir.

"We shouldn't let our guard down," Claire added. "Come on. Let's hurry and get you upstairs."

"Everything all right?" another voice suddenly called down the hallway from where they had just been hiding.

Claire's heart froze and she looked around the corner to see a guard standing at the end of the corridor. Without turning her head, she glanced back at Amir and Diego, who stood frozen in place, just on the other side of the wall. Had the guard seen them? How long had he been standing there? She could see the same question in her friends' eyes, and they moved to crouch down beside the wall.

"Excuse me?" she asked weakly, cursing the tremble in her voice.

"I asked if everything's alright, miss," the guard said, walking closer. "I thought I heard talking."

"Oh," Claire said, trying to think of a way out of the situation. "Sorry. I was just on my phone."

She thought about the timer and wanted desperately to check it. How much time did they have left? If the guard realized that she wasn't alone, it was all over. But they also couldn't afford for her to be delayed either. If Amir and Diego could get back into the stairwell, they could at least get to the third floor, and might just buy her enough time to find a way to disengage with the guard.

Clearing her throat, she took a step back slightly around the corner and reached into her pocket. With one quick motion, she pulled the badge out and threw it to Diego. Diego caught it with a look of surprise, but she didn't wait for his reaction and stepped toward the approaching guard.

It took only a second for her friends to realize what she wanted them to do, and to her relief, they quickly slunk back down the hall toward the stairwell door. She waited until they disappeared in her peripheral vision, before turning her full attention back to the guard. Now she just had to figure out how to get away from this guy and get back to them before they ran out of time. She just hoped he didn't ask to see her badge.

Amir followed Diego as they made their way to the stairwell, momentarily glancing back in Claire's direction. From the doorway, he could only see the back half of her body, the rest of her hidden around the corner. Her hands were clasped behind her back, but otherwise, her posture seemed relaxed. He hated leaving her behind, but he understood that the whole operation would be put at risk if he and Diego were discovered.

Diego, too, took a moment to look back and gave him a helpless shrug. Quietly, they closed the door and moved to the banister, one of them looking up the stairwell, while the other looked down. To Amir's relief, there was no sign of the guard from earlier.

Motioning with his head for Amir to follow, Diego began to climb to the next floor as quickly as he could without making too much noise. Amir followed closely behind, glancing over the railing to keep an eye on the stairs below. Within moments they reached the landing for the third floor and Diego peered through the little window set into the door before pressing Claire's badge to the scanner. After a few seconds, the scanner gave a quiet beep of recognition, followed by the click of the lock disengaging.

Pushing the door open slowly, Diego poked his head out and looked across the developer's floor. Unlike the previous floor, this one was just one big room filled with cubicles, though it did have a small hallway on the other side behind the offices where the restrooms and break room were located.

Diego stepped onto the familiar floor and motioned for Amir to follow.

Amir shook his head. "Give me the badge. I need to get back to Claire," he said.

"But what about the guard?" Diego whispered, looking around to make sure he wasn't heard.

"If he asks her for her badge, she won't have it. I still need her in order to get down to the server room."

Diego nodded. "Right. Of course. I guess now that I'm here, I don't need it. I can use the stairwell to get out of the building when I'm done," he said, tossing the badge to Amir.

"How long do you need?" Amir asked, glancing down at the timer on his watch. 9:04.

"Just a few minutes," Diego said, instinctively looking at his phone. "I've got just under nine minutes left. You?"

"Yeah," Amir nodded. "We're going to be cutting it close."

"That's part of the thrill, right?" Diego said with a nervous smile, stepping toward the cubicles. "Here goes nothing. Good luck."

"You, too," Amir said, stepping back and letting the door close silently.

He hated to leave him, but they were running out of time. From here on out, Diego was on his own. Turning back to the stairwell, he didn't bother to be quiet as he raced back down to the second floor, taking the stairs two steps at a time. When he reached the landing, he pressed the badge to the terminal and waited for the lock to disengage. Slowly opening the door, he peered over to where he'd left Claire.

To his relief, she was still standing there, but he noticed her posture had changed. Instead of standing still, she was fumbling around as though searching for something. Shit. He was too late. The guard had probably asked to see her badge.

Cautiously, he stepped out into the hall and snuck towards her in a crouch, trying to move as quickly as possible without making noise.

"... I thought I had it, but I probably left it in my office on the third floor. Like I said, I just came down here to look for some paper for the printer," he heard Claire say as he drew closer.

Maybe if he threw the badge at her feet, she could say it dropped out of her pocket. If it landed too far away though, the jig was up. Gritting his teeth, he coiled the badge and lanyard in his hand and tried to gauge the distance. He had to get this right.

"Oh!" Claire exclaimed suddenly. "If you call down to the security desk, they can vouch for me. I used my badge to get into the building. They should remember. It was just a few minutes ago."

"Just a second," the man said, with a slight sigh in his voice. After a moment, there was the static sound of a walkie-talkie. "Hey. It's Mike."

"Yeah, Mike. What's up?" came a metallic reply.

"I've got a lady here on two without a badge," he declared loudly. "Said she left it in her office on three. Name's… Sorry, what's your name, Ma'am?" he asked, lowering his voice to a more conversational tone.

"Claire... Javernick."

"Claire Javernick. Said she accessed the building a few minutes ago," he reported.

"Yeah. She's good," the voice at the other end replied. "Hope you're treating her well. She's kind of a big deal," the man's voice added with a hint of a laugh.

"Thanks, Steve," Claire said, raising her voice to be heard.

"You got it, Miss Javernick," the voice replied.

"You can call me Claire," she said jovially.

"Copy that, Claire."

"Alright. Thanks, guys," the guard said, ending the call. "Okay, Miss Javernick. Sorry. Just protocol. But you might want to remember your badge next time, in case you run into someone else."

"Of course. It was stupid of me. Thanks for being so understanding," Claire said sheepishly.

"Not at all. You have yourself a good night."

"You, too," she replied.

To his relief, Amir heard the man walk away, his footsteps receding down the hall. For her part, Claire let out a long sigh and turned back to look in Amir's direction. When she spied him crouched against the wall beside her, she raised her eyebrows in surprise and gave one more glance in the direction of the guard. Giving her a toothy grin, Amir held up her badge and dangled it by its lanyard. With one last glance in the direction of the guard, she stepped over and took the badge, offering Amir a hand as he got to his feet.

"Nice work," he said quietly, rising from the floor. "Very impressive."

"Thanks," she whispered. "Everything go okay?"

"Yeah, Diego's on the third floor. Said it'd take a few minutes and he'd find his way out."

Claire let out another sigh and nodded.

Instinctively, they both checked their timers. 7:42.

"We gotta go," Amir said.

"Yeah," Claire agreed.

"Ma'am," the guard's voice called again from down the hall, stopping them both in their tracks. In a panic, Amir pressed himself against the wall and looked wide-eyed at Claire, her own panic apparent.

"Yes?" she asked nervously, turning back around the corner.

Amir could hear the heavy footfalls of the man approaching and looked to the stairwell door. Would he be able to make it in time? Maybe if he ran. But then the guard might hear him.

"Don't want to leave without your paper," he said.

"Oh," Claire replied, relief in her voice. "You didn't have to do that."

"It's no problem. Supply closet is just around the corner there. Is that the kind you needed?"

"Yes. Perfect. Thank you," Claire said, and Amir could hear the distinct crinkle of plastic. "I would have gotten back to my office and then had to come back down."

"With your badge," the man added with a chuckle.

"Absolutely," she said. "Thank you."

"No problem. Have a good night, Miss Javernick."

"You too, Mike."

Slowly the footfalls receded again, and after a moment Claire turned back around the corner, a plastic-wrapped ream of paper in her hand.

Amir checked his watch.

6:53

No time to waste.

Taking her hand, he pulled Claire behind him as he rushed to the stairwell and pushed open the door. The thought of the guard they had almost encountered before barely registered in his mind as he hustled down the stairs. There was a heavy thud as Claire dropped the ream of paper and followed quickly behind.

The servers were located underground, one level below the ground floor, so they had two levels to go. Again, Amir took the stairs two steps at a time, but Claire had a harder time keeping up. He didn't wait for her. As he reached the door, he looked back at her and gestured for her badge. Pulling it out of her pocket, she slowed for a second and tossed it to him. He caught it with both hands and quickly pressed it to the scanner.

The door unlatched just as Claire reached him and together they hurried out of the stairwell. Before them, taking up the entirety of the floor, stood the server room. Behind a thick wall of glass, hundreds of servers stood in neatly organized rows, each emitting a multitude of blinking lights on shiny black metal.

Amir took a moment to look around, staring through the glass for any sign of movement. To his relief, there didn't seem to be anyone around. He moved to the server room door. Like the other doors, this one had a badge scanner. However, above it was a plastic box with a small glass square inset. The retinal scanner.

Without hesitation, Claire moved over to the door and swiped her badge, while simultaneously pressing her cheek against the scanner. Though they didn't spend much time down in the server room, they were all familiar with how access worked. Amir fished into his pocket for the thumb drive he'd brought and waited impatiently for the door to unlock.

To his surprise, the scanner made an abrasive error sound and flashed red instead of green. Claire looked at him uncertainly and pressed her badge and face to the scanners again. Again, the scanner denied them access. Claire tried again. Access denied.

Shit. Claire might not have been purged from building security, but Jia must have reset the server room's access. It made sense. Jia probably didn't know about Claire at all, and though she didn't care who entered the building, she would have wanted to make sure that she knew who had access to the servers.

This was it. Without access, nothing they'd done tonight mattered. Marcus would lose his chance to enter Sam's World. Clive would win.

Amir thought of Marcus and the disappointment and pain he would feel at learning they'd lost. His friend had changed a lot over the last few years. It was slow at first, but the closer Sam got to death, the more he saw it. Marcus needed this. If they failed now, he'd be destroyed.

But he wasn't just doing this for Marcus. Amir needed this. This was his life's work, made possible through countless hours and years of sleepless nights. And it had been taken from him. Now Clive Ellison was bastardizing it for his own amusement, and hurting the people he cared about in the process.

They were so close. Just one last obstacle stood in their way. Amir stared at the door and wracked his brain for a solution. They just needed to get past that door. But how? Desperately, Claire tried again, only to be greeted by the same angry red denial.

A thought suddenly came to mind. A possible solution. But it came with a price. It was one he was willing to pay, but he couldn't make that decision for his friends. He looked down at his watch.

3:15

He reached out and took Claire by the arm, gently pulling her away from the door. She stiffened and looked at him in confusion.

"We have to keep trying," she protested. But in her voice, he could hear the recognition of their failure.

"Jia must have reset the retinal clearance. It's not going to work."

"There has to be something we can do. We can't give up now. We're so close."

Amir nodded, a strange sense of calm washing over him. "There's one thing that might work. But it means blowing our cover."

Claire looked at him for a moment, then shrugged. "Whatever it takes."

"Can we make that call for Diego?" he asked.

"If it means getting the job done, Diego would be the first to tell us to do it," she said without hesitation.

Amir considered what Diego would say and nodded. "All right. You can probably still get out of here if you leave now. You don't need to be here. Just go out the stairwell."

"If you're staying, so am I," she said, resolutely. "What do you need me to do?"

Amir knew better than to try and convince her otherwise. "Okay. If we pull the fire alarm, all these doors should unlock as part of the fire safety code. But it…"

"…means we're fucked," Claire finished. "I get it."

"I was going to say, may not work," Amir corrected. "But yeah, that too."

Claire gave him a smile and gestured to the door. "I'll go pull the alarm, and you get inside. They're definitely going to check the security cameras the minute it goes off. We won't have long. You sure Jia won't have changed something about the security of the server itself?"

Amir reached into his pocket and pulled out the thumb drive, holding it up for her to see. "Jia might be cunning, but I'm the one who built this damn thing."

Diego watched Amir disappear as the door to the stairwell slowly closed behind him. Well, he was on his own now. Turning back to the darkened floor, his eyes scanned over the empty cubicles. Things would be so much easier if he still had his office, but he knew all his credentials had been revoked. He needed a workstation he could access. Immediately he thought of Delila. She was always forgetting her password, so he'd worked out an easy one for her to remember. One he still remembered too.

Marking her workstation, he wove his way through the warren of cubicles towards it. Everything had been so promising with Sam's World at first but had turned out so terribly. Maybe they had been naive, but he understood why Marcus had to do it. It was Sam. He'd do anything for her. They all would. But for Marcus, Sam wasn't just a partner or a lover. Diego had seen it every time they looked at each other. She was Marcus' entire world. He wasn't sure the others understood that. Not truly. But he did.

He had always loved that about them and had even been a bit envious of what they had. He wished he could find someone like that. Someone who made him feel more purposeful. Like part of something bigger. Not just a person in his life, but an intrinsic part of him.

The thought of Sam losing her memories was particularly painful, and he couldn't help but feel guilt about it. He'd seen how she'd changed. How she'd taken playing the role of Morrigan to the extreme whenever they were in the simulation together, to the point of concern. Maybe if he'd said something sooner, he could have helped stop all this. Then again, maybe Claire was right about the whole thing. Maybe when Sam died, she died for real, and Morrigan is just an echo of some sort. Hell, if they'd listened to Claire about Ellison, none of them would be in this mess. Though Sam would still be dead.

He let out a sigh and tried to push back the stinging tears that welled in his eyes. Not now. There'd be time enough later. Right now the rest of the team needed him. Of course, if Amir and Claire couldn't get to the server, nothing he did would matter anyway. He wondered just how Claire would get out of dealing with that guard. What if they had gotten detained? He forced himself to push those thoughts away. No use focusing on what he couldn't control.

The muffled sound of a hand dryer blowing from the bathrooms caused him to freeze in the middle of the cubicles and stare at the hallway behind his old office. Someone was on the floor. Instinctively, he dropped to a crouch, hiding behind the cubicle walls. The sound of the dryer grew louder for a second as whoever it was opened the bathroom door, before becoming slowly muffled again.

Cautiously lifting his head to peek over the cubicle walls, Diego stared at the entrance to the hallway in anticipation. Though the overhead lights were off, the hallway was illuminated, and the figure cast a long shadow before them onto the floor. Diego watched as the shadow grew closer, ready to duck down at a moment's notice. If it was one of the developers, or even the janitor, he could probably talk his way around being there and still get the files uploaded. Unconsciously, he crossed his fingers and a dozen faces came to mind that he willed to appear around the corner.

Instead, the face he saw was unfamiliar. What was familiar, however, was the uniform he was wearing. Another security guard. They must have beefed up security and put someone on every floor. Come on universe! What was the point of manifesting positivity if it didn't pay off when you truly needed it?

Slowly, Diego lowered himself back down behind the cubicles and tried to think of what he could do. The guy didn't know he was there. And if he could stay hidden behind the cubicles, he might be able to reach Delila's desk and still access her workstation. He just needed to be quiet.

On hands and knees, Diego began to crawl between the cubicles, winding his way down the aisles created by their tall fabric panels. Though he couldn't see the guard, he tried listening for the man's footsteps but found it difficult to hear over the rubbing of his own knees on the carpet. As he passed, he counted the cubicles, trying to mentally map the route to his objective.

Just as Delila's cubicle came into view, a heavy footfall landed on the other side of the panel beside Diego. Freezing in panic, he closed his eyes and tried not to make a sound, hoping he hadn't been seen. To his dismay, he didn't hear the guard take another step. Inclining his head in the direction of the man, Diego forced himself to crack open one eye and look.

Silhouetted against the hallway light, he could just make out the shape of the man's head on the other side of the cubicle wall.

The *back* of the man's head.

Suddenly the silence was broken by the warbled sound of a strangely human scream. The sound echoed over the floor, then happened again in quick succession. For a moment Diego was bewildered, but also thought he recognized the sound, though he couldn't quite place it.

"What in the fuck?" the guard said quietly to himself. "Why would anyone have something like this?"

At his words, Diego remembered where he'd heard the sound before. It came from a little bobblehead toy goat that Byron kept on his desk. If you flicked the head, it would bounce and give out that demonic cry. It drove everybody crazy and Oswald had been forced to tell the developer that he could only keep the toy so long as he didn't make it scream. Apparently, Byron had kept the batteries in it.

The guard flicked the goat's head again and the toy gave out its distinctive cry, but this time Diego used it to his advantage. Quickly moving behind the next cubicle, he tucked himself behind its panel and waited for the man to lose interest and walk away. Fishing his phone out of his pocket, he looked at the timer.

4:08

He had to get to that workstation.

Blessedly, the guard had his fill of the toy and walked away, muttering to himself. Diego peeked around the corner and waited until the man was out of sight, then scrambled across the aisle to Delila's cubicle. Pushing her chair out of the way, he knelt at her desk and wiggled her mouse to banish the screensaver. As her screen illuminated, his eyes were immediately assaulted by an array of folders cluttering her desktop. Unconsciously shaking his head in disapproval, he did a quick search and brought up the link to the developer's suite.

DAmperton. 123!@#321. So easy, a child could remember.

To his great relief, the application opened without issue. Searching the database, he found the hidden server identifier that designated Sam's World and opened it up. He scanned the files as he fished a thumb drive from his pocket and inserted it into the computer's USB port. In a separate window, the application he'd created to download his changes appeared. Clicking the file, a prompt popped up asking him to confirm his download.

As he reached down to the keyboard, something in the server files caught Diego's eye and he quickly scrolled through the lines of code in disbelief. What was all of this? There were thousands of lines of code. Was this something Jia had added for Clive? If so, it was beyond him. He wasn't sure exactly what he was looking at, but it definitely had something to do with the simulation's structural coding.

To his astonishment, more lines appeared as he scrolled through them. They were being added in real-time at a rate much faster than humanly possible. What on earth was happening? A thought occurred to him. The AAIP. It had been making its own changes to Sam's World, but this went way beyond just asset propagation. Just what it had written so far would take months to parse through. As much as the thought pained him, maybe their plan to wipe the server was for the best.

Diego reached into his pocket and pulled out his phone, the timer prominently displayed on his screen.

1:17

Shit. He was out of time. No time to try and figure it out. Putting his phone away, he turned his attention back to the screen and noticed a face peering down at him from over the cubicle wall.

"What the hell are you doing?" the guard asked.

"Would you believe I work here?" Diego replied, with a sheepish smile.

"No," the man said, leveling a yellow-striped taser over the cubicle wall. "Badge. Now."

"About that…" Diego said, holding up his hands.

Without warning, everything erupted in a cacophony of chaos as an alarm wailed across the floor, accompanied by red, flashing claxon lights. Both Diego and the guard looked up in confusion, trying to figure out what was happening. Just as quickly, however, they turned their attention back to one another.

"Don't move," the man said, his taser still leveled at Diego. With his other hand, he reached up to the walkie-talkie on his shoulder. "This is Darren on three. What the hell is going on?"

"Fire alarm was pulled on B," the voice on the other end replied.

"I've got a guy here I found creeping around the cubicles," Darren said. "What do you want me to do with him."

"Take him into custody, escort him out of the building, and wait for instruction."

"Roger that," the man said, turning his attention back to Diego. "Alright, you heard him. Get up."

"Yeah. Good idea. Sounds like a plan," Diego said, rising to his feet and lowering his hands. "I just need to do one thing."

"You heard what he said. That's the fire alarm. We need to leave. Now. What could you possibly need to do?" the man asked, incredulously.

"Nothing fancy. Just this," Diego replied, pressing the enter key and starting the download.

CHAPTER 28

Marcus stared impatiently at his phone, waiting for Claire's call, and tried not to imagine the multitude of ways things may have gone wrong. The plan was simple enough, so long as it worked. They all knew the building layout. They just had to get Diego to a workstation and Amir into the server room. Nervously tapping his foot, he stared at the static home screen, willing the notification of her call to display.

His eyes drifted over to Sam's empty bed, her covers unmoved from when her body had been taken away. The whole room had been left unchanged, the ventilator and monitors sitting dormant around the bedside. He imagined her lying there, as he'd grown used to seeing her over the months, smiling sleepily at him and reaching for his hand. Unconsciously, he reached out as he had done countless times before and cupped his hand around the air where hers would have been, mouthing the words "I love you."

This is it, babe.

He ran the plan over in his mind for the thousandth time. He wasn't afraid. Not anymore. Instead, he felt a sense of resolve wash over him. Whatever happened today, he would make up for what he had done. And with any luck, ensure Ellison never gained control of Synerdyne or Sam's World again.

He nearly dropped his phone as it buzzed in his hands, and he looked down to see Claire's face and name on the call notification. Clearing his throat, he quickly answered the call.

"Claire. Everything okay?"

"We ran into some trouble, but we got it done," she said loudly, trying to be heard over a loud alarm sound.

"What the hell is going on?" Marcus replied in a panic.

"Don't worry about it. We'll handle it, but we're probably not getting out of here tonight. Also, Jia's probably going to figure out what's going on. So you might want to hurry."

"Once I'm in, I won't have to worry about her pulling me out," Marcus said, but knew that wasn't the only thing Jia could disrupt. "Though the longer you guys can keep her occupied, the better."

"We might not be in the best position for that in a few minutes, but we'll do what we can. Amir says it's just a few more seconds. You ready to jump in?"

"Yeah, just say the word," he confirmed.

"Looks like thirty seconds," she said, her voice growing distant as she turned her face away from the phone.

Marcus glanced at the proxy server set against the wall, his eyes searching the little blue and green dots on its face to ensure no error lights were flashing. He reached back and ran a hand over the small scar on the back of his neck, unconsciously tracing its contours.

"Hey, Claire," Marcus said.

"Yeah."

"I just want to say I'm sorry."

"Don't worry about it," she replied. "We knew what we were getting into."

"No. Not just about this. But about everything. About the way I treated you. I'm sorry. You deserved better."

"Forget about it. Right now just focus on what's important. You and I can talk when this is all over," she replied.

"Yeah," he replied somberly.

Marcus looked back to the bedside and pictured Sam's face smiling at him. He couldn't help but smile back, and settled himself into the chair, reaching out his hand to take her imaginary one again.

See you soon, boo.

"Alright, Amir says you're good to go," Claire said. "Jump in when you're ready."

"Thank you, Claire," Marcus said. "For everything."

"Don't worry about it. And good luck," she replied, hanging up the call.

He stared for a moment at the display picture of Claire and Sam, then looked again to the bed. Sam's face smiled back at him.

Alright, babe. Here I come.

Marcus opened his eyes to take in the tavern's guestroom, the heat and humidity immediately stifling. For a moment he lingered in the bed, staring up at the heavy beams crisscrossing the ceiling. He'd never really given it much thought, but he found himself appreciating the familiar comfort of being in the simulation. For years it had been a refuge for him and Sam. A place where they could escape all the pain of the outside world and just be together. But after today, he'd never be able to return to Sam's World, and the realization left him feeling hollow.

Sitting up, he summoned the protocol menu in his vision and searched for his adjustments to the program. He let out a sigh as he found his modifications waiting for him. Diego had been successful. Reluctantly, he began his work. His first task was to confirm Clive wasn't in the simulation and was relieved to find no sign of his location marker. Good. Seemed like Evan pulled off his end of the plan, too.

Marcus held his breath as he made each selection, running through the list of protocol changes one by one. When he reached the last protocol, he let out a long sigh. Intellectually, he knew that the whole process had only taken a few seconds, but in his mind, it had felt like an eternity. Quickly, he ran through the protocols to double-check that he hadn't missed anything.

Satisfied that everything was in order, he turned his attention to Morrigan's location, using the new identifier that he had assigned her. A dull blue dot, identifying an asset, appeared on the map in his vision, located somewhere in the jungle. With a deep breath, he instructed the protocol to transport him to her location.

The tavern walls were suddenly replaced by thick-leaved plants and tall trees. Marcus looked around at his surroundings, getting his bearings as he searched for Morrigan. According to the protocol, she was only a couple of hundred yards away, and he made his way in her direction. As he drew closer, he caught the scent of wood smoke and soon sighted ruins, their vine-covered stones rising above the tall plants. He approached slowly but didn't bother to try and hide the noise of his passage.

"Morrigan?" he called out.

The plants thinned as he drew closer to the ruins, and he could see the embers of a fire set between the crumbling walls. Pushing his way out of the underbrush, he found himself in an open space created by what was left of the ruins' walls, where a pelt was laid out for sleeping.

"Who the fuck are ye?" Morrigan's familiar voice called from behind him, and he turned to find her staring at him, her spear raised warily between them. "The Tyrant send ye out on yer lonesome?"

"No," Marcus said, shaking his head. "It's me. Aer. Don't you remember? We're friends. More than friends, really," he said with a wink, taking on the affectations of his character in the hopes they would help her to remember.

"Aer?" she said, squinting her eyes uncertainly as she looked him over. "I dun know that name, though there's somethin' familiar about ye." She lowered her spear slightly, as she relaxed her posture. "Can't say I remember ye exactly though."

Marcus held up his hands in a pose of submission and stepped forward.

"I don't work for Brannock. You and I have been friends for a long time, Morrigan. Very good friends."

"Oh, is that so, *friend*?" she asked skeptically, bringing the spear to rest beside her and leaning on its haft. "If we're such good friends, why can't I remember ye, then?"

Her words stabbed at Marcus' heart, but he continued to hold to his persona and smiled at her. "Try and remember. We've known each other for a long time. No one knows me better."

"Yer talkin' like a lover there, boyo. I think I'd remember ye, iffin' we fucked."

"The Tyrant must have cast a spell on you to make you forget," he said, stepping forward. "But I think I can prove it to you if you let me."

"Ha!" Morrigan laughed. "Iffin' that's how ye get women to sleep with ye, then I know we haven't fucked."

Marcus shook his head.

"No. Nothing so extreme. But if you're scared..." Marcus said, arching an eyebrow.

"I ain't scared of nothin'," Morrigan shot back.

"No, you're not. Are you?" Marcus replied, moving to stand in front of her, only inches away.

Morrigan looked up at him defiantly, lifting her chin and arching her eyebrow. For a moment, he took in her face. Sam's face. The face he had adored for most of his life. The face that had always given him comfort, even in the worst of times. She was so close. So tangible. Staring into her eyes, he lifted a hand to her face and gently brushed his thumb against her cheek.

Morrigan's eyes watched him curiously, and he felt her body relax. Morrigan, Sam, the name didn't matter. He'd know her by any name. She was the person he loved most. His best friend. His every desire. With a smile, he leaned down and gently kissed her lips. For her part, Morrigan didn't pull away and allowed him to kiss her. Slowly, he pressed his lips more forcefully against hers, while wrapping an arm around her waist to pull her closer.

Morrigan complied with his actions, pressing her mouth to his and easing against his body, the sensation as familiar to him as breathing. As their kiss continued, she dropped her spear and reached up to wrap her arms around his neck, opening her mouth to kiss him more passionately. Lost in each other's embrace, they pressed themselves close to one another with a familiarity that transcended thought. Marcus clung to her, trying to absorb every sensation: the soft feel of her lips, the sound of her breath, the warmth of her skin, and the scent of her hair, unable to let her go.

With a painful resolution, he disengaged from the kiss and relaxed his grip, lamenting the feel of her body pulling away from his. Blinking, Morrigan looked up at him with a look of surprise, and behind her expression, he thought he caught a glimmer of recognition. Letting out a long breath, she leaned back, but remained in his arms, letting her own hands slide down to his chest.

"Well, boyo. Iffin' we haven't fucked yet, we'll have to remedy that soon," she said with a grin.

"I need to ask you something," he said, resting his hands on her hips, unwilling to let her go.

"Aright…" she said, uncertainly.

"You might not remember the name Aer, but what about Marcus? Or Sam?" he asked, staring into her eyes as he searched them for any sign of recognition.

"No. Should I?" Morrigan said, her brow twisting in confusion. Who are they? More 'friends' of mine?"

"Something like that," Marcus said somberly, not catching even a glimmer of recognition in her eyes. Despite knowing better, he'd hoped that maybe something of Sam still lingered. But the truth was, she was gone.

Staring up at him, Morrigan searched his own gaze. "Ye okay, boyo?" she asked with an uncertain laugh, stepping slowly out of his grasp. "Ye look like ye just lost yer favorite ax."

Marcus let his fingers linger on her hips as she moved away, wanting every second of connection he could have with her and hesitant to let her go.

"No. I lost something far more important than that," he said, bringing up the protocol menu in his vision.

"Well, maybe I can help ye find it," she offered, leaning down to pick up her spear.

Marcus gave her a sad smile and shook his head.

"I lost it long ago, I just couldn't bring myself to admit it until now," he said, selecting the server purge.

"Well, if ye can remember where ye last saw it…" Morrigan began to say, but Marcus reached out to take her hand.

"It's not important anymore. I thought maybe we could talk. Or not. I just want to sit a while with you."

Glancing down at his hand, she arched an eyebrow but didn't pull away.

"Well. I dun know about talkin', but I can think of a couple of other things we could do," she said, looking up at him with a mischievous grin.

Marcus couldn't help but smile, but as he began to reply, she suddenly vanished from sight. Confused, he stared at where she had just been. Morrigan was gone while the jungle stood undisturbed all around him. In his vision, the protocol menu still hovered in anticipation of his will. What had just happened? He hadn't activated the purge yet.

In an instant, the jungle disappeared and Marcus stumbled to his knees as the world spun around him. Just as quickly as it happened, it was over, and he looked up to find himself inside the castle's throne room. To his relief, Morrigan knelt beside him only a few paces away, but he soon realized they were not the only ones in the room. On all sides, they were surrounded by red-sashed guards, their weapons drawn and ready. Behind the guards, Marcus was shocked to see Clive sitting atop the dais on his throne.

"You're not supposed to be here," Marcus blurted out, still trying to process what happened.

"Thought you'd sneak in when I wasn't looking, Marcus?" Clive asked mockingly.

Marcus tried to stand but found himself unable to move, his body and limbs unresponsive.

"Did you think I wouldn't know if someone accessed Sam's World? It was the first thing I had Jia implement after you popped in on me and Morrigan so unexpectedly. I thought you were smarter than that. What could you possibly have hoped to accomplish by coming back here?"

Suddenly, Morrigan disappeared, only to reappear beside Clive on the dais. Standing rigidly, she glared in disbelief as she too didn't appear to be able to move.

"You know, you hid her identifier from me, but not yours. So, when I saw you out there in the jungle next to another asset, I figured it could only be one person. And lo and behold, I was right!" Clive said, pushing himself up from the throne. "You know it's funny. After everything you did to keep her from me, you turned out to be the one to help me find her."

Despite his inability to remove Clive's control over his body, Marcus still had access to the protocol. Bringing up the menu in his vision, he scanned through his options until he found the server purge. If he was going to act, he needed to do it before Clive decided to do something violent and eject him from Sam's World again. Hovering over the purge option, he hesitated. If Clive was still in the simulation when the purge happened there was no telling what might happen to him. He needed to find a way to convince the man to leave.

"No, Clive. You don't understand. You can't be here," Marcus said.

"You don't get to tell me where I can and can't be, Marcus.

You're not the one in control. This all belongs to me now," he replied, moving to stand beside Morrigan and run his hand down her back. Haven't you learned that yet?"

"Go fuck yerself, ye pig-fuckin' squirrel-eater," Morrigan spat.

"I love it," Clive laughed. "This is what I enjoy so much about this place. And her. It's raw and real in a way you just can't find back in reality. Honestly, the best sex I've ever had too. But tell me, how'd you get back in? I assume Evan was in on this? I thought it was strange that he insisted on meeting at such a late hour. I guess he's probably pretty confused at the moment."

Marcus shook his head, his anger rising. "Did you really think you could lock me out of my own program? My team and I built this place. *Sam* built this place. You are just a usurper who has no idea how any of this actually works."

"That's the thing, Marcus. I don't have to know how it works. I have people for that. People like you. And what I do know is people. People are easy. Everybody wants something. You just have to know what it is," he said, tucking a finger under Morrigan's chin. "Take you, for example. You're easy. You want Sam. And you know what the funniest part of all this is? I can give her to you."

"No, you can't. Sam's gone," Marcus replied, the words leaving him hollow.

"Is she?" Clive replied, pointedly looking at Morrigan. "Marcus, do you know why I took Sam's World from you?"

"Because you're a parasite, unable to create anything on your own. You just feed off the life and work of others," Marcus snarled.

"No. I *better* the work of others," Clive corrected. "People can create all sorts of things, but rarely do they have the vision or will to realize all the possibilities of their creations. People are small-minded. Including you, Marcus. You lacked the necessary vision. You lacked the will. I didn't take this place because I wanted Sam. I've already had her. And as nice as that was, my focus has always been on something greater."

"I took it because you thought you knew better than me," he continued. "And I knew, if I didn't take it, you'd just ruin it to make it a playground for you and your girlfriend. But as I told you, this place is much more than that. I thought you understood that. You accidentally discovered immortality, but you wanted to keep it all for yourself. Just so you and Sam could continue to play together."

"Sam's world. Elysium. It was never supposed to be about that," Marcus replied. "For a while I'll admit you convinced me to listen to you. But it was always about Sam. And Sam's gone. I didn't oppose you because you slept with Morrigan. It hurt, I'll admit. And it opened my eyes to who you really were beneath all your talk about the greater good. To the facade you hide behind. But it was when you started to alter the fundamental programming of Sam's World. When you were willing to experiment with the duplicants. I realized just how reckless and dangerous you and this research can be."

"Please spare me your sanctimony," Clive scoffed. "You want to call me reckless? You didn't have a problem with what we were doing while Sam's memory was still intact. I told you exactly what I intended to do. Had things stayed the way *you* wanted, you wouldn't have questioned my methods."

"Maybe you're right," Marcus said. "I would do anything to save Sam. But I realize that in the process, I doomed her. And hurt a lot of other people too."

"Progress is never easy, Marcus. Sometimes people get hurt. But we have to weigh that hurt against the good that can be done. Some people lost their positions at Synerdyne. Got their feelings hurt. So what? That's life. You know what's worse than that? Death. And I would go so far as to say that hurting some people's feelings is worth the cost when it means conquering death. I thought you understood that too."

"It's not as simple as that, and you know it," Marcus said, glaring. "It's about control. Your control. And you're not looking to just stop death. You want to control it. Be the arbiter of who lives and dies. And that level of control leads to something far worse than death."

Clive chuckled mirthlessly and shook his head. "Jesus, Marcus. Don't be so dramatic. There will always be people with control. Do you think it is any different now? Do you think I, and countless others, don't already have that level of influence over people's lives? I know you're not that naïve."

"There's a difference, and you know it," Marcus replied.

"You're right. There is a difference. One where death exists and one where it doesn't. Will everyone be able to use this technology? Probably not," Clive said with a shrug. "That's just not realistic, but it at least will be a possibility. Your choice is to just return to the status quo."

"That's just it. It's not my choice," Marcus explained. "That's what I am trying to tell you. We aren't conquering death or shaping our own reality. Not really. It's just an illusion of control."

"If that's the case, then why are you so adamant to stop me?" Clive countered.

"Because even as an illusion, this technology can be used by the wrong people to manipulate and control others. It is dangerous."

"Dangerous," Clive repeated, tapping a finger against his lips as he considered the word. "I wonder if you would still feel the same conviction if we were to bring Sam's memory back."

"It's not possible," Marcus said. "I told you. Sam's gone."

"Is she?" Clive said, looking back to Morrigan. "I mean, she's standing right there."

"No. That's not Sam. Not anymore."

"I'm surprised to hear you say that," Clive replied, with a look that seemed almost sympathetic. "Despite your talk of illusions and control, I honestly thought you believed in this project. And I never thought you'd give up so easily."

"You're not listening to me," Marcus implored. "I'm not giving up. I'm facing reality."

"Reality? You have the gall to sit here and talk about reality? Look around you, Marcus. You proved that reality can be whatever you want it to be. You faced the reality of death and did not accept it. Compared to that, what is a little memory loss? You proved that nothing is absolute. That if you have the will and the drive, you can shape reality itself."

"I was fooling myself," Marcus replied but found himself staring at Morrigan. Even though he'd come to terms with the fact that they weren't the same person, it was still difficult not to see her as Sam.

"She's right here, Marcus!" Clive shouted, gesturing to the dais. "Don't give up so easily. I still believe in this project. I believe in you. You are better than this. We are better than this. We can fix this."

"Is this why ye been huntin' me? I dun know who ye think I am, or what yer talkin' about," Morrigan growled, her body rigid but directing her head in Marcus' direction. "But ye got the wrong person. Let me go, Brannock. I dun even know who he is."

Hearing the certainty in Morrigan's voice was painful, but it dispelled any lingering doubts Marcus had about her still being Sam.

"There is no fixing this," he said, looking back to Clive. "Not the way you think."

"And what if I told you that I have Jia working on a way to reverse the damage to her memory?"

"What?" Marcus asked, his surprise causing the protocol to disappear from his vision.

"She has an entire team working on the problem. It's been made the top priority."

"I don't believe you," Marcus said, searching Clive's gaze for any hint of deception. "Why would you do that? Sam doesn't really mean anything to you."

"Again you're thinking too small, Marcus. Sam is important. She is the key to the cognitive mapping, after all. You're right about one thing. If the simulation really causes someone to lose their memory, we're not really cheating death. But if we can figure out what is causing the problem, we can fix it. And Sam is the embodiment of that problem. So it's in all our interests to fix her."

Marcus looked past Clive to stare at Morrigan. Could it really be possible? Could Sam's memories be returned? He looked into her eyes. Sam's eyes. And the thought of seeing recognition in those eyes again filled him with something he hadn't felt in a long time. Hope.

"We don't have to be at odds here, Marcus," Clive continued. "I admit, I got a little carried away before and acted without thinking. For that I am sorry. You may have noticed, but I don't like it when people tell me what I can and can't do. And I especially don't like when someone tries to take control away from me. It was never about Sam or Morrigan. And I should have realized how upset I had made you with our little dalliance."

"I told you, it wasn't about that," Marcus said, looking back to Clive.

"Sure. But let me make it up to you, anyway. Come back to Synerdyne. Let's put this all behind us and go back to the way things were before. You *and* your team. Then we can focus on what's really important. Fixing Sam."

Fixing Sam. He'd thought he had come to terms with the fact that Sam was gone. But hearing Clive say those words so confidently made Marcus wonder if he'd given up too easily. What was he doing? He had gone from striving to preserve Sam's World to now attempting to destroy it, all because he had lost control. So what if he didn't control Synerdyne or Sam's World? What did that matter? If there was even the slightest chance that they could restore Sam's memory, shouldn't he take it?

"Last chance, ye rat-lickin', toad-fucker," Morrigan shouted. "Let me fuckin' go, or I'll tear yer fuckin' cock from…"

"Yes, yes. Threats of violence," Clive said dismissively over her.

Morrigan words cut off abruptly, and her eyes widened in surprise.

"As much as I love her spirit, I think we need to let the grown-ups talk," Clive said with a knowing smile to Marcus.

Marcus looked over at Morrigan as her expression changed from surprise to rage. That was it, wasn't it? Even if they somehow found a way to restore Sam's memory, Clive would never let her be free. He'd use her as leverage. If Marcus wanted access to her, he'd only be able to do so at Clive's discretion. Sam would always be at his mercy. Just a toy or tool for Clive to use as he saw fit. They wouldn't be saving Sam by bringing her memories back. They'd be dooming her.

For a moment their gazes met and Marcus hoped Morrigan could see the regret in his eyes. This whole time she'd never had control. Not as Sam or Morrigan. Life had forced pain upon her, while Marcus had forced her to remain. And now Clive would force her into subjugation. In trying to protect her from death, he'd actually kept her from being truly free.

Staring into Morrigan's eyes, Marcus brought the protocol menu back up in his vision and activated the server purge.

Goodbye, my love.

"Clive. You need to leave the simulation," Marcus said, lingering on Morrigan's gaze. "Now."

"Marcus," Clive said with a sigh. "Your emotions are high right now. I get that. But you need to put that aside and think about what's best for Sam."

"That's exactly what I've done. I won't leave her here to be your puppet so that you can use her to manipulate me and everyone else."

"It's exactly that kind of talk that I told you I don't appreciate. I know you're just trying to goad me, but to what end? I'm offering you the chance to be together again. Isn't that the point of all this?" Clive asked, making a sweeping gesture around the room.

"Yes. That's exactly the point," Marcus countered. "Oh, you'll give me what I want, so long as I comply with your demands. So long as I do what I'm told. But the minute I don't, you hold the power to take it all away. You don't care about anyone. People are just pawns to you. To be used to get what you want."

"Oh grow the fuck up, Marcus. That's how the world works. Just because this place looks like a fairytale, doesn't mean it doesn't have to comply with reality. That's how life works! If you have something someone wants, they offer you something you want in return. How is this any different?"

"Because people's lives are not bargaining chips. They are not currency to be spent or exchanged," Marcus growled.

"Everything is currency, Marcus. That's what you can't seem to understand, and it's why you lost everything. You can talk down to me all you want, but what do you have to show for it? You built this place, but I'm the one with control of Sam's World."

"Not any longer. I didn't come here to *save* Sam. I came here to stop you. I just needed to see for myself one last time that Sam was gone. But now I realize that even if she was still here, that would be even more reason to stop you."

"Stop me? Well, I hate to break it to you, Marcus. But if that was your goal, you failed pretty spectacularly. How exactly did you think you would do that?"

"By destroying Sam's World. We added a server purge protocol to the AAIP just before I jumped in. I activated it about a minute ago. That's why you need to leave. In a few minutes, the simulation will become corrupted and wipe itself, destroying everything in Sam's World."

"What?" Clive exclaimed, his brow twisted in confusion. "You wouldn't do that… not with Sam here."

"Sam isn't here," Marcus said. "She's gone, and beyond either of our control. And I won't let her memory become another tool you use to get what you want."

"You can't possibly think you can rattle me that easily," Clive said, but Marcus thought he caught a hint of uncertainty in his voice.

"I'm not bluffing, Clive. You need to leave. Now. I don't know how long it will take to corrupt the AAIP, but Amir thinks it'll only need a few minutes. And when that happens, it may also corrupt the link to your SynAPP. That might mean you'll just be ejected from the simulation. Or it could send synaptic feedback into your hippocampus. You might suffer brain damage, or even die. You need to eject while you still can."

A panicked look came across Clive's face, but then quickly changed to skepticism.

"If that were true," he said, arching an eyebrow. "Then you'd need to eject too. But you're still here." Clive walked over to stand next to Morrigan. "However, if you came here for a different reason. One where you needed me outside of the simulation. Say, you've found a way to lock me out of the server. Then telling me some lie about destroying Sam's World would certainly be a way of scaring me into leaving."

"Damn it, Clive! I'm telling you the truth. I'm not lying or trying to manipulate you. You need to leave while you still can. You don't have much time left."

"Okay. Then I'll leave when you do, Marcus," Clive said with a smile, sitting back down on the throne.

"This isn't some game I'm playing with you…" Marcus insisted, but his words were cut short as he was suddenly released from the protocol Clive had used to freeze him and fell forward onto the floor. Instinctively, Marcus tried to bring up the protocol, but nothing appeared in his vision. The purge must be working.

Shaking off his bewilderment, Marcus looked up at the dais to see Clive's own look of confusion. Beside the throne, Morrigan suddenly stumbled forward and found her balance. Looking down at herself, she took a moment to register what had happened, before a wicked smile split her face.

"Kill… kill them!" Clive ordered, eyes wide as he scrambled off the throne and away from Morrigan.

The surrounding guards were just as confused as everyone else and it took them a moment to register Clive's order. Marcus didn't even try to escape as the men fell upon him with their swords. His gaze focused beyond them to dais. The last thing he saw was Morrigan tackle Clive to the ground as two of the soldiers' swords pierced Marcus' body and the world grew dark.

CHAPTER 29

*T*o Amir, Diego, and Claire:

I thought about writing a letter to each of you, but every time I started one, it always seemed like I had something to say to you as a group. So I apologize if this feels impersonal. Please know that there is nothing impersonal about what I want to say. I've scheduled it so that you will all receive this letter in your inboxes at the same time, but depending on who checks their mail first, you may each read this at different times. I guess that means if you are reading this, maybe assume the others haven't yet.

Firstly, I want to apologize. For everything, really. I know you've all been put through the wringer lately, and a good portion of that was my fault. I was so focused on my pain and on my need to save Sam, that I didn't consider your feelings or how difficult this might have been for you. I've always been singularly focused that way, especially when it comes to Sam. But we all love Sam, each in our own way, and it was unfair of me to assume your way was inferior to mine. It was just different. What matters is that Sam loved us. She was full of love in a capacity that still astonishes me. And that love she has for us binds us together, even more than our love for one another. And I do love you guys. For the years we've known each other, and for the love we all share for Sam.

Sam is both my greatest strength and deepest weakness. She is everything I have ever known, and the thought of life without her is maddening. That's not an excuse for my behavior, just an explanation of my mindset. Though I doubt that comes as a surprise to any of you. I'm just telling you things you already know. Okay, I'm rambling. The point is, life without Sam is not life. Not to me. It's meaningless. I thought I could save her, but really I was trying to save the life I knew. That's not to say I wouldn't have saved her if I could have, it's just meant to explain why I couldn't let her go. Not when I thought I could do something. But now I realize that I was being selfish. That I have been selfish for a while now. Unable to let go of what control I thought I still had over my life.

Amir, you think that the respawn is responsible for Sam's memory loss. And Diego, you've suggested that the addition of the consciousness mappings to the AAIP's protocol created a sort of feedback loop. While Claire, you argued that the Sam in the simulation is not our Sam, but just a duplicant. That our Sam died when her physical brain activity stopped. You might all be right. Maybe there is no way to ever return her memories, maybe she is only a tool of the AAIP now. Or maybe she's dead, and her consciousness was never preserved. Regardless, I've always believed that she and I are soulmates. Bonded in a way that transcends our physical form, or even our memories. Something more eternal.

If you are reading this, then hopefully that means the plan worked. Evan will be calling another shareholder meeting to appeal his removal as CEO and will introduce a motion to buy out Clive. He intends to use the pain protocol agreements Clive had the duplicant hosts sign as evidence of his recklessness.

Evan knows the shareholders well and thinks that will rattle any confidence they had in Clive. As for Jia, I can't say for certain, but Evan and I came up with an incentive to persuade her to our side. When she discovers what happened to Sam's World, she will have two options. She can defend Clive's actions and remain under his thumb. Or she can reveal the truth to the board, attain half of Clive's shares when he's bought out, and become a shareholder herself.

As for Synerdyne, Evan intends to continue our original mission of using the simulation in Elysium to work on therapies, as well as offering comfort for those in situations like hospice and paralysis. If we are successful, no one should be able to access Sam's World again.

Now, after reading all this, you might be wondering: what happened to me? This is why I've written you this letter, instead of telling you all of this face-to-face. Again, I want to apologize for not telling you everything about my plan. As I said before, life without Sam is not life. I've been grasping at straws, trying to keep her with me, any way I could. But at the end of the day, I still lost her. And I can't continue life without her. So I've decided to follow in her footsteps. I'm going to take the remainder of her pain medication before I jump into the simulation. I looked it up, and she had enough left over that I'm confident I won't survive the dose.

I couldn't tell you this because you would try to stop me. But for this plan to work, someone had to stay in the simulation to ensure the server was purged. I manipulated you, and I'm sorry. You're all far better people than I deserved in my life.

In the next few days, you will each receive an equal portion of my voting shares in Synerdyne. With those, plus your own shares, you three and Evan will have enough to determine what happens to the company from here on out. I encourage you to work together. But whatever you decide to do, I trust you'll do a better job of it than me. As for any expenses dealing with my end-of-life needs, I've given Claire access to my bank account. There should be enough funds to deal with everything. And whatever's left over, I want you to divide among yourselves to do with as you see fit.

Each of you has been a better friend to me and Sam than I have ever been to you. Thank you for all you've done. I love you all very much.

I hope one day we'll see each other again, wherever we may end up.

Marcus.

CHAPTER 30

Amir stepped out of the elevator and stared at the familiar rows of servers, all buzzing and humming behind their thick enclosure of glass. Walking up to the door, he pressed his badge to the terminal and stared into the retinal scanner. With a beep, the screen glowed green, and Amir stepped inside the server room, making his way to one server in particular and the terminal beside it. This place had become his defacto office over the last few months, and though most people would hate being shut away in the basement, he kind of loved it.

Taking a sip of his coffee, he put the mug down on his desk and settled into his chair. As he logged his credentials into the system, his eyes unconsciously followed the wires leading from his terminal to the server. In a steady rhythm, the little green and blue lights on its face flickered normally. Still functioning. Amir let out a sigh and took another drink of his coffee, turning back to his monitor.

A beep at the door, followed by the sound of the lock disengaging, caught Amir's attention and he swiveled around in his chair.

"Good morning," Evan said, carrying his own cup of coffee. "And how is Sam's World today?"

"As to be expected," Amir replied. "No change on our end, anyway. Though I'm sure the AAIP has been hard at work."

Evan nodded and took a sip of his coffee, his eyes staring at the server. "Any luck on deciphering what it's doing?"

Amir shrugged. "According to Diego, it's still rapidly propagating the simulation with assets. At least that's part of what we think it is doing. After it thwarted Marcus' attempt to shut it down with the server purge and severed all access both in and out of Sam's World, it's been continuing to write code at an astonishing rate. There's so much to go through, all written in a way that the AAIP might understand but is goddamn difficult for us to parse out."

"So it's not a threat to the server?" Evan asked.

"I don't think so. Not that we can tell. It definitely seems like its priority is to protect itself. The only issue might be space. Memory, that is," Amir stated, turning back to his monitor and pointing to the server diagnostic. "The question remains: when it reaches its limit, will it slow the propagation? Can it understand that? Or will it exceed its limitations and cause a failure?"

"And if failure happens, what does that mean for Sam's World?" Evan asked, concern in his voice.

"Well," Amir said with a sigh. "In a normal scenario, the server would slow down and not run as smoothly. There might be issues of loading time and the like. But as to how that would manifest in the simulation? I have no idea. Worse case? It shuts down completely."

"And have we gotten any closer to figuring out if Marcus or Sam still exists there?"

Amir turned back to face Evan and shook his head.

Evan gave a long sigh and looked down into his mug.

"What about Clive? Any change?" Amir asked.

"No," Evan said, shaking his head. "According to Jia, the doctors say his brain activity is functionally irrelevant. They have no idea if he will ever wake up."

"I'm sorry, Evan. I know you did your best to keep Clive out," Amir said sadly.

"Yeah."

Evan let out another sigh and stared at the server bank. "Could we give it more memory? Add servers to it?"

Amir followed his gaze. "Yeah. We'd have to take some of the backups offline for Elysium, but it would give us some more time."

"All right," Evan said. "Let's do it."

"But that won't solve the problem," Amir pointed out. "It'll just delay the inevitable. I don't think the AAIP is going to slow down. No matter how many servers we add, it will continue to propagate the simulation with assets. It's basically building an entire world."

"Well, we have to do something. I like to believe they're both still in there," Evan said, taking another sip of his coffee. "So the least we can do is buy them some time."

CHAPTER 31

Stepping out of his hut, Aer took a moment to stretch, lifting his arms above his head and letting out a long groan. The early morning air was not yet warm enough to bring the day's humidity and felt pleasantly cool on his skin. There was something familiar about this part of the jungle. Something that pulled at his thoughts, like a dream he couldn't quite remember. One that left him with a sense of longing. He didn't know why this place called to him, but he couldn't deny it.

There was plenty of game in the forest, and he'd become quite good with both his sword and bow. They used to cause him some difficulty, he vaguely recalled. But he couldn't remember how he'd learned to master them. There was also a stream with a small waterfall nearby that always ran clean and clear. The only things he needed to worry about were the Half-men who prowled the jungle looking for slaves to sacrifice to their brutish gods. But he didn't worry about them too much. If they came here, he'd make sure they never returned to their temple, just like he'd done with the ape.

Whenever he tried to remember his past, it all felt so distant. How had he come to this place? Had he sailed here on one of those ships in the harbor? Or had he always been here? He'd spent some time in Freeport, but nothing there felt like home. Not to mention he couldn't stomach living under the Tyrant's rule. There were times when he thought he might remember tidbits, but the moments always slipped away before he could grasp them. Yet there always remained a lingering sense that something was missing. Something part of him was seeking. Something that would make him feel whole.

As he lowered his arms, he gazed over his little homestead. The hut was coming along nicely, about half of it built, and he looked forward to sleeping with four walls around him soon. His eyes came to linger on his drying rack. The pelt there was stretched and cleaned and on its way to being cured. A few more and he could bring them to Freeport for sale.

He walked over to his fire pit and stirred the coals, pleased to find them still smoldering underneath. Grabbing some kindling and branches, he started a small fire and made his way over to where he'd hung and wrapped the remaining venison from the deer. Taking two hanks of meat from the large green leaves he'd used to preserve them, he spitted the steaks with a stick and hung them over the flames. Soon the pleasant smell of seared meat filled the air.

While waiting, he grabbed his ax and whetstone, sitting down to place it across his knees. Stroking the stone against the ax's blade, he began sharpening the tool, stopping occasionally to turn the spit. He hummed as he worked, his motions with the stone practiced and precise.

It was almost indistinguishable from the din of the jungle, but he caught the sound of rustling coming from the underbrush nearby. Continuing to whistle and sharpen the blade, he pretended to be unaware of the disturbance, watching the area for movement in the periphery of his vision.

"Ye gonna eat all that by yerself, boyo?" a woman's voice called from the dense jungle, causing him to stop his work and stand up.

"I'd planned on it, yeah," he called back. "Who's asking?"

From behind one of the broadleaf ferns, a woman stepped into view. She was tall and lean, wearing only a few small pelts that left little to the imagination. But what Aer noticed most was the spear she held in her hand. Watching her warily, he held his ax by his side, gripped tightly and ready for use.

"I am," she said with an arch of her eyebrow. "Seems ye got a lot of meat," she continued with a grin, looking him up and down. "Ye got any you'd be willin' to share?"

He stared at the woman. She was attractive to be sure, her body muscled and taut, but still curved in a way that was soft and inviting. However, it wasn't her beauty or her flesh he found himself drawn to. It was her eyes. As their gazes met, there was a spark of something that he couldn't define. Something that he thought he might have seen pass in her eyes as well. A feeling of familiarity. Of comfort.

Aer let his grip on the ax relax. If she noticed, she gave no indication.

"Aye. I suppose I could spare a little," he said.

The corners of her lips curled into a soft smile.

"Name's Morrigan," she said, lowering her spear.

"Aer," he replied.

"Well, Aer. It's nice to meet ye."

Aer couldn't say why, but a smile spread across his face.

"It's nice to meet you too."

Thank you for reading the Last Protocol.

If you enjoyed this book, please consider leaving it a review.
Every review matters and helps promote the book so new readers
might discover it.

For more MANE Publishing productions visit us at
www.manepublish.com

About the Author

Andre Segura is a Cajun transplant who traded the humid swamps of Louisiana for the snow-capped mountains of Washington State. He enjoys all fiction but is particularly drawn to the speculative nature of fantasy/science fiction, believing it has a unique capacity for exploring the human condition. After the loss of his life partner and best friend to cancer, he turned to writing to work through his own questions of existence and loss, completing his first novel, The Last Protocol.

You can find more information about Andre and his upcoming projects at: *andresegura.com*

www.ingramcontent.com/pod-product-compliance
Lightning Source LLC
Chambersburg PA
CBHW021438310726
48971CB00005B/1407